The Love Eaters

The Kiss of Kin

Books by Mary Lee Settle

The Love Eaters

The Kiss of Kin

by Mary Lee Settle

with a new introduction by the author

UNIVERSITY OF SOUTH CAROLINA PRESS

Copyright © 1995 by Mary Lee Settle

Published in Columbia, South Carolina, by the
University of South Carolina Press

The Love Eaters first published by Harper 1954
The Kiss of Kin first published by Harper 1955
University of South Carolina Press dual edition 1995

Manufactured in the United States of America

99 98 97 96 95   5 4 3 2 1

Library of Congress Cataloging-in-Publication Data

Settle, Mary Lee.
   [Love eaters]
   The love eaters ; and, The kiss of kin / by Mary Lee Settle.
      p.   cm.
   ISBN 1–57003–098–7 (pbk.)
   I. Settle, Mary Lee. Kiss of kin. II. Title. III. Title: Kiss
of kin.
PS3569.E84L6   1995
813'.54—dc20   95-32164

The Love Eaters

The Kiss of Kin

INTRODUCTION

Publishing a first novel is like walking through a stone wall you have been staring at for years and finding it is mist.

Except for a few months in New York in 1945, I had been living in England since I joined the Women's Auxiliary Air Force in 1942. By 1952, I had written five plays in four years. None of them ever saw a stage. I was wined and dined and praised and starved. I made my living as best I could, as a freelance—BBC radio reader, model, fashion journalist, etiquette expert for *Woman's Day*, and even, for a glorious little while, as foreign correspondent for the late *Flair* magazine, for which I received $100 a month. I have said that the difference between dedicated writers and the rest of the world is that writers earn money in order to work, and most people work in order to earn money. There is a deep gulf between the two. There were years of eking and pawning, and hard, hard work. Now I know that what I thought was neglect was apprenticeship.

Then I decided that if nobody wanted to do my plays, I would do the last one myself. I would be everything the theater had taught me was needed—the director, the actors, the props, the scenery. In short, before I knew what I was doing, I was turning my play, *The Kiss of Kin,* then called *Deed,* into a novel.

It was my first novel. It went to every major publisher in the United States and in England. It was refused. I got advice—I was told by my London agent that there were too many facts to the page, that there should be only two, that the "heroine" should be eighteen, the "hero" in his early thirties, preferably a war hero. I started my next book, which had none of these virtues, in a shower of rejections.

On a spring day in 1952, James Broughton, the poet and *avant-garde* filmmaker, and I were walking through the ruins of the Crystal Palace gardens in London. He was looking for a place to film *The Pleasure Garden*. Rain-rusted dinosaurs stood neglected in the tall grass and the weeds, abandoned during the war. What had been lawn had long since turned to meadow. I still see it as a landscape of postwar England, a neglected, stained, secret, romantic wilderness.

We argued as we walked, not about politics or love or where we would go to dinner but about the nature of tragedy. With the spaces of weeds that had been flower beds, and the wild trees that were, before the war, in a pruned and disciplined London park, it seemed the right place for such indulgency.

James, if I remember well enough, argued that tragedy was inherent in the act itself; I argued that it had to be recognized, as the Greeks recognized it, for any disaster to survive pathos or sensation.

Then I said, "Why if the Phaedra happened in a provincial American town, people would say that she was mutton dressed as lamb, no better than she ought to be, cradle-snatching, maybe a murderer . . ." I can't remember what else, but then I said, "I'll prove it to you." So out of that long afternoon *The Love Eaters* was born. It is the story of the Phaedra, and not one critic recognized it.

It, too, was sent to every publisher and rejected until the Viking scout in England sent it to Viking, where it was rejected, and then to Heinemann, in London, who accepted it. I was already working on *O Beulah Land.*

I was terrified. When I waited in the beautiful eighteenth-century drawing room of the publishers in Museum Street, I seemed to be accused by books, mounted to the fourteen-foot ceiling—Conrad, Dostoyevsky, Tolstoy, Turgenev, Maugham. I have thought of that room ever since as a "softening-up" room.

I went to Paris for the ten days before the publication date and holed up in a cheap hotel in the Rue de Tournon called the Helvetia. I took one book with me, *Life on the Mississippi,* and I read it over and over. In the evening I went with my friends to the cafés. One evening, as we walked around St. Sulpice, Max Steele and I were ahead, and Alfred Chester and some others walked behind us. Alfred called out, "Look at them. Just because they've been published they are telling secrets they won't share."

What Max was saying was, "Now honey, if you make a little money, put it in a liquor store. Even in a depression they don't go bust."

On the Sunday morning I was to leave, just as the train was pulling out for Dieppe and the channel ferry, Max ran down the platform, thrust in through the train window copies of the London *Observer* and the London *Times* and a jar of watermelon pickle his mother had sent him from North Carolina. I was on my way. I opened the papers.

The rest was a Walter Mitty dream. The reviews were not only very good, but that rarer thing as well—all except one came within the week of publication. That one was in the *Manchester Guardian.* When its review came out a month later, the critic said, in effect, that if people thought *The Love Eaters* was a work of genius they were out of their minds, or some such thing.

One of the second-edition jacket blurbs read "' . . . genius. . . '
The Manchester Guardian."

I went on working on *O Beulah Land* in the British Museum.
Angus Wilson was one of the heads of the reading room and a
leading literary light. He came up to me and said, "Isn't it wonderful? Now you can make your living in the literary world as a
reviewer, write articles . . ." I looked up from the huge heavy
catalogue I had just heaved onto the circular leather surface of
the catalogue shelves, and said, "Angus, I don't want to write
about it. I want to write *it*." I still do. He didn't speak to me for
several months.

I had the satisfaction after the first notices of having five cables
from American publishers in my hands at the same time asking
to publish *The Love Eaters,* all of whom had rejections in their
files at the reader level. I chose Harper.

When my editor at Heinemann asked me if I had any other
novels I said no. After all, wise heads had rejected it. Finally I
let her see *The Kiss of Kin.* It was published by Heinemann and
then by Harper and was selected as a Book-of-the Month alternate. So my first novel was my second and my second novel
was my first. The critics agreed that for once a second novel was
not a disappointment.

One day the telephone rang in the hall of the boardinghouse
where I was living near the British Museum. It was Eddie Foy,
Jr. I had never met him. He congratulated me on the Book-of-
the-Month (my publishers had not told me) and then said, "You
know, this book would make a wonderful play."

THE LOVE EATERS

To

DOUGLAS NEWTON

Contents

CHAPTER I

The Cracks in the Pavement

UNTIL Hamilton Sacks was lifted off the C. & O. Pullman by his mother and one of the porters, nobody in Canona had any idea he was a chair-bound cripple. It was October, so that even when the 6.18 came in it was already dark; his first sight of the town was of a small group of men and women standing under the cold, high, white electric light of the station platform. The bravest of them broke away and came towards him; a dark woman, with strong-looking wrists, and a Spanish bun of black hair drawn back from her handsome rather wide face. She had stripped off her black gloves and held out in front of her a hand so surprisingly slim it looked like the hand of an invalid.

"Mother, darling, it's my leading lady, I'm sure. I didn't know they still looked like . . ." Hamilton was quiet and brought all his hard-earned charm forward on his face, smiling like a friendly little boy; the woman had come within ear-shot.

"Mr. Sacks, I'm Martha Dodd. This is indeed a pleasure."

"But I already know you from all your sweet letters. Isn't this exciting?" Hamilton Sacks flicked his hand gently at his mother, both to make her push in step with Martha Dodd as they went towards the others down the long, cracked concrete platform, and to introduce her.

"This is my mother."

They shook hands a little awkwardly behind his shoulder, across the chair-back.

To cover the slight silence, Martha Dodd leaned towards him and kept her voice below the hearing of the others.

"We all thought we'd go up to the house, and get to know each other . . . but if you're tired after your trip maybe you'd like to do it another time. We can take you straight to your . . ."

Hamilton Sacks jerked the chair away from his mother's hands and flicked it round, facing the tall woman. He leaned forward in his chair.

"Get this straight, Mrs. Dodd. I'll have no over-solicitousness about my health. It's the wrong way to start. I can't stand up, that's all. I just can't stand up. If I'm going to get you to work you've got to respect what I say. You can't if you're being motherly. I have a mother. Thank you."

The rest of the reception committee had come near enough to speak, but were met with Hamilton Sacks' back, and the sound of his hammering voice; that and the sight of Martha Dodd's white face, as startled as if she'd been suddenly scratched by a kitten.

"Mr. Sacks," she tried to speak, but it came out with a gasp. "This is Mr. Trent, our stage-manager, Mrs. Trent, who likes to make costumes. She's a god-send . . ." Martha Dodd was back in her stride again. "Miss Lydia Leftwich, who's about the most loyal one of us."

"Oh, Martha, honestly . . ." Lydia giggled.

Hamilton Sacks turned the chair to them as gracefully as a swan turning on the water, and when they saw his face, with the smile again, beautiful in its aquiline way, they almost forgot the warning of the voice they'd heard.

"Let's go," said the man in the chair. "The cars must be at the other end. What a hideous station." He swung himself on down the platform before them, and they followed like children being led through a strange place, his mother with them.

The Dodds' large station wagon rested beside the mail trucks and Martha Dodd slipped down the short steps to unlock it when Hamilton Sacks had stopped the procession at the car-park. She was trembling the keys in the little bright lock and stretching quickly across the seats to all the doors. In her hurry, she felt a stocking go, and said from long habit, but more vehemently than a simple run called for:

"Oh, futch!"

"How marvellous!" Hamilton carolled at the sight of the car. "Just our thing. Now, Mr. Trent, you're my Man Friday. Put me in the back like a piece of luggage. I fold up. Any size. Mother will show you how. Mother!" he called above them to the little woman gazing over their heads to the dark, fast-moving river.

Lydia Leftwich giggled and then shut up, wondering suddenly whether he'd meant to make a joke.

"I made Jim get this station wagon for me. We just use it all the time for the Thespians." He could hear Martha Dodd explaining from the front of the car as he was being folded into the back.

"Jim must be nice."

"Are you O.K.?" Elsworth Trent surveyed him like a puzzle.

"So cosy! What are you up to, Mother?"

She stood alone, still staring, this time back toward the dark track, now empty of the train.

"I wonder what we ought to do about our grips."

"My Man Friday will see to the cases, Mother. Get in."

"Why not have a taxi take them right over to Mr. Sacks' apartment?" Martha Dodd called over the open door to the fast disappearing joyful Man Friday. He waved a hand in answer, and she turned and climbed into the driver's seat.

Martha Dodd drove like a man, but like a man who was a bad driver. She seemed sure of herself and eased in and out of traffic as if the station wagon were part of her. Yet, watching the station-yard, then the bridge, swing up and disappear behind him, Hamilton Sacks found himself clutching the arms of the chair, now collapsed into a sort of baby chair for motoring. He called shrilly:

"Mrs. Dodd, let's go slow along the river. I don't want to miss anything. What's it called?"

"The Canona River," she called back. "We forget everybody wasn't born here, don't we, Lydia?"

Lydia was too surprised at being spoken to to answer her.

The yellow fog lights along the river street painted the trees a bright high green, although they had long since turned, and were sending down leaves in a wind that shook the station wagon from side to side as it slowed down. Swirling along the asphalt, the leaves sounded like rain against the tires.

"Do you get much fog here?" Hamilton asked in the silence inside the car.

"Do we? Wait till you see it. Boy, you just wait." Elsworth Trent turned. "It comes up from the river."

There was another silence. The street reeled out behind the car; on one side the thick trees of the river bank; on the other the shadows of large solid houses, a few with white columns on their porches shining in the darkness; but most, as they rushed past, looking like high, heavy brownstone ships.

"Is this where all the coal barons live?" Hamilton called out.

4

No one answered, but Martha Dodd laughed over her shoulder.

"It's where I live," she said, slowing down. "I can even show you a coal baron." She stopped the car and got out.

"Mr. Dodd's in the coal business," Mr. Trent said as he unfolded the chair and lifted Hamilton out on to the wheeled frame.

"Oh, I hope I haven't said anything wrong." Hamilton smiled over his shoulder as Elsworth Trent began to push him up the wide, concrete walk, wheeling him without question as if he'd been born to do it.

"No, sir," Trent answered, and wished he hadn't let 'sir' slip out to a man so much younger. "Marty can take a joke. You'll find she can take a joke . . ."

Hamilton Sacks' answer sounded suspiciously like a giggle.

The house before them was so high it seemed to disappear upwards among the trees. Its porch, with four ugly, powerful-looking columns of brownstone, twelve feet around and lined in squares, was not a porch at all, but some architect's dilemma between providing a fine *porte-cochère* for his house and satisfying Jim Dodd's grandfather, who had lived on a farm up the river until he made all his money, and still liked to sit out in the evenings. It was not long enough for a porch, and far too high for a *porte-cochère*; it disappeared upwards, almost the height of the house itself. Between the columns, which had screened Dodds from seeing up and down the road ever since they had gotten rich, an empty rocking-chair still moved back and forth as if someone had left it and moved inside when the car drove up—or as if the wind had caught it to rock the ghost of grandpaw.

But inside the front door Marty Dodd had been at work. She had not painted the stained oak white, as less dramatic and more conventional women would have done to defeat the house, but had had it stripped of its dark veneer and highly polished. The walls of the hall, which had once had dark red flock paper imported from England, were now plain yellow; down them she had hung sporting and hunting prints, and on the triangle of wall below the chunky carved stair-rail, a delicate Cézanne print. Nothing jarred; in calm good taste, nothing spoke at all. It was as if she had seen all the pitfalls in the road and wisely avoided them, but in doing so had found herself lost.

"Well, here's the mausoleum." She turned to Hamilton, and he noticed for the first time that though her hands were so slim, she was a large woman, and that she had a prettiness left around her mouth, which was wide and full, that belied the severity of her hair and the set of her head.

"You'll want to wash up a little bit after your train ride. Elsworth, take Mr. Sacks to the boys' room. Come on, Mrs. Sacks, you come with me. Now the rest of you just make yourselves at home. You're not company. Jim'll get you a drink." She had turned away, stripping off her coat before anyone could help her.

"I'm not company either," Hamilton flirted with her.

"You're certainly not. You're the head of the Thespian family now," she called over the banisters. "Jim. Jim!"

It was when she raised her voice to call for her husband that Hamilton heard the twang of her region most. It was as if all the expensive schools he supposed, jealously, that she had gone to, and all the money black from coal that advertised itself in the very size of her surroundings, had not been enough to take away altogether the faint tang of the mountains, like a whiff of onion grass in spring milk.

"Jim," he heard her call again. "Where are you, honey? We're all home . . . ho-ome," she sang, almost through her nose, on two distinct notes.

6

Elsworth Trent turned him carefully into the red punched-leather dressing-room along the narrow side-hall, and he heard no more.

The stairs rose up, a square tower like a centre-pole carrying the house. Mrs. Sacks looked up and saw it disappearing up into the attic, heavy, solemn, carved. "I've tried my best to do something about these awful stairs." Marty caught her eye and apologised, a little shyly. "They won't even let me take these terrible column-things down. They hold the ceiling up."

"Oh, don't you like them?" Mrs. Sacks followed her up. "Why, it's just like Juliet's balcony, or some fairy tale." But what she told Hamilton later was, "She must have been real gawky when she was a youngin. She's still got an awkward streak."

Marty paused on the stairs, and changed the subject: "Lord knows where Jim is. You must be half dead."

"Oh, no, I'm used to trains," said Mrs. Sacks sadly, following her into her bedroom.

Marty left her there, for as they had risen to the level of the first floor she had noticed the door to the upstairs porch swinging open in the wind. She went down the upstairs hall, and, alone for the first time after the excitement of welcoming the Sackses, sighed and stood with her eyes closed for a second. The hall she stood in was high and dark, and clove the bedrooms apart like a wide, useless road. It was a part of the house, half-architecture, half-stubbornness, where the stubbornness had won.

Case Dodd knew damn well that you had to have a big wide hall open at both ends if you were going to sleep a wink in the summer time. What he wouldn't listen to was that the huge vault of attic and roof above them would filter away the sun, and that the dark woodwork, the brownstone, the sunless hollow of the big rooms weren't going to hold heat

7

even in July. So he got a cool house, but its farmhouse upper hall magnified the breeze so that it was usually like a wind tunnel.

Marty felt the wind catch at her and opened her eyes. She ran forward to grab the door before it banged again; through the glass pane as she closed it she saw the glow of a cigarette and recognised the nearly square figure standing on the upstairs porch.

"Why, Jim," she called out, tapping on the pane. "Come on in here. What are you doing out there?"

The cigarette flipped away into the darkness and he turned to come in. She had already started down the hall when she heard the door click again, and felt Jim take her arm. She turned in at her own door.

"I'll go on in here, honey. Mrs. Sacks might want something. They're real nice." She couldn't think how to warn him quickly that Hamilton was crippled, and she was afraid that in the megaphone of a hallway her voice would carry all over the house. "You go on down and give everybody a drink, honey. We'll be down in the minute." She closed the door behind her, thinking already of the sweet little old lady in her bathroom. All the time in her hurry she had not looked round and so she never knew that Jim, her square-to-fat, dandy, dark-haired, light-footed, Stogie-smoking, poker-playing, silent, rich husband had been out there in the wind, crying, and that the tears were still wet on his cheeks.

Marty sank down on the edge of her own bed, sitting sideways, expectantly, as if she were a stranger, too, in her bedroom. When Mrs. Sacks came back, she said, "Have you got everything you need?"

Mrs. Sacks sat down in front of the white-frilled dressing-table and patted her white hair with gentle little pats. "This is the sweetest room," she said. "Oh, I'm so glad to be getting settled with my own things around." She turned round on the seat and confided, "It's the nicest thing for us!"

Marty, remembering about the stairs, said, "You know, you've just *made* that staircase for me. I just hated it. But when you said that about the balcony I remembered when I was a little girl . . ."

"I love these big old houses," Mrs. Sacks interrupted, and dived into her handbag for her handkerchief, rummaging around among the mess.

Marty went on: "When I was little my father took me to a house like this. You find them all over. In our little old town there was only one. I just loved it." Marty seated herself more firmly on the bed. "All those cubby-holes and dark stairs, just like a real castle." She got up and smoothed her skirt. "I hadn't thought of it since. Just spent my time trying to lighten up this old barn."

She pulled open the door and followed Mrs. Sacks through it.

"Don't you change, though?" she said, but Mrs. Sacks seemed not to hear.

Downstairs they could hear the sound of ice in glasses, and the soft murmur of voices. As they came to the living-room door the murmur was drowned in a burst of loud laughter.

"Ham's just killing us, that's all," Elsworth Trent called out.

Hamilton, from his cosy place where he'd been pushed within the glow of the huge log fire that threw his shadow dancing against a ceiling corner of the room, lifted a hand. "Don't, Elsworth, don't call me Ham," he groaned, "not in our profession! The number of times . . ."

There was another gust of laughter.

"Jim, honey, Mrs. Sacks and I are dry," Marty said,

9

leading her to the corner bar in the library where Jim stood being bar-tender.

"If y'are it's the first time since this State repealed the amendment," Elsworth called, full of himself, in the party.

Mrs. Trent leaned forward confidentially, but all she said was, "When was this State ever dry?"

There was another loud peal of laughter.

To tell the truth, if you had traced the laughter to its source, most of it came from Lydia Leftwich, who sat holding her unaccustomed drink in both hands as if it were the pole on a merry-go-round. There was a slight note of panic though the laughter was happy—panic that seemed to say, "If I stop, and let go my glass, I'll just sink through to nothing in the cushions of this couch and somebody will sit on me."

Hamilton couldn't resist playing her.

"I see Marty's not the only one with a sense of humour in this part of the world," he said, watching Lydia.

She went completely silent and blushed scarlet, the colour rising like coffee through a sugar-lump. As Hamilton swung himself round a little so that he could see through the huge, opened french doors into the dark library, she put her glass down beside her on the floor, and didn't touch it again.

"Come on out of that cave," he called to the three at the bar, and nursing their drinks they came to the fire, Jim following the two women but watching only his glass.

"Sit here by me, Mother. She gets cold." Hamilton motioned under the parchment lamp to the easy chair nearest the fire. Lydia sank further into her corner and Marty sat down between her and Elsworth Trent, who had risen to a half-crouch to be polite when they came in. With the firelight and the lamplight brightening all their faces it made Hamilton a little blind to look over the couch into the outer darkness of the large room to where Jim stood, concentrating on his ice cubes as he swung them round and round his glass. But Hamilton's instinct for 'grouping', as he called it, made him go on watching, then call to Jim's dim figure.

"Mr. Dodd, come on and join the party. We all look like we're gathered to tell ghost stories."

"Oh, you all go on right ahead, I'm fine." Jim looked up, registering vaguely what he had said. "Don't you worry about me."

"Oh, come on over, honey; way out there." Marty sensed a slight command in Hamilton's voice which, remembering the station, she was eager to appease.

"I'm fine . . ." Jim dragged a high-backed chair near the circle, eased his large body into it and went on looking into his drink. The light from the fire caught the glitter of ice-cubes and crystal in his hand and he concentrated harder, swinging them like a tiny chandelier in the wind.

"Now let's get down to a little serious business." Hamilton set the new pace, already tired from his flash of comradeliness.

"I believe I'm right in saying," here he leaned back in his chair and folded his hands, "that the Canona Thespians have never worked for a professional director before." He didn't wait for an answer.

"So, there are a few things you should know. I do not believe that a play can be produced without as strict discipline as if you were opening on Broadway . . ."

Lydia Leftwich felt a chill of excitement and began to shiver.

"I will not countenance," here he looked almost sadly around the row of intent faces, "lateness, skipping, or laziness in rehearsals. Of course I realise that most of you, especially the men, make your living in other ways—so that

11

sometimes your work will interfere. That inconvenience we will have to suffer. The word amateur will never be used in my theatre except as a term of abuse."

He stopped, and there was silence from the Thespians— only the ice-cubes in Jim's glass, smaller now, and rounder, bumped lazily against the sides as he spun them.

"Mr. Dodd, can you stop that? This is an extremely serious moment for the rest of us and I must be able to concentrate."

The glass was still.

"Now the reading committee . . . when can I meet them?"

"It's us, Mr. Sacks . . ." Marty leaned forward into the firelight.

"Call me Hamilton, my dear, *please*. . . ."

"And there's Anne Randolph Potter, too. She's wonderful. She majored in English Lit. at Sweet Briar and she sees all the Broadway shows. They're coming for dinner, they couldn't get to the train . . ."

"Have you made plans for a first show?"

"We thought maybe *Pride and Prejudice* . . ." Lydia said, who fancied herself as Jane.

"Then we diddled around a little with *Gaslight*," Mr. Trent interrupted for obvious reasons.

"What about you, Marty?" Hamilton swung towards her, enjoying the confessions.

"We've never done that *There Shall Be No Night* or . . . you know."

Hamilton knew.

"The first play," he announced, "will be an explosion in Canona's face. The first professional performance of the Thespians. The explosion will take place after Christmas. I refuse to be confounded with Santa Claus. Besides, we need time together." He looked slowly around at his new

12

dead-silent family of Thespians. "I have several plays in mind which would do. All comedies . . ." Marty's eyes swung away and she sprang up. "Oh, excuse me . . ." She followed the bony white woman, dressed in a white apron, who had been beckoning from the library entrance and had finally caught her eye.

The clang of the doorbell threw Hamilton still more out of stride and he gave up. "Well, children, no more for now. Let's get acquainted. There's plenty of time for plans. Setting public reading dates . . ."

Lydia's eyes filled with easy tears and she looked down at her large hands.

The doorbell rang again and Jim got up to answer it. But not before it had been plunged open and a great square of cold wind let into the hall.

"*Y'awl died and gawn to hell?*" a man's voice called, and the door slammed again.

Anne Randolph Potter and Plain George, her husband, appeared in the doorway of the living-room, taking off their coats and stamping their feet as if they had come in from heavy snow.

"Boy, it's real football weather, ain't it, son?" Plain George called out.

"Gimme yourall's coats. I wouldn't have let you freeze to death, but I thought Gladola'd answer."

"She's probably finishing up dinner," Anne Randolph said, letting him peel off her coat.

"Come on in here and meet the folks." Jim brought them in and introduced them to the man in the chair and his little mother. "Mr. Sacks, your glass is empty. Can't have that in this house. Give it here." Jim, who had come awake as a man out of a heavy dream, began to fill the glasses again, swinging back and forth between the red punched-leather bar and the group at the fire.

13

"Suppose I can't persuade you to join us, Plain George?"
Plain George lumbered after him.

"You could beat me, Jim," he crowed, "I'd give in. . . .
Hey, woooah! that's too much," as he leaned over it and saw
Jim pouring a drink.

"O.K., son." He gave him another glass. "Say when,"
and when he had finished, took the large drink himself.

"Hey, take it easy, man. I thought you didn't drink!"
Plain George became confidential. "What'sa matter—is it
that little pantie-waist out there?" He took a long drink.
"He don't look so bad as I thought he would."

"Nothing . . ." Jim answered, irrelevantly.

"Cheer up, boy, it might be diamonds, or big trips, or
even women's clubs. We're lucky. . . . To our women!"
Plain George raised his glass with a flourish.

Back in the living-room, Anne Randolph had kitten-
curled herself in the seat that Marty had left, sinking a high
heel into Mr. Trent's leg. She threw her head back so that
her hair spread over the couch and gave her a thin blonde
halo, then drawled: "Thank the Lord you're here, Hamilton.
Now we can get some order into all this chaos!" She spread
her arm out as if the room itself had turned topsy-turvy and
Hamilton had come to clean it.

"You're the literary expert, I gather," Hamilton said.

"Oh, don't you believe all you hear. I just love to read,
that's all." "Awl", she said with her whole mouth.

"You're not from here, are you?" Hamilton asked her.

"Hununh. I'm from down Virginia." She buried her
mouth in her drink, drowning her top teeth, and looked at
Hamilton over the glass.

"Reads everything she can get her hands on, don't you,
honey?" Plain George came in and stood behind his wife.

Before Hamilton had a chance to answer, Marty appeared
at the library arch. "When youall are ready," she said softly,

14

so that she could move them without disturbing. "Gwan, finish up your drinks." She stood smiling at Mrs. Sacks, never quite saying that dinner was ready.

Hamilton swung around the lamp and wheeled himself past her, leading the way. They were all in the dining-room before Elsworth Trent could get his bruised leg to work again.

CHAPTER II

Night Talk

THE wind blew most of the night, gathering high beyond Canona where the mountains were separated only by a mile-deep gully, and invading the valley below; twisting around the branches and catapulting them against the sun-porch windows outside Marty's bedroom.

It was only after an hour of lying in her bed listening, trying to impose a rhythm on the crashes against the windows, that Marty heaved over and saw the light burning under the bathroom door. For a little while she tried to ignore it, half-awake, hoping Jim would see it from his room opposite.

A final slap of the branch woke her into a panic and she rushed out of bed and into the bathroom. The light was off there, but through the open door Jim's lamp was still on, and he sat at his desk, so still she thought he had fallen asleep there until she saw the cigarette in his hand.

"Jim," she half-whispered through the open door, as if her voice would disturb the nightmare of the wind outside and it would find her. "Can't you sleep, either?"

"Come on in, honey."

"Why, Jim!" She came further into the room and glanced at his bed. "You haven't even tried to go to sleep. Are you all right?"

When he didn't answer she repeated, "Jim—are you all right?"

"Want a cigarette, honey?" He held out the packet and

she took one and crawled across his bed, covering herself with the English eiderdown against the night cold.

"Look, honey," he began—but didn't go on.

Marty watched him moving around the room softly, his slippers hardly touching the carpet, his broad back bent, his eyes not seeing her as he passed, and knew better than to say a word. After the gabbling of women, her marriage to Jim had been an escape into silence and, like most marriage escapes, she knew with a feeling too reserved to be sorrow she had got what she wanted.

Between them the gulf of silence had stretched for fifteen years, not crossed by crises because there were none; no sickness; withdrawal instead of quarrelling; a quiet, rich, polite, childless marriage that Marty had never really thought enough about, living through it day by day as she did, to call bleak. She moved restlessly under the eiderdown and drew on her cigarette.

"Honey . . . I've got a son," Jim said with his back to her, and fell across the desk, his head buried and his shoulders jerking, then eased himself blindly into a chair.

"Awe, honey, awe, honey!" She ran with her hands stretched in front of her as if he were a child who had fallen. "Awe, honey," she kept saying, stroking his back, too shocked to take in fully what he had said. She had only seen him cry once before, and that was when his father had died, and he had come out into the upper hall from the room he now used himself, and bowed his head. When she had gone close to touch his arm she had seen the tears ditch his cheeks without any sound.

Not like this, not this heaving back under her stroking hands, not this man bending and falling forward like a woman who collapses from relief.

"Come on to bed, honey." She lifted him, guided him out of the chair. "You just come on over here." She steered

17

him by his upper arms as if he were drunk or blind, back to
the bed she had left, and tucked him into it. In the stillness
after the sobbing she sat beside him on the bed and watched
his closed eyes. Her cigarette, forgotten, lay burning on the
bedside tray, sending a thin line of smoke high, which only
wavered when she changed her cramped position or a
fragment of the wind shook through the window curtains.

Then slowly, like a chill running through her veins, came
the realisation of what Jim had said.

"I've got a son."

As if he knew the words had finally gone home, big Jim
rolled back to her and took her cold hand.

"I've been trying all day to tell you," his voice was calm
and shy in the night. "But you been so busy."

"I wouldn't have been too busy, honey." She rubbed his
wide, pale, fuzz-backed hand, twisting the heavy gold class
ring he still wore around and around his fat finger without
knowing what she did.

"I didn't know how to go about it without upsetting
you"; he released his hand and rubbed it across hers. "I
didn't want to upset you any——"

"What is it you've got to tell me, Jim?" She almost
muttered it, colder with fear she'd hear he was going to leave
her.

But he took her muttering to be the beginning of anger.

"I don't know what you're going to think of me, Marty.
I just don't know." And then, because her waiting demanded it, he launched into his story, adjusting himself
until he lay flat against the pillows and couldn't see her
face.

"You remember that time I went to Colorado?" he told
the ceiling, and heard Marty say:

"I just knew you went. You always told me you went."

"You know I married that girl out there."

18

"In Colorado. Yes. But I never asked you about it. You never brought it up." Marty began to shiver as the wind and fear caught her.

"You cold, honey? Yeah, in Golden. It was a little old jerkwater town then. Nothing there but the School of Mines." He felt the current of her coldness again in the hand he held. "You come on in here and put the covers over yourself."

She took her hand away. "You were out in Colorado . . ." It was hard to get him to tell a story—any story. "You know, Marty," he'd say. She knew, and she'd be the talker, the front, the voice. In the back always stood Jim, no longer quite listening, withdrawn into staring at his glass. But she couldn't tell this story. She could only draw it from him in fragments, and fit what might be her own disaster together for herself.

"I married this girl out there."

"Oh, Jim. I knew all that."

They both fell into silence so profound that the panes' rattle and the clock tick and the creaking of the house in the night rose up to fill it. Marty stared at the line of smoke now as fine as thread from the nearly burned cigarette and wanted to reach forward and squash it, but dared not even expel her breath, waiting for Jim to go on.

"I can't even remember what she looked like," he said quietly, and Marty leaned forward and squashed out the burning ashes.

"Why didn't you ever talk about it before, Jim? What was there about it?" she said, keeping her lips and her speech formal, dependable, away from the edge that might be hysteria or a shaking that would never stop.

"I didn't want anybody from Canona to know. You had to later, and so did Solly Leftwich. That was all. I never even told Dad." When she didn't speak he had to go on, like a tired rower who's lost his tow rope, as best he could.

"I didn't even tell Dad. I was planning to. We had it all figured out. When I came back in the summer I was going to tell him."

"Did you tell him?" The story was so slow; Marty began, by habit, to guide it.

"No."

"Why not?"

"Ella walked out on me. There wasn't any sense telling him."

"Jim, are you trying to tell me we're not really married? That you lied about your divorce? Is that it?" When he didn't answer, she went on, asking her own white hands, "That's what you're trying to tell me, isn't it, Jim?"

"Oh, Lord, we're married all right, don't you worry about that. I didn't even know where the little floozie had gone off to. Just went to the boarding-house one day in the spring and she'd gone off with some guy, bag and baggage. I didn't tell Dad, but I told Solly and Solly went all over the place trying to find her. She'd gone off; we didn't even know who with."

"Didn't she leave any word at all?"

Jim laughed for the first time that night. "Sure, she left a note. I'll never forget that note. It just said: 'Jim, we made a big mistake.' Hell, I didn't know anything about a mistake. She just packed up and waltzed off. I couldn't even find out who she'd gone to, the little bitch."

Marty stole a look at him, sitting up in bed by now, staring dead-faced at his own memory. "Go on," she prompted. "Tell me, Jim."

"Well, honey. Solly went all over. After all, I was legally tied to the little bitch. He got me a divorce from her finally for desertion like I always told you. I had the damnedest time keeping Dad from finding out."

"I never could understand why you never told him. You were so close." Marty knew she was getting further from the story, not nearer. Her hands began to twist as if they had their own separate decision, trying to get warm.

"I don't know now. Habit. He'd of kept me looking for her until the day he died. He'd have said she was my legal wife."

"Why have you kept it from me about the child? You know it wouldn't have made any difference."

"I don't know, honey. I tried to a couple of times, but I just didn't know how to go about it——"

She got up and began to pace the room as he had done. A slightly theatrical gesture of putting her hand to her head seemed to disturb her and make her too aware of her own movement. She let her arms hang down again. "Jim, you can carry reticence a little bit too far."

"I just didn't want to get you all upset, honey."

She said nothing, just walked back and forth at the foot of his bed.

"The thing is, honey, we finally heard something. I've got a son. His name's Selby. Selby Dodd." Something in his voice made Marty's head snap up to look at him. "Selby's twenty-four years old. It seems that Ella's dead. . . ."

"How long have you known, Jim?" She shot the question directly, almost yelling.

"Only a week, that's all, Marty."

"Why haven't you heard anything about him before?"

"I don't know, honey; that worried Solly. But he says the boy's got a pretty strong case."

"Who wrote the letter?"

"He did."

"What was his excuse for not finding you before?" She pounded questions at him at last, angry, whipping the story from him with her voice.

"He didn't know until Ella told him. She'd raised him as the other man's son."

Even the bitterness in Jim's voice couldn't stop her.

"Go on, Jim, tell me why!"

"Ella drank, honey. It seems she ran away from her own husband after a binge. They were from Denver. Her marriage to me was bigamous. He finally tracked her down one afternoon at the boarding-house and just packed her up and took her home. She didn't dare to tell him about me. I reckon she was scared. She didn't tell the boy until after he died two years ago. Even then she made him promise not to find me. She got some idea he was illegitimate. Poor little youngin!"

"Is that what he told you?"

"Yes. He doesn't blame her, though. The letter's full of understanding for her. I want you to read it, Marty."

But he didn't offer to get it for her.

"Jim, what are you going to do?" She was stock-still at the foot of the bed, her arms folded now, waiting.

"I'm going to Cincinnati tomorrow to meet him, honey. We arranged it that way. So we could get to know each other a little bit."

"Are you bringing him back here, Jim? What'll we tell people?"

Jim looked full at her then and said: "I don't know what we're going to tell people, Marty. But Selby's my son. He belongs here with me."

His tone was so final, so closed to any reason beyond emotion, that he forced her to match it, blackmailing him.

"Your only son. Go on, Jim, say it!" Marty, feeling she had failed, both in that windy night and somehow in her neat, tidy, silent marriage, threw herself across the bed and sank blessedly into hysterical moans. Jim, trying to reach

22

her, found that she had thrown her large body across his legs and he was pinioned, caught, unable to heave forward in a formal gesture to stop the moaning and slight rolling of his wife's body.

"Awe, honey. Awe, honey," he said to her, as she had said earlier to him.

By four o'clock the wind had died, and by dawn the air was so still that the white mist did not clear from the river until late in the morning. Hamilton Sacks, sitting at the window of the new apartment, listened to his mother getting breakfast in the tiny kitchenette and watched the river where it seemed suspended as a long ribbon in the air below his window. The Eldorado Apartments, built in the Spanish time of the twenties, right on the street, had the river and its bordering trees as a front yard. Almost straight down from the window, Hamilton could hear cars swish by, but he could see nothing but the river and the closed muffled tree-tops—not even the other bank. He clicked his tongue with annoyance as he rested his head against the back of his chair and closed his eyes and sighed. "Oh, my God," he moaned to the empty room.

Hamilton Sacks was his mother's fault. When he, a weak changeling boy, had surprised his sixty-year-old store-keeper father by being born at all to a young, quiet wife, his mother had seen too quickly the shocks that that hostile surprise might bear on him. Out of her terrible fear known only to herself, she had become armour. She was a shield and Hamilton flowered behind her. She had practically raised him on snatches from the cash register. They had educated him; dollars that had once made the bell of the cash drawer ring found their way to a series of addresses in New York, in California, to the intensity of a converted Ozark barn. Then it was emptied altogether for hospital

23

bills when polio had ruined his career. What the career was his mother could never quite make out nor did she really care. When he was well again, she came to look after him as naturally as she breathed, heaving a little sigh of relief as she closed the store she had tried to run for twenty-five years after his father's death—which had been so wished for except by him. To tell the truth, she watched Hamilton now as if he were a slightly dangerous miracle. Her Narcissus had never allowed anything but her takings to touch him— now he had returned, in love with himself no longer, in love with nothing, a Tiresias rather for her to watch, keep dry like powder, and wheel through small towns while he yearned for what he could never have and she did not know, except by sighs, existed.

When she heard his voice, she almost ran out of the kitchenette.

"Why, Joey, I didn't even know you were out here. Your breakfast is all ready." She hitched her robe about her and retied it as she went to the back of his chair. "How long you been up?"

"Hours, Mother; did you hear that wind? Look at the day. It's as grey as a brain."

He had long since stopped trying to make her call him Hamilton; his name between them had become an uneasy truce. In public she called him honey, in private Jo-ey, the way she always had.

"What's the matter, Joey, don't you feel good?" She fitted him in at the kitchen table and began to pour his coffee.

"How will I stand it?" He spoke to himself, including her as a part of that.

"How, honey . . ." She stopped, a little worried, but saw his mood had not grown into deep anger, was only the truculence of the morning.

24

"If anything were going to happen I didn't already know about, if anyone were going to say anything I hadn't already heard. If any sign were one I couldn't already read." Deliberately, he licked his forefingers and smoothed both blond-winged eyebrows. "Where's the sugar?"

"Oh, Lord, I forgot it." She held her robe collar, *peignoir*-like, around her and rootled into the cupboard, paying no attention since he hadn't said he was sick. "They've all done the cutest things getting our apartment ready. Look—everything." She held up a tin of Log Cabin Syrup with some triumph. "Everything good quality, too."

"The kind of thing they used to do for the new preacher, I'm sure . . ." Hamilton muttered, but she didn't hear.

"That Miss Leftwich . . ." She put the sugar on the table and forgot, as people were apt to, about Lydia Leftwich. "I think I'm going to like it here, don't you, Joey?"

"No, Mother."

"Awe, honey, I don't know what gits into you. They were all so nice to us . . ."

"Gets, gets, *gets*, Mother, *gets*!" The last *s* was a sibilant, so carefully pronounced that he faced his mother like a gargoyle, his mouth stretched. "Say it!" he ordered.

"Gets."

"That's better, Mother. I'll hear enough starting tonight. Whye Laedy Sary whur did yu git that Dook? Oh, Lawd Sawboanes, ah jist found em! God," he said again reverently as his mother giggled obediently, and stirred her own coffee at last, relieved that he had begun to joke.

"Didn't you like her? Miz Dodd?"

"Our leading lady?"

She nodded, not quite repeating the phrase, but being interlocutor enough for him to gossip happily and at least entertain himself.

25

"Like her, darling. One does not *like* the woman. Under the burden of all the negative virtues, she has grown large and kind; behind the flick of her wrist on the car wheel there is a caged animal. It is not important, for it will never be let out except in amateur dramatics. And if it were it would probably be more mare than tiger. Oh, Mother, a good woman, good figure, good works—good God! If she didn't bathe three times a day she would have a deep, erotic smell—that would be something, but even that she drowns in more respectable toilet water. Such dark *corralled* women do. Never mind. It all makes for dependability. . . . I have several things in mind for her!" He drank his coffee, waiting for a cue as formal as Mr. Bones. . . .

But his mother said instead, "I thought she was real nice, Joey. She said something lovely . . ."

Hamilton was disgruntled, and so obviously didn't want to hear anything lovely as he bit at his mother.

"Mother! That house! You liked it, didn't you? Rich Coal-Baron Gothic. Now, didn't it go straight to that National Cash Register where you keep your old mahogany dreams?" But the malice was desultory as one plays scales, without pressure or passion, just to keep loosened up.

"As for Big Jim—with his big ring and his big head and his big, rich body . . ."

She was, as she was very seldom, stung to fight back, but only a little. "I'll declare, Joey, he's a nice well-set-up-looking man . . ."

"Well-fed, Mother, well-fed, well-heeled, well-cut, and well-oiled from the looks of him. Did you see those eyes? He looked like he'd been drunk for some years, just quietly, unimaginatively, blind. I love the wealthy, they always look so wonderfully rich." Hamilton was pleased with that. He went on aloud, with what was really an imaginary conversation in *his* dream room, which was not the Eldorado

26

Apartments, slung above the mist of the Canona River, but was somewhere white, above the wine-dark Mediterranean where he had never been. "Did you see that library? I did! The *complete* Edna St. Vincent Millay—the 'best plays' series, Shakespeare, all hers. The Bible, and every national magazine with a circulation of over half a million, for him. The inside of that man's mind must look like a whisky ad. A bronze horse with a lighter up it's arse," he leaned back and closed his eyes, "a fine old pigskin jock-strap, crossed gold golf clubs rampant on a green felt heart, a Varga girl with a lace telephone, all covered with Eau de Richesse. More coffee, Mother," he said, running out of images and opening his eyes.

"I think you're awful, Joey," she giggled now because he was happy.

"As for the rest of the brave little band. I can use Mr. Heavenly Trent. That grocery boy must have made you throb, Mother. Ayun Rayondaulph will be a source of pleasure with her tired blonde hair and her rich husband and her forty-five well hidden years! That blow-george she's married to I'll keep well out of my theatre—I didn't marry his money. And as for Miss Lydia Leftwich, let's decide about her later. Such a depressing girl."

The telephone rang, and on his own wings he wheeled his way there ahead of his mother. From the doorway she smiled after him in some relief. Then she heard him say:

"Everything's heaven, Mrs. Dodd. I adored your house. . . . You *can't come!*" There was a silence, the dream burst and Hamilton's mother knew for the first time how grey the day was going to be. "Oh, my dear lady. We can't start that way. We simply can't. . . . Well, put him on the train and come right away. . . . We'll meet here and get straight to work. Will Mr. Trent call the others?" There was a long wait while he stared malignantly at his mother. "I'll forgive you this time."

He slammed down the phone. "She's got to put her slob of a husband on the train to Cincinnati. Really, can't he have his own little business trip without interfering with my affairs? I wonder if she remembered to pack his cigars. She'll come though, Mother, isn't that nice of her? Isn't it *thoughtful*—the first day. For God's sake push me to my room. I want to get dressed."

The sun was gone. The squall was raised. Hamilton's mother pushed him silently down the long hallway wishing the Marty Dodds of this world, the rich and the selfish and the amateur, could be a little more thoughtful of her dear, breakable, sickly child.

Chapter III

Manicure and Mascara

TRUE to the tradition of her profession, Irene Sigsbie was called 'Sigsbie' by her customers. As she sat hunched over their pale hands, stretched out under the spot-light on to the sterile white towel mat, they seemed disembodied to her; only their hands real, and those flaccid, waiting to be handled, petted, as she moved from nail to nail, picking up fingers separately and painting the nails like little rows of carefully coloured sea shells. Usually she made no other contact during the manicure; her customers' heads were under the roaring dryers and so shut away from her voice; but once in a while, as a blessed relief from the silent concentration on row after row of dead pink shells, someone came in to get a 'touch-up' without a 'set' at 'Dorene's'; then Sigsbie could gossip.

By the time Marty arrived for her touch-up on the Thursday afternoon after Selby Dodd's arrival in Canona, the whole beauty parlour was agog. The girls, from time to time, would peek casually out of their curtained cubicles toward the door; some holding their hands up piled with white suds; Dorene herself wiping her arms with a towel. Once when the door opened, Mrs. Marcellus Cory, half pinned-up, but with little snakes of wet hair still combed down her warm pink neck, stuck her head out through the curtain, and when it was only the mail-man she giggled and went back.

"Isn't it the very limit?" She sat back down in the leather chair, gathering her flesh comfortably under her as Dorene lifted another little strand. "If anything'll take Marty Dodd down off her high horse, this ought to."

"When I heard about it," Dorene went on twirling up wet corkscrews under her clean fingers, "I just said to myself, Miz Dodd, of all people! I think they've done it real well. . . ."

"Don't know what else they could do. . . ." Mrs. Cory caught Dorene's eye in the mirror and they both smiled.

"Well, I mean—coming right out with it like that. You know, just 'There the boy is . . . ask your questions'."

"Lord, I don't know what else they could do. You can't hide a twenty-four-year-old *man* in a bag. . . ." Each laughed into the other's image.

"Of all people, though . . ." As she heard the door swish open again Dorene shut up and went on silently piling little round pin-held curls over Mrs. Cory's head.

Marty, coming in from the cool, sunny, autumn afternoon, felt a wall of physical oppression as she pushed open the door. The electric hum of the dryers made a sleepy sound in the warm, damp, sharp-smelling rooms. Because its air was created by the whirr of the dryers; because of its smell of a perfumed bathroom after a long lazy bath; but mostly because in every place it didn't have to be clinical linen, steel pipe or glass, Dorene's parlour was blush-pink; Marty had always an air of guilt about coming there out of the sun, as if it were somehow faintly common and pornographic. She showed it by striding gracelessly on her heels, as soon as she came in, in a hurry to get away to some imaginary golf-links. Sigsbie, who was neither a fool nor unkind, smiled to herself when she saw the little act, more pronounced this time than ever, and went to meet Marty, in her brassy famous way, to put her at her ease.

30

"Well, Miz Dodd, you're a sight for sore eyes," she told her. "I'm all ready for you, honey. Lemme take that coat. My God, Miz Dodd, this is the prettiest thing I ever laid my two old eyes on. You better watch out I'll have this pussy-cat off your back one of those days and swear I never."

A curtain flicked; there was a murmur of voices, and someone shouted, "I can't hear a damned thing," from under one of the dryers. Marty turned towards the door without even knowing she had done it, but Sigsbie took her by the arm and put her down behind the manicure table, switched on the spot-light and caught her there by her long hand, half-nurse, half-jailer, while she babbled on.

"Honey, I'm going to come right down to brass tacks and say I think that boy of yourall's is the cutest thing I've ever seen in all my life. It musta jest been wonderful for you to have a full-grown handsome youngin like that to pop up right out of the blue and save you the trouble of raisin' him. Now don't pull back. You ought to know by this time I won't file your cuticle." She went on filing Marty's nails carefully, concentrating until she was used again to the feel of that individual set of fingers, murmuring, "Cutest old thing I ever laid my two eyes on." Then said, brightly, "There. Now soak that till I tell you to stop."

One of the white hands moved over and began to play absently with the slick variegated marbles in the bottom of a bowl of warm suddy water.

"Of course, the whole town was just on its ear. You wouldn't have a bit of respect for me if I didn't come right out and say what I thought. You know you can trust Sigsbie." She drew back and looked at the nails in a row, turning her head to the side. "You don't think they're too pointed, do you, honey? I don't think they're too pointed. After all, with those real long lady-like hands. God, I look at mine after you come in here and they don't look like a damn thing but stumps."

She moved the bowl. "There, soak that one." She began to dry Marty's wet hand, carefully, gently, so as not to bruise the cuticle. "Lord God, I said to myself, I think Miz Dodd's wonderful. You don't need to tell me what a shock it musta been for you, honey. But that husband of yours is the happiest-looking thing I ever saw. Honestly, when you come to look at it, you've got a lot to be thankful for. Moon-Glow, or Dream-Glow—or maybe Sin-Glow this week, just to kick over the traces?"

Marty had ceased to follow. "Sigsbie," she slowed her down. "What on earth are you talking about now?" She smiled at last, able to treat Sigsbie like a clown.

"Those are the new 'Glow' shades. Aren't they cute little bottles? But, good God Almighty, look at them names. Which do you want? Shell, pink or red, honey. Take red— go on, turn over a new leaf! Go on!" She held up the squat pinched bottle and the bright red through the spot-light seemed more alive than the hand that held it.

"I don't know. I can't take my eyes off my finger-nails if I have that."

"Well, you're going to have it, anyway. A little bright red won't do you any harm, honey. After all . . ."

"Sigsbie, you . . ." When Marty stopped, Sigsbie looked up, the red brush poised over the first finger-nail.

"What do you want, honey?"

"Nothing. You go on ahead."

After the ten red nails lay under the hot light, false as masks on the white fingers, Sigsbie leaned back for the last time. "Miz Dodd, they look gorgeous. Don't you move till they're good and dry or I won't let you have Sin-Glow any more." She crowed with laughter. "Lord, honey, you don't look a day over thirty, sitting there in your Sin-Glow—and here with a fine ready-made-grown-up boy! Lord's love, I think you're wonderful."

"He's a nice boy, Sigsbie; just as nice and polite and intelligent as I'd want a boy of mine to be. I think I'm pretty lucky." Marty, when she finally did speak, spoke carefully and seriously what she wanted the whole of Canona to repeat, knowing that to speak at Sigsbie's table in 'Dorene's' was just as public as any opening night of the Canona Thespians. As she spoke, she was aware, as of a hidden audience of familiar people made strangers by the footlights, that here were silent listeners, all down the cubicles and behind the movie and fashion magazines of this warm, woman's place. Her voice dropped; she couldn't help succumbing to her own training, when she said "pretty lucky". There was a high silence after she had spoken, but she broke it herself, saying, "Sigsbie, isn't my Sin-Glow dry yet?" She was relieved enough to laugh, listening to the buzz of gossip and crackling of dryer-literature well up again around her.

"How do you like your new watcha-call-'im? Director?" Now the interview passed on to other matters. Sigsbie had Canona's first lady literally by the hands for less than half an hour of the eventful week. She stood outside it, fascinated by a woman to whom something had actually happened, who was in the middle of a kind of sacred circle of money, leisure and crisis. There Martha Dodd sat, though, with her ten fingers still offered on the white mat, her face unchanged and full of secrets, her body slightly widened in the years. There were fragments that Sigsbie, innocently, was intent on uncovering, and the whole line of white curtains behind her still remained alive with listeners, depending on her.

"Mr. Sacks? Oh, he's just wonderful. I think he'll set us all on our ears," Marty answered. "He's turned the whole

Thespians upside down. It's real exciting." Then, kindly, "There'll be public readings for parts. Everybody who wants to can come. What about you, Sigsbie?—we need some pretty girls."

Sigsbie leaned back her blonde head and neighed with laughter. "Me? Oh, Lord God Almighty! Couldn't you see me . . . pushin' forty!"

It was just at that minute that Mrs. Cory, realising that there would be no more said about the boy, signalled for Dorene to lower the dryer over her wet head. As the loud air-whirr closed in around her ears, she spoke for the first time, not knowing that she yelled. "If Jim Dodd was any husband of mine I just simply wouldn't stand for it, that's all."

She settled comfortably down with an old *Vogue* and some movie magazines, not knowing that her voice had rung like a cracked bell around the quiet beauty parlour.

"Lord, I never felt so awful in all my born days! That big blabber-mouth. I tell you I nearly went through the floor!" Sigsbie stood, arms twined and elbows out, leaning against the doorsill of her little living-room. It was five-thirty in the evening and she was still in her coat, but too excited to take it off before she told her story.

Plain George, lying back in the one big chair, with his stockinged feet nearly into the gas-fire, interrupted, "Boy, I can see old Marty's face now! What did she do?"

"She just sat there." Sigsbie's voice went quite quiet with admiration. She shed her coat on to a chair and came and stood before the fire with her skirt hiked up at the back. "She looked real statue-like for a minute and then she said," here Sigsbie closed her eyes and bunched her skirt tightly in her fists, suffering, " 'Sigsbie,' she said, 'are my nails dry yet? I've got to go.' Real calm. I could have gone *right* through the floor. So I felt her. She was dry all right. 'Don't mention I heard it,' " she leaned over and almost whispered to Plain George as Marty had done to her. "So I just took the bit in my teeth and I said, 'Look here, Miz Dodd, you can't let that old barrel in there get away with talking about you like that.' I said that. Just said it, right out, and she said, still all calm and cold, 'Maybe you're right, Sigsbie.' And then she waltzed right back to the booths and I went right after her. I thought she was gonna have a real knock-down carry out—— Oh, Lord . . ."

Here Plain George interrupted again, "I can see that! I can see her unbend that much!" He reached over and pulled Sigsbie down into his lap.

"I went right after her"—she got back to the story, "and she started jerking back curtains until she found Miz Cory with just her chin sticking out under the dryer. But of course she could tell by the body!"

"She just said, 'Elner, I heard you. Don't think I didn't hear you.' Still real calm. Then she walked off down the shop. Well, of course, Miz Cory hadn't heard a damn word, her sitting under the dryer like that. I ran after her and I said, 'Miz Dodd, she couldn't hear a damn word you said.' I just told her, right out. And she turned around." Here the story reached a climax and Sigsbie sat straight and full of dignity on Plain George's lap, "And do you know what she said to me? She said, 'Lord, Sigsbie, I don't even care about a little thing like that.' And she *laughed*, just laid her head back and laughed."

Plain George, playing with her blonde tightly-waved stiff hair, asked, "What happened then?" just because he liked hearing Sigsbie talk.

"Oh, she just went on out, that's all." Sigsbie leaned back. "Have you seen the boy?"

"Oh, sure, I've seen him. We went down there the night

after he came. Real nice boy. Good-looking. Nice boy."

"Does he look like his father?"

"Lord, no, honey. Jim's gone to fat."

"Oh, I know that—but in the face?"

"Nope. Curly-headed boy—real nice." Plain George had his face in Sigsbie's hair by now, but she sat up, hoping to make him tell more. "What does he do?"

"I don't know, honey. Come here."

Sigsbie, who had been doing just exactly what Plain George told her to since her brother brought him home to drink one afternoon eight years before, bent her head and shut up. Plain George, warm, master, sighing with comfort and safety, said "Miss me?" and began cosily to unbutton Sigsbie's dress.

Somebody, as people do, had tried to tell Anne Randolph Potter that her Plain George had been quietly, happily, unromantically unfaithful to her for eight years. She said quite merrily, because she cultivated a merry voice, "Honey, I really think you're out of your *mind*!"

She told Marty about it later. "George! Imagine! Lord, I can't get him out of the house." She had giggled and, being the kind of woman who takes for granted that all adultery takes place in parked cars, added, "Can you imagine Plain George doing anything that *uncomfortable*?"

But at seven o'clock, while Plain George was finishing a nice hot cup of coffee that Sigsbie always made him, as a little ritual, to drink in front of the gas-fire before he had to drive away, Ann Randolph was putting mascara on even more patiently than the years of practice could account for. She did not shake her head then, but held it still, as she painted her lashes with her mouth slightly 'oh-ed' with concentration.

Downstairs in her colonial living-room fifteen minutes later, Anne Randolph sat gracefully among the traditional 'coverlet' cushions, and fumed. "Hi, honey!" Plain George called out to her from the hallway, having driven down at sixty from Sigsbie's cottage in the Hollow to where his own house spread brand-new, looking across a span of mud that some day would be a lawn. "Miss me?" he added by habit, without an idea of what he said.

"Oh, George, I'll just have to gulp my dinner down now," she wailed, coming out into the hall and going into the dining-room without looking at him. "Oh, Beulah, how many times have I told you you don't want to put the soup on the table until I tell you?"

There was no answer from the kitchen.

"Lord, I can't even get myself a drink first." He followed her in.

"You probably had plenty already."

"I had to work," he said feebly, not caring whether she heard or not.

"Well, I've got a reading tonight and I've just got to get there on time for once." Anne Randolph thawed. She never stayed mad with Plain George long, just petted him a little and forgot. "Hamilton's got this idea that a lot of new talent's going to turn up." She stopped long enough to let her face relax carefully around the eyes and mouth. "A lot of uneducated trash! He'll learn." She began to eat, hurriedly, pounding at the bell with her foot between courses.

"Marty going tonight?" Plain George looked up and spoke his first words just as Beulah stumbled in with the grey pie she made so badly and often. Anne Randolph refused it with her usual military discipline about her own slim body, leaned forward, fascinated for a minute across the table.

"She's bringing Selby." She announced, "Honestly, George, I do admire the way Marty is handling this whole

37

situation. Look at the way they've had the house full of people every single night, as if he was home from college or the war or something. I always thought Marty had a little kind of tacky streak in her. After all she doesn't have what I call the best of taste. Don't you think so? I mean—sometimes I *feel* it—intellectually."

George, his jaws stuck together with a gob of pie, didn't know which judgment he was meant to agree with, so he just nodded.

"It's just that thing that comes out once in a while—I don't know a more modern way to put it," she giggled self-consciously, "except that she's a little too 'lady-like' a lot of the time about things. And a lady," Anne Randolph said, with the inevitable swing of the corn hair that had grown down Virginia, "never let's you know she's acting like one." She was pleased at putting her finger right on the point. "But don't you think this time she's grand—just grand? Kind of casual about it. He ought to be good at the Thespians. Lord knows we need a nice-looking boy with all those shoe-salesmen."

"He'll have to come see Sally Bee Christmas, won't he?" George had managed the pie and the idea struck him as particularly bright as he tried to get involved in Anne Randolph's monologue.

"Honey, you get the oddest ideas sometimes!" Anne Randolph stood up, and he rose, too, as if it were the Episcopal Church. "Sally Bee's a baby! This boy's a man when you come to think of it. Why, he's been all over and he reads and everything. Lord knows what he'd talk to Sally Bee about, of all people! Besides, what do we know about the boy, after all?"

Plain George knew the understanding condescension that was way beyond anger with Anne Randolph, so he followed without answering and helped her into her coat.

38

"I'm taking your car. Mine's gone funny." She called back at the door, "Key's in it?"

"Sure," he called from the living-room, already mixing a drink.

The door slammed.

So Plain George, who had a large collection of reading to do, since Anne Randolph hadn't kept him home for several nights, carried his drink to his cute master's maple chair, piled *Collier's*, the *Saturday Evening Post*, the *Red Book* and *Astounding Stories* beside him on the milking-stool table, switched on the radio loud, and settled down with a sigh. But with his comforting sex and his heavy supper, before he had finished his drink, or begun to read, Plain George Potter was deep in his evening nap.

"No, Marcellus, he went to meet him in Cincinnati. *Cincinnati*," called Mrs. Cory over the noise of the radio while Mr. Cory, tired Mr. Cory, slumped down beside it and sucked his cigar.

"I always thought your family sent you to Cincinnati when you took to drink or when you had a nervous breakdown!" Dorene's manufactured curls bounced as she sat down beside him.

"Go to see Broadway shows." Marcellus Cory told her about Cincinnati, scoring a point and plugging his private smile again with his cigar.

"I saw her today."

If he didn't say "Who?" he should have, so Mrs. Cory answered him, anyway.

"Martha Dodd!" she said then and fell back against the couch to tell the story.

Chapter IV

See the Brave Thespians

HAMILTON SACKS' active imp had forced him to suggest to the Canona Thespian Reading Committee—and drive through like he did his own chair—a sophisticated comedy called *Bedtime for Miranda*. A desire to shock, to fill his theatre for his first play in Canona, and the fact that he planned to do it again at a summer theatre in the Adirondacks with a fairly professional cast, had helped his choice. It had taken him only three weeks to break down all their private dreams for the winter.

"It seems to me that our duty to Canona is to give it a professional theatre," he was saying to a large gathering of people making a half-circular group which peppered out into the darkness of the auditorium from where he sat in the aisle before the footlights, bathed in the only balcony spot. His voice sounded hollow through the darkness as Selby lifted the little light-curtain for Marty to go into the dark house and then followed her. He smiled, hearing what Hamilton was saying, but his smile was caught only by a fifteen-year-old girl who looked back, seeing the flick of the curtain, and saw his thin, nearly gaunt young face in the beam of light from the foyer which caught his fine waving brown hair and made a nimbus of it. The girl sat sighing the rest of the evening and couldn't bring herself actually to read for a part in the play—not in front of *him*.

Later she put it all into passionate speech, "He's the cutest thing I ever saw!"

"A local company does not mean a company where only those plays are done which, having failed the high test of commercial success, are now relegated to the outer provinces of those who know better. We will not strive to be 'too good' for the public we serve." Here Hamilton expected some laughter—but he did not get it. His audience had no idea what he meant. "A professional stage gathers the best from New York, from London—perhaps, not often, from the past itself; offers it to its audience and says, Here—I have done my best. Here is Theatre!" Hamilton spread out his hands in an easy gesture of offering and his mother rearranged herself with relief, knowing that when his hands left off clutching his chair-wheels, the fear and the depression over the first public meeting were over, and that he was, in his way, enjoying himself.

Marty could see only two seats left vacant in the front row, but she hesitated at the top of the aisle with Selby hovering behind her. She knew already that to walk through the house while he was speaking and command the spot-light for a minute would be an entrance that Hamilton would enjoy more than forgive. But he seemed to sense she was there after a few minutes, and called her down. Actually Hamilton had seen the shaft of light cut across the back of the dusty dark house, too, but he waited until he could control her entrance.

"Is that Mrs. Dodd? Do come and join us," he called graciously. "We didn't want to start without you, but having announced our reading for *eight* I really feel we must start on time. Come and join the Casting Committee. Selby, you may sit beside mother, but don't say a word. We want you for an actor, so you *mustn't* cast the play."

The impact of Hamilton's insult-studded, careful speech

was staggering, but he had so quietened his audience that the shock whispered across the crowd like a gust of wind instead of rising in a crescendo of noise. He had told the Casting Committee that for the first time in the life of the Canona Thespians they were not to have actual parts in *Bedtime for Miranda* but would be driven by him without any hope of the breathless first-night glory-dive. He had also ticked off Canona's Thespian backbone, money-bags, leading lady, matron-patron for being late.

But, more than all that, he had put into words that, in the eyes of the rest of Canona, Marty was at last a mother.

There were only a few evidences left that the Canona Theatre had once been a Church of the Methodist Immersion faith. Its one-time main room had had its floor tilted slightly and was fitted with spring-back seats. Its floor once had been the bane of a little group of soap-smelling, sad, middle-aged women who'd tried to raise money for a carpet out of their religious dues and the sale of their old clothes to each other. But it had been for some years now covered with dusty, ugly rubber cloth to lighten the tread of late-comers to the Canona Thespian performances. The only memory of the Methodist Immersions, so far as the auditorium was concerned, was in the Canona Thespians themselves, the building's present gallant little band, who had, with Puritan zeal, kept all the money they raised for the other side of the thick brown velvet curtain and had not put one spot of colour into the house at all.

But this was not evident. What was a real memory of the church was the small square entrance-hall, which had only been painted to match the 'Green Room' next door and had a few amusing show-boat posters, and one framed Victorian broadsheet announcing 'The Canona Thespians' in *Ten Nights In a Bar-room*, to wean it from its religious background. The square iron stove, kept from church times, was religious enough—the same old darky tended it, fed it carefully over the years, and now no one noticed it as an object at all, just a focus of heat to stand near while the outside door swung back and forth, breathing in gusts of cold air.

At the end of the reading a little, loyal group huddled about the hall-stove. Most of the strangers, not knowing the way of gleaning gossip, had gone. The little group spoke in whispers, staying in the transient hall because they were not close enough to the Thespian inner council to swing back the door and go and sit in the Green Room. The fifteen-year-old girl had finished her passionate speech, but even her screech of joy was only a half-whisper, as they strained their ears to hear snatches of the conversation going on inside the auditorium.

"Isn't he cute, though?" Another girl, muffled already and slightly red-nosed, since she couldn't get near enough to the stove, added to the picture of Selby.

"Isn't it cold, though?" the delicate little County Librarian added, changing the subject tactfully.

"Winter came on too early this year to suit me!" said her best friend, who worked as a State Registered Nurse, and knew the signs of fright in the bird-like Librarian's face.

Later, walking down by the glare of the all-night garage to the bus-stop, the Librarian suddenly stopped and blurted out, "Not a one of the rest of us could get by with a thing like that!"

Her friend, knowing exactly what she meant, tempered, "Well, Lord, I don't know what else the poor woman could do but brazen it out. He was supposed to have been married. You know, way long in the past."

"I'll bet. I'll just bet." The Librarian was quiet for a minute. "It's always the man," she announced.

"It sure is the man all right," her friend agreed.

"Think of any trouble coming to those kind of people."
The little Librarian and her friend talked no more, standing
in the wind at the deserted bus-stop.

There is a certain stage of cruelty, or humiliation, where
one is numb, where one goes through the actions of one's
expected life like a heavy dance, and nobody notices, except
perhaps a lover or an enemy, that anything is wrong. Marty
sat in this slow mood of numbness, and Hamilton, watching
her, hawk-like and avid for clues, suspected that she herself
did not know the reason for her state, for she was taking
part, making suggestions, playing at casting as hard as the
rest. Only once she faltered and said, surprised, "I'm dead
tired tonight," and yawned, covering her mouth.

"Why, Marty, you've been leading too gay a life! You'll
wear yourself out. It's you, Selby," he turned towards the
boy, smiling more gently than his mother had seen for a
while, "you've just bewitched the whole place."

"Honey!" Anne Randolph leaned over the back of the
seat and took her hand. "Don't you pay any attention!"

Marty smiled self-consciously, "Let's get back to work.
What about the Martin girl for the maid? I've got her down
as O.K. She's been trying for so long, and she's so loyal."

Hamilton struck a line across his notes through Miss
Martin. "Oh God, dear, two reasons why she'll be more
trouble than she's worth. I've had it before. All that good
intention rolled into three lines! They take more work than
any lead." His gold pencil stopped, and he looked up,
excited. "Mrs. Potter, I've got an idea. You play the maid!
You're one of our mainstays—and if you do it you'll show
the public that we're really a team and that there's no inner
circle plucking the plums."

Anne Randolph said nothing until everyone had looked
round at her. "I'd just love to," she said then carefully,
"but I don't think we ought to go against your rule about

44

the Casting Committee not having parts. I just somehow feel that it wouldn't be the thing. Not just yet . . ." she added sweetly to warn Hamilton that there was truce but no capitulation.

"You're right, dear, you're absolutely right, dear." The gold pencil danced on the paper and then Hamilton sighed. "I can't think for another minute. Let's meet tomorrow when we've all slept on it to decide finally." He began to wheel himself slowly up the aisle out of the light. As the rest were shifting to get up he whirled round for the last time.

"Of course," his voice rolled down from the back of the house, "we're all agreed on our new juvenile. Selby . . . you'll be here long enough to take the part. You won't desert us all, will you?" He knew, with a jump of his heart that to someone else might have meant they were in love, that the question of the length of Selby's stay had not been discussed. He knew by the catch of silence.

Then Marty's voice as she got up and faced the bright light, "He'll be here, Hamilton. We're not going to lose him now that we've found him at last, are we, Selby?" as the boy moved forward to slip on her coat.

Hamilton noticed with real joy that Marty's face, in the light, was as hard with embarrassment as lined stone.

Later, in his little office off the Green Room, he giggled to his mother.

"I do admire her, you know, darling, she's so noble, and she has such a gorgeous instinct for figure-headedness. I do wish she'd be a little less corny about her line reading." He threw his head back, glared fixedly at the goose-neck lamp on his desk and intoned, "We're not going to lose him now that we've found him at last," and brought out the "last" with the dying fall of a parson.

His mother, stirring the Nescafé into their 'Studio' cups

behind him, had stopped listening. Her lips were moving as a habit. "Rhubarb, rhubarb, rhubarb," she would mouth —the only habit she had ever managed to keep from Hamilton. That was because it only happened when Hamilton's malice was too much for her, when the barbs were flying from her unhappy child and she wanted neither to notice nor to answer. "Rhubarb, rhubarb, rhubarb," she said silently now while Hamilton imitated Marty Dodd.

But as she carried his cup to him, she noticed, lying on the desk, his evening notes. Scrawled across them was a heavy-uddered cow with the face and hair of Anne Randolph Potter.

Mrs. Sacks, who had packed and unpacked so much in the last ten years, sighed a very little sigh.

It was that cold night, when the station wagon in the parking lot seemed sunk toward the icy ground and refused to move, that Selby began driving for Marty. She was not sorry when he suggested it after she'd choked her engine and filled half the lot with smoke. As Selby jumped out to run round the car, Marty, sliding across the seat, caught a glimpse of herself in the car mirror where the street light shone across her face and, without knowing that she had done it, wet her lips and pressed them together.

"We ought to let it rest." Selby leaned back easily. "Cold?" He pressed the heater and the small fan whirred. When she said nothing, huddled beside him with her head withdrawn into her coat collar, he watched her. "Tired?" he asked gently, but she only nodded.

"This is the first minute I've been alone with you since I came. Do you realise that?" He kept on watching her, and when she turned to look at him, frightened a little, cornered, she found that he looked, not as she had expected, as avid for her to make a move to give herself away as the rest had been, but that he seemed as calm, as unaffected, and as casually sympathetic as she had wished for all her life.

"You've been taking a ride on account of me, haven't you, Marty?"

"Selby," she answered almost formally, "you know how glad Jim and I are to have you. Why, your father . . . She came up out of her coat, on sure ground now, to tell him how happy Jim was.

"Curiosity can be cruel. God, how well I know that!" he went on. "Look, ask me now. Ask me whatever you want to, Marty. You be curious. My God, you must be going crazy with questions you haven't asked." When she didn't answer, he said urgently, "Ask me before the engine warms up." He held the wheel and would have shaken her as he shook at it to make her answer.

"We just love . . ." she began again.

"You. I know about Jim. I knew Jim when I saw him coming down the lobby of the Netherland Plaza Hotel, all there was to know. We got along fine . . . what a dump that place is!" he said irrelevantly.

"I'd just never forgive myself if I asked you anything that made you think for one minute that you weren't just as welcome as you could be . . ." Marty began, hesitantly. "We don't want to complicate everything, do we?"

"Try again," the boy murmured.

But he had spoken too soon. She retreated back into her coat collar, apologising. "If there's anything strange to you, you talk to Jim. Men." She said weakly, "You're making him so happy." She reached out and touched his arm, safe at last. "It ought to start now."

And because of a second of safety, she failed to stop Selby's questioning and fell into the gulf she was trying to dodge.

"How much does he tell you, Marty?"

Some faces look younger in the half-dark, but Selby's looked older, older and harder because the night had drained the colour away. Turned towards her in the pale street light she saw his head darkly, and his hair, curly above his forehead, threw a dark shadow that made his eyes seem sunken, tired; they could have even been in pain.

"Why are you keeping on at Jim?" she said, louder, to keep him from watching her so intently.

Now the questioning was turned and, without realising it, Marty had grown angry with the boy—"You've got to let us get used to you, Selby. Lord knows we're trying hard enough. Why, your father . . ."

"He hasn't told you a damn thing. I wondered if he would."

"What's there to tell me? You sound so bitter."

"I don't want to start an argument," he muttered, turning his face away at last. "I thought there were things you'd want to know. God—here I butt in—a complete stranger." He tried the starter and the car gained energy, was animated smoothly under his touch. "Here we are, all complete strangers—play-acting at mother, father, son—who for? That malicious little crippled bastard back there? I could have dragged him out of his push-cart and broken his neck. How many incidents like that have you had?"

Marty felt a chill along her back when he spoke, but thought it was the cold and pulled her coat tighter. "Honey! Don't mind him. You have to make allowances, you know. He's not like us."

Selby glanced at her with a shock that was nearly fear, too surprised at what she'd said to realise that he had misunderstood. He backed the car and whirled it round in the nearly empty lot.

"Why, Selby, honey"—not understanding what he said, but recognising the youngness of his tone, Marty became

48

kindly. "Don't you give people another thought. You have to learn to ignore things." Then, remembering a word to tie to, "We don't want you to feel like a stranger. You're Jim's son. It's the same to us as if you'd been with us all your life. Now you better forget this stranger talk. Why, Jim's already as wrapped up in you . . ."

"As if I were a new baby. What do you know about me?"

"Well, I think we know all the important things. Jim said he had a good long talk with you and that he was proud of the way you looked at things; that's what he told me."

At the corner where they stopped for the signal, the strings of coloured lights and the glittering Christmas windows were making a fantastic reddish twinkle below the familiar neon signs of the shops—shining out holiday, shoes, clothes, food, movies, although the street was nearly deserted. As the signal snapped from red to bright green, a live drop of light in the centre of their night vision, Marty let the starting of the car push her gently back against the seat and she closed her eyes.

"Christmas!" she said. "It seems to start earlier every year. We must make some nice plans. After all, we've all got a lot of celebrating to catch up on. Jim and I never paid all that attention before." She smiled without being noticed. "You know—parties—but nothing of our own. Don't be surprised if he lands you up with an electric train, Selby."

The tension was gone between them. Selby, driving, had succumbed to her refusal to meet him and was aware only of the large, powerful car under his body, his hands and feet hitched to it like electrodes while his brain ran it. He heard only dimly the woman beside him, agreed easily, let her control their relationship in their ride home.

"I love trains. Good," he told her, then almost teasing her, "So I'm staying for Christmas?"

49

"Why, Selby, I guess I just took it for granted that you were. Jim talked like it."

"I'd love to. I'm having a wonderful time."

"Well, that's just fine." In a burst of confidence because they were so near home that a few hundred feet would rescue her from complication, she put her hand gently on his arm. "We're going to be good friends, Selby," she said as he had known all along she would. He turned the grin that rushed to his face into a gentle smile of complicity.

"Sure we are, Marty. And sometime I'll tell you why I'm so bitter." The car slid to a stop.

"Oh, Selby."

"You said it, Marty."

"I didn't mean to hurt your feelings. I wouldn't have done that for the world." She realised her hand on his arm and drew it away.

"Who's been considering your feelings in all this?" He reassured her, jumped out of the car and went round to help her out. "I've got some idea. Marty, you're a nice woman. You know that?"

"You're all right yourself." Marty's smile was grateful and her step, as she walked ahead of him towards the high porch, the up-hill self-conscious walk of a young, shy girl.

Chapter V

They All Lived Happily

MARTY knew better than to waste her time trying to make Jim talk to her when he was already resting in the habits of his evenings. She dreamed that night through the lazy gossip, the comfort and the night-caps; all the rituals, the adjustment of the fire-screen, locking the doors; inspection of the ash-trays, and the last shuffling of envelopes in his pockets which Jim always went through like an unminded litany while he let the music from the radio wave round him. She dreamed, and said good-night to Selby, watching him more closely; having slipped into acceptance of the 'son', she began to notice more about the person. From the edge of the stairs to the upper hall she watched him say good-night to his father, bend forward with the brush of a kiss for his cheek, turn and swing lightly into his room, his head down, shy for a second; then he was gone.

In the corridor alone, Jim raised his hand to the cheek Selby had kissed so lightly; then realising that Marty was behind him, he scratched his face and said, "Honey, he's a nice boy," and turned away.

She began what she wanted to say in the corridor, knowing that there, as he was between rooms, he was also between habits, caught in flight, easier to find. She watched with the unconscious timing of the hunter, the servant, the flirt, the child of bad parents; with the timing of women she watched him turn along the hall and, in mid-step, called lightly:

"Jim, I want to talk to you."

That way she entered for the first time since his confession into Jim's dreaming. He stopped and waited for her to catch up.

"Sure, honey, come on in, have a cigarette," and followed her into his bedroom.

Inside it was not so easy. Silence while they lit cigarettes. Silence while they sat each side of the gas-fire and watched it.

"Everything go all right tonight, honey?" he asked, to help her into words, although she and Selby had entertained him with it before, together, making him warm with contentment.

"Jim," she leaned forward over her clasped hands, but stiffly, using her words carefully, as if her thinking aloud was on a razor-edge. "I've been thinking about all this for quite some time; it's been nearly a month since Selby came, and I think that now we're all used to each other, we ought to make some decisions, and, you know, honey, things have to be regular. We have to know where we are."

"Don't we know where we are?" She did not catch the withdrawal in his voice, the suspicion that she was going to wake him up, make trouble, prick the bubble, measure his happiness out of existence.

"Well, for instance, I think that for Selby's sake we ought to—kind of regularise things. People ask me things and I don't know what to say. I just don't know how to answer, Jim." He did not catch the fear, the horror of the gulf of surprises as she begged, trying to explain at the same time; he interrupted:

"What business is it of anybody else's? Selby's my boy—our boy—this is his home. What business is it of a lot of people's? Selby's my son. He's a Dodd the same as me. Why we prit near built this damn place."

"Now, honey, don't get upset. Everybody likes Selby.'

She stood up, as he had done, to pacify him, to shout him into helping them measure the new world if need be. "I think he's as sweet a boy as I've ever known. Why, Jim," she laid her arm on his sleeve, "I feel he's mine, too."

He was rocked into peace by her expected, formal, demanded sentimental lie, and he sat down again, guided by her hand. "Marty, you don't know what you saying that means to me. I'll never forget that, honey."

"I think just for Selby's sake we ought to decide with him how long he wants to live with us."

"You said you liked him. . . . Dammit, I don't know what the hell all this is about."

"Now, Jim, you know I like him. I'm going to try to think of him as my son, too, if you want me to. But there's nothing wrong with all of us knowing where we stand, is there? You've got him to think of."

Back on the track of her thinking, he said nothing.

"Now, things like this. Are you offering to take him in with you?"

"Naturally. Sure I am."

"Have you told him? Have you asked the boy?"

"Well, I just took it for granted . . ."

"Jim Dodd." Marty jumped up and almost slapped him. "Don't you take so damn much for granted. Do you know what kind of life the boy's had? What kind of training—anything! Lord—you've got to be fair to him. Does he want to live with us? Or has he just come like a stranger to look us over and just go off somewhere, and us all upset by him being your passing son—just left high and dry. Which is he? Lord, I don't know. I don't know anything!" Marty, having been brought by her anger somewhere near to what was troubling her, only glimpsed it and shrank away from it. She could only say sitting down again and covering her eyes. "Lord, I just don't know."

"Now, honey, you just calm down. Maybe you're getting a little bit too complicated about all this." So for the second time that evening they turned away from understanding and sighed. "Don't you worry, I won't make my boy do anything he doesn't want to. But you can see by looking at him he's steady and maybe he needs us as much as we need him." He lifted her up and put his arms around her. "I don't mind telling you, honey, I want him to settle in here and just be one of us like he'd been here all his life. That's my dream."

"You know I want him, don't you, Jim? That's always in your mind," she said, leaning her head on his shoulder and gazing at the gas-fire. "Isn't it, Jim?"

"Sure, I know that, girl—I know. Now, don't you worry. Don't you worry about a thing."

So Marty Dodd went to bed refreshed, not knowing in her relief that she had asked for facts and settled for simple dreams from Jim of living happily ever after with a fairy prince for a son who appeared out of the past in answer to a wish. She didn't know that until she woke up, startled, in the cold morning light.

CHAPTER VI

The Twelve Days of Christmas

GIRLS moved in packs, eddying to and fro, clogging the aisles, attracting boys in the holiday train. They ate and waved, and stood with their hips awry in the corridors, shrieking over the clatter of the train and the rhythmic maddening tinkle of touching silver and glasses on the white Pullman tables. The Old Corn Pone Tavern dining-car, for such few evenings of the year, became, as it hurtled down out of the deep passes at dinner-time, like a speeding, well-cared-for club-house where the only badges of membership were those unmentioned ones of voice, sweater, shoes, belts, haircuts, fur-coats, and the deep-moated solidity of having enough money to go East somewhere to school.

Sally Bee Potter sat quite sure of herself and already a little drunk at a table in the centre of the car, while Terence Jameston Sowerby III, whose father had cornered Taxema, Missouri, lay asleep beside her with his crew-cut down among the Corn Pone Tavern silver. Across the table, Sally Bee's best friend, a girl from Duluth who took thyroid tablets, looked over at him with some panic.

"How're you going to move him, Sally Bee?" she asked.

"I guess he'll wake up before he gets to Cincinnati, won't he? I'm going to leave him right here. Oh, I'm so tired of the whole pattern of my life." Sally Bee let her head fall to her hands and leaned forward, exposing the round swell of her breasts to her friend from Duluth. "I love Sourball, but he's never sober . . ."

The room-mate from Duluth refused to hear Sally Bee's troubles. She was too excited.

"Aren't you glad to be going home? Gosh, I've been counting the days . . ." she confessed with some joy because she was only seventeen.

Sally Bee looked at her with what could almost have been pity.

"Really—haven't you ever been away from home before? Really—you act so *naive*."

"But I'm glad. I'm just glad. What's the matter with that?"

A boy in a checked jacket made a great pantomime of looking down Sally Bee's dress and then whistling, a long low call, but was pushed on down the car by his companion.

Sally Bee paid no attention.

"Honestly, Sally Bee, I think you ought to put that little jabot back in your dress."

"Jabot! What kind of word is that? Why don't you grow up? Why do you talk like a tacky midwesterner? You just bore me to deep oblivion."

"If you go on yelling at me, Sally, I'll leave you right here and never come out with you again."

Sally had not yelled. Their faces had drawn closer to each other and they whispered, their whispers barbed with anger as they nagged at each other across the table.

"I wouldn't give a f—," Sally Bee spat at her, and the room-mate's face crinkled with anger and controlled tears. She threw a five-dollar bill on the table and ran, forcing the waiting people out of her way, down the dining-car. Sally Bee took a last look at Sourball, flung down another bill and sighed. Then she, too, ran down the snaky train, falling against the high-backed seats as it lurched through the pass.

She found her room-mate sitting watching herself in the

wide mirror of the ladies' dressing-room; when the girl saw the reflection of who it was, she turned away and studied the V-shaped towels piled high on a shelf.

"Now, honey." Sally Bee caressed the girl's back but looked over her head into the mirror sadly. "Don't mind. You know me better than that. You know I don't mean anything I say. I'm temperamental, honey."

"I hate that kind of language." The girl's voice was muffled.

"I just reckon I'm too hard", Sally Bee said. "You're lucky. You don't know anything and you want to go home and everything. I just hate it. I just goddam hate it," she said violently and began to cry, still watching herself in the mirror.

That was early, when the first lights were being flung back out of the darkness from isolated shacks as the train rushed past.

Later on the valley widened and Sally Bee read from the twinkling bright windows of the towns, the lines of tipple lights down to the water across the river, the far distant red glow of the coke-ovens, that she was getting near home. She had forgotten her tears, and even why she'd cried them. Frantically she began to dash her face in the drunken water of the pullman basin and re-insert the little white collar and stock she had taken from her dress. She combed her short curls and straightened her stockings and danced around getting ready so much that the room-mate from Duluth began to be excited again with her.

"Gosh, you're funny. You are funny. You're so temperamental, honey!"

"Rhyme!" they both screamed, and the girl from Duluth went through the ritual, counting on her fingers, "Ten— ABCDEFGHIJ—who do I know that begins with J?"

"Maybe you'll meet a J during the vacation."

"Jimmy McTurley, oh Lord!" the girl groaned.

The train began to slow and Sally Bee rubbed a window clear of foggy moisture with her fist and pressed her face to it, scanning the track-side.

"I've got to go. I've got to go now. We're almost in. Good-bye, honey, have an absolutely marvellous time."

"Oh, I will. You too. Merry Christmas," the room-mate said in an agony of sudden embarrassment.

"Same to you. I will. Oh, sure I will." Sally Bee rushed down the aisle, tripping towards the door where the porter had put the bags for Canona.

As it was, she was the first off the train.

The room-mate from Duluth watched Anne Randolph and Plain George hurrying, all hearty and good-looking and gay, out of the high porch of the Canona station, sat back in her seat and sighed.

The platform was a babble of "Hi! Hi, honey! Why, hi, Yew!" and under the screaming of excited girls, the steady hum of the boys, some with their voices newly changed, eyeing each other carefully to see who had gone sissy, pansy, square, egg-head, damned; who had broken the code of uniformity they were being exposed to; who would in turn be broken on the rack of innocent, social taboo during the Christmas holidays.

Sally Bee, over her mother's shoulder, squealed, "Lord, look at Stumbum! Has he gone Yale! Gosh, he isn't even out of Sainsbury yet. Hi, Stum!" She rushed past her parents to a languid boy in dark grey flannel, with the collar of his camel-hair coat turned carefully up in a careless manner, smoking a pipe with the silver letter S on the side of the bowl, watching the rest of the platform with the self-conscious appraisal and disinterested disapproval of a Puritan saint or a diplomat or a *New Yorker* reporter.

"Hello, Sally." He shook hands.

"Why, Stum, I didn't know you smoked a pipe? I thought . . ."

"I took it up this year."

Their conversation drew to a stop, a little silence in the fast-moving calling groups as the train began to pull out. He puffed a cloud of smoke over Sally Bee's head.

"Why, hi, Stum boy." Plain George stuck out his hand from behind Sally Bee.

"Good-evening, sir." Stumbum unbent from his perch of judgment over the platform and shook hands again.

"We better be seeing a lot of you this Christmas, boy."

"Very nice of you, sir. I hope so." Stumbum let his eyes wander slightly past Plain George's head, but he drew his gaze back, politely, at once.

"Come on, Daddy. Bi, Stum." Sally Bee pulled her father's arm and they went off down the crowded platform to where she could see Anne Randolph's hair disappear toward the parked cars.

"Daddy, honestly, you say the most embarrassing things sometimes . . . why, just asking Stum up like nobody ever asked me out . . . or pushing or something. I'm just broken up . . ."

"Lord, honey, I didn't mean anything. We've damn near raised the youngin and I feel kind of sorry for him."

"Sorry! For Stum?" Her voice went up into a shriek of sarcastic dismay, "Oh, really!"

"Well, honey, he hasn't got much home-life. His mother's sick again. . . . Nobody even to meet the boy . . ."

"George," Anne Randolph interrupted as they came within earshot, "I don't think you ought to talk to Sally Bee about trouble in her friends' families. It only spreads gossip among the children. You've got too much lip-stick on." She climbed into the front seat.

"If you mean about his mother being a dipsomaniac, everybody . . ."

"That's enough out of you, Sally Beatrice; get in. Words like that just sound silly coming from you."

Plain George could hear their voices jabbing at each other already as he put the cases in the back, and he looked up as Stumbum walked by alone, catching in the boy's eye the look of a child that has tried to blow up yet another balloon and had it pop in his face.

"Hey, Stum, I'll play you a round in the morning. How 'bout it?" Plain George called suddenly, not knowing why.

"Yes, sir, I'd like to, sir. Ten o'clock?" The boy's face went eager, and he gasped surprised thanks.

"Ten o'clock."

Stumbum set his pipe back between his teeth and loped off.

In the car as Plain George got in Anne Randolph was saying, "What have you been drinking?"

"Nothing, Mother, just a beer." Sally's voice was sullen and far away back in the corner of the seat.

Plain George, to break the silence as they crossed the bridge, said, "I promised Jim we'd come by from the train. You know how he feels about you, honey," he called back to Sally Bee.

Anne Randolph reached into her hand-bag, got out her mirror and her pocket brush. "Lord, he treats the child like she was three . . ."

"So do you, f— you," muttered Sally Bee, so far under her breath that Anne Randolph complained:

"For Lord's sake blow your nose before we get there, you can hear it bumble," and waited with her lipstick poised until Plain George had brought the car to a stop in front of the brownstone house.

"Will *he* be there?" Sally Bee looked up with some

apprehension at the familiar high front, bit her lips hard, and then shook her soft curls to prepare herself.

"Of course he will," Anne Randolph assured her before Plain George could answer. "You better treat him like an old member of the family or you won't be Jim's pretty-bud for much longer!" She laughed as she got out of the car, and when Sally Bee giggled too, she took her arm.

Jim, hearing the car draw up and throwing open the front door, saw mother and daughter, 'more like sisters', come arm-in-arm laughing together up the walk, and was satisfied with the picture. "Lord, come on in here! I been waiting all day for my little old pretty-bud to come home! Merry Christmas, honey." He grabbed Sally Bee and she threw her arms around his neck for a big bear hug.

"Boy, have I got you a Christmas present this year!" He disentangled her and led her into the living-room. "There," as Selby got up from beside the fire. "I got somebody to give you a big rush. Selby—here she is—isn't she the cutest little old pretty-bud you ever saw?"

"Lord, honey, let the youngin get warm." Martha kissed Sally Bee calmly. "Take off your coat, honey. Selby'll put it away for you."

Selby, who had moved away to get Anne Randolph's coat, an action which put her into good enough cheer to continue the sister act, came back when he heard his name, and took Sally Bee's coat as she dropped it behind her.

"Come on, let me drive you to drink." Jim herded Anne Randolph and Plain George into the bar, now half-hidden by an enormous tree. "I'll declare that youngin gets better-looking every day."

"She is sweet-looking, isn't she?" Anne Randolph stood enraptured in front of the tree as if she'd never seen a Christmas tree before. "Jim Dodd, that's the prettiest thing I ever saw!"

"Marty and Selby did it. All I did was mix the drinks—here," he handed them glasses.

"A real tree party! Isn't that cute?" Anne Randolph turned to Plain George.

"I'm a happy man," Jim said, raising his drink.

"We ought to do a tree like that." Anne Randolph's voice was a dying fall, closing the subject, as she carried her drink back into the living-room.

"Here, children," Jim gave glasses to the two in front of the fire. "You want sweetening?" he said to Marty, sitting watching them politely.

"No, I'm all right—Selby's . . ."

Jim didn't hear her. "Do you want to know why I call this little doll pretty-bud?" he asked Selby over Sally Bee's head, and she turned and smiled like a little girl from under his shoulder, being part of the story. "She called every flower pretty-bud—even every little bit of paper caught her eye—pretty-bud this and that. As if she wasn't even going to let a flower bloom till she got big enough to bloom along with 'em. I'll tell you, she's a bloom by now." He looked down, sharing with Selby her soft cheeks, her rounded plump shoulders, the set of her head with the delicate almost blurred line of chin to hair that screamed young, young, like a death-knell to Anne Randolph as she watched the girl turn her head in the firelight.

"Jim," she called, "I'll declare you do spoil that youngin." She strode up to the group. "I don't think you ought to have a big drink like that, honey," she told Sally Bee, "you know you have to be careful about pimples." Jim had turned away, drawn down by Marty, so only Selby heard her, and at his look she hastened to explain, "She told me she'd already been drinking beer. They get sick so easily!" She smiled.

"Anne Randolph—come here. We've got an idea," Jim

said from the couch. She leaned down to them, and Selby led Sally Bee away from the fire to see the Christmas tree, reaching for a handkerchief as he saw the girl's face grow red with suppressed, angry tears.

Behind the Christmas tree she shed only a few for luck, and whispered, "I could die of humiliation. Why can't I have a drink like everybody else?"

"Want me to tell you why?" Selby almost whispered, close to her. "You're blind already. A couple of Jim's drinks and you'd be out like a light, little girl."

She could only stare, remembering to make her eyes grow bigger and bigger. "I just knew," he answered the question she hadn't asked.

"He's already got her under the Christmas tree," Jim roared laughing in the next room.

"Oh, Jim, stop that! You'll embarrass them to death," Marty's voice fussed fondly, close beside him.

"We're coming right now," Selby answered. "I was just showing her our pretty tree." He caught his father's eye, sharing the joke.

"Marty, tell me something I ought not to ask." Anne Randolph pulled Marty towards her and whispered, "Isn't Jim drinking a little more than he ever used to? Is everything going on all right?"

"Why, Anne Randolph—Jim's drunk, but not with liquor. I've never seen a man so up in the air. It scares me a little bit."

"I know just how you feel, honey." Anne Randolph patted Marty's knee. "Happiness!" She sighed, and with a little dramatic click of her fingers Marty had seen her use in an English play about a young man who got the 'flu and had to stay for the week-end, settled back to drink her drink.

"Boy, we got the best idea, kids." Jim loomed up over the fire again, into the brighter light. "All six of us going to the

63

Christmas dance at the Club." Sally Bee went tense, but as he continued, "Marty, I'll take my car. Selby, you take Sally Bee in the station wagon . . ." she relaxed and moved closer to Selby.

"We'll go in my car," Anne Randolph said over her shoulder to Plain George. "I can't get in yours in my evening clothes . . ."

Jim, who had forgotten the usually boisterous Plain George because he was so quiet, went over and dragged him into the circle of the fire. "What do you think? Drinks here—dinner together there. . . . What do you think?"

"We'll see, we'll wait and see. Don't look so surprised, George. This is Rip Van Winkle's first Christmas." Anne Randolph began to giggle, rolling her head from side to side.

"We've gone together every year for any number of times." Marty looked up at Selby, remembering to explain this one, of all their many private jokes.

Anne Randolph saved the crank to throw into the plans at breakfast next morning.

"I wouldn't have spoiled Jim's fun last night for anything in the world," she said to Sally Bee as she came half-asleep to the breakfast nook nestled in the gay geranium wall-paper, "so I talked to Marty just now." She drank her coffee, sure of herself, making Sally Bee speak.

"What about?" Sally Bee finally asked, seeming to smooth her hair so that she wouldn't get caught in a childish habit of rubbing her own dear little skull.

"Surely you don't think you could *seriously* go with Selby to that dance, do you, honey? Why he's a *man*. I'm sorry, honey," she added in a kindly way, "you're *much* too young for him—you'd have a better time with somebody more your own age."

Shock caught Sally Bee still with a sleepy smile as she realised what her mother was saying. Then her face went dark with anger.

"You jealous old twat!" she suddenly screamed, and caught Anne Randolph a stinging slap across the face before she stumbled out of the pretty nook.

Plain George, late for breakfast as usual, found Anne Randolph crying among the coffee and the morning papers. As she saw him through her tears, she moaned, "She's insane. I think the girl's a little insane. We've *got* to have her seen about! I try my best. I do, George." Plain George, who'd heard it so many times before, calculated quickly how fast he'd have to pacify her before a quarter to ten, so as not to keep Stumbum, the poor little youngin, waiting on the first tee.

Sally Bee apologised at ten minutes past ten, having made her own plans, and together mother and daughter went out to look at clothes, and meet the whole, seething, gossiping, Christmas-loaded town. In Anne Randolph's morning of new love and understanding, having kept the reins of authority from slipping off the fly-by-night frightening little girl's shoulders, she bought Sally Bee four lovely evening dresses. They picked them together, keeping Sally Bee's age well in mind. Anne Randolph told Plain George afterwards that Sally Bee's dresses had more than made up for the disappointment over the Christmas party. But when Plain George, calling out "Chrismus Gif," threw open the door of Jim Dodd's house on Christmas evening, Sally Bee was with her parents and Anne Randolph had dark blue shadows under her eyes that no cosmetic could cover.

Marty stood, like the spirit of blended Christmas, among the velvet-collared robes, the cologne, the silver smoking equipment, the nylon and the Christmas candy, and scrabbled beneath it somewhere for Sally Bee's present.

"Wait a minute," Jim called from the bar. "Lemme give it to my honey," and found the black cashmere classic sweater himself among the cascades of crackling cellophane and gilded stars.

Marty leaned out of his way from the tree. "We're going to pick Hamilton and his mother up for dinner. Of course they can't stay at the club long, but I thought . . . well, Christmas and a new place. Who's to ask them but us?"

"What's this man like Marty's asked?" Sally Bee asked Selby as they drove toward the club in Marty's station wagon.

"Oh, he's some flit they've picked up to run the local theatricals."

Sally Bee giggled. "Oh, I know what he does. Whenever mother lets up on me, she starts on him—or you." She glanced sideways at him. "That's not what I meant."

"He's a crippled flit. Now are you satisfied?"

"She wasn't going to let me come with you," she went on, paying no attention to Selby's bark.

Selby grinned, "I know. You gave her hell . . ."

"I sure did." Sally Bee's eyes welled up with misery. "It sure has been a wonderful vacation," she said bitterly. "She and Daddy. If you knew about them! How they act. Look at this dress.'. She opened her coat. "I'm nearly eighteen and she still makes me wear sleeves!" She let her shoulders round and the sleeves, set precariously on edges, fell almost to her elbows, the tight bodice stayed just covering her bust. "Look! She didn't know I could do this."

Selby saw the girl in the passing street light naked and round and young enough to bite. "O.K.," he said, slowing the car. "Put your clothes on, jail-bait, and let's go to the party."

"*She* said," Sally Bee told him, hunching up her coat

again and watching him closely, "you'd be bored to death going out with me."

"Why would I?" He was non-committal, knew that his job was only to seem to listen.

"She's a fool. What does she think I am? Does she think Jim, old as he is, pretty-buds me all the time because he likes *teddy-bears?*"

The car slowed down almost without Selby's realising it.

"Boy, how low can you get, honey?"

She slipped the coat back again and leaned against the seat, in a movement mindful of her mother, looking upwards, "I'm just being frank. You can't say a word. I want to be free—*free*," she repeated, watching him.

Selby turned the car up a darker street, shot with giggles and desire, "What are you trying to do?"

She turned her head, letting her dress settle so that the pink skin surrounding her hard small nipple showed like a dark shadow.

"Oh, my God," he said, stopping at last. "All right, if you want me to, you little fool."

"Don't kiss my mouth," she whispered, "they'll know." As his head fell forward with a slight groan towards the shadow, she was still talking. "I'll show her. I'll show the old bag," and moved Selby's hands back around her waist, with a slight sigh.

Anne Randolph had let her head fall back, too, but less consciously and for different reasons. Beyond a murmured, "That child just worries me half to death," which Plain George didn't answer, she said nothing, all the way to the club.

As Hamilton was being wheeled up the porch of the greystone club-house, the tottering, glissading shadows thrown hard against the windows by the light and the bright fire inside made him remember, with a slight conscience, the mind of Proust; but not for long. He was far too cold, cold and embarrassed after all the years, at being trussed up and delivered to the unknown lights and shadows inside the door by the square dumb man at his back.

Behind Jim and Hamilton, Marty was guiding Mrs. Sacks down the slippery board walk that was laid down in winter to keep high heels from sinking in the winter mud. But as Mrs. Sacks laid her hand on her arm, she stopped and the men pushed on, out of earshot.

"I just want to tell you, Martha, how much I appreciate you bringing us here."

Marty, whose motive had been the more selfish one of a quick surge of charity regretted all the week, hoped by not answering she wouldn't show her embarrassment. But Mrs. Sacks hardly gave her time. "And I want right here to make a little confession to you, honey. I've never been inside a Country Club before. Other places it's been, well— like the Rotary or the Lions and all that . . . but never the Country Club! I just wanted you to know how happy you've made me." She paused. "On Christmas," she added as if she'd forgotten it before.

"Why, Mrs. Sacks," the warm surge returned and it made Marty put out her hand and draw the older woman close to her. "That's the nicest thing anybody's ever said to me." Together they walked up to the high columned porch and past the vague shapes of porch swings, dead and forgotten on the frosty winter night, into the hall-lounge of the Club.

Anne Randolph stood waiting by the door, still in her coat. "The men have gone to put their coats away. If I know George that'll take an hour. I'm worried about the kids. They haven't got here yet. Do you think anything could have happened?"

The opening of the door made them draw into the shadow

68

of the huge Club Christmas tree, which bent against the twenty-foot-high lobby ceiling like a tall man caught in a low doorway. Mrs. Cory, far away in the bar, at the back of the L-shaped room, called over the sounds of drinking to her friend, Mrs. Satterlee. "Party can start now. The sacred circle are coming. Boy, don't they all stick together?"

She neighed with laughter, so that her curls wiggled like little bed-springs, and clutched the zipper of her new red dress. Beside her Mrs. Satterlee, who was the only one they could find to run Ladies' Day faithfully, put down her glass and peered over Mrs. Cory's shaking shoulder. "That's his mother, is it?" she whispered.

"Whose—the boy's? Do you mean to tell me you don't know?" Mrs. Cory stopped laughing.

"Oh, I know all that. I mean the little cripple man they just brought in."

"That's the mother."

The door opened again and Sally Bee came in with Selby.

"Isn't she the sweetest-looking child you ever saw?" Mrs. Satterlee said.

"Looks like butter wouldn't melt in her mouth," she added as she saw Anne Randolph pilot the girl into the ladies' locker room.

"Never mind about her. Look at him!"

"Who?"

"The boy! That's the boy!"

"Oh. Oh, is it? Don't look a bit like Jim, does he?"

"Doesn't even know what to do with his coat."

"He's pretty good-looking."

"Pretty good-looking! He looks downright sissy to me. Where are those damn men?" Mrs. Cory looked balefully towards the green double-doors beyond the bar, through which, except for daring escapades in certain members' adolescent years, no woman ever dared to enter.

Christmas had not reached the men's locker room, except in a series of flashes of new cigarette-cases and Ronson lighters. Selby half recognised it. The smell of a certain kind of sweat and leather, as little like the sweat of work as the tan of a sun-lamp is like the leathered collar across the farmer's neck. Tall green lockers, row on row, with the white tiled floor and the coconut mats, made a sterilised-looking tunnel of the place. All along the benches, men in evening clothes lounged and drank together, safe from the women.

At the end of the room, between the high walls of the lockers, Selby glimpsed a large table, covered with a white cloth, where an old coloured man set tray after tray of water glasses, each with a heavy chunk of ice, and opened rows of bottles of charged water, ginger-ale, Seven-Up. "Go get some set-ups." Jim gave Selby a slight push. "I got the liquor in my locker."

Selby moved forward among the knots of men, as frightened as if he had been thrust on to a stage. The din near the 'set-up' table was loud but gruff. Selby tried to find a way through.

Somebody in front of him wheeled round, his hands high, filled with glasses. "Hell-o, Selby!" It was Jim's lawyer, Solly Leftwich, who celebrated Christmas without setting foot out of the safety of the men's locker room. "Hey, Eddie, come meet Jim Dodd's boy." The rest of them who heard the name were too polite to let their voices drop. There was not even a pause in the roar. Selby was nearly faint with relief, but "Hi, Solly—good to see you," was all he said.

"Where have you been?" Anne Randolph whispered to Sally Bee.

70

"Selby doesn't want to drive Marty's car too fast. Satisfied?" Sally Bee looked blankly but bravely into Anne Randolph's eyes.

"I hate that sassy look," she answered, and swept after the other women.

Although the room they entered was called a locker room too, it was as different as a life-time from the men's. Here the paraphernalia of sport and sweat had been swept into a small back white-tiled room, and the front room, with its dark liver-coloured carpet and its three high, thin pier-glasses, set like a row of huge pendants along the end of the room, seemed to hold court among the coats, the gossip, the lip-stick, the drifts of blown powder, and the occasional flare-up into fighting, as regally and objectively as three dowagers at an evening of culture. Between them, the gilded sconces twisted up the wall, now with candle-shaped electric bulbs, which still forty years later looked out of place after the bright gas mantles.

"I can't see a damn thing," Anne Randolph complained, peering into one of the mirrors.

"Isn't it quaint, though." Mrs. Sacks looked around appreciatively.

"I'll tell you about it all," Marty said, taking her arm. "We'll go on in, Anne Randolph."

"What's the use?" Anne Randolph mouthed, lip-stick poised over her half new-painted mouth. "The men's locker room!"

"It causes more trouble," Marty laughed, thinking she was explaining enough but leaving Mrs. Sacks a little perplexed.

"Any of 'em could do anything and the rest wouldn't say boo to it." Mrs. Cory, opening the door, showed only by her quick bite of silence that she was talking about someone inside. Mrs. Satterlee caught on and followed her in, obediently silent.

Anne Randolph understood, too.

"Why on earth she has to cover her head with those little tacky corkscrews, the way she looks already," she said spitefully to shut Mrs. Cory up, and as she spoke she tossed her own fair hair in the old gesture she had not made once before that evening. Mrs. Cory, behind the door in the little white-tiled room, turned to her best friend. "What a mean, mean thing to say," she said to Mrs. Satterlee.

"Don't pay any attention, honey."

"What a really mean thing to say," said Mrs. Cory, her large chin quivering a little with deep hurt and suppressed killing anger.

Marty smiled her way through a huddled group of still fur-coated newcomers at the door of the dressing-room, clearing a path for Mrs. Sacks. They and the rest stepped aside for a second as an alabaster-faced girl, her lip-stick startling as a painted sign, rushed past them glassy-eyed into the locker room.

Marty ignored it, but a woman's voice behind Mrs. Sacks rang out.

"You'd think they could stay a little sober. After all, it's Christmas."

"Little too much Christmas if you happen to ask me——"

"Honestly!"

"After all, it is a religious holiday."

"Well, honestly I don't . . ."

They had all pushed through the door behind Marty and Mrs. Sacks and left them standing in the line of the Christmas tree. Hamilton, sitting beside the fire watching the locker room doorway, beckoned them over. Mrs. Sacks saw that he had grown impatient, but found, slightly surprised at herself as she walked beside Marty across the great high room, certain the eyes of the world were on her, that she didn't care for once.

72

"Where have you two been?" as they came in earshot.

"Really, Hamilton," his mother said archly, but he didn't notice.

"Marty, darling, sit here beside me and tell me all about everything, right down to where the heavenly 'drapes' came from and who designed the bar. Jim's gone to get us a drink . . ."

"Where do I begin?" Marty sat down on one of the huge couches that flanked the fire. "This place used to be a private house."

"The boy's bringing some drinks. What a crowd!" Jim joined them and talked to Mrs. Sacks. "Selby's coming up in a minute. Already made some friends his own age." He settled back on to his heels and felt for a cigarette.

Mrs. Sacks went on smiling socially.

"This place used to be a private house," Marty had begun again, looking at it to tell the story, letting her eyes swing around it as if for the first time.

"My God," said Hamilton.

"Now there was a coal baron if you like," Marty said, teasing him, "old S. R. Slingsby owned so much coal they made him Ambassador to . . . somewhere. Jim," she called up, and drew him towards her, "where was Slingsby Ambassador of . . .?"

"How the hell should I know, honey?—before my time." He leaned back. "Here are some drinks. He just was," he added, to be helpful—turning his back on her and taking a drink from the 'boy' he'd called, a wrinkled, smiling negro in a white coat.

Marty began again. "Anyway, he was. It wasn't England or any place like that. I wish I could remember. It's right on the tip of my tongue . . ."

"Anyway," Hamilton jogged her over her little worry. . . .

73

"Anyway," Marty copied, relieved, "back before the days of more than picnics and entertainments like that out in this part of the world, he rolled back with a lot of big ideas. Social life and all."

"Why did he come back?"

"Oh—the Administration just changed. He turned into a real legend. Of course we're all used to it now. Most of my friends' children were practically raised here, but back around 1900 it was really putting on the dog! He bought that huge stairway complete out of some old house and had it shipped here on the railroad. You see those pheasants." She motioned up to the fireplace where a procession of stuffed pheasants with belligerent dead eyes marched beak to tail in bas-relief across an oil-painted autumn wood. "Aren't they the worst thing you ever saw?"

"Oh, they're sweet!" Hamilton told her. "We ought to be able to use those . . ."

"Good heavens, Anne Randolph, did you hear that?" Marty called up laughing as Anne Randolph and Sally Bee, their faces flushed, strode across the thick rug to the fireplace.

"What?" Anne Randolph tried to sound gay, but her voice was sharp.

"Hamilton already wants to move Mr. Slingsby's birds!"

" 'Bout time somebody did!" Anne Randolph saw from where she stood that one of the more festive members had stuck mistletoe under the tail of each solemn bird.

"Honestly!" she said, but had to giggle.

"Come, sit down. I'm telling him." Marty patted the couch beside her.

"Uncle Jim, where's Selby?" Sally Bee leaned her head on his shoulder.

"He went home and left you for me!" Jim teased her, and

when she saw he was teasing they both laughed and with Mrs. Sacks grew silent, waiting and watching the crowd.

"You'd have the whole Slingsby family down on us like a ton of bricks if you moved a feather. Old Mr. Slingsby shot those birds in the company of the Crown Prince of Sweden. There's a plaque."

"Aren't they awful!" Anne Randolph watched them as if they were going to fly.

"Now you watch what you say! Hamilton thinks they're cute."

Out of the dressing-room door loomed Mrs. Cory, followed by Mrs. Satterlee.

"If it was any daughter of mine . . ." said Mrs. Cory. "She raised that girl wrong. Did you ever hear such goings-on in public. Both of them!"

"Mothers and daughters. Well, that's life," said placid little Mrs. Satterlee. "Aren't they like twins?"

"They sure are, and it serves Anne Randolph Potter right. Look at them all, hugging the fire. The rest of us could freeze our tails off," Mrs. Cory whispered as they walked through the high arch back to the bar. She whispered because she did not care to see the forks of Anne Randolph's tongue again until it suited her purpose.

"So he left the house for what he called a 'golf club', and what's more left a list of three hundred eligible names for it: 'who could understand the art of golf' I think he put it. Honestly, the will was a real piece." Marty was shy for a second, in memory of Mr. Slingsby's snobbery. "He said the pheasants were to stay over the fireplace as a symbol of sport, and the big glass conservatory upstairs that he built at the end of the ballroom had to stay as a symbol of beauty—and—what was the other one, Anne Randolph?" Marty, being hostess, drew her forward into the conversation to end her sulks.

75

"That's the killing one!" Anne Randolph leaned towards Hamilton. "The ballroom is full of those little rickety gilt wooden chairs. You know!" she waved at Hamilton's expected knowledge. "Terrible little old things. Well, he left those for what he called a symbol of grace! Grace! I think he meant you had to sit on them like a lady or choose to break your back!"

"He *did*, honey," Marty interrupted, "didn't you know that? He told Solly Leftwich's father that no girl could sit straddle-legged or humped over on chairs like that, and if he didn't make ladies of the girls in this town one way he'd do it another. It was just the time women started to ride astraddle."

"Marty, *where* do you pick up words like that? Astride, honey!" Anne Randolph was so kind that Hamilton found her bitchiness an even better target than Marty's slight shame.

"I suppose by the 'twenties all you girls were standing on them doing the Black Bottom and drinking boot-leg corn. I've always envied people who were old enough to remember the 'twenties," he sighed, rather majestically.

"Why, Ham," Anne Randolph countered, "I never knew it then! I was just a little old girl down Virginia."

"I didn't either," Marty said, and the note of belligerency, for the first time since Hamilton had known her, made him turn and stare.

"What?"

"Know this place in the 'twenties. I was too damn busy earning my bread and butter," she laughed. "Don't think I can't."

"Marty, you're a fascinating woman." Hamilton patted her arm flung down along the couch arm. "You have even learned how to be honest."

76

They fell silent, and Jim's voice finishing his version of the story reached across to them.

"Funny old man, Slingsby. I remember him years ago. I couldn't have been more than four. He stopped me and my father in the middle of Canona Street. Fine-looking old man. Dignified."

"How did you remember all that time?" Mrs. Sacks looked amazed.

"He gave me fifty cents," said Jim, and they laughed together, but fell silent when Sally Bee refused to laugh too.

"What about most of the rest of these people?" Hamilton asked Marty.

"Oh, they just take it all for granted," Marty said easily, thinking she had been complimented.

"Want to hear about the time I shot a moose?" Jim said to Mrs. Sacks.

"Oh, yes," she breathed, delighted.

"George, honestly," Anne Randolph jumped up and her voice brought them all together again. "Can't you drag yourself away from that place for a minute?"

"Hi, honey, I was just giving Selby here a little shot."

"See you've been initiated into the mysteries," Jim said. "Good boy!"

It was as he turned in the firelight that Marty first noticed the shadow of Selby in Jim's face.

"Jim, honey, find us all another drink," she said. "I'm suddenly frozen, right here by the fire."

"Hello, jail-bait," Selby whispered gently to Sally Bee as if he were kissing her ear.

"Come, sit down, Selby," Anne Randolph called from the couch. "I haven't seen you all evening."

Obediently he joined them.

"What a place!" said Hamilton, catching Selby's eye.

"Yeah, some place," answered Selby, hoping he had covered successfully his understanding of Hamilton's look.

"God, I'm hungry," Jim said. "Let's go eat. We'll get some drink in there."

"Suits me," said Marty, lifting herself up from the deep couch.

"I'm so hungry I could eat a mule stuffed with firecrackers," Anne Randolph said, cutely.

"She won't do a thing but peck." Plain George followed her proudly.

"What's the matter, kid?" Selby whispered as he and Sally Bee followed.

"I've just been humiliated to death in the ladies' john," Sally Bee whispered back. "Oh, Selby, if you only understood how miserable it all is!"

He was gentle because she wanted him to be.

"Never mind. I'll see you forget her."

"Honestly?" she said. "Oh, Selby, if I was just free!"

He suppressed his laughter and hugged her as they reached the door.

"Hello, sweetheart," he told her.

Sally Bee flung back her curls and stared at him for a second. Then she let him follow her to the table.

Marty, waving her hands vaguely about the table, motioned them down. As she sank down beside Hamilton, Anne Randolph noticed that Plain George was the only one who had brought his drink to the table. "Honestly!" she moaned, and Plain George, catching Hamilton's eye, winked and whispered, "Women!" loudly.

"I never caught such a cold, waiting in that swamp country. I'se sick for a week," Jim pulled Mrs. Sacks' chair back for her. "But I reckon that's moose hunting."

"Oh, that's moose hunting all right," Mrs. Sacks agreed.

"This part was built on," Marty talked quietly to Hamilton behind their turned heads. "Of course the old dining-room was too little for a Club, so this big porch was added on."

"I see," said Hamilton, and found for once nothing more to say. The room was so negative, with its plain wicker-chairs and it's white cloth polka dots of tables, that there was for once nothing he could say. He sighed. Even the red poinsettias placed carefully in the dead centre of each table depressed him. Only the lights of the town down the hill beyond the trees winked and blinked like a nest of fireflies in the black, cold night. Looking out, the room seemed suitably small, small enough to bear. He felt a new tiny desire to touch Marty, and so drew her attention by putting his hand over hers as she followed his look.

"Dearest Martha, it is a very beautiful view," he told her at last. "Usually I don't like views, but I like the night. I like seeing this much of it," he punctuated his giggle by taking his hand away, "sitting in a red and white Christmas card."

But the silence they had spilled had spread around the table and touched the rest. Jim, to stop it, said gallantly, "Can I get you a plate, Mrs. Sacks, or would you like to pick your own?"

"Oh, I'll come with you, Mr. Dodd," she got up so quickly she tipped her chair and Jim caught it for her.

"Mother!" Hamilton rapped from across the table, and the others got up, moving and talking to cover the sharp edge his voice had shown.

"Want me to get yours, honey?" Plain George asked, but Anne Randolph was already weaving her way among the tables to the huge buffet set along the middle of the dining-room.

"Selby!" Hamilton called and stopped the boy as he was

79

rising from his chair. "Your mother and I want to be waited on."

"I'll fix you up!" Selby promised, smiling. "You two sit tight." He followed Sally Bee among the tables.

"Hamilton, don't say that," Marty's voice was so soft that at first he didn't hear her. "I don't think you ought to call me that to Selby. It's hard for him in rehearsals and everything—if you don't mind . . ." She faltered, and Hamilton realised that her voice was fast filling with tears.

"Why, darling Marty, I wouldn't have teased for the world if I'd known you cared—I mean it, my dear. I make jokes about situations when they interest me. Oh, my dear, I will never do it again." He was shaken and frightened by her look, a look she didn't know she had.

"It's all right—I don't care. Don't misunderstand. And it isn't a situation, not like that. You can make too much of a thing . . ."

Hamilton, fascinated, drew her away gently from the brink of a scene she'd gone towards so blindly. "Let's not think any more about it. Tell me more about this wonderful mausoleum."

They smiled together, so close that Mrs. Sacks, flicking her head up for a second from the stuffed olives and more poinsettias, repeated in the shape of the tomato aspic, felt a shock of fear. She didn't quite let herself understand, and explained her sudden stopping of the slow assembly-line of eaters by saying, "Mr. Dodd, we're going to like Canona. I just feel it. Your wife is just wonderful to us. And Hamilton just feels she is a real prop to him in his work." She went on moving sideways down the long table.

"Oh, Marty's a wonderful girl. Wonderful girl." He glanced up, too, but didn't stop finding food. "Course, they've got all that in common."

"They certainly have," said Mrs. Sacks, wondering by

80

now where she could fit a slice of turkey without making her plate look heaped up and greedy.

"Poor Mr. Slingsby," Marty was saying, amused, "he must have thought he was so original! And every town in this state must have had a home like it; ferns, birds, gilt and all—they certainly put on the dog in those days. One or other took a trip out East and brought it all back. Yes," she leaned back, "Mr. Slingsby must have thought he was the height of originality."

Hamilton, remembering the yellow hall and the dwarfed Cézanne print, changed the subject to talk of his mother.

"Mother," he said, in a whole new voice, "is in heaven."

Marty, looking up, saw that she had stopped, and was making some remark to Jim.

"I hope she's enjoying herself," she said, a little worried.

"Mother has one rare feature. I mean this seriously," Hamilton said, watching her, too, so that when Jim looked up he saw them both staring at the buffet table, "she always knows what's happening at the time it happens. That is very rare, Marty. Some of us know later, some of us . . . forebode it and spend our will avoiding what's going to happen. Mother doesn't. She knows in phase, in time. Sometimes she doesn't face it, but that's a different matter."

"Does she?" said Marty, feeling called upon to answer, but not understanding why he should talk about his mother so abstractedly. Sensing it, he began to joke again, partly to put her at her ease, and partly because it had not only been his mother he meant.

"All her life," Hamilton went on, "she's wanted to live a nice, respectable, rich life—to 'know the best people', she puts it. All that dream has been centred on a place—in some towns it's the Country Club, some the Yacht Club, the Fishing Club—anyway the Club with its little doors shutting the best people inside."

Marty looked afraid he was going to be bitter and embarrass her, but he only added, "Sometimes it was *almost* the local theatre—but never quite. Mother's 'best people' can't be 'artistic'. In their perfect world there is no need to be *déraciné* and no excuse to be careless. Tonight, at last, mother is at the Country Club. Now here's the miracle. She knows it. Every move she makes, everything she hears she knows is happening. . . . Marty, darling, you aren't even listening!"

"I was wondering. I'm sorry. Go on. . . ."

Selby interrupted them, carrying plates. "There you are; Jim's ordered some wine." He was off again before Marty could say, "Ordered some wine? Oh! Jim brings up some champagne," she finished, to Hamilton, "and dumps it in the Coke cooler."

"How delicious!" said Hamilton, watching Selby's back as he wound among the tables back to Sally Bee's side.

Three bottles of champagne later on Christmas evening, the dining-room tables were hidden by a moving, celebrating crowd. Dodging and bouncing, they even obscured the night out of the windows. It was more and more evident to everyone at the table, except Anne Randolph, that there was a kind of pall over dinner that no amount of anxious gaiety could expel. People stopping at the table, shouting "Merry Christmas," or standing leaning against the chair-backs saying, "Hello, there!" sensed it; that and the two mystery men, Hamilton and Selby, frightened them into silence. They tended to drift away again without pulling up free chairs and enlarging the circle, as seemed to be going on all over the room. Anne Randolph worked harder and harder as the dinner wore on, until by the time the Satterlees wandered near the table she was like a despairing high-tension wire, shaking her hair and flashing energy, even at them. Mrs. Satterlee leaned across Jim's head and said:

"Anne Randolph, I'm coming to see you opening night. I wouldn't miss you," and was slightly surprised when Anne Randolph swung towards her and became intimate enough really to tell her anything.

"You're the sweetest thing to me, Mrs. Satterlee, you ought to meet our new director. This is Mr. Sacks. Mrs. Satterlee is one of our loyalest supporters. Of course," here she smiled conspiratorially around at Hamilton, "we all swore none of us would actually be in this play, but after Hamilton saw the talent, he just realised he had to have some old stand-bys, didn't you, Hamilton?"

Hamilton was not ready to answer and Anne Randolph went on, now holding Mrs. Satterlee by her thin wrist. "You know it won't all be old faces. You know Selby Dodd here." She motioned to Selby, taking for granted with her voice that who did not know Selby had better not dare to say so. "He's going to do the juvenile and he's *marvellous.*"

Mrs. Satterlee, knowing little of Anne Randolph's Thespian language, started to say, "Well . . . good-bye. See you later," and moved away, but before she could do it, Hamilton was ready to enter the conversation.

"We couldn't find anyone else to turn in quite the performance Mrs. Potter will. It's an older-woman-young-man romance . . . a comic situation. Don't miss it."

The silence after he had spoken was deep and Mrs. Satterlee, saying, "Well, merry Christmas, anyway," backed to safety away from the table.

Anne Randolph, still determined to be as cheerful as the day demanded, turned and laughed at the white-faced man, as if it were a joke, and said, "Hamilton, you scared the daylights out of that poor little woman!" and was watching Stumbum as he came up behind Sally Bee before Hamilton could speak again.

Away above them that faint rhythmic beat of the dance

83

band, playing its theme song, 'Dipsie Doodle', was sifting through the noise of the crowd. It sounded, from where they were, a little dead-beat already, as if it were just too tired to force its way through any more holiday noise.

"Good-evening, Edward," Anne Randolph called. "I think it's downright mean," she explained to Jim in a whisper, "calling that poor little old youngin by some awful nickname. You have no idea how young people suffer."

"Come and meet people," she said as he came nearer, treating him like the grown-up she most wanted to see just at that moment.

Stumbum said good-evening with a slight suspicion of a bow until he got to Plain George. "Come on downstairs later. Got something to tell you, boy," Plain George grinned.

"Sally Bee, the band's started, and we're all up in the ballroom. Would you care to join us?" Stumbum said carefully, but Anne Randolph broke in:

"Oh, Edward, Sally Bee's with us this evening. We'll bring her up later."

"O.K., then, see you . . ." Stumbum, rather grateful for the excuse, backed away from the table.

"Mother!" Sally Bee was horror-struck. "You made it sound like I haven't got a date! What will everybody think? Honestly, Mother, acting like I just came to the Club dance with my parents. . . ."

"Sally Beatrice, I'm sure nobody at the table wants to hear any more of the way you speak to your mother," Anne Randolph broke in sweetly. "You can dance later."

"Well, I think we're all finished. You children can be excused now if you want to," Marty told Selby. "Go on, take Sally Bee upstairs."

They got up, both watching Anne Randolph, Sally Bee triumphant, Selby slightly alarmed at the little storm which

84

Marty, usually so calm, had helped to stir up. Before they had turned from the table, Plain George was on his feet.

"Come on, Jim," he said, "we got business to attend to." Jim got up with a sigh of relief.

"Excuse us, honey," he said to Marty, "Mrs. Sacks. We'll be right back."

Anne Randolph's mouth was, for a moment after they had all gone, closed like a hand-bag. When she did speak, because she was too angry to stand even the moment of silence, she said, "Honestly, Marty, was that necessary? You just went directly against my authority."

"I'm sorry, Anne Randolph, I didn't meant to. I just want everybody to enjoy themselves." Marty looked away shyly, trying to find in the room some new object for the conversation.

"I suppose you just can't help being a little bit clumsy," Anne Randolph told her, getting up. "Excuse me." She almost ran from the room, partly because she wanted to show that she was hiding tears; partly because she suddenly wanted to catch Plain George before he reached the green baize door.

But she was too late. He and Jim had already disappeared, and she was left, to walk back and forth in the nearly empty bar, like the impotent caged tiger, too self-conscious about her timing to go back within Hamilton's orbit so soon.

"I wonder what that was all about?" Mrs. Satterlee said to Mrs. Cory as they watched the Dodds' table empty, from their own across the dining-room.

"I'll bet I know," Mrs. Cory told her calmly.

"Anne Randolph was acting up."

"It's perfectly evident why," said Mrs. Cory, and for once wouldn't say any more.

Back at the table, Marty turned, too upset to hide it

any longer, to Mrs. Sacks. "I don't know what to say, Mrs. Sacks. I don't know what got into everybody . . ."

"Don't you, Marty?" Hamilton put in before his mother could answer. "There's a great childishness about you. It's Selby," he added, shortly. "You have been watching a mother-and-daughter fight, my dear. I'll bet you it's been going on for some days. I knew she was . . . uh . . . attracted to the boy . . . not in love. You couldn't say that. That's why I cast her in *Miranda*." He stopped to light a cigarette, pleasantly confident that Marty would be too shocked at all he was putting into words, to speak.

"Of course it will be comic," he went on. "It's funny, a woman like that lives a series of small warlike engagements —which she never wins and never knows she's lost. Do you think I would have let her get by with breaking my rules if I hadn't had a reason, Marty?" His sudden megalomaniac anger went over Marty's head. She swivelled round towards the door Anne Randolph had left and murmured, surprised:

"But he's young enough to be her . . . son," and realised too late what she had said.

"Can't you think how devilish it is for her watching that child's rounded shoulders and the skin she still fits like a glove. Oh, my, my!" Hamilton began to giggle.

"Don't," Marty commanded, "don't say things like that, Hamilton. You oughtn't to put things like that into words. It makes them happen."

Hamilton interrupted, ignoring impatiently what she had said. "Marty," he said, in the same kind of worried-mother voice Marty was inclined to use to Jim sometimes. "Let me tell you something. If you're ever in trouble, my dear, come to me. Things happen—even without talking about them. Let's go back by the fire. I can't bear this room any longer." He wheeled himself out of the now emptying dining-room, while the people who were left nudged each other to make a path for the cripple.

"Selby . . ." Marty caught up with him in front of the lounge fire. "Does he have any idea?"

Hamilton thought for a moment, and she watched for a sign from him as if he were a sybil.

"I don't think Selby knows," he said at last. "I think he is a boy," he felt his way carefully, "who draws love to him, and trouble. I doubt if he is very affected by it; I wonder, when he sees the scenes coming, if he tries to resist them. No," here Hamilton answered himself. "They keep him alive. He's this year's American male version of La Belle Dame sans Merci." Hamilton stopped for a minute, pleased with himself, then he remembered the woman. "Do you know what an incubus is, Marty?"

She did not, and could not stop him telling her in his slowest fireside voice. Mrs. Sacks, before her hostess was affected by the charged atmosphere enough to ruin her evening at the Country Club, cut in to talk about ghosts, and with a hidden show of will, understood if rarely seen by Hamilton, steered the conversation in to safer fields.

Upstairs, Sambo Johnson and his 'Dixie' Doodlers had finished their theme song, and were playing a medley of old favourites, which they had done for twenty years, so that the medley by now had gone through the stages where everyone groaned when they heard it, and had become a museum piece.

"When the blue of the night," middle-aged men babaa-ed to their wives.

The first thing Selby noticed when he reached the top of the stairs with Sally Bee was the disparity of age between Sambo and his band.

"Who's the boy genius?" he whispered to Sally Bee as they began to dance around the fast-filling floor.

"Aren't they the tackiest thing? It used to be his father's, but his father died and he inherited it. Isn't he terrible— and that awful girl!"

Selby watched the boy, who swung the baton as if that were not what he wanted to do with his life; awkward, his face still covered with spots, and his arms hanging as though on worn-out springs, leading the band, whose average age was fifty, turning from time to time to smile across the floor over his shoulder almost like a spasm he could not control. The only other member of the band who was young was the singer. She sat, calmly staring into space, keeping time with her twitching fingers, her evening dress carefully arranged about the chair.

"What's the matter with her?" Selby asked.

"She's downright common," Sally Bee told him. "The boys go to see her sometimes, I think." She came closer to him, to see if the touch of her breasts and her moving thighs against him would stop him talking, and he said nothing more, until a tap on his shoulder released him from the girl and he gave her to Stumbum and went out into the conservatory to watch from behind a palm until he could cut in again.

"Well, I had to come with him," she was explaining to Stumbum. "After all, he doesn't know anybody and after all if he'd been around here longer he'd be one of us. After all," she said again when the boy didn't answer, "it is a family thing."

"I wonder where he went to school," Stum said, dancing correctly.

"Honestly, Stum, you're the worst snob I ever knew," Sally Bee laughed. "What does that matter?" and began to wonder for herself where Selby had gone to school.

"Well, it's the kind of thing you naturally wonder," Stumbum defended himself.

Out among the shrubbery, Selby patted his evening trousers gently and said, "There, there!" and sat down on a gilt chair to laugh to himself about the girl. It was there Jim found him to take him down to the men's locker room.

Anne Randolph stopped them both at the green baize door and said, "Jim, send Plain George up. I've just got to talk to him," and looked so hard at Selby that he paused between his father and the woman, wondering which grasping wish he should satisfy first, then compromised.

"Will you dance with me in a little while, Anne?"

"Why, sure, Selby," she brightened. "You gwan have your drink. I'll meet you by the fire," and went back so gaily to join Marty and Hamilton and his mother that they avoided each other's eyes as if they'd been caught talking about her.

"You're the only one I've ever seen she'd let call her plain Anne," Jim told him as they went down the stairs.

"What a way to spend Christmas," the singer said as she passed Sambo on the orchestra stand, then she turned round and smiled beyond the microphone.

"Buncha jerks," Sambo said, but the brass section were making too much noise for her to hear his answer.

So she sang *Let Me*, sending it warmly a foot over the heads of the dancers.

In the men's locker room Plain George was holding his own party, and the men around him made room for Jim and Selby.

"Come on into the place of peace, boy," Plain George waved his arm. "Everybody here knows Jim's boy," he let his arm come to rest over Selby's shoulder, and he turned him away from the group and began to walk him along between the long dressing benches.

"Anne Randolph wants you," Jim said.

"Whyn't she come get me?" Plain George roared with

laughter suddenly, then stopped just as quickly. "Don't get me wrong, son. I'm only joking. We joke about it—y'know, don't you?"

Selby, realising that Plain George was drunk, said with great sympathy that he knew.

"Sure you do, boy, sure you do. My wife's as fine a woman as you'll hope to meet. She's got the most wonderful mind, it's an honour to live with her. I'll tell you that straight, boy, it's an honour to live with her." He sank down at the end of the bench and pulled Selby down beside him. "You understand, don't you, boy?"

Selby said he understood.

"You're a fine boy," Plain George told him, slapping him gently on the shoulder and then, forgetting, letting his hand fall gently down the boy's back. Selby, at ease at last among the affectionate older men, took the gesture for granted and did not move. "Why, she's so delicate—fine-boned." Plain George went on, "That's what we call it down here—fine-boned. Christ! it makes me feel like a big slob to look at her. I'm a lucky man, boy."

"You said it," Selby told him with a warm conspiratorial smile, wishing Jim would bring him a drink.

"How do you like my little girl?" Plain George asked him suddenly, almost belligerently.

"She's all right, George . . ." Selby searched for the words to cool him. "She's a real credit to you."

"Did you hear that? Hear that, Jim, you ugly old bastard?" Plain George lurched up and caught his foot against Selby's. Selby caught him.

"What, you sonofabitch?" Jim called.

"This boy here thinks my little girl is all right. How do you like that?"

"Fine, fine." Jim came over at last with a water-glass and the bottle for Selby.

"I tell you who I don't like." Plain George didn't wait for an answer. "I don't like pantie-waists like that Sacks. I can't stand 'em."

"Oh, he's not so bad," Selby tried to keep him happy.

"What did you let Marty bring that bastard for, anyway?" Plain George was suddenly so sad that Selby thought he was going to burst into tears. He knew that the big-faced man was at that state of drunkenness where he skated like a runaway among the wilder emotions. But missing tears, he went toward anger again. "He better keep his hands off my wife. I'll tell you that much. I'll knock his damn head off."

Selby was feeling so at home that he forgot and burst out laughing.

"What's the matter?" Plain George asked him.

"I can see Hamilton making a pass at a woman, that's all," he said, sharing the joke.

The quickly sober looks that both Plain George and Jim gave the boy wiped the smile from his face, and taught him the difference between a Turkish bath and a Country Club locker room.

"There are some things we don't mention, son," Jim said quietly.

"Oh, for Christ's sake!" Selby wheeled, furious that he had been caught misunderstanding, and nearly ran out of the locker room.

Anne Randolph yohooed as he passed the little group by the fireplace, and he turned up his eyes when he heard her. But when he turned back from the stairs and joined the others, he was as calm, as gentle as ever.

The champagne, the terrible thing she had heard Hamilton say about Selby, and now the closeness of the boy made Marty move more and more carefully as if the spot-light of her own secret emotions had caught her and followed her for anyone to see.

"Selby," she said, "do you think you could find us all a boy to bring us some drinks. Jim's forgotten."

"Oh, he's in never-never land. I'll see to you." Selby moved away again, but not before Hamilton, who had been lulled into slowness by Marty's pace, by the fire, the drink and his own boredom, had sat half-upright and quipped:

"Do you think they ought to be left without Peter Pan?" knowing from Selby's easy acceptance of his remark that it was the kind of exchange he was used to.

As soon as Selby came back with a waiter and the drinks were ordered, Hamilton tried again.

"Everybody their own camp!" He watched the boy, and knew by his stony, blind look of incomprehension that he understood completely.

"If you'll excuse me," Selby bowed slightly as he had watched Stumbum do, and ran up the stairs to the ball-room.

"He forgot our dance," Anne Randolph wailed before she could stop herself.

"*That's* what I want in the second act, darling. *That's* it. Don't forget it." Hamilton, now thoroughly alive, drew the two women to him and they began to discuss the play while Mrs. Sacks watched the people pass and rested, knowing Hamilton's work was a fairly safe topic.

Mrs. Cory, seeing the boy standing at the top of the 'fine old' stairway, searching the crowd, said to Mrs. Satterlee, who was sitting on a gilt chair beside her.

"Honestly, sometimes I wonder. I do, really."

"Well, that's life!" said Mrs. Satterlee, not having the slightest notion what she was talking about.

Selby had found Sally Bee again, and cut in:

"Love me?" he asked her easily, drawing her tightly to him, as if he had been asking the same question all his life.

Sally Bee, who usually asked such questions, ignored him.

"God, it's hot in here," she said. "You sure left me for a long time. Honestly, I might have got stuck or anything."

"I had a drink with the boys."

She didn't know he was joking. "I sure would like one. Where's mother?"

"Guarding the bar," Selby told her. "Come out here with me. I'll get you a drink later. Jail-bait," he whispered as he stood back to let her pass at the conservatory door.

She giggled. "Honestly I never heard anyone talk like you before! You just have a habit of whispering insulting remarks in doorways. Whyn't you just stand and insult everybody as they go by. Honestly!"

"It's a job I'd like." Selby looked back for an instant at the ballroom. A surge of anger made him feel his drink. "Come here," he said, and drew the girl to him in the shadow of the high plants.

"Not here," she whispered, "oh, Selby, not here. Come on." She opened the outer door and a gust of air from the night caught them.

"Christ, you'll freeze." He followed her out on to the empty dark porch, holding her to him in its corner, a little protected from the wind.

Back in the ballroom Mrs. Satterlee watched them go.

"That girl'll just freeze her tail off!" she said, worried.

"I wouldn't call him *really* good-looking, would you?" Mrs. Cory asked.

"Oh, yes. I would!" Mrs. Satterlee answered.

"Hununh! Not me. A little too weak—you know, almost call it pretty. Hununh." She settled into her chair and it groaned a little.

"I suppose so," said Mrs. Satterlee.

"I think Marty and Jim have bitten off more than they

can chew. She'll get her come-uppins. Boy in the house they don't know from Adam." Mrs. Cory said all this slowly, really thinking about each word, with an air of profundity.

"Blood's thicker'n water," said Mrs. Satterlee, sagely, nodding and forgetting to stop as they turned their attention to the dancers and she caught the rhythm of the music.

Outside, stretching below the porch-edge, the empty swimming-pool was like an open grave in the moonlight, forgotten now that the life of the Country Club had moved inwards. Both the figures huddled against the porch wall in the shadows ignored it, trying to beat each other hot and explosive with their bodies.

"Selby, you want me, don't you?"

"Yes."

"Want me."

"Oh, my God."

"Say 'I want you'."

"I want you. Christ, help me."

She stood away from him, pulled her bodice up, and touched him on the shoulders. "Honestly," she said, "mother told me you wouldn't care anything about me."

"Sally," he tried to pull her to him again. "Please."

She nestled as shyly as a girl being first kissed. "Selby, darling," she told him. "I care about you. You know that. But I can't do that. I just can't. You wouldn't want me to if you really thought." She made the appeal quickly, without thought.

"How many guys have you taken in?" he said, taking her arms from around him.

"Selby, that's the most awful thing anybody ever said to me." She was almost crying with fright.

"You little cock-teaser."

"I'm not going to stay here and be insulted."

"O.K. Go on back." He turned his back and leaned against the balustrade, looking at the swimming-pool and trying to make the cold of the stone and the sight calm him.

"A gentleman would know better," he heard her voice, furious, behind him.

He said nothing.

"A gentleman would know not to let a lady walk back on the dance floor by herself."

He turned round without speaking and took her arm. His silence made her cry her own defence. She stopped among the greenery and looked up at him.

"You wouldn't blame me for the way I act if you thought sometimes what somebody else is going through once in a while! You know how mother . . ."

"Look, kid, I've got an idea," he went close to her. "Since she's your only interest in life why don't you just marry your mother and settle down? I'm sure you two would be happy together."

This time he did leave her standing alone, more frightened at being found without a date than she had been of anything in years, and walked quickly across the dance floor and down the stairs.

When Sally Bee, after five blank, cold minutes of despair, finally caught Stumbum's eye, she burst into tears of relief and let him put his arms around her to comfort her

"What's the matter, Sally Bee?" He kept on patting her hair. "You can tell me."

"It's just terrible and nobody knows. I can't tell."

"You can tell me, Sally Bee. You know you can trust me."

"I'm in a terribly tragic situation," she whispered.

"Gosh!" Stumbum said, and swallowed, hoping his swallow didn't sound too noisy.

"I've been terribly in love with somebody named Terence Jameston Sowerby," she told him. "Mother doesn't know." She sobbed for a minute silently.

"Go on," whispered Stumbum, expecting more.

"I've just found out he's been killed in Korea," she said, looking up with her eyes huge.

"Oh, honey!" Stumbum went on stroking her hair.

It was after that she told him about Selby leaving her to look after herself while he went to get a drink.

"You better put some lip-stick on before we go back. You've cried it all off," Stumbum told her.

It was not hard for Selby to apologise to Jim when he found him by the fire with the others. As he saw him from the turn of the stairs, standing a little disconsolately by Marty, turning his glass in his hand, Selby remembered his moment of anger over his father's belligerent *naïveté*, and was ashamed; ashamed and a little alarmed that the tight-wire behaviour of his visit had snapped in a few seconds of annoyance and sent him sprawling, broken. He saw Jim's face light again when he looked up and noticed him and then go cloudy and querulous. His glance fell from Jim to Marty and she was looking at him too. She had such a soft look of infinite tenderness that Selby was as repulsed as if he had really seen the Mona Lisa, or happened on his step-mother when her bowels were open and moving. The silence as her eyes caught his and swept away was broken when Hamilton looked up. Unconscious of his action, Selby whipped a handkerchief, wiped his mouth and inspected the handkerchief, making the women pop into sweeps of laughter—all of them but Anne Randolph. Protected by the laughter, Selby came across the floor and said quietly to his father:

"I'm sorry, Dad." It was the first time he had called him dad without pausing.

Jim grasped his arm.

"Lord, son, I forgot it. We all got a little bit to drink. Be funny if we didn't get across each other at all, wouldn't it?"

"Sure it would," Selby grinned.

"Hell, boy, blood's thicker'n water." Hamilton, straining to hear, separated Jim's voice from the laughter, which was prolonged because they had waited so long for the evening to catch and were trying by now to blow some life into it.

"Selby, you owe me a dance!" Anne Randolph got up and shook her wide skirt loose around her.

"You owe me one," Selby said, taking her arm, and guiding her away.

Marty caught Hamilton's eye and was ashamed because he had caught her paying attention to his dirt.

"Honestly, I don't suppose a one of us has thought to introduce you to any other girls." Anne Randolph arched her neck and looked up into Selby's face.

"I know enough girls." He caught her closer, playing the game, and swept her around the floor.

"He dances like some professional or something," Stumbum said, full of disdain.

"Doesn't mother look awful?" Sally Bee breathed. "Honestly, it's so humiliating."

The dance by one o'clock had reached a roaring stage. The stairs were full of people milling up and down them, like a painting of some suburban Last Judgment. Hamilton Sacks and his mother had made no move to go, but sat, for their different reasons, pictures of contentment. It was during a moment of lull when Selby was sitting beside Marty, trying to persuade her to dance at least once, that Stumbum finally got up nerve to speak to him.

"May I speak to you a minute?" he whispered over the back of the couch.

Selby, having had the various doors of his father's social

life opened with the traditional gift of Bourbon in a water-glass, excused himself from the others, expecting Stumbum to lead ahead beyond the bar to the green door. Instead the boy turned towards the front door, swung it out in front of him, not bothering to stop it as it swung back into Selby's face, and he had to catch it by flinging his arm up to protect himself.

"Look." Stumbum was turned round, waiting for him.

"Sure," Selby told him, "what's on your mind?"

"Uh . . . look here, for two cents I'd knock your goddam block off."

"What's the matter?" The sight of the boy growing redder in the light of the window they had backed against made Selby too curious to be annoyed yet. "What's got you?" he demanded.

"I don't know where you get your code of behaviour." Stumbum was trying desperately to be formal enough to give point to what he was trying to say.

"What's that to you?"

"I'd like to knock your block off," Stumbum said again, almost crying with the frustration of not finding the right words. "We don't leave girls in the lurch at parties. I don't know what dance-hall you picked up your manners in," he took a deep breath, "but to me you're nothing but a jerk." He, having roused no anger in Selby to help him, was suddenly horribly embarrassed before what he considered an older man. "A damn jerk," he repeated with the last vestige of bravado, trying to find somewhere to look.

"Look, kid," Selby told him, "if my manners are any of your damn business, I did pick some of them up in a dance-hall when I was about your age. You might try one. It would make a man of you. Right now if I weren't a visitor here I'd give you the first lesson." He turned away from Stumbum, with no signs of anger at all the boy could recognise.

He called after Selby, his voice rising until it reached across the cold lawn, "Whoever heard of a guy just visiting his own parents. Christ, now I've heard it all—just passing through!"

Selby had turned and caught him a blow across the cheek with the flat of his hand that sent him sprawling against the window-frame, and walked back into the hall, before the tears had blurted from the boy's eyes. Stumbum had been hit before in his life, but never a blow that finished with the mark of four fingernails dug down his plump, young downy cheek. He ran down the porch steps, wiping his eyes and nose in one winding sweep of his knuckles, and found his new Christmas convertible to go home, not wanting to show himself inside even for his coat.

Inside the hall, as if the small explosion outside had detonated a larger one before the fire, Selby ran into such a scene that no one but Marty, as pale with fright and disgust as she was, saw that he too was white and his hands were trembling.

It was Plain George. He stood in the middle of the floor, facing Hamilton, who sat gripping the arms of his chair and trying to speak through Plain George's yelling.

"I don't have to take any crap from a guy like you. I don't have to." He stopped long enough for Hamilton to open his mouth, but over whatever he said, yelled, "I'm an American. A real American. You can't tell me."

Jim, after what was a few seconds and seemed to Marty like an hour, jumped across and took Plain George's arms. "O.K., fellow, O.K. Let it alone, fellow," he repeated quickly.

"I don't have to pay any attention to this little bastard," Plain George explained loudly to Jim. "I'm an American, Jim. You know me, don't you, Jim. Don't you? I'm a good goddamned American. That right?"

People, passing, averted their heads and talked to each other harder than ever.

"Sure, George. Sure, you're a good American. Now come on home." Jim pulled at his arm.

"I don't have to pay any attention to any goddam little fancy-pants, do I, Jim?"

"No, no, sure you don't. Now come on." Jim was beginning to get him to move.

"He's not a good American, is he, Jim?" Plain George, nearly in tears, was leaning slowly over on to Jim's arm.

"I'm going to find him a bed here, Anne Randolph," Jim said over his shoulder, and led away Plain George, whose voice had subsided into a mutter without energy or passion; they still heard, "I'm an American, aren't I, Jim?" and Jim saying, "Sure, boy, you're an American all right. Sure you are, boy," as they disappeared around the corner of the hall.

Anne Randolph managed to speak first.

"Oh, Hamilton. I could kill him!"

"Why don't you?" He spoke coolly but without breath.

"I hope it won't make any difference. He's drunk. He won't even remember." Her words rushed. "I wouldn't have had it happen for the world."

"Now we'll hear no more about it. If I could have hit him, I would have, but obviously I can't." He looked at her at last. "I just hope for your sake he's got a lot of cash. Nothing else would be worth it."

"Hamilton, I've apologised. I can't do any more." Anne Randolph turned and ran into the dressing-room.

"She's the one with all the money. He's just in insurance," Hamilton heard Marty say as they watched her disappear.

Anne Randolph could not cry, not in public. She could only sit bolt-upright on one of the plush chairs, staring ahead of her. When Mrs. Cory, who had seen it all, hurried into the dressing-room after her and said, oily with kindness, with some of the vinegar of curiosity, "Mr. Cory and I were just going, honey. Wouldn't you like for us to drive you home?" Anne Randolph said, "Thank you. One of my friends will drive me home," without even bothering to look at the woman.

Marty, glad to get away from the stone-still man in the chair and his mother, who had shrunk into a corner of the couch and seemed caught frozen in the gesture of the split-second in an accident when the windshield shatters, tip-toed towards the dressing-room a few minutes later and found her there. She still had not moved a muscle.

She looked so forlorn and so much too thin that Marty could not resist putting her arm around her and saying, "Never mind, honey," as she would have to a child. "I'm going to drive you home. Selby's bringing Sally Bee and picking me up at your house. Jim's going to take the Sackses home."

"It's all so much trouble." Anne Randolph turned her hand in the air, but did not stop staring.

"Lord, it's nothing, honey. Don't think about it."

Anne Randolph finally roused herself to get her coat.

"He knows how much I hate it. Social disturbances," she said, and went into the back locker room.

Marty, having bundled the two Sackses off with Jim, taking Mrs. Sacks' thanks for the evening as sadly as if she'd entertained her at a wake or a prayer-meeting, sat alone on the couch nearly under the Christmas tree, which still cast its multi-coloured lights over the shambles of the Country Club, waiting for Anne Randolph to get herself brightened again enough to meet all those people, too drunk, too tired, too excited, or too young to notice her existence at that late, stretched hour.

"What the hell was all that about?" Selby asked, above her.

"Oh, Lord, son, I wish I knew." She looked up at him, using the classic word for younger men that women in that part of the world always use, but causing several people to turn and stare. "I'm afraid it's been a bad introduction to the Club for you. The Christmas dance is always like this. I think everybody's too tired."

"Sure, maybe that's it," Selby answered.

Home Sweet Home wafted down the stairs from the hungry, weary 'Dixie' Doodlers.

"Go get Sally Bee, honey." Marty got up. "I'm taking Anne Randolph home in their car. We didn't think she ought to go alone. Now you pick me up there . . . if that's all right," she found herself adding shyly, then explaining before he could answer, "Jim had to take the Sackses. I can't handle that thing of Hamilton's."

"O.K.," Selby said. "See you there."

Sally Bee did not show her relief that Selby had turned up to dance the last dance and take her home by speaking to him. She kept a cold silence out into the car. As they drove through the cold dark early morning, Selby tried to break the silence but she wouldn't answer.

"I'm sorry, honey," he said. "After all, you can t help being a little cock-teaser."

She burst into a fit of giggles and the spell was broken.

"By the way, your snotty young friend Stum wanted to break me in two. What did you tell him?"

"Nothing, Selby, honest. He just knew you'd gone off."

Without believing her, Selby went on, "I hate guys like that. That foggy dead-pan Eastern look."

"Oh, sure. He's just a baby," she answered, and after a pause said, "Where did you go to school?" thinking she was changing the subject.

"At my district high-school in Chicago, Illinois! You wouldn't know it."

"Gosh," Sally Bee said, "really?"

"Yeah, but you wouldn't notice it. When she was sober, mamma kept my nose very, very clean."

"Gosh," Sally Bee said again.

"Is that your final word on the social situation?" he asked her, turning into the raw new driveway of Anne Randolph Potter's dream house, and stopped the car. Anne Randolph's car was ahead of them and the lights of the kitchen wing were on.

"Good-night, Selby," Sally Bee whispered and moved towards him because she didn't have any other answer to his question. "Don't kiss me good-night on the lips. Mother . . ." she stopped talking.

"You do it every time, like a duck to water," he whispered.

They parked when the kitchen door slammed and the dark figure of Marty hurried down the drive. She leaned into the car window.

"Anne Randolph wanted us to come in but I said no. It's too late."

Sally Bee slid out the other side.

"Well, good-night, Miz Dodd. Good-night, Selby. I had an absolutely wonderful time."

"Good-night, dear," said Marty.

Selby, remembering too late, called out, "Let me take you to the door."

"Never mind," Sally Bee called over her shoulder. "Good-night."

"Good-night."

"Good-night."

She was gone.

Marty had moved around the car and got into the place still warm from the girl.

103

"Want something to eat?" Anne Randolph said when Sally Bee had come into the lighted kitchen.

"Unhunh," she answered, reaching for the turkey carcass.

"Pigs say hunh, you say, Yes, ma'am, young lady." Anne Randolph took a bite of the sandwich she had made.

"Yes, ma'am." Sally Bee sat down at the kitchen table and started to spread her own sandwich. "I didn't think the Christmas dance was half as much fun as last time."

"Well, I told you you ought to go with children your own age," Anne Randolph told her, wiping the mayonnaise from her mouth with a little lace handkerchief.

Selby drove Marty through the dark streets, silent with the houses shut, blank, asleep in the lowest time of the night. The only cars passing them were those from the dance, whisking by and disappearing as dwindling sleek shadows. The silence around them, the hum of the motor, made them sleepy, made them speak softly when they spoke at all.

"I just can't think what made everything go so wrong tonight," Marty tried to tell herself, mournfully, just letting Selby hear. "I can't put my finger on it."

"Look, Marty, I think I better go pretty soon," Selby said, as if he had been waiting for some time to say it, watching the road.

"Why, you can't do that now," Marty answered, paniced. "You just can't now."

"Why not?"

"You just can't. This is your home now, honey. Aren't you going to settle down with us? Are you just visiting?" Her voice went high with the question, sounding, in her fear, almost annoyed.

"You better wake up, Marty. You and Jim, both. I don't belong here any more than my mother did. Every move I make is wrong. Don't you see that?" He glanced at her, trying to read her face.

What he saw there shocked him and he tried quickly to explain. "You people have no idea," he added weakly.

"What do you mean, no idea?"

"Mamma always told me we were the best people on our street in Chicago. You should have seen the street. You should have met mamma."

"Awe, don't, honey, don't talk all that kind of thing."

He moved the car to the side of the street and switched off the engine so that a complete, blank silence engulfed them.

"Have you ever known a genteel drunk?" When she refused to answer he went on. "I was raised in a dream world, filled full of a lot of fool ideas about being a gentleman. I know three real things. I kept my trap shut around the man I thought was my Dad. I started earning my living so I wouldn't have to ask him for money, and I learned the right way to sober mamma up so she wouldn't die. That and a lot of dreams about being a gentleman. Do you know what happens to a gentleman on a lousy street in Chicago?"

"I'm sorry these things happened to you, son."

"I'm not kicking; I'm telling you. Just telling you what you ought to know, that's all."

"But you're here with us now, honey. You're . . ."

"No, I'm not. I'm here and I'm there. I quit my job selling shoes in a down-town department store. When you're genteel that's the kind of job you get. I used to be cruel—do bad things to her because of having to keep that job. I quit it when I didn't get home in time one night, and it was too late to sober mamma up. She hadn't been too drunk to put her head in the gas oven."

"Oh, honey, we didn't know that. We had no idea. I'm

sure you weren't cruel, you just tell yourself that. A person can only do his best."

"Well, you know now. Tell Jim if you want to. I have an idea I'm not filling the bill with him, anyway."

"Oh, Lord, child, where did you ever pick up such an idea?"

"God, I didn't make a move right tonight. Not a move."

"But everybody was so glad you were there, Selby. Hamilton . . ." She stopped, remembering what Hamilton had said.

"Hamilton wasn't in tonight's fight. Don't kid yourself. He just refereed."

"There wasn't any fight. You've got it all so wrong. Oh, honey," the words came out in a sudden welter of tenderness. "I wish I could tell you . . ."

"Tell me what?"

"We want you, Selby. Oh, we want you so much." He had finally struck the growing core that she had so carefully hidden all through the evening.

"My God, Marty, what are you saying?"

She started to cry, and he pulled her head to his shoulder and patted her hair. "Now, wait a minute, wait a minute."

"Jim and I wouldn't know what to do without you, now," she said, muffled in his coat front.

He let his lips brush her head. "We won't talk any more now. I'm taking you home."

"We didn't know all you'd gone through. We'll try to make everything go smooth." She kept on murmuring.

"Sure, Marty." His tenderness at this loss of control, this sorrow in a woman he expected to be a pond-calm receiver for his angry self-pity and the hot frustration of the night, was being slowly replaced by embarrassment.

"We've all gone through things, Selby. Different kinds

of things. We all have. But you came to us after she died, didn't you? You must have felt there'd be a place for you here." He had trouble making out her words. She had fallen further forward towards his lap, still with her head hidden. "You should have come to us sooner. You could have trusted Jim."

"I didn't know until I read the letter she left. That's how I found out, for Christ's sake. That's how." His hand was still on her head. "He doesn't know that, either. I didn't tell him that. I made up something."

"I know what you told him. I don't blame you. Oh, Selby . . ." She bit her lip to keep from saying 'Don't go' again and let her head fall further, into his lap, touching, without knowing it, the old desire the girl had left for him to remember her by.

"Oh, my God, don't do that, Marty," he couldn't help the words coming out, or his body jerking a little in that fine twinge that turns desire into repulsion.

She straightened up, her face as controlled again as he was used to. "You'll have to excuse me, Selby. I guess I'm so tired I don't know what I'm doing."

"Don't worry—I didn't mind." He started the car again. "We better get back. Jim'll be worried."

She sat so still for a few minutes that he thought she'd dropped asleep, and then, as quickly, said, "Oh, stop. Stop the car."

She was out, moving like lightning for a big woman, and around the back of it before he'd stopped it rolling. When she came back she was holding a handkerchief to her mouth.

"I'm so ashamed," she told him finally as they drove on. "I had no idea I'd had too much to drink."

The light smell of vomit got to him as she took the handkerchief away from her mouth.

"Don't you worry about it," he said, hoping he didn't

sound cold, so tired of these strangers and their uses of him that he blurted out, "Would it shock you to know that I was damned relieved to get away from her? I was nothing but a damn nursemaid. I had the whole thing on my shoulders."

"No," she said coolly, and surprised him. "It wouldn't shock me at all."

Jim opened the door for them.

"Where the hell . . ."

"Honey, I've disgraced us all. I've been sick in the street," Marty told him, as a joke.

"Who, you!" He was amazed, delighted. "Hell, I never thought you'd add to the trail of sick down from the Club dance. I'm proud of you, honey." He put his arm around her shoulders. "She's a good sport, son. Come on, let's have a cup of coffee."

Shoe-salesman! The phrase hit Marty like the throb of a hangover as she finally got into bed—Anne Randolph's favourite phrase for the dapper, the tryers, the genteel not-quites. She lay trying to remember all the times, all the remarks that Anne Randolph had made, trying to remember if Selby had ever heard her use it and been hurt, tossing in an agony of hearing the down-Virginia voice saying shoe-salesman until the morning was light against her windows.

Selby slept, pushing decision away until morning. When he did wake, it was with the step already taken in his mind that he knew he ought to take. His quietness at breakfast was noticed by neither Marty nor Jim, each of them still drifting into consciousness from having had so little sleep. As it was, the winter sun had switched the boy's cold shadow eastward by the time he had walked all the way to Hamilton's apartment.

It was Hamilton, not his mother, who answered the

long ring, so slowly that Selby had turned to go away again.

Hamilton didn't wait for him to explain his visit. "Mother's ill," he told him angrily, and swirled round, his back to Selby, wheeling himself fast into the living-room, where he waited until the boy had slipped by, and reached back and shut the door.

Neither spoke for so long that Mrs. Sacks' timid knock sounded clear in the winter room. She put her head around the door, and said, before she noticed Selby:

"Who was it, honey?"

"Mother, darling, do go back to bed. It's only Selby. Now you trot back like a good girl. We'll make you some tea." He looked over his shoulder at his mother and Selby was surprised to hear him speak completely without malice. She slipped away, pretending that she had not noticed the boy, embarrassed at being in her old kimono, but what she left behind her was the realisation that he had been taken completely for granted by both the mother and the son, that he had been accepted as if he were home again.

So the first thing he said, the edge of his thought, was, "I don't know why I haven't come here before," and he sat down as easily as though he'd settled in for good.

"I could kill that man," Hamilton told him, finishing a conversation that didn't need to take place.

Selby took a deep breath. "What a crew," he agreed, and then shut up, realising that he had spoken too loudly.

"Thank God *you're* here, anyway." Hamilton wheeled himself nearer and took the boy's slim hand in his. "It wasn't easy for you, either, was it, dear?"

Selby, set alight by the touch of Hamilton's hand and by his modulated sympathy, could not trust himself to answer.

"You've tried so hard," Hamilton went on, "I watched

109

you playing all things to all men last night. Is that the way you are, Selby? Is it?"

"I wanted them to like me. What's the matter with that?" Selby's voice was edged with challenge, defending himself already.

"And by today you couldn't care less." Hamilton helped him over the first flush of anger.

Selby echoed by habit, "No, I couldn't care less," and looked away.

"But you will tomorrow, won't you, dear?" Hamilton spoke so softly that Selby thought he was completely in accord with his own pity for himself, which had grown through the night to make him feel like a flayed man. He nodded and looked down at both their hands.

"Well, I won't, child. I know you too well. Something in your life has put you on the outside looking in. What it was doesn't matter. It would have given a strong person compassion." Hamilton was still.

"And me?" Selby whispered to start him again.

Hamilton didn't answer. He said instead, "I couldn't love a man like you any more than I could wheel myself into the bathroom and cut my wrists. You're the one who's bleeding to death. You need the constant flow of other people's love through your soul to keep you alive. You won't have that from me, but you'll have my understanding, Selby. You see, it's really all I can muster."

Although his words left much to be considered, the fact that he was talking about him at all acted on Selby as a balm. He grew calm, as a man who feels the caress of a drug through his nerves at last. He rested the whole afternoon with Hamilton, and made tea for his mother.

Chapter VII

People Tapping on Windows

ON the fourteenth of February, at 8.30 in the morning, the children were going to school clutching handfuls of last-minute Valentines. Some of them hoped for love cards with lace and velvet hearts; some of them for power—more cards than anyone else in the room; all of them secretly feared malice—the vile, thin, crumply pages with big heads, rhyming all the terrible mistakes of jut-bones, crossed eyes, big feet, freckles and smells. It was at that moment that Mrs. Marcellus Cory leaned down for her morning milk and toppled out of her back screen-door, drowned in the revolt of her own blood.

The news began slowly to wander around Canona even before Mr. Cory had begun to cry, while he was still standing in his cheerful, newly-decorated hallway saying to the doctor:

"I can't understand it. She didn't feel very good this morning, but she didn't feel very bad, not even bad enough to stay in bed!"

On the same morning Anne Randolph did stay in bed, the play over, with that curious let-down like the loosening of bandages; Sally Bee back at school, but the watchfulness hanging about her new house like the sound of a phone bell that has finally stopped ringing. Anne Randolph lay still, listening to Beulah stumble around the living-room, already waiting huddled, tense, for the crash of her clumsiness. She was not resting. She was clinging to her bed like a floating spar, half-realising that the power of her own compulsion would whip her around her house until by evening, when she wanted to look her best, she would be so charged and exhausted that her whole body would sound to her inner ear like the hum of terrible little bees and a silent scream would tear to get out of her head. She turned enough in bed to reach out her oiled and naked hand to the little calendar on her spindled night-table, looked at the date, and sighed. It was the date a sensible woman would stay in bed until noon.

"Beulah!" she called out, hoping to make her hear before she started the Hoover. The heavy flat tread of feet plastering the stairs told her she had been successful.

"Yes'm." Beulah stood, a monument to that fat, slovenly insolence known as 'a character', in the doorway.

"I don't feel very good, Beulah," Anne Randolph told her, apologising. "Do you think I could have my coffee in bed this morning. It's probably my time . . ."

"Yes'm." Beulah displaced her mass from the doorway.

"Can I have the paper?" Anne Randolph called to the big vacant space she had left.

There was no answer. Anne Randolph heaved herself up to punch her pillows. It was then she saw Plain George's heart-shaped paper velvet box on the foot of her bed.

"Oh, my God, it's Valentine day!" She lay back and buried her head again in the pillows, fighting the compulsion, which had come back stronger than ever, to get up, to wander, search, pry until everything was understood and she had answers to all the questions she hadn't dared to formulate, and could doze in peace.

It was while she was reading the funnies, not because she liked them, but simply on such mornings to make the paper last longer, that she remembered she had not yet had a look through Sally Bee's toy box. All the drawers, every scrap of paper, even the few books the girl had in her room had been shaken, the backs of the cushions of the chairs prodded until Anne Randolph had nearly ruined her finger-nails—all in secret, all with the growing sense of urgency—urgency without direction now that the play was over and the child had gone. She threw down the paper, forced herself into her pretty pink dressing-gown, almost ran into Sally Bee's room, and went to her knees, shaking, beside the toy box.

Once she'd found a diary, twice letters, once a typewritten chapter of a novel, a hideous thing, a thing which had sent her to bed reined in with barbiturates for a week. She had sifted through old corsages, football programmes, College colours in a tangle of bright ribbons from V.M.I., 'the University', the Ivy League, and several she refused to recognise, through junk heaps of old make-up cases, and cascades of discarded underwear. Now she threw Sally Bee's cute little collection of raggedy, stuffed, and furred animals over her shoulder into a bedside sheepskin known to the trade as a 'Snuggle-rug'.

But when Marty Dodd, that same morning, heard the school bell ring for Iroquois Grade School, and had to stop while crowds of children rushed past her into the iron-wire gates with lateness pushing their bottoms forward, she realised that she had already been out walking the Canona sidewalks for an hour. She watched the children form into patterns in the yard, grow gradually quiet, and file in, out of sight; she felt lost, suspended in the empty street, as silent suddenly as if some Pied Piper of universal literacy had lured the children all away.

She was almost glad when she heard her name called from the curb and saw that it was Mrs. Satterlee, bending out of her car to attract her attention; she finished her thoughts aloud, as people will do when they are interrupted.

"I'll declare, I never knew it made such a difference, the

children just disappearing out of the world like that." She stepped out of the way of one haunted straggler as he flung himself towards the gravel path and ran towards the school buildings. "Honestly, you see a whole nother world . . ." She had to laugh. "How are you, Miz Satterlee? I've taken to walking lately," and as she leaned into the shadow of the car, really saw Elizabeth Satterlee's face. "What in the *world's* the matter, honey?"

"I've just got to have some help, Marty. Elner Cory's . . . Elner's . . ." She slid over in the seat, and put her head down awkwardly towards her lap and began to shake with sobs.

Marty ran round the car and slid in and started it. "You'll have to tell me which house, I never can tell."

"I'm glad I found you. I'm so glad I found you. I've got to have some help," Elizabeth Satterlee said as her sobbing quieted down and she sat dejected, making little hiccuping sounds.

"When did it happen?" Marty asked.

"This morning. Half hour ago. I was just going down. I've never dealt with things in Canona before. At home when mother passed on I knew everything to do."

"You show me the house." Marty slowed the car.

"I just don't know what's got into me," the woman beside her moaned.

Marty, giving her up, looked for a clue herself along the street. The houses along it were not exactly the same. It would have been better if they had been. Like half-made embarrassed gestures of recognition they turned just slightly this way and that, some a little toward the Dutch, with heavy square columns on the brick porches, some a little toward the Colonial, with thin, round, white-painted columns on the same porches, and others with columns curling upward, still from the same porches, with the barest nod to the Art Nouveau. But basically they were brick, square, and extremely solid, as if having made their bows one time they would make up for it by being even more staunch and ugly for the rest of their long, long promised lives.

"It's there, where the car is," Elizabeth Satterlee got hold of herself enough to point out, and Marty slid to a stop behind it.

The Corys' house had Colonial columns.

Walking up the concrete walk, Mrs. Satterlee said, "They'd just paid off everything, and owned their own home. Elner came into a little something . . ." The tears began to course down her cheeks again in the same pink channel, but without sound.

They opened the door quietly, in the presence of the dead, tip-toeing, but ran straight into little Doctor Adams as he came out of the living-room and slid the big doors shut behind him.

"I've given Mr. Cory a sedative and he's dropped off a little in there. Mrs. Cory's upstairs on her bed. I've called Lightfoot's Funeral Home. They buried Mrs. Cory's mother last year and she seemed pleased with things. They'll be here any minute. I've got to go. Can I leave things to youall? Marty, you and Elizabeth know what to do." He pushed past them without waiting for an answer and shut the front door behind him. Through the gathered gauze curtain over the oblong of glass, they could see him hurrying off; upset or angry or just in a hurry, they didn't know which.

Elizabeth Satterlee sank down by the telephone on the only hall chair and, seeing what she had done, said, "I guess I ought to start calling up people. I thought we'd have to . . ."

"You start calling up." Marty began to wander through the hall—Elizabeth Satterlee's voice followed her.

"She just had all this part done up, and the kitchen——"

Marty pushed open the kitchen door and went in, shutting out the other woman's voice, which had already begun, "Miz Coleman. I just don't know how I'm going to tell you, but . . ."

The kitchen was too quiet. The new tin-topped table was set for two, neatly, with the papers on one side. On the new rubberised sideboard sat the percolator; either it had never been turned on or someone had remembered to turn it off, for there was no smell of coffee. It was as if a busy housewife had just slipped out to answer the door—or get the milk, and disappeared off the earth.

But the back door was ajar, held open by broken glass. Marty looked down to where blood, milk, and glass were mixed and flung like some terrible vomit across the back porch. She realised that she had sunk on to one hand leaning on the table, and took her hand away. It made the table top jump like a rifle shot in the quiet room. Marty jumped too, but only from the noise. Somehow the mess of death was so real, so without mystery, that she took it quite calmly. She only lifted the top of the percolator, then shook it, and, finding it already prepared, switched it on, finishing what Eleanor Cory had begun, and went back out into the hall. Elizabeth Satterlee was saying, by now in a kind of rhythm:

"Mamie, I don't know how in the world I'm going to tell you . . ." Marty saw beyond her, through the door, the discreet ambulance draw up. By the time the white-coated attendants reached the front door another car had arrived, and one of Mrs. Cory's neighbours hurried across the dividing patch of lawn.

When she opened the door to the two quiet young men and said, "Upstairs . . . I don't know which room," the neighbour listening behind them broke in as they swept past carrying the stretcher with the precision of chorus boys.

"Good Lord, Miz Dodd, what's the matter? Anybody sick? What are you doing here?"

"Oh, Mrs. Browning, it's Eleanor Cory."

Mrs. Browning knew by the unspoken language of death that the use of both her first and last name in such a final way meant that fat Mrs. Cory, corkscrew curls and all, was not being carted to the hospital, but to the lysol-smelling back part of Lightfoot's Funeral Home.

"What can I do to help?" she demanded, pushing her way in.

"I don't know," Marty faltered. . . . "I don't know what to do myself. The doctor took care of . . . Elizabeth here is phoning. I made some coffee. Mr. Cory obviously hasn't had any breakfast. He's in there. . . ."

Mrs. Browning had already pushed back the living-room door.

"The doctor gave him . . ." Marty called out.

But the woman's voice inside told her that poor Marcellus Cory had been waked up again.

The doorbell rang.

As she turned to answer it she heard Mrs. Browning say in a tone of sympathetic exasperation:

"Why the Lord didn't you call me, Marcellus? Somebody's got to take charge of things at a time like this. Now you just lie there and I'll see to things for you. I don't know why people can't be practical. . . ."

Marty turned quickly and glanced at the man on the couch, trapped by the woman, shrunken and groggy with grief and drugs, trying even to smile to thank her.

She opened the door and two more women whom she did not know filed past her as if they were coming into a church, so solemn that the first one did not see that she was walking straight into the man at Eleanor Cory's feet.

"Look out," Marty called in time, and they stepped aside

to let the stretcher pass, bowing their heads, so that Marty, who had felt the touch of plain and final death in the kitchen, but not yet the atmosphere of formal passing-over which covers the obscenity and hallows it, remembered to slide her head forward too.

Gratefully, she saw that the body passing below her eyes was entirely camouflaged under a white cover.

"We're from Mrs. Cory's Auxiliary," one of the women said sadly when they had watched the body out. Another car had just drawn up; enough now for a bridge party, and looking quite the same, parked casually along the 'residential' street.

Mrs. Browning's voice, behind her, full of orders, said:

"Martha, take your car and go and get Mr. Cory's pastor. He's calling for him."

There was no sound from inside the living-room.

Marty said, "I haven't got my car . . ."

One of the newcomers cut in, "I'll go. I'll go. My car's right outside. I want to be some help in all this . . ."

As Mrs. Browning shoved the woman out of the front door ahead of her, Marty felt a tug at her arm. She looked round and saw that it was Marcellus Cory, motioning with a little bird-like gesture from a wide crack in the folding-doors. She slipped through it into the living-room, where someone had drawn the blinds, and there were in the dimness shapes of a heavy upholstered living-room 'suite'. The smell of the evening's fire and Marcellus Cory's last cigar of the night hung in the airless warm spaces.

"Will you get me a glass, honey? All these people. All I want is a drink." He peeked out of the crack, which he'd pulled narrower into an eye-hole, and watched the hall, stuffed with tip-toeing, murmuring women. "I can't go out there myself, can I?"

"Wait a minute." Marty edged through the gap and

118

closed it behind her. Someone else was answering the door; Mrs. Satterlee was still tolling the telephone bell, her face red from rubbing and attempts to control herself enough to talk. No one noticed when Marty passed behind them into the kitchen, turned off the now hard-boiling coffee, which had made the room come alive with morning at last. Someone, she saw, had cleaned up the mess on the porch.

She slipped back with the glass into the darkened room.

"Boy, I sure need that." Mr. Cory poured a drink for himself and sank back in his chair by the radio.

"Honey," he said, his voice full of wonder, "ain't this the God-damnedest thing to have happen?" and he fell forward on to the chair-arm, scattering all his weekly magazines, last night's paper and his new-poured drink all over the floor. When Marty ran to lift him he muttered, "Oh, get out of here, honey, and lemme alone. Just lemme alone for a minute."

She backed out the door and met Mrs. Browning again.

"Let him sleep," she whispered when she felt the woman push her aside, and when that didn't stop her beginning to roll back the door, said, "For God's sake let the poor man alone," so loudly that she stopped all talking in the hall, and there was dead silence.

Mrs. Browning only stared.

Between calls, Marty caught Mrs. Satterlee. "You've got plenty of help now. I'll do whatever I can, but there are just too many people here," she whispered.

"I sure see what you mean." It was the first completely unemotional remark Mrs. Satterlee had made that morning.

"Call me if you want the least thing, and make them leave that poor little man be." She touched her shoulder.

"Thank you, Martha, for all you've done." Mrs. Satterlee had become solemn again, realising where she was. "I'll never forget this."

Marty smiled weakly and was gone. She did not begin to shake again until she had walked far down the February street through the deceptive spring day.

After she had gone there was a silence, and then a woman whispered, "Doesn't she look *terrible*!"

"Never seen a woman go to seed like she has; matter of weeks."

"Well, if you happen to ask me . . . she's going to land up with a serious operation!"

Someone poked her head out of the kitchen door. "Somebody's made some coffee." Several of the women filed through to the kitchen.

In the deserted living-room Mr. Cory had indeed gone off into the deep sleep of shock, sprawled across the chair-arm, with the litter of his secure and solid world scattered about his feet.

Marty finally reached home again as noon struck. She knew, with a slight unaccountable thrill, by the sound of the children spilling out again into the street for lunch time, and was a little sorry, as she pushed open her own house door, that this was the first day she'd noticed how the day divided its silences in winter. They came, skidding and yelling and scraping their feet down the street, and she shut them all out and leaned against her door, exhausted at last.

"Miz Dodd, what in the world's the matter? Where you been all morning?" Gladola's voice, so near her, made her jump and open her eyes.

"I just been for a little walk, Gladola."

"You been out since eight o'clock. You ought to go on upstairs and lie down, Miz Dodd," Gladola began to whine, "you're white as a sheet."

But when Marty began to move, she found herself staggering. "I've just tired myself out, that's all." She leaned on Gladola to keep from fainting. "Lord, it shows you how you need exercise." She recovered herself and started up the stairs, Gladola, worried, close behind her.

"Anybody call?"

"Yes'm. Miz Potter, three—four times, and that new man once."

Marty knew that the new man was Hamilton. Gladola, who was a thin, capable, nervous mountain woman with very few prejudices, had one bit of waywardness which Marty fully respected. She refused to clutter her slightly over-wrought mind with the names of people she did not like, and though positive criticism never passed her lips, Marty knew by the habit that from November on she had not liked Hamilton.

"Mr. Dodd and Selby are coming home to dinner."

"What on earth for?"

"I don't know. The office just called up. One o'clock."

They had reached the door of Marty's room when the telephone rang again.

"Don't worry, I'll get it." She sank down on the bed, kicking off her shoes, as she answered on her own extension.

Anne Randolph's voice was a worried whirr on the other end as Marty leaned back at last. "I've been trying to get you for hours!"

Marty broke in, knowing that Anne Randolph wanted to talk about Mrs. Cory, but trying to stop her.

"Oh, Lord, honey, for some reason I've been down there all morning. I went for a little walk . . ."

"Down where?"

"Haven't you heard yet? Eleanor Cory died of a heart attack this morning. Just dropped dead on her own back door-step . . . I was . . ."

"What?" Anne Randolph screamed, then was still; then unbelieving, "But I just *talked* to her day before yesterday!"

Marty wanted to laugh, but dared not do it; she wanted more to fall into the first deep sleep for weeks, but the telephone had started making noise at her again.

"The poor thing. Isn't it terrible, though," and then, irrelevantly, "of course I never really got to know her. You went right inside the house, did you?"

Marty jerked slightly when she heard Anne Randolph's voice lilt up higher into a question.

"What?"

"What was the house like?"

"Oh, very neat. Just as neat as it could be."

"No taste at all, I bet."

"No, honey." Marty changed the subject before Anne Randolph, now that she was used to the news, could sharpen her teeth on it. "Gladola said you'd called before . . ." She left the question unsaid.

But when Anne Randolph answered, quiet with doom, "Honey, I just don't know how in the world I'm going to tell you . . ." the now familiar refrain of the morning woke Marty again entirely, and she waited, tense, for Anne Randolph to go on.

When she did not she prompted her, as she had once prompted Jim. "Go on . . ."

"Of course I know you'd just be the last person in the world to want anything to go wrong."

"Yes?"

"I always say you and Jim are closer than any kin we've got . . ."

Marty waited. The silence caused Anne Randolph to rise up in her own bed and groan, "Marty, you've just got to help me! I don't know what to do!"

"What in the world's the matter?"

Anne Randolph sank back mournfully into the crumpled pillows. "Honey, I just happened to be in Sally Bee's room this morning and I accidentally ran across something—I just don't know what to do."

"What was it?"

"Well, it was a syringe." Anne Randolph said 'shringe' in two syllables, in almost a holy voice of terror.

"Honey, I don't understand what you're getting at."

"A shringe! A shringe! A *swirling shringe!*" Anne Randolph's face screwed up as she panted the words into the telephone. "Oh, Marty, do I have to say any more? Do I have to draw it all out for you? What am I going to do?"

"Why don't you have a quiet little talk with her when she comes home? You don't want to jump to a lot of conclusions you'll be sorry for later, honey . . . now you just . . ."

"Marty—you don't think she and Selby were *doing anything* at Christmas, do you? Do you? Marty—you've got to find out. You've just got to! I'll never rest a minute till you find out for me. You've just got to find out."

"Well, I don't know, honey." Marty had sat up too, fully alert to the naked, tearing jealousy in Anne Randolph's voice. "I don't think Selby would. I just know he wouldn't. Sally Bee's only a child. He wouldn't do a thing like that."

"How do we know, Marty? What do we know about him? Just turning up like that. Oh, he seems all right—but let me tell you, if he's laid a finger on that child of mine, I'l have George Potter run him out of town on a rail . . ."

"Oh, Anne Randolph, for heaven's sake calm yourself down."

"If you think for one minute we're not going to protect our little girl I don't care whose son he is . . ."

"Now, Anne Randolph, don't say any more."

"I'll say what I please, Marty Dodd . . ."

123

"*Don't say any more.* I can't stand it. I just can't stand any more of it."

"*You* can't stand. What about me? What about . . ." There was a faint click. Anne Randolph was yelling at the empty air. When she tried to dial again Marty's phone was busy.

Marty woke, startled, remembering dreams, and saw that the room was already dark. She felt a terrible weight—a weight of apprehension, of dry aloneness—but, fighting through to consciousness, put out her hand and found that someone had covered her over with a thick quilt. The only light, cutting across the muted darkness, was a line from the half-opened door. Marty fought upwards and switched on her lamp. When she saw the telephone she wondered who had placed it back on the hook.

"Marty?" Selby loomed at the crack in the door and Marty drew the cover high up over herself again and fought back her heavy panic. "Marty, you awake yet?"

"Come on in, honey. Lord——" before he could talk any more, "I don't know what came over me. I've been asleep for hours. What time is it?"

"About six . . ."

"Jim," she went on, looking away from him but finding her eyes travel back always to his face, now nearer the bed. "Where's Jim? Did you all come home to lunch? Why didn't somebody wake me up?"

"He wanted you to sleep. He told me to stay here and see you didn't get up. We were going to Cincinnati just over-night on business. . . ."

He was standing so close now that Marty waited, not daring to breathe, for him to take her pale hand lying too near him on the cover.

"You want anything? A hot-water bottle?" The boy

backed away slightly, cool with a revulsion he couldn't hide.

"Oh, Lord, son. You don't mean my doing this made you miss your trip? I am sorry. Jim didn't need to ask you to stay."

"He lent me to you." Selby smiled, wandered past the bed and stared out of the window.

"I'm sorry," Marty couldn't keep herself from saying again. "You go on out. Don't you worry about me. I'm fine. I just had a long walk this morning."

"Wasn't it O.K. for me to take the car?" Selby turned quickly from the window as if he'd touched his funny-bone.

"Lord, yes, honey. I've just taken to it. This winter— it's the funny weather," she said quickly.

The room was still again. Marty felt the heaviness return, pressing her down, down into the bed, and dared not speak at all for fear of hysterically calling for help. He went on looking out of the window. Weakened from sleep, she let herself watch his back, not knowing that the black night against the polished glass made a mirror of it, so that he had to turn yet again, to avoid catching her eye without meaning to.

"I don't want to go out. I'll just stay here and read," he said, moving to the mantel and letting his fingers wander among the objects, mostly books and boxes that Marty had let gather there and Gladola never moved.

"I expect you feel a little bit at a loose end now the play's over. Why don't you call up somebody? I'm sure . . ."

"Are you sure you wouldn't mind?" He turned, eager for the first time since he had come into the room.

"Good heavens no. Will you ask Gladola to come up?"

"Sure, Marty. Sure there isn't anything I can get you?"

"No, child, not a thing. You go on have a good time."

When he was half-way out of the door, her voice winged after him. "Thank you for staying. That was real nice."

He fled from her across the hall into his own room, closed the door, and leaning into his own mirror said to it carefully, "Oh, my God, what a sheiss you are! What a lousy little sheiss!" But went on, long after he had spoken and even the after-sound of his voice was gone, watching himself carefully in the mirror, inspecting dispassionately the deep set of his eyes, the pleasing hollows of his cheeks, the sharp angle of his jaw.

Chapter VIII

The Nightmare

SELBY had scared drowsiness and peace away from Marty's room, and scattered in its place a heavy charge of his own absence. She heard the front door close and thought he had already gone, without even waiting for dinner, turned her head away from watching the door, and said brutally to herself aloud:

"Why the Lord shouldn't he, you old fool?" and tried to read a book of essays she had thought for a long time she ought to, but failed.

When Gladola brought her dinner on a tray, with even a flower, taken from a still blooming Christmas plant, leaning thin and alone in a drinking glass, Marty played at being drowsy, so that she wouldn't stay and talk.

But Gladola, to whom the rumour of illness was a tonic, would not be put off. She tendered her advice, standing solidly over her with her bony arms folded and her thin face working with concern. She even said it.

"Miz Dodd. I'm gonna tender you a little bit of advice. I wouldn't feel right if I didn't. You don't talk much about yourself like some I might mention. I never heard you complain. But you been going to seed since Christmas. Yes, you have, and at your age you just can't let yourself go like that. When you're younger they ain't nothing a little pink powder and lip-stick won't cure, but you're too late for that. You gotta go deeper. One day you wake up and everything's just gone—all broke up . . ."

Gladola never made long speeches, and the effort of this one made her seem taciturn. She shifted her feet, getting an even firmer grip on to the floor. "I spoke out to Mr. Dodd about it. I told him you ought to go see the doctor. Your age you jest gotta be careful—if you don't take yourself in hand you're gonna need more than a little bit of paint and powder . . ."

Marty, watching the huge shadow of Gladola's head on the ceiling bob up and down like one of the comic shadow animals made with moving fists, wondered when she'd stop laying down the law, but said, to please her:

"You're as nice as you can be to worry about me so much, Gladola. I'll go see the doctor. I'll go see him right in the morning."

"Somebody's got to . . ." Gladola muttered, as she closed the door behind her.

Marty, to keep her from coming to talk to her again, made herself go deep into a half-waking dream when she had finished her dinner, so deep that when the door opened again she barely heard it, kept her eyes closed. When someone leaned close over her to take the tray she realised with her whole body, half suspended in sleep, that it was not Gladola, but Selby bent across her.

And then, because it might so easily have really been a dream, she was so protected from herself by sleep, reached out her arms and drew the boy down so he lay flat across her, both their bodies so stiff, not breathing, they might have been deep under water. She let him go almost at once, still quiet, but now frozen with shame at what she'd done, and he bounced away from her like a swimmer fighting to a surface where he could breathe again.

Fully awake now, all her excuses flicked away as useless by her cold shame, she dared not open her eyes. At least, then, because he saw the colour ebb from her face and her lips stiffen as she woke, and the wrinkles around her eyes web out suddenly like broken glass as she fought to keep them shut, he took her hand as if he'd been her doctor, not her sickness, and said:

"Poor Marty. Poor nice woman. I would have to turn up like the fairy prince, wouldn't I?"

Still she kept her eyes shut, trying to shut out what had happened.

"Why do I have to be everybody's goddam fairy prince?" When he saw that she would not open her eyes, he put down her hand, patted it, picked up the tray and started to tiptoe out, but said, before he left, "I couldn't go off and leave you feeling like you do. I'll be across the hall if you want me."

He thought he heard her mutter, but it might have been only a gasp from trying to breathe again. He closed the door quickly, hoping she had indeed gone off to sleep.

No matter how quiet she tried to be through the night, he was too wakeful himself to miss the fact that she was not sleeping. The click of her bathroom light; the high-pitched whistle of her toilet flushing, which ebbed into the night noises and left its whine in his ear long after he knew it had stopped; the crack of floor-boards as she paced back and forth across her room, were more nerve-racking because he could tell by the silence she had stopped, stiff, like a frightened animal, whenever she had stepped off a live board; then, later, the opening of the french door on to her sleeping porch, and then an outer window, letting in the wind, which whistled and jollied the night currents of the house so that even the papers on his own bedside table quivered a little so far away. He jumped up, fully awake, and snapped on his light, straining to listen, afraid to hear, not daring to run to her for fear of her, then sinking back still listening, and hearing nothing, drifting finally off to sleep, too drowsy all the time to know that the sudden light from his own window, flung like a banner across the black garden, changing the position of the skeleton trees, had chased Marty back to her own bed afraid too.

Then, when the morning was sunny and Gladola made her stay in bed for breakfast, and stood while she called the doctor, and fussed around her while she got dressed, she found even in her kindness a feeling of false content that it was a sickness, a simple sickness, which the doctor was to exorcise by giving a name to take the sting of magic out of what was wrong. The content lasted until she got down into the hall and saw that Gladola had even fixed Selby, waiting there, to drive her down to the Canona River Building. Gladola handed her over, pleased, and scurried back into the kitchen still ordering.

"Now you take real good care of her, Selby. Take her down there, and you wait for her, you hear me?"

"Sure, Gladola, I'll look after her." He took her arm, and then came closer, urged, and closed both his arms around her, holding her close but so gently she let him and couldn't in his care so completely draw herself away. It was only a hug, after all.

"We'll be all right, Marty. Don't worry about anything. Now, come on," he led her, with his arm across her back, out to the car.

It wasn't until he put his hands on the wheel that she spoke to him for the first time since the night before.

"Why, Selby, I didn't ever notice you bit your nails!"

This time it was Selby's turn not to answer, and reading the ravages of the night decided to tell her later, at the right time for talking, that this time he had really decided quite unselfishly to go away.

Even the clean black and white marble entrance tiles of the

Canona River Building had an antiseptic ring to Marty as her heels clicked across to the lift, which ran up and down to doctors' offices with a suppressed sigh, depositing patients. Marty had had her whole self patched in the building for years—her feet to the first floor, her teeth to the second, her eyes to the fourth. But good old Doctor Adams was all the way up to seven.

She sat down in the brown waiting-room and flicked idly at the piles of magazines, old, curled edges, that a patient had left strewn beside her on the leather couch. But Doctor Adams' nurse, Bah Salter, didn't give her a chance to read them.

"Lord, Marty, you haven't been in for years! How long is it? You must of been keeping in good shape." She laughed, and then peered. "How's Jim? I heard all about things. How is he?"

"Oh, Jim's fine. Just fine, Bah. Fat as he can be."

"Fat and sassy, eh?"

"Fat and sassy."

They looked at each other in a minute of silence.

"Doc'll see you in a minute, honey," the nurse told her, and went on out of the office door on her interrupted errand.

Doctor Adams' office was as brown as the waiting-room. He still sat at his large roller-top desk, with his swivel-chair in front of it, out of which he was always half pushing a faded chintz cushion with his dapper, wiggling little rear. Behind him, high on the wall, was a sepia-print called *The Doctor*. Marty had first noticed it there when she was very small, and she had wondered why the young doctor was sick at his stomach and if the little girl wasn't uncomfortable on the two chairs. She found herself wondering still as she caught sight of it again. Nothing had changed in all the years. Nothing but Doctor Adams, who had grown smaller and a lot franker as a privilege of age.

131

"Lord," said Marty to avoid talking about why she'd come, "how do you and Bah keep so healthy? She looks fine."

"Oh, Bah's fine. Bah's just fine. She does a lot. Women of yourall's age ought to do a lot. Takes care of that whole triflin' bunch. I don't know how she does it on what I pay her . . ."

"I went to school with her . . ." Marty began.

"Hell, honey, I know youall went to school together. Every time you call up Bah tells me, every time you come in you tell me. What the hell were you doing at Marcellus Cory's yesterday morning? I didn't know youall were that close."

"I just happened to be passing and what's-her-name— that little friend of hers—got hold of me. Wasn't it a shame?"

Doctor Adams' chair swung round and he stopped it with military precision, and sat staring out of the window over the street through the naked wires of neon signs with his back to Marty. "I reckon that's what it was, Marty. A damned shame. I felt real bad. I'll tell you right now—I shouldn't have lost Eleanor. Leaving Marcellus like that without a damned soul to look after him. She ate too much. If I told her once I told her a thousand times. All that weight—your heart won't stand it . . . anybody ought to get their blood pressure down when they're warned." He got over his sad anger and swung round again to Marty.

"What's the matter, honey? What you got wrong with you?"

Marty hesitated, trying to muster what she could tell, what wouldn't sound hysterical or shamming or silly in this brown room where serious business went on and even her own friends could be condemned to face facts.

So she said, "I don't know. . . ."

"Hell, honey," he told her, "you have to tell me things. I ain't a horse doctor." Then he softened, let her talk while he turned a pencil over and over in his scrubbed hands.

She looked past him then and tried to tell what she could to the sepia engraving. "I've been overtired lately. I thought maybe I didn't get enough exercise. So I took to walking. That helped for a while—but we've had all that excitement, we've all got so much to catch up on we stay awake till all hours. There's been the play and a lot of company."

The pencil went on turning with precision in his fingers.

"Yesterday when I got home I lay down for a minute on the bed and I went off until dark. Why, I've never done such a thing before in all my life. When I woke up I felt heavy— as if I was half dead myself—it was awful, Doctor Adams." Marty tried to convince him and herself that that was what was really wrong. "It happened several times in the night. Is there something wrong with my heart?"

The pencil stopped. She wanted to jerk it out of his hand and wind it in her own fingers.

"Martha, how old are you?"

"Forty-six. I'm forty-six."

"Any pains in your legs——"

"Well, a little—just a little."

"Breasts?"

"Only at certain times."

"Ankles swell——"

"I haven't noticed."

"Headaches yet?"

"What do you mean—yet. I have them sometimes."

"Martha, honey, you're your mother's daughter—most down-to-earth sensible woman I ever knew. I'm going to be perfectly frank with you. Have you looked at yourself lately—had a good look?"

"Well, I suppose so. I can't think." She was near to tears.

"Next time you take off your clothes, have a good look. You've changed shape. You've begun to look mature. Now if a woman is sensible, it can be a good time for her. One of the most beautiful times of life." He threw back his head and began to wind the pencil again. "For a sensible woman her fall of the year can be very beautiful—any trouble with your periods?"

"Well, they're a little irregular."

"Get depressed? World turn bad over-night?" He smiled at her.

"I guess so." She smiled back.

"They all do." He suddenly leaned forward and said, closer to her face, "Want me to tell you what I did last night? I went out three times in the middle of the night. Three heart-attacks. All people you knew, Marty. I'm sixty-eight years old and I still go out in the middle of the night. Do you know why? Every time an Eleanor Cory keels over, everybody her age and over looks in the mirror and sees the reaper. They see the old reaper and they hear him, and they lay down on their beds and they even feel him. Nine times out of ten they ain't a damn thing wrong but fright—just plain fright. When one of you dies, you all start looking over your shoulder. At least you didn't call me up in the middle of the night. Now I'm going to examine your heart—but I'm not going to find anything wrong. You're worn-out and you're due for your change. I've been expecting it for about three years now. Your mother had it at forty. I don't think you'll have anything to worry about." He motioned her to the black leather examining table covered with the fresh laundered sheet, and began to gather his stethoscope, to unwind the wide black band from the sphygnomamometer. "Of course it would have been better if you and Jim had had some children. Funny you couldn't. We tried so many things I always wondered if it wasn't Jim. Of course, now I know better. Isn't it funny? Big strapping woman like you. Take your blouse off. I can't get to you."

He went on talking bending down behind her, not waiting for her to answer. She could feel the cold flat metal press against her back.

"You and Jim were always happy together, weren't you, Marty?"

He heard her Yes hum under her back.

"Sex life all right? Of course I think they lay too much store on it. Hell, they ought to see how ordinary people live. What's sex to most women? Bunch of kids, prolapse, change, old age. Lay down. You're lucky, honey. You got a nice husband. You got money. You can get away when you want to. Wouldn't hurt you right now. No. They ain't a damn thing wrong with your heart. That weight you felt. That's just sluggish—blood slows down. You know what they call that—incubus. Doctors used to think that heaviness came from a little sexy devil sitting on your chest so you couldn't breathe. Let me have your arm. You go on take a little trip. Take that boy of yours if Jim can't go. Never hurt anybody to get away . . . I always think of a little poem." Pump, pump. "Something like 'After all the stress and strife, the autumn of a woman's life'." He let the pump out a little and watched the gauge. . . . "Something about beauty." Pump, pump, pump. "I forget it . . ." He let the pump fill with air. "Go see that sensible mother of yours . . ."

Selby had not waited for Marty, but had driven the station wagon furiously away as soon as her disappearance into the marble hall had left him free.

Mrs. Sacks motioned over her shoulder down the long hall to the living-room, followed him only a little way, saying politenesses but hardly hearing herself do it, she was so used to him.

"Gwan in, Selby. Make yourself at home. Joey's in there." But she was so much slower than Selby that she had not reached the kitchen before she'd seen him throw himself face-down on the couch and Hamilton had wheeled over from the window and slammed the living-room door, shutting her out, so that she shuffled back into the tiny kitchen.

It was only later that she made out, over the shut door and her own lack of interest, what was being said. Hamilton's voice intruded, filled the hall, even through the shut door.

"You couldn't wait. You just can't help it, can you, you little innocent? Everybody has to love Selby! You went to work on that love-starved woman that minute you got here. Everybody's juvenile couldn't be satisfied with sending half the town. It had to be her, too. Oh, God! that poor sad woman!"

CHAPTER IX

On a Hill Far Away

"WE'RE English blood, all right. Pure English. Your paw always swore his grandmaw was a Jew—but I don't believe it. I seen her plenty times. She was just real dark English—like you. Even sprouted a little moustache like a man when she got old—you'll get yours. All the side of the family you take after do."

As Marty half-watched her mother, sitting huddled in her coat, rocking and talking on the Sunday porch, she saw little change in her. She registered vaguely that her mother was smaller than when she had seen her last—but, as with every return she had made, they seemed to take up conversation, prejudices, and a sort of candid relationship which had grown up between them as Marty herself had grown up, where they had left off, ignoring the long time they had been apart. That Marty had gone thinner in the face her mother saw at once, but, looking at her through the eyes of her own past, saw no reason to get riled about it. Having watched herself in the speckled mirror grow harder and more angular with the years, and turn from the smooth, tan, country skin that she'd been secretly a little proud of, to parchment which didn't even fit but only loosely covered the witch's change of her face, she was already shocked beyond surprise at what the flat hand of age could do.

"I'm glad you come up to see me, Marthy. I got something I want you to do." She rearranged herself in her chair, pulled her shawl tighter, and almost stopped rocking. She then began to give her instructions carefully.

"Now I want you to go up to the State House, and I want you to tell Alec Little that Ebbie's been laid off the road commission gang. I can't get out of Sary Corine why they laid him off but it ain't nothing important. Now I don't want you to call up on the telephone, I want you to go right up there. You tell Alec to give the youngin some other kind of job. I don't care what else. I just don't want Sary Corine belly-achin' around here any more botherin' me. I wish you never had of high-tailed off from a good job at the State House like you did and gone to work for them Dodds. I don't know what got into you, Marthy, with all that business training and all this bunch of kin on my neck."

It was an old refrain of her mother's, who distrusted marriage anyway, that Marty had ruined her future by leaving her government job, but even after all the years it never failed to make her snap back.

"Lord, Mother, anybody who'd of taken on more people than Jim did would of been a downright saint. Why he's laid himself out all his life finding jobs and land and Lord knows what for my bunch of triflin' relations."

Her mother was completely unmoved. Perhaps she didn't even hear what Marty was saying. She just went off rocking at the same small pace, waiting for her to stop talking. "There ain't nothin' like a government job. Safest thing in the long run. Our family always believed in getting a little something with the State. That don't fail you, come hell or high water. Bottom don't drop out of it. Course, there's always that chance of the ministration changing, but you have to take it. Nothing's sure-fire. Four eight twelve years ain't long to wait you got some little piece of property to wait on—I'm seventy-eight years old, ain't seen one of us starve yet . . ." She began to ramble a little, then with an abrupt switch brought her attention and her talk back to Marty.

"You're due for your change, Marthy. Lemme see. Well, you ain't started sproutin' no whiskers yet. Now don't go gettin' yourself all tar'd out. Your Ant Teeny, now, she took after the same side of the family as you. Lord, you'd of thought nothin' would of riled old Teeny—real feet on the ground. Six feet tall—held a real important job as the telegraph operator. Now Teeny was just as smart as they come. Well, come forty-eight years old one day she just put on her Sunday hat and prissed out of the house calm as you please; only trouble was she didn't have one blessed stitch else on. Poor old Teeny—she was real simple from then on. She got a moustache, too." Marty's mother rocked a few times. "Now my side it don't show much." She was still for a minute, watching out over the wet, brown front yard, which had begun to show the ice-breaking awakened signs of early spring. No green yet, no softness even in the air to cover the hardness of the brown earth and the ugly farm-yard where even at the best time of summer the few stunted bushes took on a dusty look; there was only the wet in-dignity of the breaking of spring, like sex in sad women.

"I been to see old Doc Adams lately," Marty told her mother.

"Lord, I haven't seen him two three years. How's he keepin' himself?"

"Same as ever. He told me wasn't anything to worry about. He says I'm fine."

"Bah still there?"

"Yes, ma'am. She's fine, too. He said I ought to take a little trip." Marty slipped in the news about her projected holiday obliquely by habit, as she always had, when she wanted to be able to say to her, "I told you twice, Mother; you just weren't paying any attention."

But with that true capacity of children, the old, and the deaf for never failing to catch the whisper of secrets, her mother heard, and made a sound as near a chuckle as a skinny old woman can.

"Don't know what you'd want with a vacation. You don't do nothin'—ain't he an old fool, though? If he said it once he said it a hundred times, 'Miz Collins, I don't know why you don't have a nervous breakdown all you do.' I said, 'Lord, Doc Adams, I ain't got time for no nervous breakdown.' He said, 'I know just what you mean, Miz Collins, only rich people got time and money enough to get sick and go off.'"

"Oh, Lord, I never meant to go!" Marty defended herself jokingly, changing her mind even as she spoke, the worm of shame moving slightly in her that she'd ever dreamed of doing such a thing—especially in the winter, for no reasons but her own.

"What you come up here for?" Martha's mother suddenly turned on her, almost belligerently.

"Nothing, Mother, just thought it was time for a little visit," Marty said easily, at home, spreading her knees, and rocking a little, sprawled and comfortable, Martha Dodd with her married world thrown aside like a girdle, resting in her mother's house again—isolated and toughened to the kind of unthinking woman's brutality she was born in—or at least toughened while she was in it—like a fighter whose eye does not turn black until the fight is long over.

"Just thought I'd ask," her mother said, "thought you's after something." She protected herself, watching Marty for any clue what she might want to 'get out of her', not realising in her bird-like awareness that she had long since ceased to possess a vestige of anything to give her daughter —that daughter who was neither the oldest nor the youngest of the six, who she remembered as leaving home for Canona as soon as she got out of her high-school middy to go to business school, who had appeared from time to time since, bringing little and then bigger presents, who got her picture in the Canona social page from time to time, which pleased her mother and gave her something to talk to people about.

She said aloud, when Marty had not answered, "Whyn't you bring the boy? We all want to see him. I seen his picture in the newspaper, real play-actor. Nice-looking boy, though. You get on all right with him?"

"Why, sure, Mother—I'd of brought him up to see you only he works every day with Jim now."

"Steppin' right in, is he?" Marty's mother found that extremely funny, and laughed so that her hawk face split, exposing a wide expanse of grey-pink empty gums.

"Mother, why the Lord don't you wear those nice teeth we got you? I've taken you down five six times to have them seen to, but you never will wear them."

"Oh, I wear 'em to eat. That's what teeth are for—to eat—ain't they? I'm too old and too poor to put 'em in for beauty's sake. Wouldn't do me any good." She cackled again. "Walked right in and took over, has he? I always knew you'd get yourself into some kind of situation—marrying all those kind of people been out East, drinking and everything, and all that play-acting . . ." The play-acting made her forget Selby and she switched again. "You was always pretty good at elecution, though. Didn't you get some kind of prize or something once, or was that Essie Corine? How's Gladola?"

"She's fine. Just fine."

"Whyn't you bring her with you so's she could see her folks?"

"Oh, Mother, I always bring her. This time I just wanted to come by myself."

"You *did* come up here after something"; she sprang forward in her rocker and seemed to peck at Marty.

Marty looked quite squarely at the old woman sitting bowed in her grey-black coat, with her shawl huddled high about her skeletal neck, and her strands of white hair pulled into a knot but hardly covering any longer the greying skin of her head. She saw behind her the brown yard, the ugly fences of the farm without even a coat of whitewash to lighten the gloomy boards, and away behind them where the now brown hills rose barrenly, ploughed over and treeless to the horizon. She followed the dirt road, with its deep rills of constantly running drain-water off the hillside, which connected the square wood-house where she sat, with its gingerbreaded, wooden, paint-peeled Sunday porch, to the next house just like it, but out of sight on the other side of the hill. She let her eyes come back to her mother and, with an easy weakening which made her examine her own strange new awareness as if it were something outside herself, she let herself hear old Doctor Adams' voice, "Go see that sensible mother of yours . . ."

"No, Mother, not a thing. I just wanted to ride by myself."

"Might have remembered Gladola's bus fare. It's a hundred miles. People get rich forget things like that."

Marty said nothing, just numbly rocked as if, even with the hardness and ugliness, the home and its people that she had once run from so blindly could not hurt her any more. Even, with the years, she had softened her picture of it all when she was away from it. She forgot a little the Puritan blindness and replaced it in memory with a few anecdotes of her mother's country common sense. She forgot even the look of the place, and was apt to endow it (when she called it up, as one does, in one's mind's eye, all distorted by wishing) with a certain homespun, cosy charm, the sun sifting on to the weekday porch, the chickens cuttering among the raspberry bushes, the smell of 'good' farm food. She forgot the prejudiced diet of starch and coffee, the linoleum-covered bedroom floors, the meeting-house, rickety straight chairs, the gnarl-handed, straight-laced, black-coated, ugly saints like the one who sat opposite, who had planted a worm of shame in her worse than the Catholic's original sin, which she would never escape, which confession only fed and contrition watered, and which intruded into her walk, into the selfconscious way she held a cigarette, into the hard shell of self-contempt that she had learned to clap over her offending emotions. She forgot all those things, she even after a time forgot her mother's homing capacity for recognising and gouging at the quick of her secrets when she had a chance.

"You never did tell me what you thought of the boy."

The old woman was homing at last, and Marty knew it. She also realised suddenly why she had asked Selby to let her use the station wagon and come all the way to see her for the first time in a year—a hundred miles over the grey road through the low farmed-out hills. She had come to taste the secret bitter aloes of punishment, for the Puritan God can afford mercy—his saints deal out none.

"He's a real nice boy," she said again and waited for her mother's tongue.

"What's he look like?" Her mother watched her avidly. She seemed to have forgotten about the picture.

"Oh, nice-looking boy—just as polite as he can be. Of course Jim's just crazy about him. He's a new man. Selby seems to be so quick about picking up the business, Jim says he's real useful already. He's paying him a salary. . . ."

"How much?"

"Oh, Mother, I don't know how much. They don't even talk to me about it."

143

"Hunh." Her mother snorted.

"Oh, Jim thought he did. But you know what he's like—talks all around a thing and never hops right in and says what he means. He probably thinks he'd had a lot of real good advice from me about that boy's pay and all—I couldn't hardly make head or tail of what he was talking about." When Marty spoke about Jim, which she did so seldom, she did it with such an air of joking affection toward him that no one could ever have accused her of complaining, even her mother, who was so quick about the rest.

"Is he fat?"

"Jim? He's not any fatter than he was when you saw him. Jim's not really fat—he's, well . . ."

"No, no, no." The old woman clicked her lips with impatience. "The boy."

"Oh, no. Selby's slim, he looks just like Jim must have when he was real young. I can see such a lot of Jim in him." She sighed, and, just for a second, forgot her mother. "Course I never met Jim until he was over thirty. By that time he'd widened out just about like he is now."

"Well, you just watch your step, my girl. Take a little bit of advice. Don't you go making a damn fool out of yourself with a boy in the house like that. I know what I'm talkin' about, I ain't been alive a hundred years for nothin', and I tell you there ain't nothing worse than some fool old woman running round like she was in heat over some little old spalpeen."

Marty didn't stop her. She couldn't. She'd come a hundred miles on her doctor's orders for this bath of cruelty and brutal fact which has made truth bc called naked, and sense, common.

"Don't she have any idea what she looks like?" Her mother was getting excited again, "all baggy—mutton

144

dressed like lamb—disgusting. I never did hold with all that elecution you do, Marthy. Get a lot of dirty ideas. You just watch—your—step!"

"Mother, what are you talking about?" Marty made herself say quite firmly. Her mother's depth of craving disapproval and foul-mindedness astonished her sometimes and she tried to steer her away from the subjects that were already making her old eyes glitter.

It did no good. The old woman leaned back, began her series of rapes, incest-born children, the generations' urge toward each other.

"There was that old thing up Kitty Creek; she married a young feller young enough to be her grandson. Oh, it's awful the way some of these trash act." She rounded back to the point. "You just better watch your step. It'd serve Jim Dodd right," she laughed, "ain't right for some people go through life not a damn thing ever happen to 'em. He'd holler like a stuck pig!"

Marty was almost drawn to defend Jim against her mother on his behaviour in a disaster that would never happen. She knew it wouldn't happen because she, Martha Dodd, was too good a woman to let it happen—that thing which had sent her sick with loathing when it had intruded like an ugly beast into her regimented thoughts. She was not a damn fool; she was not some old woman in a poke bonnet with an ageing trashy itch up Kitty Creek. She was Martha Dodd, safe with Jim, a self-constructed woman who had made herself everything she wanted to be and channelled away the messy-mindedness that had made her unhappy when she was a girl with an interesting, hard-working hobby. Nothing could happen to her. Jim wouldn't let it.

She got up, almost smiling, to say good-bye to the old woman—and left the Sunday porch refreshed and surer of herself than she had been in weeks.

When she was disappearing down the road, Ebbie slouched round the corner of the house. "That Ant Marthy gone?" When old Mrs. Collins didn't answer, he said, "Did ja ask her?"

"Oh, I asked her all right; I don't want you hanging around here for me to feed." She shooed him away with her hand.

The boy—he was twenty—slouched away again, feeling too murderous to answer.

The old woman promptly forgot him, and forgot Marthy, too, her third daughter, who'd left home so early, but turned up once in a while to see her and do a few errands for her. She forgot them, because she was seventy-eight years old, and afraid to die, sitting alone out there, watching the other hill with not a damn one of them around—no children she cared much about, no husband, no God she could really trust when it came right down to it—nothing. When Ebbie had long gone the hopeless mood began to lift, and to make herself feel better she began to sing herself a hymn.

"Oh, I'll cling to the old Rugged Cross," she quavered, partly from age, and partly because the hymn moved her so:

"Till my burden at last I'll lay down,
    Yes, I'll cling to the old Rugged Cross,
    And exchange it some day for a crown."

Ebbie, away out leaning against the corn rick, heard her, pegged his jack-knife again towards the hard ground, and said aloud, "She don't care. . . ."

Marty drove fast and sure along the hill road, miles up through the woods. She was congratulating herself on her new clear-sightedness, on how much good a little trip had

146

done her; her mother had seemed to enjoy it, and the ham and candy, though she'd rather die than show it. Marty smiled into the windshield and saw reflected the movement of her face across the road, remembering affectionately her mother's pride. It was then her own face changed into another face, and she was caught before she knew it in the recurring wish, so that she had to pull the station wagon up under the trees beside the road and lay her head back against the seat and let her body find peace in it, lying there as she had sprawled in her mother's rocker, awash in a sweet daydream.

Chapter X

In the Dark House

"MISS LEFTWICH, answer me. Are you a bird?"

"No, Mr. Sacks."

"A little dog, maybe?"

"No, Mr. Sacks."

"Well then, what are you, Miss Leftwich?"

"I think I'm a servant—maid, I mean."

"You think you are a servant. Well, that's very bold! You are perfectly right. That's exactly what you are. Now. How long have you been a servant?"

"Twenty-five years."

"Where?"

"Well, here." She whisked her arm vaguely around her. "Wasn't I?" she added hopefully.

"That's right. Now, do you think that after all that time you could be expected to know where the front door of the house is, and that you might react to the doorbell without fluttering like a pet bird, or bounding down right like a pup? Take it again, Miss Leftwich!"

Far from being reduced to quaking anger or tears by these insults hurled at her from Hamilton, Lydia Leftwich took it all like the lamb she was. She was even fairly happy. At last, in the third play, she had been given a part. It was not much. It was only one line. So she peered politely into the blinding rehearsal lights, set in deep blackness, searching for Hamilton, whose voice seemed to be disembodied and to fill the void. When he had finished, she tripped back across the dirty grey stage to stand poised above an old green baize card-table waiting for Selby in the opposite wings to call out, "Riiing!"

Anne Randolph stood in the wings behind her, tapping her foot, and blowing cigarette smoke so impatiently that little clouds passed from time to time across the lit stage like ghosts.

"Madam's expecting you," mumbled Lydia Leftwich from across the stage. Hamilton gave a low groan, but called out, "Cue, Mrs. Potter."

Anne Randolph stamped out the cigarette and swept on to the stage.

"Stop!" screamed Hamilton. "What have you got in your hand?"

"Why, my sides, Hamilton," she called out, as if the auditorium were a stadium. "I just can't work without my sides. After all I have eighty sides. I can't be expected to go without my book in a week!"

She heard the whirl of the chair coming down the aisle toward her.

If Anne Randolph seemed to use the word 'sides' often she was not the only one who did it. It was such professional slang, after all their years of shamefully calling those floppy little typed books 'scrips', that they hung on to the word to get used to it. All but Lydia. She, having referred to her bit of paper as her 'side' since, in truth, it was a single line, was treated to such withering scorn from Hamilton she never dared to use it again. From the wings Selby heard Hamilton's voice lash out at Anne Randolph. "Mrs. Potter, I see by the way you are standing that you have seen a moving picture called *All About Eve*. . . ."

Selby turned both his attention and himself away from the stage and walked back to where the fire escape made a lace shadow up the darkened wall, flung there by the stage lights. He felt for a cigarette and lit it, but stayed, staring at the wall without turning, for he knew that the striking of the match had drawn Marty's attention and he could see her thin face in his mind's eye, staring, staring, when she knew he wasn't looking. No annoyance passed his face; he seemed to take it completely for granted; he only decided against going to sit with her, and turned instead through the stage door into the dark house, and wandered alone up the aisle, waiting for Hamilton and Anne Randolph to finish their usual and inevitable rehearsal quarrel, which they did as if they had both promised.

Marty, standing in the dark behind the canvas wall, waiting for her entrance, turned her eyes from where Selby had stood, the light shedding only on his face, making it stand out floating from the back-stage darkness like some angel in an Italian painting. She stamped her own cigarette out, and waited for the formal pattern of the inevitable argument to work itself out. It was then she glanced at Anne Randolph's back with the first feeling of awareness she had had since she was a child that was as sharp as the glanced flick of a knife. She remembered Anne Randolph's question about Selby and Sally Bee for the first time since she had asked it and realised as suddenly why Anne Randolph had never asked again. Anne Randolph's vanity was a shield as strong as a diver's suit. Whatever did not feed it, although it might be noticed for the moment, was forgotten at once. . . . As Sally Bee receded in fact, so she did in Anne Randolph's memory. She would not be considered again until she was a present danger to her shield of self-love, or a reminder of the weaknesses in the shield. Marty knew, watching her back as she leaned arguing with Hamilton, that she was showing off for the rest, for Selby especially, and wanted to smile. At least Anne Randolph was successful at living her own life, all communication which would hurt her stripped and tucked inwards—stream-lined. Marty saw another image—a fat woman, all outwards, all tentacles to snare affection, wrap around approval, even the cork-screw curls an effort—a pitiful effort to construct her outside as her inside hoped the world saw it—the red dress, the newly-painted kitchen, the blood and the milk. Marty saw Mrs. Marcellus Cory for the first time since her death, as stripped before her mind as if she'd told her all her secrets, and felt the numbing sensation of that complete compassion which is to slip tripwise and end for a second behind some-one else's eyes. That person dead and past all help stood for a second in Martha Dodd's shoes, and she saw through the eyes of an ageing, fat, loveless, tacky woman.

When Hamilton swung himself back up the aisle he found Selby lounging against the back row. "O.K. Let's go!" he called over his shoulder. "Riiing!" called Selby from the back of the house. Lydia dropped a ruler she'd found to represent her feather duster with a boom that made Hamilton murmur, clutching for Selby's hand, "Darling, she'll break all the Ming."

Anne Randolph swept in, unsubdued, and called, "Cyn, Cyn, come down here at once!" in her best stage voice.

Silence.

"Oh, Jesus, Selby, Mother's missed her cue again. Go get her. I really can't bear this."

Selby leaned close to Hamilton's ear, brushed it gently with his lips, then murmured, "Some day I'm going to break your neck for calling her that, you crippled bastard," and was off down the aisle, calling, "Marty!"

She passed a hand across her eyes and snapped into place again when she heard his voice. "Did you call me, honey?" she asked politely, coming into the glare of the stage, her eyes tilted toward his voice in the dark.

He spoke to her with a patience as embarrassing to the rest as listening to a married couple whose simple public disagreement opens gulfs so private that one wonders they can bear to be together: "Marty, you usually come on here." Then, realising the waiting silence of the others, laughed and was almost cosy—"Watch it, O.K.?"

She did not even notice the silence or the change in him. "I'm sorry, Selby. I better keep my eyes open. I'm so sorry."

Hamilton called from the back and interrupted, "Marty, dear, you look really drab. Now, keep that. Remember how your body felt. That's the way Cynthia feels when Nell accuses her. Not noble, darling, just so goddam worn out with it she can't think. Now, take it from Marty's entrance again and try to hold the feeling." His chair whirled down the aisle again, and in the excitement of his working they slipped into being willing pawns, as acquiescent as women dancing, letting him manipulate them.

The rehearsal, caught up in timelessness, stopped an hour later.

"Marty," Hamilton clasped her hand as she came up the aisle, as withdrawn from the rest as if they were people of another country, "you'll be O.K. My God, your hand's like ice."

"Hamilton?" she said, questioning, but didn't finish the question, just withdrew her hand.

"Honestly, Selby, I think you and I ought to have a little talk." Anne Randolph stopped the boy in the doorway and laid her hand firmly on his arm. When he didn't answer, she said, "What in the name of God's the matter with Marty? She's wandering around like a ghost, and she doesn't remember a thing I say to her. Intellectually, it scares me. Let's try to help her." She came closer. "We know what's the matter, don't we?"

"Do we?" he questioned, standing so still that his arm hung within his coat and she felt her hand on an empty sleeve.

"Honey, can't you see she's just dying of jealousy—after all, you've just taken up Jim's whole life, and you've walked in here and practically run the place with Hamilton. Honestly, none of us know what we ever did without you— all except Marty." She couldn't help a little grunt of laughter. "She is a little inclined to dramatise herself after all. We all know that, don't we?" She waited for an answer from the still boy, but, receiving none, rushed on tumbling against her own wish into apologising. "After all, if I wasn't so close to her, why, I don't know when I've been so close to anybody. I really feel I understand her. We ought to help her; get together. We can't just stand by."

"What do you think we ought to do?"

"Oh, get together and decide about things. Maybe persuade her to go away."

"She won't go. There's the play. Ever since she went to see her mother she won't go."

"I think she is afraid she won't be missed. It's terrible not to feel needed." Anne Randolph sighed the sigh of a woman who, living in an isolated world of one, is absolutely indispensable, if only to herself. "I've never been jealous," she added quite gently. "It must be terrible. We ought to get together."

"What will we do?"

"Just get together, honey. Get together and talk it over." She backed out of the stage door into the narrow street. "You call me or I'll call you."

"All right, Anne Randolph, soon."

"We'll just get together, honey," she called over her shoulder, walking off in the dark street towards her car.

"The hell we will," Selby muttered aloud, and turned back into the theatre again.

When Anne Randolph turned to wave and shouted, " 'Bye!" the doorway was empty.

"Christ, dear, do you have to crucify that poor Leftwich girl every time she rehearses?" Selby burst into Hamilton's office without knocking. "What do you do it for?"

Hamilton looked up mildly and nodded his head towards Marty, so slightly that she, catching the movement out of the corner of her eye, thought he was only agreeing with Selby.

"Oh, I'm sorry," Selby quieted down, "did I interrupt something?"

"No, honey, of course not," Marty said quickly. "I was just going."

"Don't you want me to take you home? I won't be a minute." Selby turned, expecting her to wait. "Hamilton, that slow curtain . . . it's awful trying to get it down by hand without jerking. I've . . ."

"I'll go on, honey. I feel like the walk." Marty edged behind him out the door.

"Marty!" Hamilton motioned over Selby's shoulder for her to stop. "Darling, listen. Come and talk to me whenever you want to." He paused, watching her like an oracle. "I'll be here."

Marty had already stopped listening. She was waving at Selby to keep him from moving toward her. "No, honestly, I'd rather walk. See you at home." She finally touched him with a single pat of her hand, and walked out, shutting the door behind her.

"Do you want Martha Dodd to know about you and me?" Hamilton turned on Selby, furious, but almost whispering.

Selby paid no attention to him, but sat on the desk,

swinging one foot out so that he stopped the chair by touching the crippled man's chest. "What are you going to talk to her about?"

"Marty and I are great friends, Selby. If she wants to say something to me . . ."

Selby kicked up off the desk. "You're such a good friend for a girl to have," he told Hamilton intensely. "You let her alone. What's everybody trying to climb on Marty's back for, anyway? I just listened to that Potter woman unload a lot of crap about her. O.K. So she's in love with me. Is that so terrible? She'll get over it."

Hamilton watched the boy wander back and forth, throwing his gestures a little more than Hamilton really cared for, being honest, and told him to shut him up: "You wouldn't know, you little tart, how terrible it was."

"Would you?"

"Oh, come here, and shut up." Hamilton, having to say it so boldly, sighed.

Outside on the sidewalk Mrs. Sacks was trying, unsuccessfully, to roll up her knitting. She caught Marty as she came out of the door. "Honey, come here a minute and hold my bag." She deposited her soft bag in Marty's arms and dived away, following strange lines that stretched in several directions into the dark. Having at last found the errant balls of wool, she wound her way patiently back and forth between Marty and the darkness and the light over the door where 'Canona Thespians' was printed in brown and dimly lit.

"It's called Argyll knitting. It's Scotch, and sometimes it jumps out of the bag in all directions," she said, replacing the last ball of wool. "You can't see a thing but they're all different colours. Very complicated."

"What are you knitting this time?" Marty asked the inevitable question.

"Oh, it's another sweater. I don't know who I'll give it to." She fingered the wool and looked at it critically. "I love doing the pattern. It's so complicated. But Joey thinks it's terrible, so I can't give it to him. And I can't give it to Selby because Joey wouldn't let him wear it." She sighed. "I guess I'll just send it away like I always do."

"Why, I didn't know you did so much." Marty forced herself to speak.

"Lord, honey, I suppose I've sent fifty sweaters to charity from different towns. Joey says I'll have every orphan in America looking like a sampler. He says they have to wear what they get." She was silent for a minute, and then reached forward and took the bag from Marty. "Honestly, I do like to do them, though."

That familiar feeling of painful awareness that she had felt in the wings swept over Marty again as if her nerves were exposed to cold air, and she put up her hand unconsciously to ward off the touch of the old woman's threads of love all knitted into sweaters for strangers.

"Oh, Mrs. Sacks, I love knitted sweaters. I don't suppose you could find time to knit me one, could you? One of those what-you-call-it, Scotch ones?"

For one half minute only Mrs. Sacks let herself be blinded by pleasure.

"Lord, Martha, I'd just love to, honey," then patted her shoulder. "Aren't you a sweet thing? Honey, I know they're tacky. Nothing to worry about." She tucked her bag under her arm as if to tuck the subject itself away. "You waiting, too? I wonder how long they'll be?"

"No, I'm going home now." Marty tipped down off the door-sill, then turned again as if she'd been pulled back. "I forgot something; I've got to ask Hamilton something," but found, when she tried to come in, that the little old lady half her size was barring her way.

"You gwan home, honey. Whatever it is will wait. You look wore out."

She was so sure of herself that Marty stopped, contritely. "Only a minute. I wouldn't be a minute, Mrs. Sacks."

"You wait here till I go talk to Joey," the older woman commanded. "I'll ask him what he wants me to do. Now, you wait a minute. You stay here."

She had barred Marty for the moment as effectively as if she'd shouted 'Stop.'

Mrs. Sacks almost ran through the Green Room and knocked loudly on Hamilton's office door. Without waiting for an answer, she called out, "Son, Martha hasn't gone home. She's waiting outside to see you. She's waiting right outside."

"All right, Mother!" Hamilton's voice was irate. Behind Selby as he opened the door, Hamilton caught Mrs. Sacks' eye. "Let her come in, Mother. I knew she'd do this."

Mrs. Sacks ignored Selby and marched up to her son, staring bravely down at him.

"Joey, it's about the play, isn't it?"

"What business is it of yours what Marty wants to see me about?"

"Joey, you tell me."

"No, it's not and you know it's not. Honestly, Mother, you leave me alone." Hamilton stared at her as defiantly as a small boy who's been caught lying.

"Joey, you let that nice woman alone, talk about let alone!"

"Really, Mother, between you and Selby here you'd think I had designs on poor Marty." Hamilton suddenly grew up again, with a will, and ordered them both to move. "Now, get out, both of you."

"Don't you dare talk to her about me," Selby ordered in

echo, but Hamilton ignored him. He almost ran out of the room.

But Hamilton's mother was not beaten yet. "Every miserable person, you hang on their coat-tails just for the ride, Joey!"

Selby, too infuriated to speak, rushed through the Green Room, and almost sent Marty sprawling.

"What the hell are you doing out here alone in the dark? Come on home, Marty." He grabbed her to steady her. "Pull yourself together."

"I just want to speak to Hamilton for a minute, honey," she said mildly, as if it were the most natural thing in the world.

"Why don't you talk to me? Come on home, now, you talk things over with me." But though his voice was soft, his arm, still full of fury at Hamilton, was harsh across her shoulder, and made her twist away.

"I won't be long, honey," she said distantly. "Gwan home, put some coffee on. I'll call a cab." She disappeared into the inner hall before he could catch her.

Inside the office Mrs. Sacks, hearing the street door swish inward, said a final word to her son.

"Joey, if you interfere in her business and then just drop her I'll pack up and leave you flat."

"Honestly, Mother," Hamilton laughed at her, but with a special tinge of admiration, "I do believe you would."

"It's happened before, it can happen again."

"Mother, do go on home. You're talking more nonsense than ever tonight. What do you know about me?"

Mrs. Sacks was saved from answering that question by Marty's knock on the door.

"I'll go on home if you'll drop Hamilton, Marty," Mrs. Sacks said, opening it to her; "he'll call his usual driver."

"Of course I will, Mrs. Sacks." Marty, looking at Hamilton behind her and seeing only his expression of pure sexless sympathy, hardly heard her or was aware of the door shutting as Mrs. Sacks went away. What she did not see was the driving curiosity that made him look so kind.

"Marty, darling!" said Hamilton, and waited for her to tell him what had happened to her.

But instead the strange way he looked at her, and his strange air of waiting, threw Marty into a fit of vagueness, and she could not remember whatever simple question had brought her back.

"Honestly, I'm sorry, honey—my mind's like a sieve any more. It was something I wanted to get straight. Everybody to-ing and fro-ing drove it right out of my head."

"Sit down, darling. Have a cigarette."

Marty sat down and, when neither of them had spoken for too long, said, "We ought to call your cab in a minute——"

"Never mind about the cab."

"Now it's right there on the tip of my tongue. My mother always said if you forgot it was to keep you from telling a lie." She smoked, and let a silence engulf the small office, so that the clock ticked into the room and she could hear the leather of Hamilton's chair squeak as he sighed.

Across the light of the lamp he watched her carefully, as curious when she was still and herself as he had been professionally an hour before when she had moved awkwardly across the Canona Thespian stage, as if she were looking for a rift in the reality of being herself to slip through and be the woman some playwright somewhere had dimly seen. Now, when he could see more of her body than her face in the light beam, he realised, with a shock, how much she had sunk into herself in the last months, her body forcing down until she seemed squashed with misery, her hips widened, the line of her breasts pointing straight down, her hands tired and still in her lap. Even her cigarette seemed to be of lead when she raised it to her lips and, for a moment, held it trembling in her mouth. The fullness he had noticed around her mouth when he had first seen her was, in the few months of the winter, completely gone. It was as if he had first seen her face in the last autumn stages of its bloom, then he had watched it caught, as still as stone, to shrink and cleave as inevitably as the disintegration of a shell under the ruthless movement of the sea.

"Oh, Marty," he sighed deeply, still watching her mouth. "I think you and I are getting old."

She laughed. "Hamilton, you're nothing but a boy. What would you know about it?"

"I think," he said, so carefully he seemed to be reading it, "that the first time you are reconciled to the terrible unfairness of disappointment, you are getting old."

"It chips at you." Her last word was caught in a yawn, and she covered her mouth at last.

"Oh, my God, does it not!" He slammed down his hand on his chair, forgetting to be careful because he was so surprised that she caught, as if his mind were a mirror, his image of her face. "Here am I in this frustration of a wheel-chair, so ambitious that I still cry sometimes at night. I am ashamed, but it's worse than that. I find long periods when I am reconciled. When I realise what I could have been, Marty, I am as dangerous as a snake. The things I could do . . ." His hand cracked down on the chair-arm.

When she did not answer he turned towards her with an angry flick of the wheel. "Christ, are you reconciled? Isn't that what's killing you, Marty?"

"I don't know what you mean." She spoke so quietly that he hardly heard her and it only made him angrier.

"Look at you—you have been carefully building a prison

for yourself, and when you've stepped in and slammed the door . . ."

She had found her hands, and was tracing the veins along the back of one softly with her other forefinger.

"What prison?" She did glance up then, as if she hardly dared to hope that he would throw out any scraps of truth in his violence that might help her.

"Marriage is a prison," he said finally. "Construct your best self, and your best home, and your best terrible attempts that go under the heading of culture. Force a man to be a good husband. Force yourself to be a good wife. Force your children . . . but you didn't quite succeed, Marty. You aren't cold-blooded enough to be a model woman, no matter how hard you try. You're not dead enough yet to be satisfied with that daily disappointment known as a good husband. . . ."

"If you're talking about Jim . . ." she cried at him.

"Look, Marty," he was touching her soft lap. "What's happened to you? Look, dear, you've fallen in love with a boy—why does it happen?"

She watched him, staring for so long he thought he had made her too angry to speak, but when she did try to answer she only caught back a sob, and shook her head to show she couldn't say a word, and bit her lips together.

He leaned back then satisfied, having thrust through the cold wall between the woman and the little world around her which he'd watched her build so painstakingly out of her shame, and her training and her past. He sighed a satisfied sigh and was as ready as a nurse to receive her when she began finally to speak, but all she could say was, "Oh, Hamilton," and then begin to shake her head and make little moans of unformed words. He did not know that what she was really trying to tell him was about all the women in love, of the strange experience of the night, of seeing with the eyes of other women, and that pity had weakened her and made her simple.

"It's so complicated, darling," he said. "Can't you tell me?" She shook her head again, still staring.

"Marty, you've got to talk to somebody, my dear. You'll tear yourself to pieces—tell me—what is it that hurts you so?" But she only stopped looking at him then and turned away both from Hamilton and the light, so that he could only sympathise with the wing of her dark hair and the shadow of her lined face.

"My dear Marty," Hamilton was exasperated at last with her silence, "that boy isn't worth all this. You must know that." But she never moved. "You're like a child. You've only fallen in love. My God—it happens. It just happens. Selby's like a piano—he makes the noises if you play the tune. Sometimes I think he's only alive in terms of the rest of us. Take him, for God's sake—just take him. Thousands of people do it. There's nothing," he said, "like getting to know a person, to break the charm. It won't hurt him, my dear. He's used to it. Selby's that kind of a boy." Hamilton couldn't keep from smiling. "He's used to being suffered over."

She got up, still with her face away from him, and moved faltering towards the door.

"Oh, my dear," he swung forward and pulled her arm, "I'm only trying to help. Please let me help."

She stopped only when she got to the door. "I can't remember what I came in here for."

When she had left, Hamilton pulled his chair back to the table and picked up a pencil.

"Suffering is like . . ." he wrote under his rehearsal notes, and then wrote the three words again. Then he scratched a shaky line through the words, threw down the pencil, and called his taxi.

Chapter XI

April Fools' Day

WHEN Marty got downstairs in the morning, Gladola had thrown open all the windows to April. The whole house seemed to be moving gently in rhythm with the warm breeze. A letter slithered across the big living-room table and came to a stop against the lamp. All the curtains seemed trying to shake the winter out of themselves. Somewhere upstairs the whirr of the sweeper meant that Gladola had left the breakfast on the table for them, and was already making good every moment of the new spring.

She heard Jim's laugh before she opened the door, but when she went in and sat down, both Jim and Selby were so quiet she knew she had interrupted a joke.

"Don't mind me, boys." She poured her coffee. "What's the joke?"

"Marty, honey, big news! I just don't know what you're going to think." She glanced up when Jim spoke, the coffee-pot still raised, and saw that he had put on a serious look. "Our boy's gonna get married!"

She put the coffee-pot down, very carefully.

"Why, honey," she turned politely to Selby. "I hadn't *any* idea. Who *is* she? When?"

When Selby didn't answer, Jim went on for him, "Well, she's a real nice girl he's been seeing something of in Cincinnati. Real nice girl." He was still for a minute, watching her. "Well, what you got to say?"

"Why, I don't know. I hope you'll be very happy, honey."

Jim exploded with laughter. "There, I told you so, son. Told you nothing could rile Marty. April Fool, honey! She believed it, though, didn't she, Selby? She sure was fooled."

"Lord God, Jim, I didn't even know what day it was." Marty smiled. "But you didn't fool me for a minute. If you were going to lose Selby here so quick, you wouldn't be that sassy about it. You couldn't fool me."

"Couldn't I? You forgot to pour your coffee. Look, Selby. She forgot what she was doing!" He laughed again, and wiped his eyes and mouth with his napkin. "It was his idea——" He flicked the napkin at Selby. "I haven't thought of playing jokes on April Fool for twenty years."

Marty turned and watched Selby so gently that he smiled.

"Come on, son," Jim got up. "Let's sell some coal. We'll come on home for lunch, honey," he said, and pecked a good-bye kiss on her cheek.

"Selby," Marty held him back with her eyes until Jim had disappeared, then she nearly whispered, "that was your idea of a joke."

"Oh, you know Jim, Marty. He wanted some fun." He was smiling, but his eyes were insolent with boredom.

"Why did you do it?"

"Why did you hole up with Hamilton last night? I'll teach you to say things about me, Marty." He waited for her to reassure him, having flicked the truth about the night from her.

"Why, you little upstart," she said instead, so softly that he wasn't sure he had understood her.

"Selby," Jim called from the front hall.

But when he saw her face, he knew he had understood, and turned without another word and slammed the door behind him.

He stood, for a minute, alone in the inner hall, feeling the need for a scene as urgently as some men need women.

By one o'clock the sky was dark, and the spring rain had been falling heavily for an hour, landing so hard that it danced up again along the mirror-wet pavements. Marty saw Jim turn up his coat-collar when he stopped the car in front of the house, jam on his hat, and run huddled through the rain up to the front porch. She had the door opened for him by the time he got up the steps. He was alone.

Neither of them mentioned Selby. It had hung at Marty's lips to ask where he was, but when she saw Jim's face she said nothing, just turned and went through into the dining-room. When Jim came in after her, he had a drink in his hand.

"You don't usually drink at noon, honey," she made herself say. "Don't you feel good?"

"Selby's leaving." He slammed the drink down on the table.

Gladola, hearing the tinkle of glass, stuck her head around the door. "Youall ready?" she asked.

"No. Not yet. I'll call you." Marty motioned her away.

"Look, Jim," she said, "when did this all come up?"

"You know damn well when." He turned finally and looked at her. "What did you say to him?"

"What do you mean?"

"You said something to hurt him, and now he says he can't stay here. He says you don't like him, and he feels unwanted."

"He's very wrong and he knows it. Something's upset him. He'll get over it," she said easily.

"Well, you should have seen him. Poor youngin. Now, listen here, Martha, I'm not having my home upset by a lot of damned picking and disliking behind my back. He's my son, and by God you're going to learn to get along with him."

"Haven't I?"

"Not lately, you haven't. You know damn well you hardly exchange a word with him any more. Hell, don't you think I know what's going on? I hoped things would change and I wouldn't have to go into all this; I thought if I didn't say anything everything'd smooth over." He was walking up and down the dining-room, passing Marty without seeing her, speaking his thoughts and his anger with the same isolation as if he'd been alone and talking to himself.

"Day in, day out, I've had to watch you moping around hardly listening to a word anybody says to you. What the hell are you trying to do, break up our family? I'm not going to have our family broken up. By God, you're going to get along with my boy."

"Jim, I'm sorry if I seem to have been moping around, but I haven't been feeling too good, and what with the play . . ."

"Oh, hell, Martha, who do you think you're fooling? You damn women make me sick. There's nothing wrong with you. I called Doc Adams and he told me so. You never used to mope around . . ." he said, and halted sadly. "I don't know what's come over you. You never been like this before. If it's this theatricals business, you can both stop it right now. I'll set my foot down. It takes Selby out too much, anyway. You got him into that."

"He was interested—I thought you wanted him to . . ."

But Jim had not listened. He was off again, walking and flinging words towards her. "Nothing for a man to do, anyway. Why don't he come up to the Club more? Why don't he do some of the things I like to do for a change? He's my son."

"Jim, honey. Sit on down and eat your lunch. I think you've got yourself all upset over nothing. Now, just quiet down and tell me why Selby didn't come home."

"He wouldn't tell me. However bad you've made him feel, the boy's loyal. I'll say that for him."

"But you managed to find out, anyway." He did not catch the coldness in her voice.

"Hell, yes, I found out. You hurt that boy bad, Marty. You women never will let a man get a little peace and quiet. Look at Plain George, has to have two homes just to find a place to put his feet up and feel wanted."

"I didn't know you knew that about George."

"I'm not a damn fool."

"So you're comparing me now with Anne Randolph."

"Stop twisting things around."

"I thought I'd made you a better wife than that."

"Oh, Lord, stop turning things around!"

"I've been trying to protect you, Jim."

"I don't need any protecting. All you women think about is yourselves. . . ."

"Do you want to know what I called Selby?" she asked him then.

When Gladola heard the front door slam again, and came to see whether Selby had come in, she found Marty huddled beside her chair, nursing her cheek with both hands.

"Did Jim Dodd hit you?" Gladola demanded. She clawed Marty's hands down from her cheek. "Get upstairs. I'm going to put some wet towels on that. Now, come on." Marty came, so docile that Gladola knew she was unaware of what she was doing or saying. "I never thought the day'd break when I'd see Jim Dodd lay hands on a living soul, much less you. I don't know what in the devil's eating everybody. You skin and bone. Him acting like

somebody up Kitty Creek. The devil got into both of you."
She guided Marty into her room. "Lay down there. Don't
you worry. I'll give Jim Dodd a piece of my mind when he
comes home. I ain't afraid to, neither."

"Don't, honey," Marty murmured, "don't. It ain't Jim's
fault. Something come over him."

CHAPTER XII

In the Corridors of Light

PLAIN GEORGE was setting his foot down.

"Awe, honey," he was saying, standing in the doorway watching Anne Randolph make up, "I just don't want you to stay down there after the show's over. You know I don't like that guy."

"I can't see that it's any business of yours."

"Well, I'm going to make it my business, that's all there is to it. I didn't mind your going before when I could take you—but you know damn well I can't go down there now."

"George." Anne Randolph set her powder-brush down and swivelled round on her pink dressing-table stool. "Since when did you decide that you had any right to interfere with my cultural activities? I can't help it if you're not interested in that part of my life, but you're certainly not going to keep me away from the things I care about."

"Cultural activity—I'd like to know what's cultural about tying one on with a bunch of flits and stenographers. You always come home half sick. Awe, honey, I wish you'd pay some attention to anything I say."

"Don't sit on the bed cover. You know you'll squash the fluting."

George said something about the fluting, but got up.

"What did you say?" she asked.

169

He told her he hadn't said anything. "I was just clearing my throat."

"After all," Anne Randolph's voice came muffled from her closet, "it's your own fault, George. Don't you think it's humiliating enough for me to have to go by myself without you making any more fuss. I didn't start it."

George escaped before she got round to mentioning the Christmas dance again.

When she came out of the house, he was waiting in her car.

"George," she was furious, "curtain's in an hour. I haven't any more time to argue, the subject is closed."

"I just thought you might like for me to drive you down."

"Oh," she said, deflated.

"After all," he started the car, "you won't want to drive a car back that late, honey. You go on have a good time. Call a cab bring you home."

"All right, George."

When she got out of the car, she leaned back to make peace, and asked, "Sure you don't want to see the play again?"

"Awe, honey, I've seen it twice," he begged.

"All right. See you later. Good-bye, dear." She caught the eyes of Mrs. Sacks and Marty on her from the stage door, and gave Plain George a kiss. Marty waved, but turned quickly inside.

"Lord, honey, what in the world's happened to your face?"

"My tooth hurts," Marty told her. "I'll be all right made up. I'm supposed to look like a beaten-up wreck, anyway."

"It's funny but I haven't lost a single one of mine." Anne Randolph swept past her into the outer dressing-room, through it without stopping to talk to Lydia Leftwich or the State Registered Nurse, who was playing a nurse in the play. They both sat, making themselves up as gingerly as if every touch of the make-up sticks burned their faces. The inner dressing-room had been a large closet, but it was now fitted with a narrow bench, a long make-up mirror and two chairs. Since most of the plays picked by the Thespians had quite obvious 'first' and 'second' leads, it was inevitable who should use the inner room. Marty and Anne Randolph began to undress, murmuring apologies in the small space.

"Marty, honestly. I don't know what to do about George." Anne Randolph covered her fresh home make-up with great pats of cold cream and began to take it off again. "You live such a quiet life, you wouldn't know what it is."

"What what is?"

Marty's slightly swollen face in the mirror, slick from cold cream, looked back at her like a stranger. "I look like somebody's cook," she said.

"You know. Not seeing intellectually the same as your husband. George tried to *forbid* me to come tonight to the party. Isn't that cute?"

"He just doesn't like Hamilton, honey," Marty answered. "I can't say I blame him."

"Why, Martha Dodd, I thought you and Hamilton were the greatest of friends."

"Oh, really, Anne Randolph, how could we be?"

Try as she might, Anne Randolph couldn't get Marty to say any more.

"He just doesn't realise how important it is," she finally said.

"Who doesn't what?" Marty caught the remark, having heard little of the rest of Anne Randolph's one-woman discussion.

"Why, George and activities, honey—you know."

171

The warning bell rang for the first act curtain.

"It's just like a real theatre!" Lydia couldn't help saying to the Nurse, who didn't answer, since Lydia had already explained twice about the bell.

The last-night party was one of the Canona Thespian traditions that Hamilton Sacks had found no reason to change.

"In weeno wereetas," he had said to Mrs. Sacks after the first one of the season, "it's like a performance. I know them all. Miss Leftwich said a wicked word."

"Oh, she did not, Joey!" Mrs. Sacks had giggled.

"And the grocery boy flirted with me."

"Joey!"

"Sorry, Mother."

But by the last night of the play on April 1st, Hamilton had lost interest in that aspect of the parties and was moody with his mother in the office, waiting for the last-night audience to clear, and the trestle tables to be put up within the 'country house' brown stippled canvas set of the play. A lucky few, who had been invited to the party, were squeezing through the door from the auditorium to backstage. In the dressing-rooms, men in undershirts, wiping cold cream on to brown-stained towels, were already drinking from Elsworth Trent's flask.

"Do you think anybody would mind if I slipped off home?" Marty was asking Anne Randolph.

"Awe, honey, don't walk out and leave me with all these kind of people. Please!" Then she said something which made Marty really decide to stay. "Everybody will wonder why."

"Look, Marty," she said later. "Of course it's none of my business, but is anything the matter? You know you can tell me, don't you?"

Marty had her back to Anne Randolph so that, when she didn't answer, Anne Randolph took it for granted she hadn't heard.

"What are friends for if you can't confide in them?" she asked.

"Honey, something's happened to us. We're not very happy together," Marty said softly. "Anne Randolph, I haven't got a soul to talk to."

"Well, if you ask me, honey, I think you ought to pull yourself together and count your blessings." Anne Randolph looked very serious. "Marty, honey, you have to be more intellectual about things. After all, you have that loyal husband and the cutest boy in town, with interests in common and everything. You ought to look at that side!"

"I don't know. Never mind."

"Oh, Lord, honey, if all you want's sympathy! I thought you wanted advice! Oh, honey," Anne Randolph brushed her aside and reached both arms up into her evening dress to the hanger. Her voice was muffled under the taffeta skirt, ". . . all you've got."

It was understood that, wherever they went later, the whole party would assemble first on the stage. "It takes the magic out of it, you see," Anne Randolph was explaining to Solly Leftwich when Marty slipped out into the light from the dim back-stage corridor. "You just live in a different world in a play, don't you, Marty?"

"Hi, Solly." Marty went up to them.

Solly Leftwich was as thin as Lydia, but, unlike Lydia, he was in full possession of his control. If there was any trace of effort in his detachment, it was only shown by slowing his voice down until he seemed to creep precariously along a high track of words. He was the kind of bachelor who only needed two dresser drawers for all his personal possessions.

"Anne Randolph here's been telling me all about it."
Solly waved a drink at Marty. "Lemme get you one."

Marty stood close to Anne Randolph, but though she
seemed still, Anne Randolph could feel the twitch of her
hands knitting together behind her back as her arm moved
against the taffeta. She moved over a little.

"Where's Jim, honey?"

Marty didn't hear her, her eyes were moving across the
stage, taking in the party. Selby stood near the punch-bowl,
where a group of girls who had volunteered to help with the
painting had gathered around him.

"Everybody's already having a good time," she said.

"Why do the stage hands always stick together?" Anne
Randolph said a little sadly.

"Hamilton hasn't made his entrance yet."

Anne Randolph just turned round to stare at Marty, far
too surprised to speak. Over heads of the fast crowding
stage, Solly held three glasses high and twisted and turned
back to them.

"Here y'are, girls. Yale Punch. Elsworth says it's got a
real kick. Brandy, rum, whisky, God knows what he said,
all mixed together."

"He always does just try to murder everybody." Anne
Randolph sipped. "It tastes like fruit juice."

"That ain't fruit juice, that's joy juice," Elsworth happened to hear her and called out.

A circle of high laughter rose above the noise on the other
side of the stage, lingered a minute and then subsided to the
general level of noise again.

"That sounds like a dirty story," Solly grinned.

"How you like my apherdesiac?" Elsworth came closer
and slapped Solly on the back.

"Hell, this ain't one of them. This here's a soporific!"
Solly drawled at him.

174

"Honestly, youall," Anne Randolph flicked her eyes up as she drank.

"Solly, if we get a chance later, let's sit and talk for a minute." Marty clutched his sleeve.

"Sure, honey, haven't seen you for too long. Where the hell's Jim and George? They can't walk out on me like this."

Anne Randolph had turned her attention full on Elsworth Trent, for what was probably the first time in their acquaintance, to keep from answering. "Elsworth, honey, you've just outdone yourself this time. Can I have another one?"

"Boy, you go easy, little girl like you, this is joy juice." Elsworth managed to jog her elbow playfully, but disappeared with the glasses.

"Jim couldn't make it this time," Marty answered. "I'm not going to stay long enough for him to bother, anyway."

"Selby seems to have made plenty of friends." Solly looked away from her.

"Why, Solly, what's the matter with you?" Marty accused, catching a note of coolness. "Don't you like Selby? Everybody else is crazy about him." She caught herself beginning to giggle.

"Well, honey," he answered so slowly that she thought he's never finish, "I wouldn't say that exactly. No, I wouldn't put it like that. I'm nothing but an old small-town lawyer, honey; all this kind of going-on is just not up my street."

"Solly, come here." She took his arm and dragged him through the corridor, and the house-door, down into a seat in the dark empty house. From where they sat the brightly-lit stage looked like some pageant where everyone had forgotten their places in the tableau and were milling around trying to find them.

"Now listen here, Solly, I've been wanting to talk to you,

but you know I wouldn't go behind Jim's back. I hoped you'd come to me, but you never did."

"Look, Marty, I'm Jim's lawyer—whatever has to do with the law is my business. Whatever don't, I don't meddle into."

"Solly . . . you don't suspect anything wrong, do you?"

"Course not, honey. That boy up there is as positively Jim's son as the law can make him—but, hell, honey, the law ain't every damn thing."

"He knew you didn't really approve of Selby coming."

"I didn't say so." Solly looked at her surprised.

"Jim says you can show more disapproval by clearing your throat than most people can with a big stick."

"Oh, he makes me sound like a kill-joy. We just been friends too long. Marty, I don't want to see that fat slob trip up anywhere."

"Neither do I, honey—you make me wonder. I just took it for granted everybody thought we were walking on air."

"I'm not a damn fool, Marty."

"You and Jim always say that, don't you?"

"Oh, we always did." Solly settled back in the hard seat to watch the stage. "I hate these damn things, but Sis won't stay away, and won't let me."

"Welcome, children!" Hamilton's voice rang out.

"Jesus H. Christ!" Solly breathed.

One of the stage hands screamed.

Hamilton was standing upright at the top of the wooden stage stairs that ran up the top right corner of the set. He held to the stair-rail with his hands, while he looked down with a kind of comradely insolence on to the crowd below. "There now, children," he said, when a dead silence had dropped over the party. "Have a good time at the party.

Selby, you and Elsworth come up here. The surprise is over. April Fool to all."

Selby rushed up the stairs and found Mrs. Sacks huddled on the small entrance landing behind the door with the chair.

"What's all this about?" he whispered to her.

"I don't know, honey. He just set his mind on doing it." She was nearly crying from the surprise and the exertion of getting the chair up to the landing. Elsworth behind him crowded the platform and made it sway.

"For God's sake watch what you're doing," Hamilton told him, annoyed that the shock was over so quickly and the crowd were tuning up again, ignoring the little group in their embarrassment. When he was safely back in his chair, and Elsworth and Selby had lifted it down into the party, he had already recovered his throned dignity and was being helloed from all sides as if he had arrived that way.

"Mr. Sacks, how would you like a little drink?" Elsworth hovered over him.

"I would like many little drinks, child," Hamilton ordered. "That's what I came for."

Somebody near the chair giggled, and everybody around it laughed.

Elsworth pushed his way through the mob to find that the huge earthenware crock he'd bought especially for the party was already empty, except for a still large chunk of ice.

"You lap all this up, Lydia?" he yelled at Lydia Leftwich, who was standing within two feet of him.

"Oh, El!" she shrieked.

Mrs. Trent called from behind her, "I can tell you who did!"

"Don't!" somebody begged.

Elsworth lifted the crock over his head, parked his cigarette in his mouth and managed to move through the crowd, letting them carry the stage-left entrance nearer to him like waves heaving the shore forward.

"Where's it hid?"

"Wouldn't you like to know?" Elsworth Trent was through the door, but in the dark on the other side ran with his whole body smack into the little Librarian, who had been invited to the party by her friend the Nurse.

"Lord, I didn't see youall. What you hiding out here for? Go on—dive in." He wormed past them and closed the door to the men's dressing-room with some ceremony for a man standing in the near dark, calling out to the two figures, "Don't let anybody in! I'm in here mixing my secret atom bomb."

The Librarian giggled obediently, but the Nurse ignored him and went on with what she'd been saying.

"How you think anybody would notice is what beats me."

"Well, look at her, free-for-alling around out there in that half-naked evening dress. I didn't know people were supposed to dress up."

"Nobody is, Irm. Look there—overalls and everything."

"They're stage-hands. After all, I have been in the cast!"

"Awe, honey. Never mind. Let's try have a good time."

"Oh, just look at me." The Librarian pecked at her arm and looked up at her, more bird-like than ever. "It's my best suit and I feel just tacky in it now. Everybody'll notice."

"I think you look just fine," the Nurse said, gently and loyally. "You're the neat, little type. Not like her!" She motioned with her head at Anne Randolph, who had moved to the centre of the stage, near Selby.

"I'll bet you it didn't cost a cent less than a hundred dollars," the little Librarian said.

There had been a sound like rats scurrying among old newspapers behind the shut door of the men's dressing-room, punctuated by the cracking of ice. Now Elsworth Trent threw aside the door and heaved the crock along the floor. "Le' me at 'em. This make 'em smack their gram-maw!"

He went past the two women into the light. "He's plastered," the Nurse whispered.

". . . Smack your grammaw." They heard his voice above the crowd.

"Drinking like a bunch of maniacs," said the Librarian.

"Well, I don't know," the Nurse said. "They're just having a little fun. Let people have a little fun." She got as near as she ever got to criticising her friend.

"I'd swear I smelt smoke!" The Librarian's face went up as if she were pointing.

"It's just all this crowd of cigarette smokers, honey. Don't get nervous!"

"I'll swear it's coming from the men's dressing-room."

"Oh, Lord, you can't go in there, Irm!" The State Registered Nurse was shocked. "Come on down, sit in the audience. You're just nervous."

"It's not the audience. It's the house," Irm whispered as they picked their way through the ignoring people.

"The audience to me."

"Mr. Sacks says house."

"Mr. Sacks says a lot of things," said the Nurse as she held open the door for the Librarian and they went out and sat down in seats near Marty and Solly Leftwich. By now the party had moved out, as if in an hour it had grown too volatile for the little stage and had boiled over into the rest of the building. Through the stage-door, as the Librarian held it open, Marty saw the flash of the chromium-plating of Hamilton's chair, being pushed along the

179

dark off-stage corridor to the ladies' dressing-room.
"Excuse me, Solly." She faltered up to follow, not knowing or caring why. "Be right back."

"Sure, honey. I wonder when Sis is going to get tired of
all this high life and let me go home?"

It was not until Marty got to the outer dressing-room
toilet that she realised by the voice that it was Selby who had
been pushing Hamilton, and that they had gone into the
inner dressing-room and shut the door behind them. They
were beginning to bicker and Marty knew at once and
completely that the method and the subject the two would
use would have to be kept from anyone else's ears. She
settled down in Lydia Leftwich's chair near the women's
toilet.

"There's someone in there," she lied to the first person
who tried to come in. "Use the men's." She motioned
down the high, empty back-stage corridor. Then she got up
and quietly closed the outer dressing-room door.

"Well, apropos of that," Anne Randolph was teetering
back, talking to a very tall stranger whose name she hadn't
caught. "Did you see any of the road companies of
Oklahoma?"

"Give me Kern. Give me Kern any time!"

"Aren't you going *back* a little way?"

"I guess I am for you. Let me get you a drink." The man
disappeared towards the table, and Anne Randolph smiled
after him completely happy.

"You can get a better view from here, anyway," said the
Librarian sadly as they made themselves more comfortable
in the hard seats.

"We better go soon. I don't want you to get too tired."
The Nurse was watching her face like a worried mother.

"I won't get too tired . . ."

"Crowds aren't good for high-strung people like you."

She patted the Librarian's hand and settled back to watch.

The man was back with the drinks before Anne Randolph had stopped smiling. "I've presented the Thespians with a little token. Would you like to see it?" She conspired with him. Somebody stumbled and spilt their drink. A little of it splashed against Anne Randolph's taffeta skirt and she started back and yelped. The man had a large lawn handkerchief out and was carefully wiping the drops away, kneeling at her feet. The girl in pigtails and jeans stared awkwardly and said, "Gosh, Miz Potter, I'm awful sorry." Her own shirt was dripping.

"Oh, it's nothing at all." Anne Randolph was gracious. "Come on," she said to the man, and when he rose she took his arm. "I'll show you the collection. It's in the Green Room."

"What collection's that?" the man asked urbanely. He was too drunk to remember whether the strange woman had told him or not.

"Why, my old theatre programmes," she said. "I've saved them all and presented them to the Canona Thespians." She guided him down through the dark house to the Green Room.

The little Librarian was laughing for the first time that evening. "Was she non-*plussed*! I bet it ruined her dress," she said to her friend.

Marty could hear Hamilton's chair creak and his caressing voice go on reaching out like circles in the water to where she sat in the dead-still outer room.

"It isn't as if you didn't know what you're doing, my dear. You do. No one knows himself better than you. You watch every move you make with the deep satisfaction of a lover."

"Oh, Hamilton, why am I so cruel?" Selby's voice was muffled.

181

"Think of the flies Narcissus had to swat when he was gazing at himself in the pool."

"I don't get that."

"They interrupted."

There was a long silence—the far-away noise of the party began to seep through to Marty. Somebody had tried to start singing, but it hadn't worked, and they had subsided into the general noise.

"What happened when he went home?" Hamilton asked, so familiarly that Marty realised that every moment, every nuance of the winter had been repeated to him. She remembered the moment when Selby had reached across her for the tray—remembered it as if it were happening again, and let her head drop down on her arms trying to shut out the sound of their voices, then strained to listen again when Selby started to answer.

"I don't know. I do know one thing. He's *on my side*. Whatever happens he's on my side. I could walk out tomorrow and he'd give me anything I wanted." He sounded drunk; Marty knew he wouldn't have said it if he weren't drunk.

"You think of everything, don't you, dear?"

"Oh, Hamilton," Selby sighed. "I've been so horribly poor."

"They all wanted you, but I got you, dear. The funny thing is I hardly even care."

"You got me because you understand me. It's a kind of blackmail. I can't fool you."

The room was silent again except for the creak of Hamilton's chair.

Selby whispered, she thought. It was a single endearing word, or it was again the chair creaking; there they were sighing in rhythm, both of them like people falling. Her head rolled back and forth in her arms and she felt the skin of her face and arms—dry, dry, dry, as it moved. It was Selby who broke the silence. "Have you got a cigarette?" he asked.

"You haven't given him a thought, have you?" Hamilton suddenly brought it all up again.

"Who?"

"Jim Dodd."

"Why should I? What's he ever done for me?"

"I thought you were going into coal," Hamilton giggled. "I love the way they say in coal or in oil. I'd like to be in diamonds."

"Can't you see me! Anyway, why should you care?"

"I just like to watch things happen. People. Sometimes I think it's the only thing that really moves me. After all, he's hardly my type.

"Marty's so moving," Hamilton added after a little while.

"I can't think why I was so cruel this morning. Poor Marty, I'm really so fond of her." Selby sounded sad.

"Poor darling," Hamilton said.

The Green Room was alive with noise. Under it Anne Randolph and the stranger sat turning the pages of the leather-bound programmes.

"That's a cute idea to bind them up like a book," the man was saying.

"What did you say?" Anne Randolph had to yell.

"I always roll mine up and ruin them. Just throw 'em away."

Anne Randolph stopped, caressing *Mourning Becomes Electra* with her newest shade of nails.

"I remember that," the man said brightly. "It lasted almost all day, didn't it?" He moved closer to her on the couch, to hear better.

She paid no attention. She still looked at the programme. "I was just thrilled to death," she said, softly.

"Now I'll bet you had a lot of ambition," the man joked, glancing at her face.

"I thought nothing could stop me," she said sadly. "Nothing in the world."

"Yeah, nothing like being young," the man said, trying to catch her mood. When he couldn't, he said, to change the subject, "Boy! These things sure go back a hell of a way."

"My parents used to take me to New York when I was a very little girl," Anne Randolph recovered with a shiver and told him, her head slantways. "We stayed at the Plaza Hotel. There was a big statue of General *Sherman* outside," she turned her shiver into a pretty one and made a little face. "Imagine!"

"Boy, you people sure do keep all that up, don't you?" the man said admiringly. "Real traditional!"

"Oh, I'm not from here!" She giggled slightly. "I'm from way down Virginia!"

Marty never heard the inner door open.

"How long have you been here?" Selby's voice came from behind her. She raised her head then and caught his eyes in the make-up mirror.

"I think I'd better go," Hamilton said at the door.

Selby didn't answer.

"Somebody's shut the door!" Hamilton said, surprised. Then, when Selby didn't open it, stretched up and opened it for himself. His mother, coming down the dim, high corridor, saw him and almost did a little jump. "I've been looking all over for you, son," she said. Then, over his shoulder, she saw Marty, too, and reached forward automatically and closed the door again.

The chair started with a jerk as her hands took the power

from Hamilton's, and he found himself pushed fast along the side off-stage space, through the dim side aisle, and across the Green Room, where Mrs. Sacks ignored the party as if it were the crowd in a railway station.

"What's in there?" the man with Anne Randolph asked, when he saw them disappear.

"Oh, that's Hamilton's private office. Sanctum sanctorum!" Anne Randolph flirted.

But the man (whoever he was, she never found out) was too drunk and too impatient with her flirting to be subtle any more. He placed his large clean hand firmly on her taffeta bodice, and whispered, "Come here, honey."

"I *beg* your pardon!" Anne Randolph jumped up, horrified. But she found herself blocked on to the couch by a solid wall of people, so she just had to stand there, embarrassed, her back to him, but right against his legs.

"Mother," Hamilton kept begging her to speak, "please tell me what's the matter!"

"Can't you see I'm drunk, Marty?" Selby was begging. "Can't you tell I'm not saying anything I mean?"

She watched him now, not in the glass, but turned so that she could look up at him. His face had gone pale when he saw her. Now it was as slick as glass.

"Poor little youngin!" she finally spoke.

"Oh, Marty," he bent down to put his arms around her, but straightened up again halfway through the gesture. "You know I didn't mean anything! Hamilton makes me talk like that. You know what he's like."

"You don't want Jim to see you, honey." She scanned his face as anxiously as if she suspected chicken-pox.

He turned away then and looked at himself over her shoulder. "God, I do look terrible!" he said, concerned, then came back to his fear.

"Please, Marty, what did you hear?" She looked away quickly, without having to answer. "Please—oh, my God," he rushed into the women's toilet. She jumped up and ran after him. He was being violently sick. "I don't want you to see me like this," he begged, afterwards, exhausted.

"Lord, honey, don't mind me. You've held my head before." She helped him into the inner dressing-room, and let him collapse in her chair like a rag-doll when she stopped holding him. "It's that terrible stuff of Elsworth's." She ran her fingers, lifting his wet hair up from his forehead. "Just rest a minute, you'll be all right. Sleep for a minute. You don't want Jim to see you like this." She guided his head down to the make-up bench.

"I'm trying to act like his son. Christ, I'm trying . . ." He tried to clasp her hand, but she drew it away until his own had dropped into his lap again.

"I know, honey, I know. Don't you worry about a thing. I won't tell Jim. Don't you worry."

He couldn't tell from her voice whether it was the drink or what she might have heard that she would keep loyal about, and decided, not from her dead face, but from the lightness of her voice which belied it, that it was only the drink.

"Good old Marty," he murmured. "You're on my side, aren't you?" Under her fingers, and away from the shock of finding her, he was letting himself retreat toward sleep.

"Elsworth can't have a successful cast-party without everybody getting soaked," she said to explain him.

But Selby couldn't answer. He was already asleep, his head pillowed safely in his own arm.

"Lord God, honey," she told him then, knowing he couldn't hear and be hurt. "You nothing but a little old dream-boy, are you?" She went on stroking his fair hair so gently until it came back to her what she had heard. Then

186

she leaned down and let her lips rest against his temple for as long as she could bear to do it. "It's a crying shame!" was her very weak-called defiance to the whole thing. Then she went out carefully, and locked the door behind her, so that nobody could stumble into the 'stars'' dressing-room and find the boy there, like that.

"Well, at least give me some clue to why you wheeled me in here!" Hamilton nearly screamed at his silent mother.

"To tell you the honest truth, Joey, I don't know," she answered him then, calmly, and went on with what she was doing—packing up her knitting as a sign she was ready to go home.

Marty stood, undecided, at the stage-door. But Solly saw her—and loped up.

"Want me to take you home? I've finally rounded up Sis."

"No. No, thanks." She turned her head away in the dark so that he could just hear her and not judge her face. "I've got to wait for Selby. Jim'll expect us to come home together." She went on standing in the dark doorway, too lost to move.

It was nearly two o'clock when the little Librarian sat bolt-upright.

"I don't see why everything has to be so *psychological!*" She fussed at the Nurse. "I've been saying for hours I smelled something burning. It's not anxiety. It's smoke!" she gasped.

"I can sure smell the cigarettes. It's all over. Look how it billows out over the footlights!" the Nurse said to pacify her. Then she too sat up. "There *is* something the matter. That smoke's coming from one direction!" She was out of her seat, up across the footlights and had reached the door of the men's dressing-room before the little Librarian could quite grasp she had gone.

But the Nurse didn't need to try to open the door. The brass knob, when she grasped it, was hot enough to burn her hand.

How she made herself heard above the party on the stage, she said she never knew.

"Everybody quiet!" she yelled. "There is a very little fire in the men's dressing-room. There is no reason to panic. Please walk out the stage-door and stand outside in the street until you are told you can come back in the building." She saw Solly standing below the lights. "You, there," she called. "Go get those people out of the Green Room—tell them there's no danger." Solly was running up the aisle before she had finished. "Stop that running!" she yelled after him, and he slowed to a walk.

Already the people nearest the outside stage-door had begun to push through it. The authority in the Nurse's voice had defeated panic, but it had not touched the urgency which ran like a strong electric circuit through them all. It was the urgency that kept the pack in the little hallway from letting Marty cross them; the urgency that swept her out of the stage-door, before she had any idea what was the matter.

Mrs. Sacks had just opened the door of Hamilton's office when she heard Solly's voice, and saw him beginning to herd the crowd out of the Green Room and through the main door of the theatre. "Oh, Solly!" Anne Randolph clutched him as she was carried past by the crowd. "What's happened?"

"Nothing serious. Nothing serious," Solly answered, and was still saying it when Mrs. Sacks had passed, pushing Hamilton through the door.

He did not recover, with the drink, and the events, and

the curious behaviour of his mother to deaden him, to the full danger of what was happening, until he reached the cool, safe air of the street.

"Try and rescue something! All that stuff is valuable!" he kept saying, his hands tight-fisted from trying to make someone listen. But no one heard him. They had changed in a few minutes from being a riotous party to a sober and saddened crowd, wondering whether it was really serious, whether the party was over for the night.

The little Librarian stood shivering in the dark, while she watched her friend doing a kind of Jacob and the Angel tussle with someone who looked like Martha Dodd at the stage-door. "Nobody's going back in! That's all there is to it," the Nurse was yelling. The fire-engine's siren filled the air, and the first fireman spoke to her by instinct. "Across the stage—left-hand door—still closed," she ordered. "Everybody's out. We've checked."

Marty caught one of the firemen by the arm, and at last realised that she had found someone calm enough to listen. "Listen, listen," she clutched his arm tightly. "I want . . ." then seemed to remember something, seemed to try to say something—then just shook her head as if she was saying No, and fell against the man in a dead faint.

What he had not noticed was the key that fell from Marty's hand and was lost under the feet of the crowd, who were being forced back, first by the fireman's load as he picked Marty up and wormed his way through them; then by a great blast of hot air that seemed to shimmer suddenly around them and fling them back faster. A large crowd had formed from the dark streets and the lost members of the Thespians pushed around it, trying to make contact with each other.

"Out of the way, Sister," someone yelled behind the Nurse, and she was pushed away by a returning fireman.

"Call another truck!" he yelled into the dark. "That big curtain's caught!"

The little Librarian turned to the woman next to her and burst into tears. It was Anne Randolph. They threw their arms around each other and cried, like broken-hearted children. "All that work!" the Librarian kept saying. "Everything we've built up together." Anne Randolph shook with sobs.

Plain George, who'd been waiting for her to come out all evening, found her still clasping the Librarian, and simply turned her and let her cry in his own arms until she quieted a little, then walked her carefully, as if she were sleep-walking and he were guiding her, back to her car. She snuggled down beside him, and while she murmured and sobbed he kept patting her shoulder and saying, "Never mind—you're my own lil baby. Never mind. You have to act big in front of all those people, but we know you're George's lil baby-bye. Never mind," until she had quieted down completely, close against him.

But when they reached home she wouldn't stop clinging to him, not even when he carried her like a child up to her room. She wouldn't let him leave her even then. So he stayed, for the first time in several years, and neither of them saw it when the sky above the valley flashed with a great pure pink glow.

It was the Canona Thespian theatre. It seemed to poise all alight in its own furnace, stripped of all those paper, canvas, costume ornaments that had been the little theatre; without the velvet curtain; the seats consumed. Then, for just a moment, it was the Methodist Immersion Chapel again. It paused, leaned in toward its own centre and began to fall, helping to put its fire out with its own walls.

CHAPTER XIII

The Stir of the Sleepers

"I'LL tell you before God, Bah, it's the longest night I ever spent." Gladola still stood against the window, squinting out at the bright morning light that seemed to buzz against her dry, sleepless eyes.

"Gwan go to bed, Gladola. I'm here now. I can take over. Lord's love, there ain't nothing I can't do." Bah Salter was not, at that moment, doing anything yet. She had just arrived with Doctor Adams and had come straight back to the kitchen to wait for him, and, in the meantime, to find out what she could. She still had her brown jacket she wore to the office on over her white Hoover apron.

"They brung her in about three o'clock. We thought she'd just fainted. I'd been standing out there, right out there by that tree." Gladola shook her head towards it, not loosing her tight-crossed arms that she seemed to lean on from the waist up, making a tired bow of her back. "I'se watching the light in the sky. It woke me up, to tell you the truth. That or the door slammin'. They's back in and out so much last night. They brung her in and he wouldn't even go upstairs with her, Bah. He wouldn't even do that." Her face crinkled up as if she'd felt a sudden pain. "Them two never was real close, honey, but they wasn't never downright mean to each other before. He kept on walkin' up and down in there. You could tell he was wonderin' where the boy was—seemed like he already knew. I heared him go up, down stairs a couple of times. But he never went to her room—only the boy's. He's up there opening drawers and looking in the closet when somebody come up the walk. I'se listening in here. You can't help hearing ever last creak that late at night. I heared him openin' and closin' drawers, and then I heared them footsteps coming up the walk out front. He heared them too, and he come down and opened the door before they's any knock or anything. Bah, I'll swear he knew. We both knew it wasn't the boy."

Her face crinkled again, and this time she couldn't stop herself working loose from her control into sobs. "They'd brung the news, Bah. They'd found Selby. Only . . ." Bah caught her and held her tight and tighter to help her. "Oh, honey, they can't even bring the boy home. Won't let us see him or nothin'."

Doctor Adams opened the kitchen door and looked in; then when he saw Gladola he came in, fumbling in his pocket and brought out a tablet. "Get a glass," he told Bah over her shoulder. Bah guided Gladola to the table and helped her down. As she was giving Gladola the medicine she explained. "She hasn't had a wink of sleep all night. Hasn't hardly been to bed."

"Thank the Lord you know all of them so well, Bah." Doctor Adams studied Gladola as if in her sorrow she had gone deaf. "I'm going to leave you here until I can get the right kind of nurse. Better somebody she knows. I want you to alternate with Jim Dodd. Change every two hours. Don't let her out of your sight for a minute. Gladola, can you hear me?"

The woman barely nodded.

"You're to gwan upstairs get some sleep. You might have to sit with her again later till I can get somebody. Now, listen here—she won't be like last night. She might be awake—don't try to tell her anything—don't start on the boy whatever you do—just be calm—and agree with her—and don't leave her for a minute. Understand?"

She nodded again. When he had hurried to the door she made herself speak. "Doctor Adams, is Miz Dodd gonna be all right?"

For once Doctor Adams lost the impatient brusqueness that had stopped people asking him fool questions for as many years as the woman before him had lived. He said, "I think so. I think so, Gladola. Some people just get to the end of their rope, Gladola. Just call it that. The end of her rope. I wish to God I'd of known she was so near it. What I can't understand is this—she couldn't know about the boy. Nobody's told her. They haven't, have they?" He stopped, suspicious.

"Oh, no, Doctor. None of us would have done that after what you said last night."

"Then it must have been the shock of the fire. Lord, you wouldn't think a little thing like that. . . . After all, it was only something to do—all that make-believe and play-actin'." He had forgotten that he was talking to the women and wandered out through the swinging kitchen door, still thinking aloud to himself. Bah followed him out.

"You want me to go up now?"

Her voice behind him caught him when he was nearly to the door.

"Yes, honey, go on up and relieve Jim Dodd. Bah, honey," he caught her wrist as she started up the stairs, "you aren't the kind to be upset, are you?"

"Why, Doctor, me?" The question made her pause and turn, surprised.

"Bah—she's up there thinking all kinds of fool things. Oh, Lord, Bah, I don't know!" He suddenly dropped her arm and was himself again. "Go on up. Get Jim to go to bed if he will. I'll get a nurse trained for it by this evening."

He had turned and was off down the hall and out the front door with the decisive stride designed to put disaster in its place, before Bah got up the stairs.

Jim sat beside the bed in the room where the blinds were drawn, making it dim and green, like a room under water. He had shrunken into himself so that to Bah he seemed, for the first time since she had known him, a small greying man. It was an illusion. Jim creaked up from the chair when he heard her, as big as ever, but he never stood quite upright, just turned, still bent slightly so that she couldn't see his face, and started through to his own room.

"Doctor Adams says you're to go to bed—I'll call you," she called softly after him.

He nodded once without answering, and with his head down, as if he had walked himself completely exhausted, he wandered away and only paused to shut the door behind him. Bah turned then to go and sit beside the bed.

Marty was asleep.

It had been a long night—so long that Marty had grown to look more like her mother than Bah would have thought possible. Her face had sunk into its frame, so that her eyes closed deep in dark sockets, and the bridge of her nose showed white and sharp as if the bone were ready to break through. Bah made herself lean towards her to see if some shadow she couldn't trace had fallen across her face, but it was no shadow. The long night had drained her colour; she was grey against the smooth white sheets. Her head seemed to burrow down into the centre of the pillow, but around it was smooth. Marty had been docile since someone had plumped it and put it behind her. She had obviously not moved her head at all.

She still seemed so deep in sleep an hour later that Bah saw no harm in letting the blind up a little so that she could look out once in a while and keep herself alert. She tiptoed over to it, letting it up with the gentlest click she could, but the atmosphere had gone too dead with silence. The sound woke the room.

"Who's that?" It was a thin whine from the bed that Bah heard—so tight and thin she hardly heard what Marty said, but hurried back and bent over her again.

"Hello, honey, it's Bah."

"What you doin' here, Bah?" If Marty's face had grown old with the night, her voice had grown as young. It seemed the weak querulous voice of a sick young girl. It was Martha Collins's unmarried voice dragged up out of her childhood, without one note remembered from the years between. "Lord, honey, I ain't seen you in a long time. How you keepin'?"

"I'm keepin' fine, Marthy, just fine."

"How's your folks?" Marty's voice was a thread.

"They're fine, too." Bah had sunk down beside the bed and let herself be carried forward when Marty clutched for her hand and held on to it with her own cold thin one, tight. Her head was so near to Marty's that they talked together in near whispers, the buzz of girls telling secrets in the dim sick room.

"Bah. We went to school together, didn't we, Bah?"

"Sure we did, honey."

"You're my best friend, aren't you? You wouldn't tell on me, would you, Bah?"

"Lord, honey, you know old Bah wouldn't tell a thing. Now, why don't you try go on back to sleep."

She thought Marty had. Her eyes closed, sunk again. But in a little while she whispered:

"Bah?"

"I'm right here, honey."

"I'm sick." The corners of her thin mouth began to quake.

Bah stroked her head. "You're going to be all right in no time," she told her. But the stroke of her hand meant more than her voice. It seemed to make Marty content.

"Can I tell you something, honey?"

"Sure, you tell me anything you want to."

"I've got to tell somebody, haven't I, before I just die?" Her voice rose in a curious parody of a youthful excited pitch.

"Now you just rest a little, honey. Shhh!"

"Bah, Jim Dodd and I are married! What do you think of that?"

"Well, that's real nice, isn't that real nice?" She went on stroking Marty's head in the same rhythm, quietly.

"You wouldn't tell Maw, would you? She'd tan my hide."

"No, no, you gwan to sleep now."

Later, when Bah tried to release her hand from Marty's, she felt the grip tighten like a vice.

"I'm sick, Bah." Tears welled up from the deep closed eyes and fell along the furrows at her temples.

"Sure, I know, honey. I know."

"If you won't tell a living soul, I'll tell you something. I've got to tell somebody."

She didn't open her eyes, or speak again. Bah, wiping the moisture lightly from her face, thought she had really fallen asleep. But she had not freed her hand—and when she tried, "Bah!" Marty called out, then moaned. "Oh, God, I was going to have a baby, honey. I was going to. I've got to tell somebody. Don't you tell."

"No, honey, you know Bah."

"I did something, Bah. I wanted the baby, but I did something. It would have made everything so complicated. Jim . . ."

"Sure, honey. You go on sleep."

"Jim likes things just like they are. I know Jim, honey. He don't want nothin' changed. Don't let him know I'm sick, honey. He just hates anything like that. He's my boss. I have to know how he likes things. I've got to protect him from things gettin' all upset, haven't I, honey?"

"Sure you have, honey."

"Oh, Lord God, Miss Agnes, my belly hurts though." Marty let go Bah's hand to rub the bed-clothes over herself. "What I need is a little bit of gin and water."

"I'll get you some." Bah opened the box of tablets left beside the bed, and consulted her watch at the same time. "Here, take this, it'll be better for you." She held Marty's head up to the drinking glass. When she did that Marty's eye caught sight of her mahogany bureau.

"Bah," she told her as she sank back, "I made things for it and all—without anybody knowing—look in the bottom drawer. Go on—look."

Obediently, to quiet her until the sedative worked, Bah leaned down and opened the drawer a little. Like most bottom drawers, it was a catch-all—old albums, piles of theatre programmes, a hand-out for the Canona Thespians like the Victorian broadsheet which had hung on the foyer wall of the theatre—that was all she could pick out of the junk.

"Do you like them? Do you think they're pretty?" Marty's voice was going almost too drowsy to divide her words.

"Sure, honey, they're the cutest little old things I ever saw," Bah said absently as she closed the drawer.

Below in the hallway the doorbell sounded. Bah, stopping to see if Marty was indeed asleep, stepped across the bathroom and knocked on Jim Dodd's door. "You'll have to go, Mr. Dodd," she called through it, "I don't dare to leave her for a minute. Gladola's up in bed. She won't hear a thing." When she got no answer, she said, "I'm sorry, Mr. Dodd," and went back to sit beside the bed.

It seemed minutes later that she heard the hinge of Jim's hall door squeak a little and his footsteps go off down the stairs.

It was Plain George.

The two men stared at each other quite silently, almost belligerently, as if they were strangers. Then Plain George put his hand out flat, and held Jim's arm. "It's all right, boy. O.K.," was all he could find to say: but he stayed for four days and buried Selby Dodd.

It wasn't until the fifth day that Jim talked about it. Then it was in the half-dark of the living-room at night when neither of them could see the other's face.

"I can't figure out how it happened, George."

"They say he must of run back in. That's what they say."

"Maybe that's it."

"They say he must of come out. Solly was there. He said he must of."

"Everybody come out."

"Then he must of."

"Then he must of run back in," Jim said. "He must of wanted to have a last look. Do you know where they found him, George?" Before Plain George could answer, Jim went on. "They found him in the little dressing-room. You know what I think?" He could not make George answer then. "I think he went back to make sure Marty was safe."

"I guess that's what happened."

"He thought of her like a mother." Jim straightened up then, and crossed the dead fireplace to the light. His face, for the first time since the accident, seemed alive. "It's not quite so bad, George, when you look at it that way."

It was later that night that Marty spoke about the fire.

"Mrs. Dodd's asking for you." The starched nurse with strong arms stood in the shadow.

"Jim got up and went upstairs, so slow and heavy that he sounded like he was lifting a trunk up," Plain George told Sigsbie later.

"I could hear something going on up there. I didn't know whether to go on up after him, or just sit and wait. I reckon he wasn't up there more'n ten, fifteen minutes. When he come down, boy, old Jim looked like a truck'd hit him."

Plain George was still for so long that Sigsbie didn't know whether to move or not herself, didn't know whether he'd finished or not, or whether he wanted to go on with it. But then he laid his big hand on her head and started rubbing her hair without more than half knowing he was doing it, and went on to tell her.

"Honey, I couldn't do a damn thing. He just sat down there and then he told me that Marty had seemed to come to for a minute. She was up there raising the roof, and calling out for Selby; that big strong-armed nurse couldn't hardly hold her down. Then when Jim got what she was saying, well, he realised then that Marty was worse off than ever. Somehow the fact that Selby was dead had filtered through to her."

"What was she saying? Did he tell you?" Sigsbie was a little bit ashamed of her curiosity, but she couldn't stop herself asking.

"Awe, honey, poor old Marty got some damn-fool idea in her head she was responsible. She kept yelling it. It was pretty terrible for poor Jim. She wouldn't even let him touch her. She had this idea. They finally got her quiet. Jim come down and sat there in the living-room. He said

199

she must of felt that way because she and Selby had had some little fallin' out the same morning. He said she made up all kind of stories, Sig, honey. Why can't things just go on along? What in the name of God have Marty and Jim Dodd done to deserve this?"

"I wouldn't talk like that if I was you, George. The Lord works in mysterious ways. . . . Martha Dodd was the finest woman I ever knew." They sat together, sharing the one big chair in Sigsbie's little living-room, both of them too sad to talk any more. It never occurred to either of them that they were thinking of a living woman as already dead.

It was easier for the chair to whirl down the long thin hall after the rug was up. Hamilton burst into the denuded living-room where Mrs. Sacks sat among the packing-boxes, wrapping up all her own little things and putting them away again. It was as if her little attempts at personal touches had been like her own light fingers brushed over the ugly room. Now she sat, withdrawing them all, and the room was lifeless again around her.

"They've taken the rug in here, too!" Hamilton was explosive.

"I didn't want you to get up. That's why I brought you your breakfast. I knew they were coming this morning. They've got to get the apartment ready for the next tenants." Mrs. Sacks' voice was as dull as the room.

"They could wait! They couldn't be *that* subtle—this foul little town. God! how I loathe it. God! . . ."

"Oh, shut up, Joey."

"Why didn't you *tell* me?"

"Shut up, Joey. Just you shut up." Mrs. Sacks sprang up, and her pretty little ash-tray shaped like a sombrero lurched out of her lap and across the floor. She rushed after it with a gasp of panic, but when she picked it up, it was still all right. She kept rubbing her hand over it to see.

"What on earth's the matter with you?" Hamilton tried to attract her attention.

"Joey, go on out of here and leave me alone. Just get on out, will you?"

"Really, Mother!"

"Listen here, son, in fifteen years this is the thirteenth time I've packed my things. I don't want to talk right now." She came as near to yelling as she ever would in her life again. "Because if I do I'll start back some years, and I'll say an awful lot. Now, if you don't want to hear, git on out of here and let me alone!"

"You sound like everything was *my* fault, Mother!"

The whole winter hung between them as they looked at each other over the packing-cases.

"You don't have the first idea, son, not the first idea," was all she said.

"I suppose you do," he said, almost to himself, as he tried to manœuvre the chair back around the door. She just had to go over and steer him right.

CHAPTER XIV

Coda

WHEN the 6.18 came in on the fifteenth of June, the sun was just setting behind the Canona hills, and turning the cold tan bricks of the station pink and warm. The sun hit the water and made the roof of the platform, reflecting undulating fragments of light, seem awash in the last rays thrown up from the river's surface.

Sally Bee, jumping off the C. & O. Pullman for her summer vacation, had to squint so much she didn't see Anne Randolph and Plain George until they had almost run into her. They all hugged, and the room-mate from Duluth waved again as the train pulled away west into the sun.

"Youall go on. I've got your bags," Plain George yelled over the noise of arrivals and the blast of the moving train. He motioned to a coloured porter, stopping while he picked up the bags, lingering so obviously that Sally Bee looked back over her shoulder and called, "Come on, Daddy!"

"Listen, honey." Anne Randolph was so solemn and nice, putting her arm across the girl's back, that she went cold with fear of what her mother might have found out. "Jim's out there in the car. We thought we ought to tell you. We brought him down to cheer him up. He's so lonesome since Martha went to Cincinnati and he thinks of you as practically his."

"Oh, Mother, what'll I say to him?" Sally Bee stopped, awed.

"Just tell him how sorry you are, honey. That's all a person can say. He's looking at you," she whispered and they both turned on summer smiles. "Jim!" Sally Bee lunged towards the man in the back seat, and gave him a bear hug, covering over the moment of embarrassment in a squeal. "You come to meet me!" She dropped down into the seat beside him and snuggled, never catching his eye.

"Lord, child, don't climb all over him. It's hot as Hades!" Anne Randolph got into the front.

Sally Bee subsided, but only for a second. She jumped forward and leaned into her mother's hair. "Mamma, can I go to Virginia Beach in July this year instead of August?"

"What in the world for?"

"Some people I know are, that's all. It's tacky in August, anyway."

"We'll see about it. We'll see about it later," Anne Randolph told her, closing the subject with a snap, so that she wouldn't be caught in a promise until she'd had time to think about it.

"Same little old pretty-bud. Prettier ever time I see you," Jim spoke at last, and, to tell the truth, Sally Bee had a little catch of shock. It wasn't that the girl expected him to sound different, not sepulchral or anything like that, but she didn't think it would sound exactly the same.

"Honestly, Jim, don't make her any worse than she is already! So swell-headed now we can't get her in the house." Anne Randolph craned up and caught Jim's eye in the car mirror and winked. Sally Bee didn't mind. It was all compliments, even if one was back-handed.

Plain George could avoid the car no longer. He attacked the driver's door, threw it open and hoisted himself over the back seat to hug his daughter again. "Lil' old string-bean. How are you, honey?" he hollered. "Ain't she the ugliest little old youngin you ever saw, Jim? '

"Sure is." Jim seemed easy—very quiet, but easy.

"Daddy, can I go to Virginia Beach . . ."

"Sally Beatrice, we'll talk about that *later*." Anne Randolph set her foot down.

Later, driving along the river road under the green roof of the meeting trees, Sally Bee said, "Where are we going, Daddy?"

She felt Jim's hand on her arm then and looked at him at last.

"Look, honey, we're going up to my house, just like you always did when you came home. We didn't want you to be disappointed. You just wait, pretty-bud—everything's going to be just like it always was. Selby came for a little while, and God took him away pretty quick. But He took him like a real hero, don't forget that, honey. A real hero. He went back because he thought more of others more than himself. That's what I care to remember about my son." The car ran on smooth, the people in the front seat so quiet they were hardly breathing. "His mother's prostrated with it all, honey. She took it mighty hard, but she'll be all right, too. You wait. She'll be reconciled." The last word hung in the warm air. Jim had no more to say.

Sally Bee didn't dare to stop looking, or wiggle away, but she was embarrassed. Why, his face had gone terribly thin!

THE KISS OF KIN

TO MY MOTHER AND FATHER WITH MY
LOVE AND THANKS FOR ALL THEIR HELP
WHILE I WAS WRITING THIS BOOK

CHAPTER I

JESUS IS COMING—ARE YOU READY?
When you've seen this sign, whitewashed high on the
blasted cliff-face above the hairpin curve of the mountain
pass, you will know you've reached the Holy Roller
country. The bare rocks are so high and jut sometimes
so far over the deep-cut gorges that you find yourself
imagining, as you swing around the sickening but well-
graded highway, that the people who care about catching
you in such mountain danger to both your soul and your
body have flown up like birds in their astounding faith
to paint the warnings.

Abraham Passmore, driving over the mountain west-
ward, missed the warning sign which flashed above his
line of vision as he took the curve at a careful, controlled
sixty. By the time he came down to the bridge over the
Canona river, and had left the gorge behind for the flat
river road, the afternoon sun was full in his face, so that he
missed the turning and had to go five miles back up the
river again.

After the cool of the mountain pass, the creek road was
hazy with summer dust, which tanned the bare boards of
the store porches and deadened the bright advertising
posters nailed to the shed walls. The houses of the scratch
farms looked blanketed and asleep. Abraham saw a few
men in overalls perched on unpainted railings, staring at
the road, completely still. All the way up Clear Creek to
the house of his grandmother, he saw no movement, even
among the animals. It was too hot.

By the time he reached the house, the chromium clock
on the dash-board read a quarter past three, so he pulled

his Buick into the weeds of the roadside and settled back to watch the shut doors.

His first impression was bitter disillusion. The clapboard house, set sideways of the creek, needed a coat of paint. The yard on the creek-side was full of crab-grass and bare brown patches. Although in the front some attempt at a broad lawn had been made, it lay sunbrowned and tired-looking between the front porch and the branch. The far side of the house had been built so near the hill behind it that it seemed to grow from the steep slope itself and still lean on it for support. The front door, shut against the heat, had hung on it a large wreath, curled and dead from having been in the sun in the morning, but now drooping in the afternoon shadow of the porch. Down beside the deserted path to the front gate straggled dusty tiger-lilies.

The long kitchen ell, with its high porch all around it, was awash in the sun, but even under the pall of heat the back room of the main house had its windows tight shut. In the front room, Abraham could see that the dark blinds were drawn; little winds puffed and sucked them in and out of the open windows. Down behind the house, along the side-road, there were five or six cars, he couldn't see how many, only that there was no room for him to park. The whole stillness of it, even the stillness of a small girl in the distance, squatting down by the back steps, was like the outside of a church during the service, a breath-holding stillness, hot, suspended.

Abraham leaned back and lit a cigarette; the disappointment at the smallness of what he saw brought his dark face down into an almost childish scowl, which he inspected in his car-mirror, then let the inspection carry over into an examination of his dark chin. But he could not keep his eyes away from the farmhouse for long. He

2

found himself staring at the corner of the yard where the clapboard outhouses and the hog-pen seemed to teeter backwards towards the creek water, top-heavy, awkward, and all of it little from across the creek, too little for Abraham Passmore's peace of mind. He sighed and said, "Oh Jesus!" and began to comb his thick brown hair.

Inside the kitchen, big, spare-boned A'nt Elemere stood stirring the green-beans and trying, when she could remember through her own numbness, to keep the children quiet. She stood in the shadow of the coal-range, where the three-o'clock sun, stretching through the side-yard screen-door and the big screened windows, could not reach her. In a circle above the huge, empty kitchen table drowsy flies hung in the air.

John Junior, eight years old, yawned widely and let his mouth stay opened to whine.

"It feels jist like Sunday." He watched A'nt Elemere's board-straight back, and then concentrated on her black right ear to see if he could make her turn round and pay some attention to him. He began to kick the low cabinet under one of the windows where he sat with his feet dangling heavily over the edge. She still didn't pay any attention even when he increased it to a heavy drumming. The sun threw his shadow across the floor, made a halo of his tow-head, caught the rims of his glasses as he turned towards A'nt Elemere, complaining because even the kicking had failed.

"I haven't got anything to do!"

"Shhh . . . up." A'nt Elemere was miles away from him, but he had at last managed to drag her back for a second to her duty.

"Why don' you jist shut up?" she asked him, over her shoulder.

"When are we gonna eat dinner?"

"You had a big samich."

"A samich is nothin'," John Junior muttered, and looked around the room again for something to do. This time he noticed the wall telephone and jumped down from the cabinet.

"I'm gonna call up somebody." He said it tentatively, expecting her to say 'no, not to,' but she only tasted the beans.

"Reach me the salt."

He handed it to her, running across the room from the kitchen cabinet. When she took it from his hand, she did it slowly, without even looking, just groping for it, so obviously far away where her eyes were staring, that John Junior was awed for a second, but he soon got over that, and said, almost whispering, so he could swear he told her, "I think I'll call up Digby."

He stretched up to the wall telephone, pulled its mouth down with his lips almost inside it, and pushed the receiver hard against his ear. Then he carefully put his elbow up on the lever, holding it down to ring, winding, three times softly.

When he got his answer and spoke, his voice smacked wet and urgent against the black mouth; he remembered to whisper, so that what he said sounded frighteningly important. "Hello, Digby, this is John. I can't come out today. My grandmaw's dead." He obviously wasn't satisfied with the comment he got. "I'm not bragging, I just thought I'd tell you again."

A'nt Elemere heard him and interrupted softly. "Passed over, honey, passed over."

"She had a stroke. I don't know what it is. Well, just a stroke, that's all. Well my grandmaw did die of hers even if your grandmaw didn't die of hers. I don't know whether she went all stiff or not. Nobody wouldn't let me

4

see. Do you want to go down to the creek tomorrow?"
The answer made him defend himself hotly and con-
ventionally, "You have not! You've only got to stay in
on the day if they die! They're having the funeral right
now in the dining-room. It is not funny. Grandmaw's
coffin is too big and expensive to get it out the living-
room door. I heard A'nt Amelia . . ."

A'nt Elemere rushed furiously and grabbed the telephone receiver, slamming it down on the hook.

"Gimme that phone! You jest shut up that there kind
of talk!" She was almost crying, so her voice made John
Junior apologise, quietly, "I didn't say nothin'."

She coached him by habit, as she had heard the white
women do a thousand times.

"Innything."

"Honest, I didn't do innything. Stop fussing at me."
But she had already stopped caring. She sank down at
the big kitchen table, and he realised she wasn't going to
fuss, or even see him on such a day.

He wandered away from her then and leaned gazing
out of the side-yard screen-door at Mary Armstrong, who
was playing at the porch steps. He couldn't see what it
was she had in her hand; she had a secretive way of
playing. All he could see was her back as she squatted
daintily, prissily, on pointed feet in the grass.

Abraham, seeing a shadow in the doorway, thought it
was the funeral over and stubbed his cigarette, wondering
just how he'd start it, how to break in. But when no one
appeared but a little boy he settled back again to wait,
staring down the road, coldly.

John Junior, watching Mary Armstrong with her eyes
half-lidded, already sneaking up a secret in his mind,
interrupted her.

"Whatcha doing, Mary Armstrong?"

5

She didn't turn round, but she remembered to speak in a loud whisper. "Nothin'," she said. "Get away." Her talk was as prissy as her feet. She spoke carefully, as if more people than little old John Junior might be listening.

"Can I play?"

"No. You're too dirty. You say too many dirty words and I can smell your socks when you get too close to me." She smoothed her own smocked dimity, and went on to scratch her bottom.

"You can not!" John Junior was elaborately casual. "Anyway I don't want to play innything."

But his curiosity was overwhelming because he was bored.

"What's that?" He didn't bother to open the screen-door, just pressed his face against it, craning to see what she had in her hand.

"None of your beeswax," she closed her fist.

"Any other day you'd be itching to play with me."

"Well, I'm not today," said Mary Armstrong, conscious of a power of choice she didn't often feel.

"Come on in here!"

"I can't." She bent down almost double to put whatever it was under the step. "Mama told me if she caught me inside the house today she'd tan my hide."

"Can you see innything from there?" John Junior rolled his face sideways against the screen and tried to look down the long porch.

Mary Armstrong straightened up and took on a grown-up, solemn air as she tiptoed to see through the dining-room window.

"A little bit," she whispered. "Isn't it terrible, though?"

Then she was too interested to remember that the occasion was a solemn one; she stretched and stared.

"Mama's crying into her handkerchief. Ole A'nt Mary

6

Lee's looking all stiff. A'nt Cinnybug's acting like crying but she's really peeking through her hands at Mary Margaret. I'll betcha she's trying to remember her top so's she can make one like it. There's little old Sary Jane. She got to go and she's as young as me. It isn't fair."

Mary Armstrong laughed with a 'heee' and covered her mouth.

"Sary Jane's picking her nose like anything. My mama says it's trashy for youngins to go to funerals."

But John Junior had already grown bored with what he hadn't spirit enough in the heat to open the door and see for himself.

"Do you want to know a secret?"

"No." She was impatient with him, intent on the funeral as she was, using him only to tell it all to.

"Cousin Cad's crying."

"He would."

"That Julik looks bored."

"Oh well, he don't know innything. He's not even Amer'can."

Their voices, forgetting, growing stronger, reached through A'nt Elemere's sorrow for a minute. She roused herself to call.

"John Junior, come on in here!"

He ignored her, because at last he had Mary Armstrong nibbling with interest in him, like a little fish.

"Don't you want to know what the secret is?"

"What?"

She came to the screen-door, smoothing her dress against her stomach all unawares, although she'd been caught so often before.

He whispered, a wet hiss through the screen. What he whispered caused Mary Armstrong's face to open, then to pucker up. She began to yell.

7

John Junior having finally succeeded in luring her there could think of little nasty enough to punish Mary Armstrong for having ignored him for so long. But, having a natural talent for obscenity, he managed.

"I'm gonna tell my mama on you!" She went on howling.

A'nt Elemere jumped into action. She flung John Junior out of the way, pushed open the screen-door and grabbed Mary Armstrong.

"Mary Armstrong, shut up. I'll jist naturally maim you if you holler like that agin."

The dining-room door opened slowly; a sanctimonious voice could be heard for a minute, reciting in a silent room: "For this corruptible must put on incorruption, and this mortal must put on immortality . . ."

The voice was shut out as the door was closed again, and Amelia Passmore Edwards, Mary Armstrong's mother, tiptoed into the room, looking just about worn out. She was in green-black mourning, a kind of drab fancy-dress, got together from odds and ends for the day. Her plump, white face showed all the signs of silent, handkerchief-gagged crying. She was twisting the damp knot of her handkerchief in her hands as she leaned against the door, to feel it close behind her softly.

"For heaven's sake, A'nt Elemere, can't you keep these youngins quiet? You can hear them all the way in there!" in a gentle plaintive voice, but when she turned to find Mary Armstrong the slight whine was gone. She sounded as though she meant business. "Mary Armstrong, I thought I told you to keep away from that door!"

Amelia looked round the door for her, her whole body poised to go on fussing; but there was only John Junior, standing caught in the sun. She sank back into the shadows and heaved a big sigh. Mary Armstrong at the first sound of her mother had run tiptoe, and her path was marked by a squawking runcus as she dodged through the chicken yard.

"I'm sorry, Miss Amelia, I don't reckon I was payin' 'em enough attention," A'nt Elemere told her, looking at John Junior. Her whisper was light to match Amelia's, then she called, stridently but quietly, to John Junior. "Now git on outside, John Junior, and if I hear one sound out of you I'll jest naturally pull you apart."

John Junior moseyed out of the screen-door, letting it bang with a quiver behind him. Amelia didn't see him go. She was too intent on bending down to the low cabinet to pick out a shot-glass, and carrying it carefully to the kitchen cabinet. She poured the last of a drink out of a bottle of corn whisky, balanced the drink in one hand, crossed the room and threw the bottle neatly into the garbage can under the drain-board. Then she seemed to wilt down to the table, carefully resting the shot-glass on it as if she were doing some secret balancing trick.

"I can't go back in there without a little something to buck me up," she muttered, more to herself than to A'nt Elemere, as she took off her black hat, fluffed her marcelled, once blonde hair up from where it had lain damp against her sad face. A'nt Elemere went and stood so near that she could feel the heat from her big body, a hotter shadow than the sun had been on her back.

"Miss Amelia, I wouldn't do that today if I was you." She spoke so that the boy wouldn't hear, touching her shoulder to get her attention.

But Amelia only waved her out of the light, then turned to squint up at her, still waving monotonously, shooing her, saying, "Let me alone," and again, more strongly,

"A'nt Elemere, let me alone!" She picked up the glass with her little finger crooked tea-party and delicate, paused, then knocked the drink back.

When A'nt Elemere didn't answer she went on, complaining, "It's none of your business. You make too much around here your business lately."

"All right, Miss Amelia." A'nt Elemere shrugged and turned away, giving up, too numb to care anyway. "Don't git riled at me," she said by habit; then she spied John Junior leaning on the screen-door again, and took it out on him.

"Quit hangin' around that door. I thought I told you to run on out there and let me alone."

John Junior paid her no mind. He sidled into the kitchen.

"I forgot something." He came close to Amelia.

"What you drinkin', A'nt Amelia?"

"Nothin'. Just a little tonic."

"Can I have a taste?"

"No. John Junior, go on outside!" Amelia begged him wearily, and turned her face away by habit so that he couldn't smell her breath.

"I haven't got innything to do," he hummed by habit, almost leaning against her.

She edged away from him. "Well, go and find something."

A'nt Elemere interrupted, worried, "Don't you think you better go on back in there?"

Amelia's head sank into her hand, propped up by her elbow on the table, spread-eagled. She touched the shot-glass again, turning it.

"I can't go back in there. I'd be sick." Her voice was so low that A'nt Elemere had to move nearer and nearer to hear the weary whispered complaining. "They've shut the windows so's to keep the flies out while the service is going on, and the smell of all those store-bought flowers makes me sick. Oh Lord, what a day. . . ." Her head was sinking nearer the oil-cloth table-top as if it were too heavy to hold up any more.

John Junior settled down across the table to stare at her. All of the grown-ups had been avoiding him all day and he was fascinated by this withdrawal into sadness which seemed to shut him out.

"That's your mother in there, isn't it?"

"What a funny thing to say, son! You know very well it's Mother." Amelia's head went erect with surprise at his odd question, and she sounded pathetic suddenly, saying 'mother' for a woman so newly dead, knowing he had heard her shriek another name at the old woman as she lolled crazily drunk over the stair-well quarrelling with her not one month ago.

"Now you know that, honey," she said again, finding death embarrassing in front of the child.

"Did granmaw hit you when you were a little girl?" John Junior was so curious his bottom twitched.

"Don't talk like that," Amelia told him, sternly, "it isn't nice."

"Why not?"

"Well, she's dead, son." All at once she just couldn't be bothered. "Now go on out and let me alone."

John Junior started to go. He began at least to unwind from his chair, but slowly; he was not satisfied.

"Well, did she?"

"Yes. Sometimes. But she was worried. We all got on her nerves." He had made her remember, and she sounded for a minute as prissy as Mary Armstrong. "She used to take after us, with a stick."

Amelia closed her memory then like a book, and added

because she thought she ought, "But she was a mighty fine woman, don't you ever forget it."

"In this kitchen?" John Junior was too fascinated to be put off.

"Sometimes in this kitchen."

"Like you do Mary Armstrong?"

Amelia swept her hand out towards him, half shooing, half hitting at the air, angry, "Go on out and play, John Junior, before I take you in hand!"

John Junior moved just out of the range of her arm.

"I haven't got innything to do."

Amelia forgot and almost shouted at him, "Git on out of here!"

Before he could move A'nt Elemere had bunched him up in one arm and, holding open the door with her foot, shoved him like a bundle of dirty laundry out on to the porch. He ran down the steps, and stopped, remembering that Mary Armstrong had hidden something under them. He squatted down. It was only a pebble. He shoved it into his pocket and ran off down the side-yard.

The dining-room door opened again and Amelia was warned of someone coming by the minister's voice, now intoning on his sad notes:

"Deal graciously, we pray thee, with those who mourn, that casting every care . . ."

The door shut out the minister's voice.

When Amelia saw that it was Mary Lee, she twisted the shot-glass quickly into her damp handkerchief and cupped the whole into her closed fist. Mary Lee, her lips like a dry slit, and her temples banging so that Amelia could see them throb, had not slipped over yet into fury; the whole situation was too formal for fury. As she looked at Amelia, sloppy in the heat, her back straightened like a ramrod.

"Well, I think at least you might drag yourself back to

come to the grave." Grey-haired Mary Lee had developed
a voice as biting and cold as the chop of an axe. She used
it now, full force, on the blonde, fat woman slumped
against the table. "What are people to think with you
running out in the middle of the ceremony?"

She had to stop looking at Amelia, and it weakened her
disapproval, but she could see the criss-cross pattern of
the oil-cloth table-cover when she did, and the lines
trembled and became alive at the corner of her eyes,
which were already seeing flat visions in the still time
before the storm of a migraine. She tried to bring her
mind back to her duty, getting Amelia up out of the chair.

But Amelia was too tired even to be bullied. She only
muttered, "A funeral isn't a ceremony. It's a service," as
she stuffed the handkerchief into the pocket of her short
jacket. Mary Lee didn't bother to notice the gesture.

"Don't think ever' last one of them didn't know exactly
what for!" she told Amelia, to make sure she didn't think
she could ever fool a soul.

Like a magician keeping up the trick sadly after he has
lost his audience, Amelia took the now empty handkerchief out and wiped her forehead and begged the skinny
judge who stood over her, keeping the sun away: "Oh,
Mary Lee, don't keep harping on things today of all days.
Can't you see I'm upset?"

"Don't you think I'm upset, too?" Mary Lee was
impatient. "I nearly cried right in the middle of the
service. Come on and don't give in to yourself so much."

This time she took hold of Amelia's arm and piloted
her back into the dining-room. After she had let go, and
settled down among the others to pray in the hot, airless
room, the marks of her fingers stayed through the rest of
the funeral on Amelia's soft, white arm.

13

"A'NT ELEMERE! A'nt Elemere!" John Junior ran to the screen-door, calling in a breathy squeak which was the nearest he could come to a whisper. He was far too excited at the thought of the parade to remember that it was a death march, for he went on, big-eyed, urging her to the screen-door by flapping his hand at her. "Come on quick. They're fixin' to carry it out."

A'nt Elemere hurried across the kitchen to where a small, three-cornered piece of mirror hung on a string, half hidden behind the kitchen cabinet. She stood in front of it, adjusting her high black felt hat, the tears streaming at last, without any damming sobs, down her black face. Then she took her stand, solemnly adjusting her skirt, inside the screen-door out of the way, to watch the procession pass.

John Junior lingered just outside. "Why didn't you go in there to the funeral?" he asked her, having asked the question already several times, but hoping in the new excitement finally to get an answer.

A'nt Elemere opened the door and pulled him in to stand beside her.

"Because the Southern Episcopal Church ain't suitin' to me or Miss Anna Mary," she told him. "All them books, and them writ-down prayers. Standin' up. Settin' down . . ." Her voice died away as she saw a black-suited man opening the dining-room door on to the porch.

The Reverend Beedie Jenkins eased himself in through the back screen-door just as the first of the procession carrying the coffin started out through the dining-room

14

door and down the side porch through the sun. He was a tall, raw-boned white man, his face burned Indian colour by farming in the hot sun. He had on a black suit too, but it was shiny at the elbows, with the sleeves coming to just above his long, skinny wrists. If his suit was too little for his body, his eyes seemed too big for his gaunt head. They lay deep in their sockets, snap-black, the livest thing about the man.

"Sister Elemere," he whispered, but came in at the same time and stood beside her.

"They're jest bringin' 'er out." A'nt Elemere's hand went up to brush away a fly, and came away from her face wet with tears.

A few men with pale office faces, and dressed in sober winter black, came by the screen-door silently, looking behind them crabwise, as if in front, they knew they ought to be behind the coffin.

Brother Beedie looked down at the floor getting ready to pray, but mumbling first.

"Sister Elemere, we ought to of beried 'er."

He spoke slowly, deep into his chest like a mountaineer.

A'nt Elemere began to nod her head.

"Brother Beedie, this ain't right. It jest ain't nothin' like Miss Anna Mary would of liked." She kept on nodding, forgetting why.

"Yep," he went on, "we ought to of beried Sister Anna Mary. She was ourn and we ought to of done the job."

"It ain't right," A'nt Elemere whispered.

"He works in mysterious ways," said Brother Beedie. "If she'd of lived longer, she'd of constructed a tabernacle of truth like she always said she would. We woulda done it from thar—right."

"She meant to, Brother Beedie, she meant to."

"I knowed she meant to."

15

The heavy black casket, shaped like a Georgian serving dish with tasteful heavy bronze handles, its pall-bearers straining at the weight, started past the door.

"I didn't mean it wudn't on her mind. I knowed that," he said.

None of the pall-bearers had yet begun to match their paces, so they shuffled heavily as if they were moving furniture. The pink waxy rosebuds on the living pall, given by all Miss Anna Mary's children, bobbed like little bells.

A'nt Elemere began to sob.

Reverend Jenkins whispered. "We will kneel here in prayer. There ain't nothin' else we can do."

A'nt Elemere knelt down, her head resting against the screen-door. Mary Lee, passing the door, saw her there, and she whispered to a pale, dark-haired, sad girl who was walking beside her, pushing her out of place in the procession. A'nt Elemere began to pray.

"O holy and humble Jesus of the many mercies, look down on Sister Anna . . ."

The girl slipped through the door and bent low over them.

"A'nt Elemere, youall get up from there. Mother'll just naturally wring your neck. Come on, now."

A'nt Elemere heaved herself up to her feet, crying. Mary Margaret Rosen, Mary Lee's daughter, having done exactly as she was told, sat down exhausted at the table making no move to rejoin the procession, which had by now become orderly, as it filed past the screen-door. Men and women stared into the kitchen as they passed, some very old, some bent, all but ten-year-old Sary Jane, holding her grandmaw's hand, dressed in her Sunday School dress and clutching an old beaded bag. She didn't dare look in like the rest for fear of catching John Junior's eye and giggling, not wanting to . . . it just happening . . .

Mary Margaret turned in her chair to A'nt Elemere, not noticing her anger because her face was so still.

"Is there a cup of coffee for Mr. Rosen?" she asked, "I know he'll feel awful after that service." She turned away again, taking off her black straw hat and ruffing up her dark bangs just as Amelia had done.

Brother Beedie opened the porch door, and asked before stepping out, "Ain't you followin', Sister Elemere?"

A'nt Elemere looked beyond him to where the casket was just being turned, awkwardly, through the back gate.

"No, sir, I done changed my mind," she told him and turned her back on all of them.

Brother Beedie slipped out of the screen-door and joined on at the end of the procession, bowing his head and clutching his hat to his stomach. A'nt Elemere couldn't help but watch for a minute, and then, knowing that Mary Margaret only did what her mother told her to like the rest of them, decided to forget her interrupted prayers and pour some coffee.

"Ain't you goin' up to the vault, Miss Mary Margaret?"

Mary Margaret from behind her sounded far away with fatigue. "No," she said, "I ought to, but to tell you the truth I'm too tired to face the climb. How they can do it . . . Anyway Mr. Rosen's not too well."

"Now ain't that jest too bad?" Ant Elemere began to mutter.

"Aren't you going up?"

The question made A'nt Elemere remember that she still had her hat on. She went across the room, back to the slip of mirror in its private place, took off her hat slowly, inspected it, and hung it up again, then went back and handed Mary Margaret her coffee, looking at the girl closely. With her wide black skirt and her neat black shirt, Mary Margaret managed without knowing it to bring another world, a world of cut hair and ballet slippers, into the kitchen. But that wasn't what was bothering A'nt Elemere. What it was she wasn't saying. Instead she kept on muttering in a voice so low that Julik Rosen, pale as a ghost, neither heard nor saw her when he staggered in from the dining-room.

"That was the hottest hour I've ever had to spend. Christ!" He sat down in a chair where a corner of the table cut into the shade, his thin face white enough to move anyone but A'nt Elemere, who was glaring at him from behind both their backs.

"Drink this, honey." Mary Margaret gave him the coffee. A'nt Elemere silently poured another cup and set it in front of her.

"What a day! Christ, what a business it all is, Mary!" Julik's hand waved to and fro, in and out of the sunlight.

"Mary Margaret," A'nt Elemere began to mutter the name to herself, hating Julik because he'd shortened it so that it sounded just plain Yankee, and used the Lord's name in vain twice in the few minutes he'd been in the room.

Julik heard her then. He seemed to forget the heat for a minute, fascinated by her, obviously wanting to be friendly.

"Why weren't you in the dining-room, Mrs. Freeman? Is it because you are a negro?" He tried to put his sympathy into words, to show her what side he was on. "I think it's pretty bad when they don't let a woman who's served them always come to a funeral."

A'nt Elemere was bored with him before he began. She stared through him, not seeing him for the sun-glare between them. She said, "Oh, don't talk foolishness, Mr. Rosen. I jest didn't want to. That's all."

"The reasons would interest me." He was ready to defend her.

"Would they?"

"I've heard of this kind of business, plenty. But well, you see, I never seen a place like it before. My family . . ."

A'nt Elemere cut him off with a loud, "Un-hunh!" sullen and abrupt.

Mary Margaret felt unaccountably ashamed of Julik, knowing that he was only trying to be amiable, and that A'nt Elemere was acting like a sullen old nigger. She touched his arm, and spoke to him as if he were a child, without kindness.

"Don't you think you'd better have hot milk, instead of that coffee, Julie?"

He really looked at her then for the first time since he had come into the kitchen, suddenly annoyed with her because he felt he had failed with the old negress, and couldn't understand why.

"Look, Mary. Stop fussing," he told her. "You'd think I was on my last legs! It's coming down here, it never does you any good. You . . ."

"I've only got one grandmother." Mary Margaret found it as easy as breathing to slip into the natural blackmail of the remark, and was surprised at herself.

"Don't start that," Julik almost laughed at her; "I've never been through anything like that damned funeral. This place—geez—— Did you get a look at those aunts of yours, all like Hamlet's mother, assuming virtues . . . ?" he leaned forward ready to dissect the experience with her, be objective, play at details, exorcise it with a good laugh.

But Mary Margaret said, "Shut up," so quietly that Julik wasn't sure he'd heard her until she apologised.

"Oh, Julie, I'm sorry." She reached across the table

and let her hand rest on his, both of them together, white hands without sex, telling secrets—hers flaked and dried with wringing-water and air, his tubercular fingers, still. "I'm not making sense. Don't pay any attention to me."

He didn't. "I'm sorry," she'd said, in her high, swinging voice, which sounded so sweet, though her mouth drooped down at the sides with sadness like a sorry clown. Julik sniffed, taking in more of the kitchen.

"Something smells funny."

"I expect it's the odor of bacon dripping. A'nt Elemere's always got beans on."

A'nt Elemere interrupted with great dignity, "Hog fat don't make no odor. Only people makes odors. This here's jest a plain smell of hog fat. Shame you don't like it."

Julik didn't like it. He finished his coffee with a gulp. "I'm going upstairs to lie down."

Mary Margaret got up to follow him. "I'll come with you."

"No, Mary, don't. I can wipe my own nose." He went out through the dining-room door, leaving her standing.

"What in the world you had to go and marry that unriz biscuit for I don't know. I jest don't know." A'nt Elemere launched into what she considered to be her rightful set of opinions, mostly because she'd half raised the girl. "Look at you! Twenty-seven years old. Pretty, jist wasting yourself. You ain't half the size you was when you went up there; little old skitty witch . . ."

Mary Margaret turned on her, angry, but she didn't raise her voice: "I never asked your opinion, A'nt Elemere."

A'nt Elemere paid just enough attention to her to mutter again, so she only half heard, "Comin' back down here with a lot of Yankee words and talkin' like an Irish woman. . . ."

"You never heard an Irish woman talk in your life. You're just repeating all the nasty things you've heard about me and Julie from the family. Julie's sick. I have a terrible time making him look after himself. You don't try to understand, any of you. . . ." There were tears coming into Mary Margaret's voice, but she tried to stop them, and so stopped speaking at all, and turned her back on A'nt Elemere.

A'nt Elemere's eyes found the ceiling. "For the love of the Lamb, look who's climbin' up on her high horse!"

There was only one cure for high horse. "Here, you sit back down and have some more coffee." She sat Mary Margaret down again, gently, and poured for her, but went on complaining because she hadn't had her whole say and no amount of tears was going to stop it.

"Odor! I been keepin' you from makin' a jackass out of yourself for twenty-five years and you don't expect me to quit jest because that there railroad takes you up north too easy. Odor! Who ever heard tell!"

But Mary Margaret was no longer even listening. She sat with her eyes unlit, not seeing the coffee. A'nt Elemere's pottering got slower and slower, until finally she leaned, elbows akimbo, watching the empty yard out of the window, her stomach flat against the low cabinet. The kitchen seemed to have run down into some kind of false peace.

Abraham, having got over the shock of watching the straggling little procession wind out through the back gate when he had expected a large funeral, sat and stared after it all the way up the branch road to the hill. He moved at last, slowly, when it was out of sight, and got out of the car. As he walked round it to cross the creek, he saw the little boy fall flat, and stopped again.

Mary Margaret broke the silence in the kitchen.

"There's only one day like this in the whole of our lives."

A'nt Elemere went on watching out the window, wondering who the tall man was, leaning on his car across the creek, who obviously couldn't make up his mind whether to come in or not. She saw John Junior fall for the tenth time that day, and paid no attention, but answered Mary Margaret.

"Ours, honey, not nobody else's. They don't even know what's happened yet. Neb mind."

She blew out a great whistling breath and picked herself up to meet John Junior, who was screaming his way up to the side-porch.

"I hurt myself," he wailed; his face was streaked with dust and tears, and his mouth was wet and pink and stretched with fear. A'nt Elemere stooped, caught him, examined him, and began to fuss all in one continuous habitual gesture.

"When are you gonna outgrow makin' all that noise ever' time you graze yourself? Here, let me see! It ain't nothin'. Git on out of here." She pushed him back out of the screen-door, and he stood outside it, his hurt forgotten, gaping in.

It came suddenly to Mary Margaret, like a revelation!

"He ought to have had hot milk."

She jumped up from the table.

A'nt Elemere was disgusted. "You jest spoil that man rotten, Mary Margaret, I ain't never seen the like of it. It ain't good for men to be fetched and carried for like you do him."

Mary Margaret was already putting milk on to heat. She knew it was no good being as furious as she felt with A'nt Elemere, with all of them for that matter, so she was deadly patient.

"A'nt Elemere, you just can't ever understand a man like Julie. None of you people down here could ever understand him. A'nt Elemere, he's a genius! They aren't like other people. They're something to be cared for. Rare things."

She stooped, looking for a cup in the low cabinet. A'nt Elemere wasn't paying much attention to what the girl was saying. She took it for what it sounded like, an apology for heating milk for a grown man in the afternoon.

"How could any of you understand?" Mary Margaret went on, explaining defensively. "I'll bet you've never heard anybody play the violin at all, much less lose himself in Brahms the way Julie can. Why he's . . ."

A'nt Elemere had had enough. "Your milk's boilin'," she said ungraciously, not bothering to take it off for Mary Margaret.

Mary Margaret rushed to grab it where it spread over the gas flame, and pour what was left in the cup she'd found, moaning a little.

"Oh, what a shame! Julie hates it with scum on it." She went out, still fussing a little in her soft way, through the empty house.

"Git away from that door. Quit that hangin' around my skirts. Go on." A'nt Elemere got rid of John Junior, who scuttled off down the path, almost knocking into a strange man. He turned then to stare, offering no information. Behind him in the kitchen, A'nt Elemere began to talk, strictly to herself.

"Well, ain't that jest too bad?" she started, banging Mary Margaret's cup and saucer down into the sink. "For the love of the Lamb, maybe I never did hear nobody play the fiddle like what he can, but by golly I know a nocount when I see one. Lord's love, I done seen enough of 'em around here in my time, so's I got some experience of 'em."

23

CHAPTER III

SO, as he'd always been told he would, Abraham Passmore, having stepped aside to avoid John Junior, heard
A'nt Elemere's voice laying down the law in the kitchen as
soon as he set foot on the back porch. At first he hesitated,
then when he saw through the screen-door that she was
alone, he let her rave, enjoying it, leaning at last up against
the door-jamb, waiting for her to discover him.

"We done raised more pure-bred nocounts up this here
creek than you could shake a stick at. He don't like scum!
Hunh! Poor white trash! He oughta know about scum.
It jest beats me the way my Mary Margaret done turn
herself into some kind of nurse for that nocount!"

Then she saw the stranger, standing in the shadow side
of the back door.

"How long you been standin' there?" She jerked open
the screen-door to peer at him, slowly registering his
height, the Passmore slant set of his eyes, the wide Passmore cheek-bones, the big mouth, the curiously feminine
tilted chin. "Lord God Holy Jesus! Come in here! I
know you!" Her voice was already filling with surprised
tears; she pulled him into the sun.

"But I don't know you." She felt a sudden sick twinge
of disappointment at the mistake she'd made; then she
understood and brightened up again. "Oh Lord! If it
ain't a miracle happened too late! Ain't you little
Abraham?"

"Yes. Abraham's son."

A'nt Elemere was beside herself with joy.

"Well, I'll declare, you're the spittin' image. The spit
of your paw. Sit down and have some coffee."

She sat him down carefully at the kitchen table, as if she were afraid he would disappear into the shadows again, and went on to tell him:

"You wouldn't remember your grandmaw, honey, but she passed over, Glory Jesus, two days ago. Here's some cream. She'd of jest given anything to see you walk in that door."

She stood watching him. "Young Abraham! Well, I'll declare! Same big bones. Same hair. Well, I'll declare!"

Abraham interrupted to answer the news about Miss Anna Mary, "I know about my grandmother. That's why I came."

"You're jest too late, unless you want to go on up to the grave-yard. They've opened the vault up there and they're layin' her in beside your grandpaw. Now you wouldn't of ever seen him. He died before you was born. He was a fair-size man, too," she added, taking in the breadth of Abraham's shoulders approvingly. Then she asked sadly, "Whyn't your daddy come, honey?"

"I'm standing for my part of the family," Abraham told her; then realising that he sounded already like a lawyer-called meeting, he changed the subject, grinning. "No. I don't think I'll go up to the grave-yard. I watched them all on the way in."

A'nt Elemere was curious, curious and worried. "Did any of 'em see you?"

"No," he caught the worry and reassured her. "They were being so sanctimonious they missed me." He was bitter. "I picked out every one of them from the stories I'd heard."

She chose not to see the bitterness, not yet. She was too pleased to see him. She almost crooned. "Well, what do you know? You was took away from here when you was knee-high."

25

"It was all hearsay. I don't claim to remember much."

Mary Margaret swept open the dining-room door and she stooped down to search in the cabinet under the sink without having seen Abraham, scrabbling through it with both hands, setting bandage, Flit, a can of Three-in-One oil out on to the floor.

"Is there any poultice in here?"

A'nt Elemere watched her, wondering at her panic. "I don't know, honey; what do you want it for?" Then, anxiously, "You ain't hurt yourself?"

"No. We've had an accident, though. Julie threw his hand back when he lay down on the bed, and hit the knob of that old brass bedstead. I would have thought they'd have gotten rid of it long ago. It's going to swell if we don't poultice it, and Julie's got an audition next week. It just can't swell! A'nt Elemere, please help me find some poultice."

A'nt Elemere didn't move. "You try some horse-linament," she advised.

"A'nt Elemere, this isn't just a hand. It's one of the tools of Julie's trade."

Abraham had got over his surprise at being interrupted by a neat little city girl as out of place there as a pug-dog. He smiled at the self-conscious excuse for art that went with the home-made, brave little dirndle. He'd heard it so often, so many places, but never before trotted out to apologise to somebody's cook in a way-to-hell-and-gone kitchen next to nowhere.

"Oh, I can't find a thing in here. Why can't you be some use?" She straightened up, and saw Abraham.

"Who are you?" She was rude with embarrassment, and couldn't stop staring at him. At first glance she took him for a man in an advertising company, because he seemed so young to be wearing such a well-cut suit. Then she remembered where she was, and was conscious of being out of context somehow—confused. All the time A'nt Elemere was explaining in her own terms, which she did with gusto.

"This here's your, now lemme see, your second cousin, once remove, same kin as Mary Armstrong and John Junior to you. This here's Abraham!"

"Abraham?" Mary Margaret was too startled to keep the words from slipping out. "Why, I never thought you'd . . ."

"You never thought you'd see one of my lot here again. Is that it? Seems you were wrong." He grinned at her, a lazy, 'squatter's rights' grin.

She found his studied insolence so childish and out of place with the rest of his bearing that she saw him for a second as a double image, a brat in advertising man's clothing. It was not hard for her to see which kept control most of the time, for his fine clothes were still uncreased after what must have been a long, hot drive and his general air of almost ruthless self-assurance and poise seemed to bring him into focus and tell her who was boss, even as she watched him. But even so, there was his brave little-boy mouth, a stern slit, as if he'd fixed it that way once to keep himself from trembling like a sissy, and then had let it become a habit. Mary Margaret felt a twinge of disgusted awareness of that mouth.

But all she could muster to say to him was:

"I think you're . . ." What she really thought he was she never said, because A'nt Elemere interrupted, as proud as an old hen.

Mary Margaret forgot to go on looking for the poultice. She just stood there while A'nt Elemere remembered her whole history.

"This here's Mary Margaret. Her maw, the one you'd

call A'nt Mary Lee, is daughter to Miss Anna Mary's half-sister by some man name of Elecky." She obviously disapproved of this union, made sixty years before. "She ain't really your a'nt. He come from up some creek. Miss Mary Lee married a Longridge." But she did not disapprove of this one. *A Longridge*, she'd called him, not *one of them*, or worse, *some*. "That's Mary Margaret's paw. He ain't dead yet, but he's pore. Been that way for years. Had something like fifteen stomach operations. Mary Margaret lived here when she was a youngin. Miss Anna Mary that she calls her granmaw ain't her grandmaw atall, but her great a'nt." Now the history ended with deep disgust. "After Mary Margaret growed up, she went up north and married some man."

Abraham, wanting to upset this silly girl who stood as balanced as a plate on the edge of a table, asked, to stop her gawping at him, "Is that your kid who's hurt his hand?"

"No, my husband. It's my husband." She found herself explaining, not wanting to, but doing it anyway. "It's my husband. He's a violinist, so, you see, he must be terribly careful of his hands."

But Julik flung the dining-room door against the wall with his shoulder, and now he came in, holding the hurt hand in the other like an egg. He saw that Mary Margaret was doing nothing, just standing in the shadow, staring at a stranger.

"Mary!"

"I've got to go now," she apologised to the man, hardly hearing him call.

"Oh, Mary, haven't you fixed anything yet? Please, you know how important it is."

Abraham walked between them, taking the hand in his own, looking it over. "Let me see."

28

"Be careful. Don't touch the swelling. Are you another member of the family? My name's Rosen."

Abraham looked up. "I don't see any swelling. Yes, I'm a member."

Julik was disappointed. "I guess you think I'm making too much of it." He tried to grin apologetically through his worry. "Did Mary tell you I'm a violinist?" He kneaded his hand and winced. "It hurts like hell."

It was impossible for Mary Margaret not to compare them, standing together, both looking at Julik's hand. Julik's more intense face, with its long thin jaw, and the high backward sweep of his hair, gave him a softer, gentler look compared to the squarer, browner face so close to him, a face more cruel, and more naïve, than his had ever been. A'nt Elemere, on the other hand, compared them without any qualms. To her, as she beamed at Abraham and then wiped her face quite blank to look at Julik, Julik was nothing but a long, pale drink of water, and Abraham Passmore was simply the way a man of the family ought to be.

Abraham, sensing the scrutiny of the women, did what he thought they expected of him. He took over, began to give orders.

"Well, the best thing you can do is to soak it in salt water for a while. Here," Abraham went to the sink, moving as easily in the room as if he'd always known it, and poured out a dish-pan of hot water. "Where's some salt?"

A'nt Elemere handed it to him, because he was Abraham, not because she approved.

"That'll keep the swelling from coming at all. Sit down here."

Julik obeyed, and Abraham took his hand gently and put it in the water. "Now don't move it out until I tell you to."

Julik watching his hand settle, remembered to look up and smile his thanks. Sitting undulating his hand through the water, he was comforted, and bursting with talk. "There's something absolutely nerve-racking about this house." He looked up at Abraham. "Have you noticed it yet? It fascinates me, but I can't stand it. Mary, could we possibly leave by the five o'clock train?"

"Julie, you know we can't." Her voice, despite herself, took on a slight note of secrecy. "We've got to stay this evening," Mary Margaret went on, tired of telling him, tired of the whole damn thing.

Julik ignored her warning. "Have I soaked it long enough yet?" he asked Abraham.

"No."

He went on, waving his hand through the water, watching it, thinking aloud. "Why can't you have a talk with the lawyer when they come back and tell him I've got to get away?"

Mary Margaret turned her back, hoping to stop him. "I don't think that would make much difference. Cousin Cad thought too much of grandmaw. I think he's awfully upset at having to read her will on the day she's buried anyway." Then she found herself explaining to Abraham. "But everybody thought it best . . ."

Abraham, realising what the fuss was about, said to A'nt Elemere, "Well, look at the little kittens in for their share of meat," and laughed at his joke, not caring that A'nt Elemere didn't laugh with him.

Mary Margaret knew more about him then. "You've just come down here to make trouble, haven't you?" she said. Suddenly she was annoyed, because he was there at all and because she had hoped to go through this day carried by the strangeness of formal events and reactions in a place she knew so well; carried through it like dead

Miss Anna Mary under her trembling pall of rosebuds. She had hoped to end up on the train to New York, shuttling through the dark, and then wake up, far away enough by then to be safe. But here this man had come, who she knew wasn't the kind who'd let sleeping dogs lie.

"I think the best you could do, Abraham, when we're all so upset, is to come with the right attitude to our feelings." In her anger she sounded so like her mother instead of her gentle self that A'nt Elemere started up, surprised.

But it was Abraham who interrupted—"Oh, I have, kid. I'm a real funeral pie—" and ruined her moment of righteous anger by suddenly laughing out loud again.

The noise of it aroused Julik from weaving the water around the bowl. He thought from the laughter that Abraham was taking it all as lightly as he did, and went on to explain to him, "Maybe it's because I can't wait any longer that I'm so on edge today. If you could only realise all the time we've been hanging around . . ."

Mary Margaret heard him, and her anger vanished. She felt a wave of happiness, like a sudden temperature. "Never mind, Julie," she told him, as tenderly as if they'd been alone. "It won't be long now."

He paid no attention, but went on dreaming and weaving the water. Something in his own mind, or in Mary Margaret's words, had touched off a wave of bitterness he made no attempt to stop.

"If you had any idea what it's like. People of no talent went past me. All the goddamned snobs ignored me. Not that they matter, but you know . . . The number of times I stood around and watched a lot of fools . . ." He was still for a minute, aware that he himself was being watched too closely at the moment. So he tried to make a joke of it. "Who said money doesn't talk? I ought to know."

31

Mary Margaret interrupted, "Julik, why don't you . . . just shut up?"

Abraham and A'nt Elemere were too embarrassed to say a word.

Without looking up at her, just hearing Mary Margaret's voice, Julik knew he had made a terrible error.

"Do you have to talk to me like that in front of other people, Mary?" he said, mild with patience.

A'nt Elemere threw in her two-cents' worth: "Seems to me you're talkin' pretty free yourself," she snarled.

Julik was angry, mostly because he was a little shamed and frightened at being in the centre of a lack of ease where no one was daring to look at anyone else. "Oh, I suppose it embarrasses you because I talk about the things that matter to me! I suppose you think a man's dreams are embarrassing in a bourgeois society like this. All you goddamn people with your goddamn polite breeding. Why does everything always turn shameful to people like you?" He was suddenly furious. "I was raised in a slum. Do you have an idea what that means? Do you know? It means ambition, the kind you people don't know about —when you're raised on nothing, in a slum." He had taken his hand out of the water, but now he put it back and sat silent.

A'nt Elemere crowed, seeing it all, "Wait till you hear these here people git to tearin' at each other over that there will with their maw not cold in her grave, and you'll git a bellyful of polite breedin' to remember 'em by!"

Julik's voice went low in a solemn litany. "We never had quite enough to eat."

Abraham interrupted quietly, to shut him up, "Lots of people haven't. I didn't."

A'nt Elemere was horrified. "Abraham, honey, what are you sayin'? Lemme make you a samich!"

Abraham grinned at her, "Never mind, A'nt Elemere."

"You eben knowed my name!"

"From Mary Margaret. But I was told all about you."
He talked fast to cover for the humiliated man sitting at
the table. "I was told I'd walk up to that door and that
I'd hear you laying down the law inside; it wouldn't make
any difference whether there was anybody else in the
kitchen or not. I was told you'd be laying it down anyway. You were. I won't say what about." Then he
forgot why he had begun to talk, and slipped over into
being hang-dog and boyish. "I was told you were the
only decent person in this house."

A'nt Elemere knew ahead there would be trouble. "Well,
son, you wasn't told quite right there. Not quite right,"
was all she said.

"I'll decide about that." He turned to the screen-door
and looked out into the side-yard.

"Haven't I had it in long enough now?" Julik called
Abraham back into the room, grateful to him and afraid
of losing him for an ally.

"What? Yes, long enough." Julik couldn't tell by that
whether Abraham was still sympathetic or not. It made
him awkward, made him slow down a little. He prodded
his dripping hand, kneaded it, excited. "It's gone! The
pain's disappeared. Hand me a towel, Mary."

She had already found one, and held it ready for him.

"Oh, how can I thank you enough? It was very nice of
you to take so much trouble with me. Wasn't it thoughtful
of him, Mary?"

She only heard her name. "What?"

Julik had hoped she'd forgotten. But when she spoke
he realised he'd still have to deal with her, caught on a
point and needing dislodging.

"Mary, for God's sake, can't you get your mind off that

point? When I'm successful, all that will work of its own
accord. . . ." He forgot there was anyone else in the
room, and begged her to see. "Can't you see I'm right,
Mary? You're just a woman; you can't imagine what this
all means to me. Try not to be so selfish!"

Mary Margaret was lodged, stubborn, hurt.

"You don't know what the other means to me."

Abraham there, sizing him up with every word, A'nt
Elemere, watching him flat-eyed with dislike, were not
enough to stop Julik. Too much was at stake. "Look at
it this way, Mary. Here's the tag-end of a family, about
to fall apart anyway. Here they have a chance to help
somebody who's really worth it. Jesus, what have they
ever done before? Look at it that way, please, Mary. God
knows after all my effort I deserve it." He so believed it
that for a second Mary Margaret saw beyond her own
hurt and was almost persuaded.

"I see . . ." she began.

A'nt Elemere exploded. "Well, I doesn't! I disremember when I ever heard such . . ."

"Stop it! Stop it!" Mary Margaret was so near to tears
that her voice made the other two begin to move towards
the door, even before she ordered. "Stay out of this for
once. Abraham, A'nt Elemere, please go on out, both of
you. Please!"

Abraham took A'nt Elemere's arm and piloted her
unwilling bulk out of the screen-door to the edge of the
porch. "Come on, A'nt Elemere, let them alone."

The door slammed behind them, and they stood teetering on the porch edge, squinting into the sun.

"Why the Lord everybody has to use my kitchen to do
their fussin' in—always did do it—lettin' the beans
burn . . ." A'nt Elemere mumbled and ended with a grunt,
too disgusted to be bothered with any more words.

"We better stay out on the porch, anyway." Abraham still kept tight hold of her arm.

"We kin hear jest as good out here."

But Mary Margaret's voice was so quiet with a new surge of fury when she took in the full insult of Julik's argument that they could hear only a murmur, and the rhythm of her talking. Then her voice rose until the words could be made out: "Don't you ever let me hear that kind of talk about my people again." Her voice subsided and went on murmuring. Julik had not said a word.

A'nt Elemere darted down the side-yard when she saw what John Junior was up to.

"John Junior, you let that dog alone!"

She caught him in front of the smoke-house.

"I didn't do nothin'!" he yelled. A'nt Elemere slapped him hard.

In the kitchen Julik had managed to interrupt at last, and had pulled Mary Margaret down into a chair, putting his arm round her, leaning over her.

"Now listen to me, darling. Listen. Are you listening to me?" He waited judiciously until he had caught her curiosity and made her nod. Then he spoke carefully as a mother or a doctor. "You know it's bad for you to come down here, don't you? You shed all this stifling family thinking until you come back. Then the phrases creep in, and you can't see straight or think straight. You know I'm right, don't you?"

It hadn't had quite the right effect. She started to wave her hands in the air, explaining, trying to make him see. "I know you're right, but you're not right for the right reasons, Julik. Don't you see that? You don't try to understand these people at all." She ended in a wail, and the last 'all' was nearly sung.

But she had only turned Julik back to the isolation of

his own perpetual anger. "When did they start trying to understand me?" Anger enough to take the lid off the argument and come to the point at last. "But skip that. Let's get to the point. Nobody's mentioned Ethel yet. You know you only want to spend a lot of money on a divorce that's six years overdue because of some kind of phoney sensibility you pick up when you come back down here. I wish to God you'd listen to me and stay away. It's poison for you."

Julik had begun, long before he finished with the truth of the matter, to pace up and down the room, gesticulating, being logical, making points with his hands flat and sensible against the hot air of the kitchen. Any place else it would have worked: in the kitchen of their apartment on West 83rd Street with yesterday's *Herald Tribune* always on the floor for the dog, in the only really good Italian restaurant they'd found and been loyal to in New York, at Bill's place down-town, or Bertie's up-town, everybody would have joined in and had an interesting discussion. But here, Jesus, the girl was a stranger, his own docile Mary Margaret; here in a hot and unimportant kitchen with the past spun round her like a thickening chrysalis of old attitudes, old fears he couldn't understand.

Mary Margaret was hardly even listening to him. She sat, rocking slightly, her thin arms crossed in her lap, her fingers weaving without her being aware of any movements. "We hadn't decided. We hadn't decided," she kept repeating, like a little girl, cheated.

"Don't go stubborn on me, Mary. Jesus, you're not a baby any more!"

"The concert or a divorce from Ethel," she said flatly, looking at him at last. "How many times we've talked it over, planned first one and then the other like some couples plan a house or a family. You were only fooling

36

me, all the time. You'd already made up your mind.
Julie, you ought to be ashamed of yourself. I wouldn't
have lived with you without marrying you unless I'd
thought you would do something about it as soon as you
could."

She looked so like a quietly scolding little teacher that
Julik capitulated and made an excuse to fit her mood.
"We're married in the sight of God, honey."

Mary Margaret had a sudden desire to grin, like a spasm
of her mouth. "I want to be married to you in the sight
of man, Julie. I always have." She threw off her tired
primness in a panic. "It even makes me sick at my
stomach. You know it makes me sick at my stomach,"
she accused.

"Look, Mary." Julik had had enough. "Aren't you
being a little babyish? Did I ever say I wouldn't do something as soon as I could?"

Mary Margaret had veered away already. He couldn't
catch up with her. She begged, as if that was what they'd
been talking about: "Julik, please, please, help me!"

Julik couldn't help then but be very tender with her.
She was obviously too upset to make sense. This time she
felt his arm across her shoulders.

"Who's upset my girl this much? There's something
else, isn't there, honey?"

He lulled her into admitting what it really was. "It's
Mama. She knows, and she's just been watching me like
a cold fish ever since we got here."

Julik patted her. "You're probably imagining it, darling.
Don't think I don't sympathise. I'm scared of her too."
He laughed a little.

"It's painful." Mary Margaret sighed, her head against
his shoulder. But the position was giving him a crick in
his back, so he stood upright and let her go.

"Well, you try to forget it. Don't make things up. Christ, you're a big girl now. What could she do to you?"

He thought, when she didn't answer, couldn't put fear into words, that it was all over and made right. "Now everything's O.K., isn't it?" He started out of the room to have his rest at last. "I'm going to lie down." A new thought made him turn, worried. "Do you think they all noticed when I didn't go to the grave-yard?"

He had withdrawn his sympathy too soon and he left her stranded, panicked, as if he had closed a door and shut out the light. She could only be as waspish as she knew how.

"I'm sure they didn't notice, Julik. We've had a death in the family. We don't notice much right now." Her mood had already switched again. "Now that man's turned up. I don't know . . ."

"I'm going upstairs until you're in a saner mood. I'm fed up." He went out, slamming the door.

CHAPTER IV

MARY MARGARET put her head down on the table and began to cry, letting the tears fall, with her head almost in them, not because of an old problem, a decision, a quarrel, or even a death of someone she loved, but just because of being caught and made to wake up in the middle of a hot afternoon. But too much trouble had made her dull with sleepiness. When she heard the screen-door open behind her, she thought it was A'nt Elemere.

"A'nt Elemere, gimme a cup of coffee. . . ." She rolled her head back and forth between her arms to cool her face.

Abraham answered her, hardly hearing her muffled voice, walking up close behind her. "She's down with a stick after the boy. Just to make herself feel better, she said."

She forgot that she'd been crying in her surprise at being caught by Abraham, and looked up at him, curious, ready to yawn.

"What did you come here for?"

"Oh, I don't know. I guess I thought I'd find out a few things. . . ."

"Why you weren't mentioned? Why you never came here before?"

"Maybe. Do you know anything about it?"

She decided he was being sly, and answered him as formally as she could. "No. I only know your father was a relative I never saw. No mention of anything."

"And about her?" He wasn't looking at her.

"Who?"

"My mother." Then he was, and she found she couldn't protect herself by being dignified.

"Nothing about her. Never." She was so near him that they found themselves almost whispering to each other. He walked away from her, not liking the intimacy, and raised his voice. "A'nt Elemere will know. That black witch will know. I'll get her alone. Some way I thought you'd tell me."

"You think I know."

Abraham was not whispering any longer. "I know damn well you do. When something happens in a house like this, everybody knows. It seeps out from behind closed doors. The children take trouble into their skin. There was some kind of trouble. O.K. So you won't tell me."

"I don't know. Maybe I wasn't here yet. It must have been a long time ago, whatever it was."

"Over twenty-five years ago."

"I wasn't here yet. That long ago? How in the world could it still matter to you?"

He defended himself with more violence than her question needed, because he wasn't quite sure himself why. "It matters to me. Leave it at that, will you? You'd have told me if you'd known, wouldn't you?" He was still suspicious of her.

"Of course I'd have told you. What do you think?"

He went close to her again. "I think this house is woman crazy. If I hadn't seen them all ploughing up the holy path, I'd swear one of them was listening behind every door!"

"It's only the buzz of the flies you hear. They drive you wild if you stop to listen."

"They will all gather this evening to discuss property. I can't wait." He smiled to himself, thinking of the women.

40

"So that's why you've come?"

He smoothed the oil-cloth of the table with his flat hand, leaning down to her. "I was sent for." Satisfied at her surprise, he stood up again.

"Why didn't your father come?"

"It was me they sent for." He seemed to be listening, but not to her. "When I was a kid I used to dream that a big house like this was on fire. I used to hide so nobody would find out it was me who burned it."

He wandered round the room, touching the furniture, the coal-range by the dining-room door, past the door itself. He opened it a fraction, and, seeing and smelling the high-banked flowers in the oven-hot dining-room, closed it again. He passed the sink with its damp drain-board under the sunny window, paused to drum his fingers over the dirty screen of the door to the side-yard, where beyond the big pine tree the smoke-house, the milk-house, the corn-bin and the chicken-run that he'd seen leaning towards the creek looked now like a toy street, and were casting long shadows across the yard to the kitchen porch. He even looked idly inside the low cabinet under the second big window which matched the sink window and made the side of the kitchen like a huge cage.

"I can't remember as much as I thought I could, now that I see it." He stopped in front of the second screen-door to the back gate where he'd come in first, and leaned beside it, watching nothing, remembering. "The flutter of white dresses is something I'll never forget. Oh, and the sound of women's voices going higher and higher sounding like a lot of squabbling chickens. I left here in my pyjamas, all wrapped up in a blanket. I remember because I was scared someone would see me going on the train like that. . . ."

He turned to inspect the kitchen cabinet, touching along

41

the enamelled tin surface as if he were trying to charm some memory out of it.

"It all looks so damned different, though."

"Didn't your parents tell you anything?"

"Nothing much. I picked up remarks, naturally. But not enough. Never enough to show me what really happened here. Whatever it was, I hated it. I used to come in the house from school and realise the minute I hit the door when they'd been talking about it, turning it over, both of them edgy." He was still for so long she thought he'd finished. Then he added, "I still hate it, whatever it is."

He turned finally, coming back into the room to where she sat. "I came to find out about it, if you want to know the truth."

She wanted to giggle at him because he was so naïve, and he talked too much, and he was being drawn in, just like some damn man, more than he had any idea of. All the big talk. She couldn't stop herself, realised how numb she felt in the middle of the slight giggle which had slipped out and turned it into a yawn.

"Oh, excuse me. It's the day." She tried to apologise, and yawned again.

"What were you laughing at? Haven't I got a right . . ."

"Sure. Sure, you've got a right, Abraham. It's just happening again, that's all."

"What?"

"The house. It's got you, too, but you've not even been here since you were two or three years old."

He saw the yawn begin again, the girl helpless, involved in numb, hot desire for sleep, and did the first thing he knew to wake her up. He picked her up from her chair, kissed the funny mouth which made her look so childish, and then held her head, tight, in his hands, while she stared. Then he said the other thing that had been on his mind.

"Why, you're not in love with that man!"

"You stop. Stop that!" She tried to turn her head away, but he held her.

"You told me so." Abraham was triumphant. She didn't try to move away from him then, only stood there, studying his face.

"You are down here to destroy this house," she decided and told him solemnly.

"I will destroy this house." It was his turn to laugh at her, mimicking her. "Cousin Mary Margaret, you're too little to act so damned solemn." This time he held her close, talking into her hair. "Let's you and me stick together. We'll open the cupboards and take down the books, clean out the smoke-house, rattle the bones . . ."

Mary Margaret giggled, this time sharing the joke, cosy against his chest.

Over her shoulder, he looked out of the screen-door to the back gate. A little huddle of people had gathered there, saying good-bye. Two figures in black turned towards the house, head down. He could just hear one of them say, as she turned, "No. There's nothing you can do. It's all done."

"Here come the big cats," Abraham whispered, then, with a quick compassion at the tiredness and lifelessness of the two women coming up the path, he added, "They'd better know I'm here before they see me," and disappeared through the dining-room door towards the front of the house.

CHAPTER V

MARY LEE and Amelia filed past Mary Margaret without speaking, as she ran to hold the door open for them, wiping her mouth. Some of the dignity of the funeral hung about them as they drooped; that, and exhaustion from standing in black clothes too long in the sun.

Amelia collapsed into a chair and took her hat off to fan herself with it. Mary Lee stopped, rigid, in the middle of the room, intent, as if she were trying to remember why she came into the kitchen at all.

Mary Margaret walked back to her, letting the door swing behind her. She knew from the stance, from the greyness of her mother's face, from the way she had seen her sweep her hand across her eyes, that by midnight Mary Lee would be pacing the cool attic with the migraine tightening around her head. She knew too that by morning the thin sick wreck of her would be over it, in what was for her the rare state of being weak and vulnerable, moving carefully about like a woman who has been blind drunk.

"Mother," she tried to sympathise, to jar her from her frozen position in the middle of the kitchen. But she had gone too close without warning. Mary Lee turned, savagely, using the voice and the slam of the screen-door to release her sorrow, which had by now turned to anger. "Why weren't you at the grave? Why didn't you come on after me?"

"I couldn't, Mother. I just couldn't."

"What do you mean by flaunting yourself the way you're doing?" Mary Lee's attack veered to what was really on her mind.

44

"I don't know what you mean," Mary Margaret defended herself, feeling hot with fear like a caught little girl because she'd been kissed by Abraham and her mother might have seen it.

"What I may and may not mean has nothing to do with it!" Mary Lee's shrill voice was as much to the point as her words irrelevant; she accused Mary Margaret in little gasps, fighting for air in her stiff corset of a chest. "I don't know how much you're trying to hide from me, but let me tell you, if you bring that man you're living with in fornication down here any more, there'll be a different kind of welcome. We're decent people."

"Oh, Mother, is that what you're talking about? Julik?"

"I can't pronounce his name. What are these people to think?"

"Oh, Mother, why can't you believe anything I say? You ought to try and understand. Julik and I are married!"

"In the sight of God, I suppose! You always were exactly right, Mary Margaret; always had a fine excuse for yourself."

"Mother, please don't . . ." Mary Margaret would have said one of the sympathetic phrases she knew would help to stop the tirade '. . . upset yourself any more . . . worry yourself with all you've got to do . . .' but Mary Lee cut her off, her voice edged and shrill.

"Don't talk to me any more. You upset me so much I can't stand it." She rushed by her out of the room.

Mary Margaret forgot her as soon as she had gone. The repetition had become long since a kind of dope, where she could close her mind at the sound of her mother's voice. Now she stepped in the same place her mother had stood, wondering where she wanted to go to rest, and found herself yawning again.

When Amelia had relieved herself by pulling her corset out from her flabby thighs and releasing a puff of air, she went to the kitchen cabinet. "Where's some soda? I need some soda," she talked to herself, rummaging through the cabinet, expecting Mary Margaret to overhear her excuse. But Mary Margaret only asked, "Where's A'nt Cinnybug?"

"She's out there in the back-yard talking to your Uncle Jelly. Lord knows what they've got to talk about after twenty-five years. I reckon Cinny just wears everybody else out, talking so much as she has, to finish up with Jelly."

She found what she wanted, turned the bottle up behind the door of the kitchen cabinet, and drank. With a heaving sigh she sat down again, dusting and blowing the flour from her black sleeve. She flopped back and let herself be sad again.

"You'll get used to it, days like this, Mary Margaret," she began to reminisce softly, feeling a cosier sadness as the drink blossomed inside her. "I remember when your Uncle Charles was taken. It was a day just like this. A hot day, with this kind of sleepy afternoon, the day of the funeral. Do you remember Uncle Charles?"

The memory of Charles Truxton Edwards had been more present in the house than ever Charles himself had; Mary Margaret could not remember a time when any happening had not been seen for Amelia as only a stick to stir up memories of the past she half lived in.

"No, ma'am, I don't think so," Mary Margaret answered, hoping, just today, to stop her.

But Amelia was launched into her story. "Well, there, you never would have seen him more than two or three times. It's too bad. Charles Truxton Edwards was a very fine man. A very fine man."

Mary Margaret softened toward her plump, sad cousin. The day and the hopeful dread of the coming evening had not isolated her, as it had most of the others, stranded in their own desires, waiting. Instead her senses seemed to yearn for contact, and she found herself wanting to listen to Amelia. "Were you so happy with him?" she asked the old lone bore.

"Happy, honey?" Amelia interrupted her, wondering. "Of course I was happy. You're happy when you're married, aren't you?" She began to dream again. "We had a little house with a front- and back-yard. It was the cutest little old thing you ever saw. We lived in Tennessee, just over the North Carolina border. Charles Truxton's work took him there. He was in tobacco. Happy! I should say I was!"

"A'nt Amelia, tell me something. Sometimes . . . did you forget you were in love with Uncle Charles?" She leaned hopefully on her arms, watching, asking for more of the theme song, hoping for guidance as women rustle until they find the Sunday horoscope in the newspaper, clutching anywhere for certainty.

"Never for a minute of the day or night, honey. It's my happy memory. It's what I live on now."

Amelia belched carefully, and hoisted herself in her chair. "Excuse me," she murmured, then brightened. "Let me tell you about our house . . ."

But Mary Margaret had had her answer, and she was in danger of crying again because of it, so she pushed open the screen-door and called over her shoulder, "Some other time, A'nt Amelia, I'd like to hear all about it . . ." and ran off down the side-yard away from the women's voices.

Mary Lee kicked open the dining-room door and elbowed herself through it, grasping in both hands a bowl of tight, waxy, long-stemmed roses, wired so tightly they stuck up like long quills. She set them in the sink, and

47

twisted the cold water tap until the water splashed hard.
over them.

"Who was that went out?" she called over the noise of
the water.

Amelia didn't bother to bend round to look at her, but
she knew better than not to answer, "Mary Margaret,"
already weary and bored again.

Mary Lee craned her neck to take in as much of the side-
yard as she could from the window. "Humph! Running
off towards the creek. I reckon she's going to enjoy a good
cry. She always did when she went down to the creek.
That girl sure is one to hug her own miseries." She
slapped at the screen. "This place is just alive with flies!
Where's the Flit?"

She bent down to the cabinet under the sink, taking out
the Flit gun. It was then that Amelia saw the flowers.
"What are those things doing in here?" She could hardly
find her voice to ask. She sat, frozen, as if she were in a
nightmare and couldn't wake up to scream. So what she
said was whispered, but Mary Lee heard enough to turn
and look, and then ignore the silly woman.

She started to 'Flit' the room furiously instead, as if
there were virtue in it. "Well, somebody had to look after
them." She offered the information while she sprayed the
air. "It might as well be me. It always is in the long run.
There wasn't room for them on the coffin and there's no
use to waste them."

Amelia watched them, as if she expected them to come
alive, coil, and strike at her. She managed to whisper
again, "Mary Lee, please get them out of here."

Mary Lee stopped attacking the flies and stood in front
of her, watching. "What are you going on for?"

"They make me feel sick," Amelia whispered, and
begged, "Please, Mary Lee, take them out again!"

48

"Well, I never saw such goings-on over a little vase of flowers."

Mary Lee swept over to the sink, shut off the water, and wrenched the dripping vase up into her hands. "You're just nothing but a damn fool, Amelia."

She carried the flowers over and set them down in the middle of the kitchen table.

"There!" wiping her hands on her skirt, "I'm putting them right there and don't you act like such a fool. There's not any use to waste them and they'll just die out in the dining-room with nobody to see them."

At first Amelia was too frightened by the flowers, set almost under her nose, to move at all. Then she started up. "Take them away, Mary Lee, I warn you I can't stand it."

"I never saw such damn foolishness in all my born days. Just over a little bunch of flowers!"

Mary Lee grabbed Amelia's arm tightly as she finally struggled out of her chair and tried to pass.

"You're not going out because of them! You've been drinking licker all day, that's what's the matter with you, damn you, Amelia!"

"Let go of me!" Amelia pulled away from Mary Lee; still not looking at her, but only at the flowers, she staggered through the dining-room door.

Mary Lee, having said what was on her mind, moved busily and almost happily, getting the kitchen in order again. She took the few cups off the table, put them in the sink, marched to the stove to 'look at' the beans, jiggled the heavy iron pan belligerently. Then she swept it up and struggled with it to the sink.

A'nt Elemere saw her as she heaved up the back stairs to the screen-door. "What chew doin' with them green-beans?"

Mary Lee told her, over her shoulder, "I'm just putting a little water on them." She lifted the pan and staggered back to the stove with it. "They were set to burn. If you'd look after your own cooking once in a while, A'nt Elemere, it'd be a little added strain off my shoulders. Heaven knows I've got enough to worry me without you letting things burn all over the place."

"Well, I like to know when it woulda been polite for me to come in and stir my green-beans, please, in the last twenty minutes, with all the goings-on!"

"A'nt Elemere, don't you talk back to me." Mary Lee didn't wait to hear A'nt Elemere's answer. She had already gone into the front of the house, jabbing the door with her skinny, bony arm. A'nt Elemere made herself clear to nothing but the creak of the door as it swung behind her.

"I don't see why I can't ask a simple question once in a while. I know why. There just ain't no plain, simple people around this place to answer 'em." Then she laid eyes on those flowers.

"I'd like to know who put them store-bought flowers on my clean table. Well, they can jest go right back where they come from, that's all." She picked them up. "Look at that there ring!"

She swished the water from the table with her apron. "I ain't havin' no funeral blooms in my kitchen and that's all there is to it."

So, just as Mary Lee had brought them in, A'nt Elemere took the roses back again, her elbows akimbo to catch the door, into the empty dining-room which seemed to buzz with silence and be forgotten, now that the intensity of death had passed beyond it to other rooms, spread out as separate burdens as the family had wandered all over the house.

The long mahogany table had been pushed back against

the wall, and assorted chairs from the living-room, the bedrooms, as far away as the attic, were still set in snaggled uneven rows where people had leaned forward to pray or look or ease themselves. In the ten-foot-square space where Miss Anna Mary Passmore had rested in the early afternoon on a bank of rings and roses and half-moons of tight, long-lasting store-bought flowers, her old shrivelled head powdered and marcelled like a doll, there were now only three naked quilting trestles in a line. Behind them against the summer-sealed fireplace, a criss-cross of flower-stands leaned together looking like a sold-out church bazaar. A'nt Elemere put the flowers down on the flat oak sideboard, forgot them at once, and set to work gathering up the quilting horses to take them back to the attic, trying to restore the familiarity of the room again before she succumbed to its dead silence.

CHAPTER VI

CINNYBUG LAMB prissed up the back path, her voice going on as steady as breathing, talking to Jellicoe over her shoulder. She carried in her fast, bouncing walk the memory of a body that had once been cute, little and slim with dimpled knees, a beauty which by now everyone had forgotten. Her voice was a nostalgic caricature. Where it had been breathless, now it was edgy; the trill of expectation of her youth had long been replaced by a shrill apprehension. She still wore her hair bobbed; cut by the same barber in Palmyra who had always done it, finishing with the clippers. All of this meant to most of the unnoticing people around her that Cinnybug had changed least of any of them.

On the other hand Jellicoe, lounging behind her, had just about run down. He had grown querulous, the old candy-ankle, sorrowfully lazy, apologetically weary. He spoke somehow like a plump, ageing woman.

As Cinnybug went on with her hands in the air in front of her, Jellicoe looked as if he had long since stopped listening, but was following her with his head down, so that if she happened to glance his way, which she seldom did, she would suppose he was deep in thought about what he would answer, if he ever got a chance.

"Jellicoe, what do you think, I just want to know what you think that's all; after all, you've got to live in it too. . . ."

They reached the screen-door and walked into the now empty kitchen.

"If I take most of the furniture out of the living-room I feel lonesome with you gone so much and if I put

52

it all back I feel cluttered when there's two of us in the room."

Jellicoe collapsed at the kitchen table, wiping the sweat from around his eyes.

"I don't know, honey, you gwan do whatever you want to." He yawned until his jaw creaked faintly.

"Jellicoe, I wish you'd take a little bit of interest in the house. I'll declare with all my worry and fussing over it I don't think you really look at it from one year's end to the next."

"Oh, I like it, honey, you gwan do whatever you want to; I'll like it." He began to finger his chin, and then round his mouth, thinking.

"What's gotten into you today, Jellicoe?" Cinnybug finally looked at him. "You're hardly listening to a word I say."

Jellicoe looked worried. "Nothing, Cinny, nothing. It's just hot, and I don't know whether I ought to have took the day off or not. You know what Mr. Crasscopper's like most of the time."

Cinnybug turned and began to search through the kitchen cabinet, uncovering plates, scrambling through the back for hidden things to eat.

"Mr. Crasscopper!" There was a world of new contempt in Cinny's voice. "After tonight we can say booturkey to Mr. Crasscopper." She smelt something in a tin, but made a little face and put it back.

She had surprised Jellicoe enough for him to take notice of what she said for once. He was shocked. "Why, Cinnybug, I wouldn't talk like that if I was you. You know Mr. Crasscopper's my boss."

She found a plate of cookies and began to 'taste' them, nibbling at the edges, and crumbling them thoughtfully in her lips. "He's more'n your boss," she told Jellicoe, blowing a little cookie dust before her. "He's practically owned us for the last twenty-five years. Meely musta made these cookies. They've got more sugar than Mary Lee puts in."

"Cinnybug, you know times were hard right after that. Things never did pan out. Mr. Crasscopper's been pretty nice about that loan all these years. You ought to see how he treats some people."

In his weary way, Jellicoe told about the loan, as he'd told about it almost every day for years, saying the same words. By repetition he hardly heard them any more himself; Cinnybug didn't hear them at all, only the name, the name like a red flag that tilted at her, starting her off for the thousandth time.

"Jelly, there's one thing I just never can understand about you. You're scared to death of Mr. Crasscopper, and yet every day you have to go collecting money yourself. I'd be a lot scareder of people that owed money." Her voice slid on the word: Cinny said 'money' like a whiney little girl calling her mommy. She settled back and examined Jelly all over, her mouth hidden behind a cookie. "I reckon you're just scareder of Mr. Crasscopper than you are of them. Here, have a cookie."

"Now you leave me alone, Cinny. I know what you think of me, you needn't try and hide it."

"Gwan and try one," she interrupted, not questioning what he said; after all, she'd never tried to hide it, so the whole accusation was false.

"No, I don't want a damn cookie," Jelly wailed, explaining, "Now you listen to me, Cinnybug: you know it wasn't my fault and you know I've worked as hard as I could for the last twenty-five years."

"Why, honey, what's got your goat?" she worried at him; then sternly, "Jellicoe, have your bowels moved today?"

"Oh, Cinny, there isn't anything the matter. Mr. Crasscopper's been at me lately, and you know how it gets my goat when both of you get started on me."

"Oh, never mind about that!" Cinnybug reassured him, as she got up from the table and carried the empty cookie plate back to the cabinet. "Cousin Cad told me I need not to worry when I went to see him last week—that I'd own my own home after tonight." She stopped dead, the cookie plate poised. Out in the side-yard, the dog set up a fine yapping, filling the kitchen with it.

"Own my own!" Cinnybug loved to say it. "It's what I've waited for, for twenty-five years." She shoved the plate into the cabinet. "Oh, I know it wasn't your fault, Jellicoe, don't look so hang-dog." She studied him, sitting there slumped in his seat, pucker-faced and red with apology; but she kept on turning away from him until the sight of herself in A'nt Elemere's mirror made her stop, and edge closer to inspect herself.

"What do you think I ought to do about the neck of this dress? It looks so washed-out-looking. What's eating that dog?" She waved her head from side to side, stretching her neck of scraggy tendons and chickeny bones, studying it quite objectively. "Do you think anybody'd mind if I just pinned a little white collar on it? Some people put white on mourning clothes."

"Oh sure, honey, I don't think anybody'd mind."

"You don't!" She said it out of the side of her mouth, because her neck was wound too tight.

"Unhunh." Jellicoe had stopped listening again and roused himself at last to get coffee. Cinny saw him through the mirror.

"Pour me a cup, honey. Oh, for the love of God!" She rushed to the window, where the dog's barking almost drowned her voice. "I can't even see it. John Junior," she yelled, "where are you?" Then she saw the Buick, sleek, high-coloured, and long, parked across the creek. "Lord's love! Whose is *that*?"

Jellicoe took out two cups and went back for saucers and went back for sugar, and then went back again from the table because he'd forgotten the cream. As he poured the coffee, he moaned, "I sure could use a shot!"

Cinnybug realised that the dog had stopped barking, and turned back into the room.

"Well, there won't be any here," she told Jellicoe. "Mary Lee won't allow a drop in the house on account of Amelia finding it. It stops everybody drinking but Amelia. I think I'll copy that collar off of Mary Margaret's dress. She sure does have some nice ideas in clothes when she comes down."

She came and sat down beside Jellicoe and he pushed her coffee towards her. She sat winding her spoon around it, thinking about Mary Margaret, for when she spoke she lowered her voice, but not enough.

"Do you like that foreigner she married?"

"Who?"

"Mary Margaret."

"He isn't a foreigner, is he?"

Not enough because Mary Margaret came slowly on to the porch and heard all she said.

"Well, practically," Cinnybug rejected Julik with a twist of her mouth. "His father was born somewhere out like Poland or Hungary or somewhere. That's about as foreign as you can get to. Of course Mary Margaret's husband was born right here, but I always say you can't make a silk purse out of a sow's ear. I wouldn't call them real Amer'cans, would you?"

Mary Margaret had stopped first because she was too embarrassed at catching them to interrupt, but when

Cinnybug stopped, she flew at her, scratching the screen-door out of her way.

"A'nt Cinny, never let me hear you make another remark like that about Julik, do you hear me?" Mary Margaret's voice went low and shook with fury and it swamped and froze the two lounging at the table.

Cinny looked at the girl wide-eyed, holding her breath. Then she almost screamed trying to hush her by explaining, "I didn't mean anything by it, Mary Margaret! It's just my way of talking."

Jellicoe nodded wisely, not catching the shock between them: "Sure, Mary Margaret. It's just her way of talking. She didn't mean anything by it," and went on nodding, forgetting to stop.

Mary Margaret didn't take her eyes from Cinnybug.

"Do you know what kind of pain that sort of remark can cause? Do you know how it can twist a person, twist them into a kind of cripple? You wouldn't know what it's like to be hated and alone in this country." She was getting closer to Cinnybug, panting every word, bitterly. "You're the ones who belong some place. You belong! You've got no right to be so cruel!"

Cinnybug fought her away because one of her words had struck home. "Oh sure, we belong!" She began to shriek, "We belong to Mr. Ebenezer B. Crasscopper, don't we, honey, don't we belong to Mr. Ebenezer B. Crass-copper?"

By the time she had finished the tears were running down her face and she was crying loudly, square-mouthed like a child, with her face getting red with effort. Jellicoe jumped up and began to pat her back, thumping out gasps and sobs.

"Help me, Mary Margaret! All this going-on has been too much for her. You know what kind of a day it's been.

You know . . . awe, honey . . . awe, honey . . ." Cinnybug's fists pawed the air in front of her, and her cute shoes
drummed the floor, beating time with her sobs.

A'nt Elemere rushed in from the dining-room, like an
angry hen.

"Love of the Lamb, what has somebody been doin' to
my lil baby?" She fussed as she scooped Cinnybug up
and held her thin body jack-knifed in her strapping arms.

"Here you, Mr. Jelly, open that door and let me
through." Jellicoe was hovering, making little vague
gestures of holding out his arms.

"Can I carry her, A'nt Elemere?"

A'nt Elemere didn't bother to look at him: she was too
busy trying to quiet Cinnybug, who was filling the
kitchen, like the dog had, with noise. "No, I don't reckon
you could, Mister Jelly. You jest stay down here and let
me see to her; poor little thing." She went past him,
crooning to calm Cinnybug.

Jellicoe turned round to Mary Margaret when they had
gone and the kitchen was still again. Mary Margaret
stood where she had stopped, inside the door, her face no
longer troubled, but numbed by the noise.

"Well, I don't know. I don't know what made Cinny
do that. She's real calm most of the time."

"It's today—and tonight to come. That's what's the
matter with her." Mary Margaret watched the door; the
noise had already stopped and she took a step to follow,
to apologise, then shrugged a little and changed her mind.

"You know I'm sorry you heard her say that, Mary
Margaret," Jellicoe was explaining sorrowfully. She
hardly heard him.

"What in the world's the matter with Cinnybug?"
Amelia saved Jellicoe from having to try any more with
Mary Margaret by coming into the kitchen so much faster

than she usually moved that even he noticed it. When he looked at her, he forgot to answer her question about Cinnybug: her face was grey-white, drained, taut, as if plump, gentle Amelia had seen more than she ought to for her own good.

"What in the world's the matter with you, Amelia? You look like you've seen a ghost!"

Amelia brushed into Mary Margaret, quivered against her shoulder for a second without even noticing her, and flopped down at the table. But when she did speak, she ignored Jellicoe and spoke to her.

"Get me a drink, honey—in the flour bin. Don't for Lord's sake tell your mother it's there, will you."

Mary Margaret rooted out the bottle and blew the flour from it, gathered a shot-glass from the cabinet as she passed, and handed them both to Amelia. "I wouldn't tell her, A'nt Amelia."

Amelia poured a drink and threw it down her throat. She looked at Jellicoe, standing with his mouth ajar, staring at her. "Here, Jelly, you look like you could use one, too." She pushed the bottle and glass at him. "Oh Lord, I just don't know," she began, then took another drink instead.

When Jellicoe had poured a drink, which he was far more interested in, worn out as he was, than Amelia's news, Amelia reached for her bottle, slammed home the cork, and handed it back to Mary Margaret.

"Do you want me to put it back in the flour bin?"

"Sure, honey, put it back." Amelia forgot her again and turned to Jellicoe. "I just don't know what to say," she went on.

Suddenly Mary Margaret, as if she'd been told, understood what had shocked Amelia so.

"You've seen Abraham."

59

"I've seen Abraham, stretched out in the hammock; just lying there, on the front porch, asleep. It was Abraham, and it wasn't Abraham. The spittin' image; he would be twenty-nine or thirty now at least. Young Abraham, lying asleep in the hammock, just like his father." She was suspicious of Mary Margaret. "How did you know?"

"I know. He came when you were all gone to the grave. I came into the kitchen and there he was, talking to A'nt Elemere."

"Why didn't one or other of you tell us? Why didn't somebody let us know?" Amelia had taken up the empty shot-glass and was twisting it rapidly round and round in her hands. "Oh Lord in heaven, I don't know what to think. What Mary Lee's gonna cut up like I don't know. Well, she'll just have to keep quiet for once. The boy's got a perfect right to be here, the same as the rest of us."

Something about Amelia made Mary Margaret try to question her carefully, asking it into the air, shading her hand at the same time and looking out across the side-yard as if she were drawn to something under the trees. "A'nt Amelia, why would Mother cut up? Why would she cut up over Abraham coming back?" When Amelia didn't answer she went on, "She must have known one of that part of the family would come back to the funeral. What's behind it all? He wants to know."

She turned then at hearing no answer. Amelia's eyes had glazed and she was smiling slightly, neither listening nor answering such questions as that even to herself.

"A'nt Amelia."

"Unhunh?"

"He wants to know."

"Does he? Well, I don't know. Nothing. Just nothing." She laughed and put on sweetness like a coat. "Isn't it nice? Soon as he wakes up somebody had better go talk to him. Make him feel at home."

She struggled up out of her chair.

"I'm going to lie down. This has all been very upsetting."

She stopped as she passed Jellicoe and clutched at his shoulder for support and attention. "Jellicoe, the vault was the coldest place! Did you notice? All those stone platters, and there we all were, kicking just a little too hard to get shovelled on to them. I want to lie beside Charles Truxton." She smiled, and nodded her head. "He was a very fine man."

She was gone, weaving away from the kitchen where people asked so many questions, to lie down alone and doze in the cool and let the liquor take over.

Jellicoe had already started for the kitchen cabinet before the door stopped swinging. "She'll be so potted she won't be able to move by evening. I'm gonna have another shot of her liquor."

He took the bottle back out of the flour bin and blew it. "Keep her from wasting it on herself anyway."

CHAPTER VII

"UNCLE JELLY, oughtn't somebody to tell Mother before she just meets up with Abraham?" Mary Margaret waited, half-poised, half-decided to do it herself, but still ready to be told she needn't bell that cat in the heat.

Jellicoe wasn't worried. "Aw, honey, I been watching this bunch of women scratching too long to take any notice of what gets after 'em most of the time." He stopped to yawn and went on speaking with his words full of air: "This Abraham'll have to take care of himself."

He lounged over and looked out of the back screen-door where he could see Cadwallader still leaning on the gate where the others had left him watching down the road, looking from the back too tired to unbend.

"Hey, Cad," Jellicoe yelled, and the figure began to straighten up. "Come on in here and have a shot. You look all in."

Cadwallader turned slowly and came up the path, his eyes down, his hands clasped together, only looking up at Jellicoe when he reached the steps.

"It's the heat," he told Jellicoe, wiping his face with a clean handkerchief, "I never could stand a sun like this. It makes my head ache."

Cadwallader did look 'all in', from his winter black suit to his Panama hat, for which he'd stopped at the haberdashery in Palmyra and bought a black ribbon, thinking about it for a good long time, and then fitting it on himself in his office. He looked dog-tired with sorrow and the general business of being a cousin at the funeral, expected to be sorry, but not bowed down enough as a cousin not to be able to take over. So he had taken over, for the simple reason that he hadn't been able to see who else in the world would do it but him. In the hot sun, he'd seen to getting the few cars parked, then seen to the undertaker's men having a place to stand, seen to the Company people getting seats in the dining-room; even at the end he had paid the preacher, with the tears ferreting down his thin face and fogging his gold-rimmed glasses so that by that time he could hardly see his change.

"I'm the kind could get sun-stroke—usually inside a cool, green office—room lined with all those dark green tin deed-boxes just about as cool as you can find any-where; then I have the fan on, too." He bowed his head to come in at the door, although he no longer needed to. It was easy to see where he'd got his permanent stoop, though. Stretched out he would have been six feet five inches tall; not that anyone had ever seen him stretched out, unbowed, strutting down the road, in his life.

Mary Margaret noticed that he had forgotten to wipe under his glasses before he came into the house, and that the tears he had been crying, out over the back gate, still lay damp in the furrows under his eyes. The sight of him made fresh tears spurt suddenly from her own eyes, and she had to turn quickly away and lean on the side of the kitchen cabinet.

"Mary Margaret," Cad was talking to her, but she listened with her back still to him, "you saw one of the finest women you'll ever hope to meet buried today, and don't you forget it. It makes me proud to think that I enjoyed her confidence. Oh, I hope everything tonight goes smooth. It's too hot for everybody to get to picking at each other." Cadwallader began a grin, like a nervous twitch, then stopped, putting himself already in a mood to force everything to go smooth.

63

Jellicoe, who loved peace as much as Cadwallader, but for his own lazier reasons, caught the warning note and asked, "Is there any reason why everything shouldn't go smooth, Cad?"

Cad sat back in his chair and studied Jellicoe, like he studied clients, calmly and slowly from under his eyebrows; a lawyer look, an ethical, moral, confidential, judicial, client-squirmer of a look he'd picked up at Law School and used, the same as he'd used a Panama hat, ever since.

"Jellicoe, I wouldn't, even if I could, divulge one bit of what's in A'nt Anna Mary's will. I will tell you this much, though. She disposed of her property as she saw fit and proper for all concerned." Then he wasn't bothering to look at Jellicoe any more, just sitting there remembering.

"I remember it like it was yesterday; she come all the way into Palmyra, a day as hot as this. There she sat, all dressed up; she could be a fine-looking woman, you know, when she tried—before she begun to be taken bad all the time. She sat there with her veil blowing nearer and nearer the electric fan. 'Cad, son,' she said— she called everybody son—'I figured out how to deal with my property fair for all and yet not foolish.' Well, I couldn't stand it any more, I said, 'Miss Anna Mary, if you don't git away from that fan you'll be sucked in, veil, hair and all, and you won't have a chance to make a will.'" Cad chuckled and shook his head. "She just said, 'Shucks, Cad, I'm too tough to be sucked up by some little old new-fangled machine.' You know, she went down to the Flora on the corner there as soon as she left me and pushed her way right through all those kids standing around slopping up sodas the way they do, and just give orders for some damn-fool boy waiting behind the counter

64

to bring her what she called a wind-machine. I tell you that soda-jerker hopped to it, though! It's there beside her bed now."

He got up. "I'm going to lie down a little while. Heat of the day, you know. It's best."

He wandered away slowly into the cool of the house. Jellicoe began to complain, gently, before the door had swung shut.

"Ever' time Cadwallader gets upset he'd talk the hind leg off a mule. Other times you can't get a word out of him." Jellicoe went on as he tipped the bottle back into the flour bin, smelling into it before he finally closed it. "Boy, the fumes from the biscuits'll get even to Mary Lee if Amelia don't find someplace better'n this to hide her stuff."

He looked longingly out of the screen-door, and Mary Margaret gave him the push by habit that he seemed always to demand. "Don't you want to go and lie down, too, Uncle Jelly?"

He moved towards the door, grateful. "Yes, honey, I think I will. You know, you don't get much chance, when you work in an office, for a little afternoon nap, especially when you work for a go-getter like Mr. Crasscopper." His apologies were muttered mostly to himself, for he was out of the screen-door and around the porch nearly to the swing by the time he finished.

Alone then, after all the to-ing and fro-ing, Mary Margaret sat at the table, her elbows out and her hand half shading her eyes. The whole house around her seemed sunk in summer sleep; all but the kitchen, where the silence was high-pitched and the sun on the side-porch beat through the dust. Over the table the flies wheeled a little, even though the house had run to a stop for a time. Mary Margaret went on staring at the same space, seeing nothing, sunk in it, not moving her eyes, hardly breathing out enough to disturb the heat around her. Then slowly she put her head down in her arms and tried to sleep, too.

CHAPTER VIII

ABRAHAM, half awake himself, having been caught in the hammock by the sun and roused just enough to make him move, came round the house, taking in everything aimlessly. The old tar barrel used as a rain-barrel; the rocking-chairs on the porches, all wheewhawed but so that you could see what just might be coming down either creek from them; the clumps of striped tiger-lilies; all swam by him, unfamiliar. He felt the ground rise under his feet and, looking up, saw by the stone sun-dial on the grass mound that it was somewhere near four o'clock.

The quietness of it all besieged him. He felt outcast by it; found the house, with its mothering porches, as for-bidding as an empty house; so he walked, without caring or knowing why, back to sit in his own car for a while. He looked back half-way across the creek bridge, and the house seemed small again, as he had first seen it.

Then it was easy to slip back to the disappointment of his first view of it. Nothing. Not a damned monument. Just a clapboard farmhouse with the dun-coloured paint peeling and the trellises sagging under the heavy burden of their ragged old rambler roses. Not a place at all, from right out there across the creek, where you could find your-self kissing a baby-faced stranger just to get the numbness out of her head and your own. But all he said aloud to himself was, "I thought it was gonna be bigger than this," and knew for the first time in years the easy physical urge of wanting to cry.

John Junior, inspecting the Buick, unscrewing what-ever he could find loose, thought of course from the

67

centre of his world that Abraham was talking to him.

"It's the biggest car I ever saw from way off. When you git up near it don't look so big."

Abraham slouched over to the car, let himself be drawn into John Junior's questioning, answered one for every dial, and finally to stop them said what John Junior wanted him to, "Do you want to go for a ride?"

"Yeah. I reckon so." John Junior ran round the car and got into the front seat, keeping his enjoyment strictly to himself, getting in and slamming the door with a gesture of half-bored ownership.

He settled himself, and refused to answer Abraham when he asked where he wanted to go, just waited for the car to start.

Abraham turned it back towards the main road the way he had come, beginning to wonder as he drove if it was really true that children took in so much of what was going on. So he realised why he'd taken the trouble to bring John Junior for a car-ride. He looked down beside him and watched the boy as much as he could, driving.

John Junior was slouched back in the wide seat, his legs not touching, but his arm stretched up to where he could let it lie along the window rim, his eyes hooded, trying to look used to it, hiding a high excitement. As they passed a boy in blue jeans and galluses scuffing barefoot along the dirt side of the road, he lifted his arm and waved like the King of England.

The little boy stopped and waved back wildly, his mouth wide.

"Want him to go for a ride?" Abraham asked, slowing down.

"Oh no. He don't care nothin' about cars. He wouldn't want to go, too."

"Friend of yours?" Abraham stepped on the gas.

68

"I jist know him. His name's Digby or something. I don't know."

They went on down the road past a few houses, more shacks, some high up on the side of the hill as the little creek valley narrowed from time to time almost into a hollow. John Junior took out his nickel-plated harmonica and began to play, trying Abraham to see how far he would go before he'd start the grown-up racket of asking questions and bossing. He sucked air in and out in long wails, making a noise like a piano trying to breathe.

"Can't you play anything?" Abraham said, the noise filling his head.

"This is something."

"Well, don't play it right now. I can't drive." The silence after the harmonica was embarrassing, each of them waiting. Abraham finally asked casually, "Think everybody was surprised to see me?"

So the bossing and the questions started just about together.

"I don't know," John Junior answered, and fingered the harmonica in his pocket.

"Did you hear them say anything?" It was like sticking a foot on to hard ground and finding it was made of mush. It had happened with A'nt Elemere, it had happened with Mary Margaret, and now it was happening with this four-eyed brat. Abraham kept his eyes on the road, taking the turns swinging. "Well, did you?"

"Don't remember nothin' about it. What are you asking me for?" John Junior watched out of the window as the familiar houses, the barns, the fences, the little unpainted Jenny Lind shacks sailed by like new things from a new speed and a new window.

He couldn't contain himself any longer. His joy bubbled

out. "I been down this road about a thousand times," he confided, bragging.

It was Abraham's turn not to answer.

John Junior started to sneak the harmonica out of his pocket again, but Abraham saw the glitter of it out of the corner of his eye.

"Put that goddamned thing away," he said, not bothering to look any more.

"You sure are a dangerous driver," John Junior told him, admiring him at last.

"There's nothing dangerous about driving fast," Abraham said, slowing down. "There's the main road. Want to go back?"

"I don't care," John Junior said, carefully.

Abraham slowed and began to turn.

"There's a real good dog-wagon down the main road a piece if you're thirsty," John Junior told him.

"Make up your mind." Abraham swung the car back round and circled into the main road and down it along the river. He saw for certain that the brat was too fly and too wise and too plain mean to treat the way you'd treat most children; a lot of little chips off an old dumb block, who drew forth meaningless phrases from bachelors; phrases like 'I'll bet you wouldn't take anything for him', over their heads to their parents. Abraham wouldn't have given three cents for John Junior Passmore, even dead.

"A'nt Amelia said it was all the same to her," John Junior told him when they were safe out on the main road.

"Thanks," said Abraham, watching out for the dog-wagon.

"She's high as a kite."

"Where's this dog-wagon of yours?" Abraham was still wary of his little cousin.

"Down the right, right yonder, where that thar sign is," John Junior pointed, speaking hill-billy self-consciously. "Boy, she's stinking as a billy-goat. Boy!"

"Is that any way to talk about your aunt?" Abraham pulled the car to a stop, swerving it off the road. "Here you are."

"You was thirsty," John Junior pointed out, and disappeared into the dog-wagon ahead of him.

Joe Poppelino's dog-wagon had begun to grow from the seed of his own kitchen table, where, during the 'twenties, he'd started serving a little of his own quite good home-brew, principally because the bottom had dropped out of the coal business and there was no other way for him to make a living for himself. But what Abraham saw, over twenty years later, was a long, thin, low building, with a high narrow false front made of clapboard, on which was painted *JOE'S*, in letters that had once been red. As soon as he bent his way into the door he realised what it was—an old caboose, with home-made tables in between the coupled wooden seats.

That had been added to the front of his shack in 1932, just before Joe, who was as unlucky as he was smart, had been picked up for boot-legging and sent to the penitentiary. When he came out the Eighteenth Amendment had already been repealed for nine months. He went back to the dog-wagon and started serving three-point-two instead of his own home-brew. After he came out of jail he started saving all the human-sized cardboard advertising girls that were sent to him over the years, so that the only colour Abraham could make out in the gloom was a shadow-world of bathing-suited, pert, laughing, dusty girls, some of them in twenty-year-old styles. They were the only women Joe had ever burdened himself with. The only art work he had added was a sign reading

71

'*No use to Ask for Credit*' over the dirty, tiny counter.

Abraham slid into one of the dingy caboose seats opposite John Junior. "What do you like to drink?" he asked the boy, and looked around for someone to bring it.

"Joe!" John Junior yelled.

"What'cha want?" came from the door behind the counter.

"Coke."

"O.K." Joe Poppelino, hot and old, worn out by his weight and the summer day, came in through what had once been his own front door. Abraham could only hear him; John Junior, in full view, had made him stop. "John Junior, you got any money?" he called out, bending over the ice-cooler.

"Sure I have. I'm with my cousin."

"Down for the funeral, eh? Ain't it too bad ... ?" Joe kept on muttering.

"It's Abraham, my cousin Abraham," John Junior called proudly. "He's got a big car."

Joe was uninterested, popping the top off the coke. "I don't want you hanging around here without no money no more, John Junior. I'm gonna tell your A'nt on you. You goddam kids." He knocked on the counter with the bottle, signalling for John Junior to come and get it. "Don't your cousin want anything?"

"Get me a beer." Abraham flipped fifty cents across the table; John Junior grabbed it before it stopped clattering.

"How old are you?" Joe called.

"Twenty-nine. Old enough, mister."

"Oh, excuse me. Now ain't that funny? What do you know about that?" Joe grabbed a bottle of cold beer on his way round the counter, bringing an opener with him in his hurry to see Abraham. John Junior, forgotten for a minute, got his coke and slid back into place with it.

"Pay the man, buster," Abraham told him. "Can I have a glass?"

"A glass?" Joe was surprised. "Oh, sure. I get used to these kids comin' in here. It ain't good for business, I tell you. Comin' in here."

"Joe's been in the pen. He's scared of getting pinched all the time," John Junior said, sucking at his coke.

"Shut your dirty little mouth." Joe slid back round the counter again and back into his front door.

"What did you say that for? The guy might not like it," Abraham asked the boy.

"Well, he has. It ain't nothing. Everybody around here went to jail for bootlegging. Still do." He hopped up from the table, grabbed a bag of potato-chips from the counter, and scattered them over the table.

"You don't miss much, do you?" Abraham watched him, wondering if the time had come to question him again.

As if he'd caught the scene in his mind that Abraham wanted to force him back to, John Junior began to brag again.

"They can't fool me, that bunch of old, skinny women. I'm gonna git myself some money and I'm gonna leave this old place. I know whur I kin git it, too, I jist gotta whustle." He 'hill-billyed', and wiggled and pushed potato-chips around the table, watching them.

"Do you?" Abraham asked, waiting.

"Sure I do. My dad'll give me anything I want. Anything . . ." He forgot to play with the potato-chips and sat very still, looking at nothing.

"I hate this place and I hate this school. I'm the smartest boy in my room. I have three hundred beer bottles. When I git five hundred I'm gonna sell 'em to Joe and I'm gonna buy me a ticket and I'm gonna do

73

whatever I want to." John Junior finished in a high voice, having recited himself back into confidence again. He sat with his big, spectacled eyes full on Abraham and went on skidding potato-chips.

But Abraham drank his beer slowly, not wanting to ask any more questions.

CHAPTER IX

WHEN Abraham stepped back on to the empty porch, empty because it too was full of sun now, so that the sleepers, knowing the habits of the sun, had not gone there as they would when the evening came, he saw Mary Margaret move her head in her arms, then grow still again. He opened the screen-door softly and went in.

"I can't sleep." She looked at him, drowsy, worried.

"Why is the house so quiet, Mary Margaret?" he asked her, a little disappointed because he had already prepared himself to face the hullabaloo that the news of his arrival would cause.

"They're all asleep."

"They're sleeping off the funeral. It does that to people . . ." then decided against the reminiscence. "What about you? Why can't you sleep?"

"I don't know."

"What's the matter?" he asked, as if he knew, and grinned, so that she wanted to slap his face.

Instead she was rude. "I said I don't know why. Honestly!"

"Don't you?"

"All right. I was afraid to wander around the house because I might meet you. That's why. We might just meet . . ." she ended feebly.

Abraham was laughing at her now, but quietly.

"Don't you care anything about anybody else?" her voice rose at him, "coming down here . . ."

"Nobody who gets in my way in this damned place," he interrupted her. He sat down and leaned his chair back, watching her. "When you want a man it makes you afraid, honey. Maybe you haven't wanted one for a long time. You know, it doesn't have anything to do with whether he hurts his hand, or whether he has talent or . . ."

"Let him alone!" Mary Margaret woke up at last, sat up straight. He caught the movement and tried to help her up from her chair, hugging her; but she found him too heavy on her, disturbing. She twisted away from him and sat back down. "Let me alone, too, Abraham. I can't understand you. Who are you. . . ?"

"I'm your cousin, honey."

"Why are you like this?"

"Like what?"

"Overpowering. I'm a grown woman . . ." she added carefully. ". . . you're acting like a squatter. You've got a perfect right to be here, the same as the rest of us," she explained in an echo of Amelia, and then, suddenly realising whose words she copied, paused. "You don't have to act like that," she trailed off.

When he didn't answer she tried again. "What kind of a place do you come from that you. . . ?"

"Me?" he interrupted her, looking down at her. "A lot of different places. I've worked a long time."

"What doing?"

"I messed around. I got through college washing dishes, so I learned how to wash dishes. Then I got drafted. After the war I went wild-catting. That's where I finally found out I had some talent."

"What kind of talent?" she asked, smiling as if he'd confessed to being a part-time artist, which being of her own world she thought he had.

"My kind, sister." He understood the smile. "I can smell oil when the wind blows, and feel natural gas when

I put my hand on the ground like you can feel Paganini's pulse. But right now I'm curious," he added, and changed the subject impatiently, as he changed his pace up and down in front of the table, making the screened-in kitchen look more like a cage than ever.

"You? I won't ask about you." He looked up her plump arm to her hair and reached out and touched it, tenderly. "You're the kind who gives up things—any-thing . . ." and almost added 'My mother was like that,' but, angry at his own thought, said instead, violently, "Martyrs herself to anybody who'll have her."

It was all he could do to keep from pulling her hair under his hand. "You've got the rot of this house worse than I have. Boy, oh boy, you just wait for what's coming, you and this house. I'm going to smoke you out."

He looked at her, hating her as much as the rest, so that when Cinnybug burst in from the dining-room at her most hysterically social, they might have been strangers for all she could tell. She rushed up to Abraham and kissed at him, missing and smacking the air behind his ear. Then she held him out at arm's length, like she would have a little boy, only she had to look up, not down, at him, jabbering all the time.

"Well, if it isn't Abraham, after all these years! Just think! I'm your A'nt Cinnybug. Why, we'd of been right here to welcome you, one of the family like you are, if it hadn't of been that we were up to the vault when you came. Well, let me have a look at you! Isn't this nice, Mary Margaret?"

She turned to Mary Margaret, twittering, "I'll declare I had NO idea he was coming! I wish it could have been at a better time, but never mind, it's an ill wind . . ."

Even Cinnybug ran down at last. She was silent, staring, smiling uncertainly from one to the other of them, wondering when somebody would say something, then adding feebly:

"Here we all are."

"Who told you Abraham was here, A'nt Cinnybug?"

The question was enough to set her off again happily. "A'nt Elemere told me, honey, why, tired as I was I just had to get right up and come right down here to welcome you. After all it isn't as though you were a real stranger even if none of us did know you, blood's thicker'n water. Not that we wouldn't, of course, you look just like your father, a chip off the old block. I reckon ever'body tells you that. I'll declare it's been a long time. How's your father? Why didn't he come?"

"I was the one told to come."

Cinnybug went cold all of a sudden, and she could not hide it. "Told?"

"A Mr. Cadwallader Williams wired me two days ago."

"The very day. Did he? Well I never! Cousin Cad!" Politeness and panic raced in her voice. "Well, you just make yourself right at home and I'll try and find some of the others."

She ran out through the dining-room and stood at the hall door, bawling.

"Amelia! Mary Lee! Jellicoe, where are you?"

Mary Lee could be heard coming nearer, trying coldly to shut her up.

"What are you yelling around for, Cinnybug, today of all days? If you don't have any respect for your own mother . . ."

For once Cinnybug interrupted her.

"Listen here, Mary Lee, do you know who's in there?"

"Who?"

"Abraham, that's who!"

Mary Margaret tried not to look at him, but there he was, listening calmly, taking it all in.

Cinnybug went on, "So you'd better just dry up that kind of talk and get in there and behave to him. . . ."

Mary Lee sounded bitter, more bitter than even Mary Margaret ever heard her. "You tell me why I should after . . ."

"I'll tell you all right! It's not the father, it's the son. Cad sent for him to come. It means he's been remembered!"

"Remembered!" They threw the word at each other like stones. "I might have known. Remembered! Huh! Mighty fine words swallowed to come back, I'll bet! Well, a little promise of money sure does work wonders. . . ."

Mary Lee swept into the kitchen, followed by Cinnybug, straight up to Abraham, while Mary Margaret tried to make it all right by saying:

"Mother, this is Abraham."

Mary Lee stuck out her long hand, blue-backed and lumpy.

"Glad to see you, son. It's a bad time. We should have met in easier circumstances. . . ."

But Abraham was not behaving as he ought. He dropped her hand, and left her high and dry with even her small effort.

"What words have I got to swallow?"

Mary Lee was far too surprised to do anything but meet him on his own kind of battleground. After all, you listened, but you didn't stand up and brag about it.

"What do you mean? Do you mean to tell me you stood there and listened to what I was saying? I never heard such downright brass in all my born days . . ."

Abraham's anger mounted with hers. "O.K. Just tell me what you meant."

"You ought to know what I meant. If you were too young to remember you musta been told. Your father walked through that door one day a long time ago, leaving a lot of fine words about what he thought of us all behind him." She stopped explaining to Abraham and began to accuse him, throwing her hands outward with disgust. "Oh, mighty fine words, scorning everything, talking big; telling us all just what he thought of us. What we had to sit here and listen to was more than your grandmother could stand." Then gradually her attack centred on his presence in the room. "He said he'd never come back, but I notice he wasn't too highfalutin to send you when there was any chance of things being shared out. You'll have to forgive me if I talk in a way that isn't very welcoming, but we're all upset today, and I reckon we say what we think easier."

Abraham mused, forgetting her for a minute.

"It's beginning to clear, what I came here for."

"What's beginning to clear? I should think it was pretty simple, what you came here for. Money."

"A picture."

Mary Lee understood them completely, at once, and took Abraham for as big a fool as she'd taken his father.

"Abey asked you to get something. He always was a sentimental old fool." She flopped a hand outward again, giving him the whole house. "Well, carry away all the junk you like. There's nothing here but a bunch of junk."

Cinnybug couldn't stand it. She complained quickly, whining, "Now, Mary Lee, don't you talk like that! You know Mother promised me the early 'mercan sideboard, why, I had my dining-room designed for it twenty-five years ago just so some day I'd have room."

Mary Lee didn't bother to look at her.

"It's just some junk he wants. Sentimental junk." She pushed open the screen-door.

"Now excuse me. Any other time there'd be a little more to your welcome. But today we're all a little bit on edge."

She went out, letting the door plonk behind her; she sat down straight, folding her arms and her lips, but letting her legs hang limp in the rush-seated rocker, and began to creak gently back and forth, forgetting them, watching out beyond the few trees where the land bent down to the creek.

Cinnybug edged closer to Abraham, too pleased almost to ask, "Do you mean you don't want any money?"

"I didn't say that."

Cinnybug kept from crying. She just said, "Oh," and it was like a little sigh.

Abraham looked out of the door to where he could see Mary Lee's legs bending and straightening in the rhythm of her rocking.

"He always hated being called Abey. He never allowed me to be called by it."

Mary Lee's voice sounded farther away than just the porch. "Mary Margaret, come here. I want a word with you."

"Yes, Mother."

Abraham held her back by both arms, almost hugging her, ignoring Cinnybug, and said, "Don't go if you don't want to. She only wants to bite your arm."

Cinny was surprised enough to forget about the money for a minute. "What kind of talk is that?"

Amelia, hearing voices, quickened her careful navigation of the dining-room and burst in on them, swaying a little but determined at last to carry off a decent welcome. "Hello, Abraham!" She waved her arm like a lone cheerleader. "Welcome to our city!"

Abraham smiled. "Hello, A'nt Amelia."

"You knew me!" Amelia shook her head at him in some surprise.

"I knew you the minute you bent over me in the hammock."

"So you weren't asleep."

"No."

"Just playing possum." She smiled again, less certainly.

"It would have scared you if I'd said anything. You looked all in."

Amelia, the smile not quite gone, just forgotten, began to sidle towards the kitchen cabinet. "Has Mary Lee seen you yet?" she asked over her shoulder.

"Yes."

"Where is she?"

"She's right outside the door." Abraham had recognised Amelia's crab-wise sneaking and he warned, grinning with an understanding which made her fat face coy with complicity. She had arrived at the kitchen cabinet, but at his look she took her hand from the handle of the flour bin, turned, and flopped down at the table. Mary Lee called out again, this time with tight impatience, "Mary Margaret, come here at once!"

"Yes, ma'am." She almost ran out of the door before Abraham could stop her.

He exchanged glances with Amelia and she grunted a little laugh. "Well, the pore youngin's only twenty-seven years old."

Abraham sat down beside her. They both ignored Cinny, who was fidgeting in the shade of the sink, listening.

"I don't get it," he said. "Mary Lee seems to run things, but she's not even a daughter."

"No," Amelia told him, shrugging it all away from her, "it just slipped to her. You know how it is. Cinnybug

82

there was too young. I was just married and only coming back for little stretches. Mother had to have somebody here with her. Your father and mother were here for a little while, right after the war. Then they left." She was already getting tired of explaining, finding excuses. "John went out to Persia in oil. We've been getting letters for a long time. Then he come home and left his youngin here. His wife died out there. Never met her. There just wasn't anybody else. Mary Margaret's father spends most all of his time in one hospital or another. So Mary Lee got to taking over. It was the best thing. This is a big house to run."

Abraham glanced again at the thin legs, bending and straightening as Mary Lee rocked, talking to Mary Margaret in a voice that for once no one else could hear. "That woman would drive me nuts in a week."

Amelia said, following his eye, "Don't pay any attention to her. Mary Lee's all right. It's just her way. Nobody else . . ." She shrugged.

"How long have you been back?" Abraham forced her then to look straight at him and she began to defend herself.

"My husband died! Seven years ago now. I came back for a few weeks to get over things. Buried him here, but not in the vault because they all said that was only for the immediate family. Get over things." She clung to the phrase, trying to remember what it was she had started to tell him. "There wasn't much of a place for me to go. Not with a youngin. Not with Mary Armstrong. So I been here ever since." Then she remembered what it was, waked up a little and really looked at Abraham, proudly.

"I got plans for opening a little antique shop. Not a big one, just a little one, with little tiny things in it." She

83

made a small space in the air with her fingers and looked at it lovingly. "I just love nice things. It's never happened yet, but someday it will. Charles Truxton was a very fine man, and he was as good to me as he could be."

What had been for so long a habit-phrase suddenly sounded defensive. "He left me seven hundred dollars. I was going to start a little store."

"But you never did."

"No. I never did. Charles was very good to me. No. Never did."

"And now you haven't got the seven hundred dollars."

But Amelia had slipped completely away from him. She got up and brushed past him, saying as impersonally as if she had touched a stranger in the street, "Excuse me," and then passed on forgetting both the person and the touch. She wandered away, her footsteps sounding out through the house.

CHAPTER X

WHEN Cinnybug realised she was alone with Abraham, she began to babble across him as she fluttered to the door where she hoped Jellicoe would be dozing on the porch.

"My, my, I must find Jellicoe and tell him you're here. Jelly!" Her voice pierced at the curtain of sleep around him, and he turned in the hammock. "Come around on this side! Come on!" She heard a grunt from him in answer. "We've got a big surprise for you!" She peeked round the screen and saw him beginning to pick himself up like a heavy load out of the old hammock made from bed-springs, covered with a matted-together mattress and scraps of rug.

"Jellicoe always lays around there out of the sun when he can shoo the dog off. He dudn't get much time for naps," she explained over her shoulder to Abraham.

Then, when Jellicoe hadn't come, she jumped to the next thing she could think of.

"Have you had anything to eat?"

"Yes, I have." There was another silence. "Some potato-chips," Abraham added, and wished he hadn't.

"Oh," Cinnybug sighed.

Jellicoe was at the door, inside it, smothering a yawn, then holding out his hand and saying the wrong thing.

"Hi, boy. I heard you'd turned up!"

"Like the bad penny. Yes." Abraham shook his hand.

Catching Cinnybug's eye, Jellicoe stopped the beginnings of a grin and started to apologise. "Now you know I didn't mean anything like that, Abe."

"Nobody ever calls me that." But even though Abraham

tried to soften his answer, Cinnybug gasped with embarrassment, and Jellicoe was afraid to say anything more. They stood there, the three of them, watching each other until Cinnybug couldn't stand the silence any longer. She giggled, and the sound tailed off into words, "It's been a long time."

"A'nt Cinny . . ." Abraham started to speak, but Cinny interrupted him with another giggle, because he was standing nearly a foot over her and calling her 'A'nt'.

"What were the words my father should have swallowed?"

Cinnybug tried to pass it off as something silly. "Oh, I don't know what Mary Lee was talking about. She gets things on her mind. You know!"

"You mean you do."

"Honest, I don't, do I, Jellicoe?"

"Why didn't I ask Amelia?"

"Oh, she won't tell you anything!"

"So there is something to tell!"

Mary Lee, hearing it all, called out to Cinnybug before she could make any more trouble than she had already.

"Cinny, come out here."

Cinnybug fled, stumbling out of the door. "—Sure, Mary Lee, sure, I'm coming."

Mary Lee only said, "Now sit down here and see how long you can keep your damn-fool mouth shut." Then there was silence on the porch. Abraham turned towards it to go out after them, and even Jellicoe knew that somehow he had better slow this man down before he'd started something that wouldn't be finished until the migraines clamped and the doors all slammed and the voices were pitched almost high enough to make the dog howl.

"What do you do for a living, Abe?" Then he stopped short, remembering too late about the name.

But Abraham was turned to him, looking as happy as somebody about to start off on a trip.

"I make things."

"Oh yeah. Things."

"Trouble. I make trouble." Abraham's desire to laugh was so great he had to turn his back on Jellicoe. He added weakly, trying to control it, "What is it around here . . .?"

Jellicoe looked all round, not understanding, even at the ceiling, where he saw only the same old kitchen paper and the wheeling flies. "What you looking for?" he asked politely.

But when he looked down again Abraham was staring at him so that he felt caught in a joke.

"The bomb. Before the blast there's always a silence. Just like this. Everybody waiting . . ."

"Oh, you were Over There! I couldn't go. I . . ."

There was a thunderous knock on the screen-door to the back gate. It made both the men wheel round. A boy of about fourteen, grown out of his jeans and high-coloured shirt in all directions, was standing peering through the door into the familiar house, which for the day had become a strange and almost sacred place. He remembered to say "Telegram", holding the yellow envelope up beside his head.

Jellicoe opened the door and reached for it. "Hi, Tig, what is it?" he said, worried.

"Condolences," the boy told him, now taking in the stranger. "Oh." Jellicoe fished in his pocket and found a dime. Tig pocketed it and ran off, wondering all the way what you ought to say to people in grief, whether you ought to say thank you, thanks a lot, or something like that.

Mary Lee had come in from the porch at the sound of

the boy's voice; she grabbed the telegram out of Jellicoe's hand and began to rip it open in little fast jerks. "Here, give the thing to me. I'm the only one capable of reading it today. Taking it in." She was silent for a minute, reading for all of them. "Oh."

"What's it say?" Cinnybug had to ask before Mary Lee was ready to tell.

Mary Lee wiggled her shoulder impatiently to shut her up, and went on reading. Then she was ready to tell.

"It's from John," she began and she was right back to her funeral weight. "He says he just got our telegram. Listen. He says here, 'To the Passmores, prostrated by news stop my condolences in time of deepest grief stop sorry too far to come to funeral stop love to John Junior signed John'." She held the telegram still where she'd read it, poised, but no longer looking at it.

Cinnybug began to cry. "Poor John. He loved his mother. Isn't it just awful he can't be with us today? Mother would have wanted him here. Mother!"

Jellicoe found his handkerchief somewhere and began to dab at Cinny's face. "Never mind, honey, never mind." He put his arm around her shoulders. "Never mind. Everything's going to be all right!"

But Cinny found his arm too heavy; after all, she'd been so nervous all day she'd wanted to scream at the weight of her black dress and her shoulder straps; the thought made her voice rise, made her forget tears. "I just can't stand any more. I just can't."

Then she let out, as if they all didn't know and have it weighing on their minds too, what was really upsetting her; what was bolted down in her mind as solid as a rail to a tie while everything else flittered through.

"Abraham!" like a cry, "what do you do for a living?"

"I drill oil-wells."

Cinnybug felt suddenly sick with joy. "You mean you've got money?"

"A lot of money."

She was over the edge into hysteria and she began to babble, laughing, with the telegram tears still falling down her face.

"So you really did just come down here to get a picture! He really did, Jelly, he did just come to . . ."

Mary Lee crushed the telegram in her hand and forced it into her pocket. "Shut up, Cinny!"

Cinnybug was completely silent.

A'nt Elemere, pushing her way through the group still standing at the door as they'd gathered to hear the telegram, muttered, " 'Scuse me," and tiptoed over to the stove.

Mary Lee watched her go. "A'nt Elemere, what are you doing pussyfooting around in here right now?"

A'nt Elemere got out a big spoon and began to stir the beans again, not bothering to turn round but answering, "I'm taking my green-beans offn your shoulders, Miss Mary Lee."

Mary Lee had found something besides a piece of paper to take her painful spite. "You're getting sassier every day."

But A'nt Elemere wouldn't crush like telegrams, or daughters, or flittery cousins. "If I wudn't here, you'd be calling me a sassy nigger," she said complacently. "Seem like they don't nobody but coloured people use that word no more."

Abraham ignored the rest and went over and leaned on the sink beside A'nt Elemere, watching her potter around the stove while he ignored the others.

"A'nt Elemere, what did my father say when he left here?"

Her face went blank of every personal thing about her. There was just coloured woman left, but not A'nt Elemere. "I disremember. He said so much I disremember it all."

"You're a liar." But he couldn't change her.

"Yessir."

"You didn't hate them. They told me so."

He couldn't even blackmail her.

"No, sir."

He admitted defeat.

"But you're not going to tell me."

"No, sir."

"Why not?"

A'nt Elemere drew herself up from her bosom, her elbows stuck out while she felt for her knot of brown-black fuzzy hair, straightening it, and, in the process, putting a large hairpin in her mouth and talking through it as if she'd given up paying any attention to anything he might have to say to her.

"Good servants dudn't repeat what they done pick up from time to time," as if any damn fool ought to know that.

"A'nt Elemere, you're an old fraud."

She stuck the hairpin back, wilfully misunderstanding him and both of them knowing it.

"No, I ain't, Mr. Abraham. I ain't never stole no money in all my life, Lord Jesus listen to him!" She clucked on to herself, grinning.

Mary Lee marched past Cinnybug and Jellicoe and stood stock still in the middle of the room, ready and impatient to 'get it over with', 'have it out once and for all'.

"If you've got anything on your mind, young man, I wish you'd come right out with it instead of talking all this foolishness. You're just like your father. It's just him coming out in you. He always was grinning around like he knew some joke. What are you sniffing around for anyway? If you want to know anything, whyn't you ask your father?"

"He's dead."

A'nt Elemere dropped her spoon on to the floor with a clatter and hid her face in her hands.

Cinnybug talked.

"Oh, how awful! We'd of come if we'd of known! Nobody told us!"

Mary Lee was furious, not about the death but about the conventions of the death. "Do you mean to tell me that that woman didn't even bother to tell us when one of Miss Anna Mary's own sons had passed away?"

"He didn't want her to."

Mary Lee snorted. "You mean he was downright ashamed to talk about us!"

"He died laughing at you."

Mary Lee went white, sick-looking, but before she could answer, Cadwallader, innocent and sad, came in from the dining-room to do his duty by Abraham, still pulling down his shirt-cuffs after putting his coat back on.

"Well, if it isn't young Abraham!"

He was delighted, reading nothing in their faces.

"You'd know him anywhere, now, wouldn't you? Welcome home, my boy. I'm sorry I wasn't here when you came, but . . ."

Mary Lee interrupted.

"Cad, what on earth do you mean by not telling us that Abraham was coming?"

Cadwallader began to apologise long before he decided what to say.

"Well, Mary Lee, I didn't know for certain. You know

how it is. All the arrangements to be made, I reckon it just slipped my mind."

"Slipped your mind!"

Cadwallader's apology faltered at her disgust. Then he went on:

"Well, I didn't think you all ought to have more to think about on a day like this. I just didn't want there to be any more trouble than there need to be."

He pleaded for peace, turning to Abraham, "You understand, son. All that there was to do, and you a close relation they hadn't seen in so long."

He went closer and touched Abraham's shoulder, forgetting even Mary Lee.

"One of the last things your grandmother said to me was: 'Son' (she called everybody son), she said, 'Son, you get that boy back down here,' she said, 'I'm sick and tired of all this trouble,' she said, 'I'm an old woman'; but she was a handsome woman, just as handsome as you could imagine, almost up to her passing. 'Get him home,' she said, 'I'd like to see the boy. If I can't, I'd like him to know I don't bear no grudge.'"

Cinnybug had been trying to ask, finally interrupting, "How did you know where he was, Cousin Cad?"

"We been in touch. After Abraham died . . ."

Mary Lee stepped closer to him and he dropped his hand from Abraham's shoulder.

"You knew? You knew all the time?"

"Well, Mary Lee, I'd sworn to Miss Anna Mary not to tell you all. She was more than strong-minded, as you all know. She said, sitting right in that big overstuffed chair in the living-room she liked so much, 'Cad,' she said, 'I can't stand them youngins talking about Abraham again after all these years. Let him rest in peace.' Then what else she said is still private."

He'd always known that sooner or later he'd have to deal with Mary Lee and he was determined she wouldn't get him riled.

"Cadwallader, you're one of the purest-bred damn fools I ever heard tell of." Her voice was still low. That was one thing. "Do you mean to tell me you let that old woman wrap you around her little finger so you kept everything from us?"

"Now don't be like that, Mary Lee. It's all long past. I don't see any sense in stirring up a lot of old trouble and neither did Miss Anna Mary."

It was the wrong time for Julik to come in, all set to be sociable after his nap.

"Did somebody call me?"

"No." Mary Lee was so off-hand that Julik, half asleep, couldn't yet hear the sting of that small word.

He smiled, explaining, "I thought I heard somebody call me. I do that sometimes. I . . ."

Mary Lee's mouth went awry with scorn.

"Call you! Hunh! I couldn't pronounce your name!"

Julik stepped back and looked square at her, surprised at first; then he turned away and almost ran out of the screen-door to the side-yard.

Abraham had hardly seen it all. He was intent on keeping Cadwallader to the point. As soon as the door slammed, he attacked him.

"What old trouble? Tell me, what old trouble?"

Cadwallader tried to head him off the point in the past, just as he had Mary Lee, standing between them and making half-finished calming pats towards each of them in turn, missing them both with his useless-looking scrubbed hands.

"Now, son, you better forget all that. It's a long time ago and I'm sure everybody's sorry. You know, one time everybody lets their temper run away with them, and then there's trouble none of us want. She wouldn't have wanted it all brought up again."

Mary Margaret came in from the porch and touched her mother's arm gently to draw her attention.

"Mother," she whispered.

"What?" Mary Lee shook her hand away and ignored the girl, interrupting at a time when she couldn't be bothered with her.

But Mary Margaret was so still in the room, after the strength of men talking and the rising of the argument, that she created a silence, drew their eyes to her and even her remark, as intimate as a secret, spun round the room and included them all.

"What did you say to Julik?" she asked her mother.

"I didn't say anything to him. I hardly even spoke to him."

"He's out there and he won't talk at all. He's white, like somebody had slapped him. What did you say to him, Mother?"

Her question hardened, and Mary Lee jerked herself out of her grasp.

"Mary Margaret, how dare you use that tone of voice with me?"

Amelia, swinging open the dining-room door, caught the two of them for a second, frozen in a pantomime on the edge of quarrelling.

"Oh, oh, what's all the shootin' about?"

Mary Lee shut her up. "You keep out of this."

But the question had unfrozen them, toppled them into fighting.

"Tell me what you did!" Mary Margaret forgot her calm pitch and let out a woman song.

"I didn't do a damn thing," Mary Lee sang with her.

"You did. You turned your viciousness on to Julik. He's the one person in the world I'd protect from you. Let him alone, do you hear me? Do you hear me? I won't have you hurting him. Julik is worth more than all of you put together!"

Mary Lee looked round the kitchen at the silent watchers.

"Are you all going to just stand there and let her talk to me like that?"

Amelia laughed with a snort: "We been waiting for somebody to for twenty-five years."

Mary Lee spoke then, remembering where she was and who were all ears, with an icy dignity, thrown on as quickly as a coat.

"You'd talk to me like that! Talk to your own mother like that in front of the kind of people I despise. After all I've been through; you ought to be ashamed!"

It was the loathing in her look that made Mary Margaret realise something she oughtn't and weaken with sorrow at it, so she tried to make amends.

"Oh, Mother, I didn't mean to. Oh, Mother, I'm sorry if I hurt you." She reached a hand to touch her, but Mary Lee twisted away, too breathless with anger to do much more than whisper, "Don't put your hands all over me. Hurt me! You couldn't. You just disgust me."

John Junior bolted in through the screen-door like a sudden gust of wind, blinded by his own tears, howling as he breathed. He felt a way through the kitchen full of grown-up legs to A'nt Elemere and clutched her apron, bowing his head as if he'd been whipped. She took him by the shoulders, gently this time, and spoke as lovingly as she held him: "For the love of the Lamb, little sweetheart, what's the matter?"

John Junior's face was streaked with dirt and tears and

snot. His glasses were filthy from rubbing it into a mess of shame and sorrow with his tight grimy fist.

What the matter was all came out, with just time to sob between the shoals of trouble. "A'nt Elemere, my grand-maw's dead and Mary Armstrong says I won't be able to live here any more and she says my socks always stink and nobody will play with me and nobody likes me!"

She took off his small gold-rimmed spectacles and started to clean them on her apron-corner behind his back as he buried his head again deep against her thick legs. Mary Lee couldn't stand it any longer. She grabbed John Junior, lifted him by the arms, and thrust him in front of her on to the table, screaming over his sobs to stop him.

"Shut up! Shut up! Shut up! John Junior, what's the matter with you? Stop that noise and tell me! Tell me, do you hear? If you yell like that you'll be sick and I'll give you castor oil! Castor oil! I'll give you castor oil!"

Then she was quiet, shaking, and so was John Junior, blind-eyed and new-born-looking without his glasses, staring at her.

CHAPTER XI

AMELIA thought she heard somebody on the sun-porch, but wasn't sure. "Lord God Almighty, it's hot," she said, not caring whether they heard her or not. She stripped off her shoes and stockings and flung herself down across the bed. Nobody answered her, so she forgot, lying down, and sighed to herself. Far away in the downstairs hall the clock whirred and chimed six times. A little evening breeze from the hillside, almost within reach of the window, caught the long net curtain, then her hair. She turned her cooled head as if it had been stroked, already half asleep.

Julik knocked lightly, then, getting no answer, louder, and stuck his head in at the door. The room he saw was like the one that he and Mary Margaret had slept in, so like it that for a minute he didn't realise he was in the wrong room. The same white carved-wood bedroom fireplace with gas logs; the same brown and chrome criss-crossed linoleum, with slippery woven mats flung over it in patches; the same net lace curtains, still with a jaunty air as if a long time ago they had been 'the very thing'; but even before he saw Amelia on the bed, Julik knew it was not the right room.

It was the dresser that told him. It was made of ivory wood trimmed with thin gilt lines, and to see it there was like discovering a frilly parasol blown down a warehouse street. It was covered with a lace mat under glass, and on the glass, like toy ships on a model ocean, were Amelia's belongings; her pin-tray of imitation ivory, her pin-cushion made like a hard red heart, her snapshots, birthday cards and Valentines, and a few 'studies' of the family,

97

egg-shaped on squares of white paper, some in silver frames, and some stuck into the mirror, and long since curling outwards with age. But among the whole collection there was not a single one that could possibly have been Charles Truxton Edwards. Amelia had spilled powder sometime across the surface. It covered the objects with a thin film-like age. The powder-box leaned crazily against the pin-tray it matched, celluloid with a dirty puff on a stick thrown across it. It looked so neglected, so personal, that Julik backed out again as if he'd happened on a woman dressing and didn't want to be caught.

But Amelia struggled up, frightened, and called, "Who is it?" It brought him back into the room.

"Oh, it's you, Mr. Rosen! Lord, there don't nobody knock around here. Come on in."

He still stood, half in, half out of the door. "I was just looking for Mary." He saw her bent and bunioned feet, and for a second felt sorry for the poor woman, whose name he couldn't remember, lying propped on one elbow on the bed.

"Haven't seen her, son. Come on in." Amelia helped herself up, and fumbled her feet into her shoes.

"Well, if you want me to," he hesitated, his injury coming back. He sat down in the rocking-chair by the fireplace, but kept it from rocking, watching her.

"Lordy, it's hot," she said, twisting round so that she could see him.

"Not so bad as it was," he told her carefully; then, launching his hurt, belligerently, "I guess I'm not very welcome around here."

Amelia was surprised. Then she remembered. "Lordy, son, you don't want to go taking every little thing so seriously." She snorted. "You won't last long around this boarding-house if you do. Mary Lee was just teasing you." She was sure he didn't hear her. "What do you care, anyway, smart as you are?" When he still didn't answer she gave him up and lay down again, talking this time to herself, but letting him hear if he wanted to.

"I remember . . . Lord, it doesn't seem more than yesterday. I started getting myself all dressed up to go out with my best beau. They thought they'd play a little joke on me, so Mary Lee offered to frizz my hair. She liked a little bit of fun in those days. Boy, did she frizz it! I went out of here looking like a singed chicken's ass. Abraham . . . that's the boy down there's father . . . he didn't think it was so funny." She was silent for a minute, wandering off on her own dreamy track, then she turned her head to Julik again. "That was the day my beau bought me flowers for the first time . . . store-bought flowers. He sure did put on the dog!"

Julik's chair creaked as he leaned forward to interrupt, "She wasn't kidding me!"

"That was just before he took me to Tennessee. Have you ever been to Tennessee?" She gazed at him through the brass pattern of the bed-end.

"I hardly been outa New York. I been working too hard since I was fourteen . . ."

"Tennessee's so pretty, right up near the North Carolina border. We had the cutest little house. Wait a minute, son, I'll show you a picture." She got up and walked carefully round him, sliding her untied shoes. "It's not very good. It doesn't show the lovely slope down at the front." She blew powder from a snapshot in one of the silver frames and handed it to him, pushing it between his fingers as she hung on to the chair-back and nearly made him rock with her weight.

He glanced at it politely, seeing a little white clapboard cottage, with a front porch, nothing to rave about, just like a million others even in places like New Jersey that he knew about. He was so annoyed with the woman that he nearly told her so. But when Amelia, gazing at the picture over his shoulder as intently as if she'd never seen it before, sighed and said, "My goodness, it was a pretty little old place," he didn't answer at once, but leaned across her and set it back, carefully, on the dresser.

Amelia looked down at him as if she'd just discovered he was there at all, and smiled. "Mr. Rosen, how would you like a little drink?" she asked him.

"I'm thirty-four years old and I never been farther than Jersey City when I met Mary," he answered.

"Isn't she the sweetest little old thing? Now I'm going to pep you up with a little drink."

"You people down here . . ." he began, and stopped.

"Just a little shot to perk us up." Amelia carefully hoisted a bottle out of the closet and poured a drink into a water glass.

"Thanks," he said, when she handed it to him. He thought of asking for water in it and then decided against it. Behind him, Amelia tipped the bottle up to her lips, then went back to lie down.

"Aren't you having one?" Julik turned the glass in his hand.

"You go ahead," she said, lying down again. "Gwan! It's good for you. The little things of life." She began to shout, "To hear her go on, you'd think it was a damn crime for a person to want a little peace and quiet once in a while!"

"Who, Mary?" he asked, trying to follow.

"Mary Lee!" Amelia flung herself back on the bed and was quiet. "What's the matter with a little fun once in a while?"

"I never had much time for it," he told her. "You wouldn't know. You've never had to teach. I hate it, all that time wasted." He tipped his drink back and finished it. "Maybe it's over."

Amelia watched him lazily. "Mr. Rosen, you're not a bad-looking man if you'd put a little meat on your bones."

"My mama was always trying. So does Mary. It's worry. I can't get enough sleep." Amelia let her eyes go past him and stop, staring at the vacancy of the ceiling.

"Charles Truxton ate like a horse," she interrupted, and went on staring, now out of the window to where she could nearly touch the trees on the hill. "When Charles Truxton was home . . . but then, he travelled so much . . .

"You travelled much?" she asked politely, remembering for a second that she had company. Julik looked at her, smiling there, slouched across the bed, and realised at last that she had been drinking.

"Charles Truxton covered the three states—weeks on end." She laughed. "Mary Lee's sure horsing around today. Lord, she gets my goat sometimes, horse-arsing around. She's just born to organise trouble. . . ."

"Well, thanks for the drink," Julik said. "I'd better find Mary. . . ."

"Aw, don't go off like that!" Amelia jumped up from the bed. "You let that youngin alone." She came over between Julik and the door, suddenly as mad as a wet hen.

Julik started round her. "Look, lady, lay off!"

But she caught him by the arm. "Now you just sit down, Mr. Rosen. We're going to be friends." She pushed him back towards the chair. "What's your hurry, drinking my liquor?"

"You people . . ."

"What about us people?" She stood over him.

"Nothing."

She sat back down, forgetting she'd pushed him, as soft as she'd been hard the minute before, swaying and dreaming again.

"I've always wanted to go to New York. It's one of my secret ambitions. Tell me all about New York."

Julik tried. "You've got to live there. Get caught up in it. It's tough—tougher than you people down here know. First thing I remember" (he started to rock at last) "was an eight-storey tenement with only one toilet."

She had lain down again and closed her eyes.

"Nobody ever flushed it," he called to her. "It stank up the whole hall."

But she didn't open her eyes.

"When my dad died, Mama moved in with my grandparents. Things were terrible, too many of us, not enough to eat—terrible. I was ashamed; you people have no idea. All those dark red lampshades with fringe, how could I explain what they meant? The smell of grease right down the hall when you were coming home, and everybody screaming so you couldn't think. Then my grandfather would step in and shut everybody up. He was the boss, always the boss. I was his favourite. At Passach he would choose me. You see, I was the youngest. And if he had a nickel to spare, even a dime . . ." Julik was rocking slowly, caught up in his story, telling it carefully to himself, taking for granted that the woman on the bed would listen.

"We were more cultured than most of the others; little bit better people, you know? My grandfather started me on my music. Mama said it was crazy, but he was the boss. He's still alive, still believes in me. He says to me, You start out good anyway in music. At least you're a Jew. . . ."

Amelia rearranged her back on the bed without opening her eyes.

"He isn't afraid of talking about the soul, things like that, you know?"

She sat up politely. "Why, Mr. Rosen, I didn't know you were Jewsh! Well, I'll declare . . ."

"Didn't you?" he grinned at her self-conscious pronunciation of the word. "Say Jew," he ordered her.

She was as solemn as she could be and still be half-drunk, and slopped all over the bed quilt. "Lordy, you've got a chip on your shoulder all right!"

"I'm just telling you the facts. When you grow up with it . . ."

She interrupted, not hearing him. "Mary Lee said you were foreign, but she didn't say Jewish."

"My grandfather doesn't speak a word of English. Yiddish, Hebrew, Russian. He's a smart man."

"Well, what do you know? I reckon you think we're just plain dumb. All those languages." Amelia made her eyes wide to seem interested. "Would you like another little drink?"

"No, thanks," Julik got up again. "Now if you can spare me, I'm going downstairs."

"We've been around here so long we just don't bother . . ." She didn't get up.

"Yeah, you stuck yourselves in, you people." He was at the door, "Thanks for the drink, anyway."

As he closed the door behind him, Amelia shrugged and got up. "Oh, Mr. Rosen, you bite like a dawg," she said happily to the mirror, patting her marcell. Then, as she listened more carefully for footsteps, she found the bottle again.

CHAPTER XII

U P in the attic, still hot with the last of the sun, though it was almost evening and the rest of the house had grown cool, Mary Lee squatted on her thin haunches and tore paper. Before her on the floor stood boxes, piles of old magazines, and a book or two, swollen twice its size with having things stuck between the pages.

It took two long rips, with her hands turning as if she were wringing out clothes, to divide one of the thick letters, already grown yellow, hardly legible for age, but something, like all the rest spread around the floor, that had belonged to Miss Anna Mary which she'd put away a long time ago and forgotten or not. A pile of playing cards, big ones with bicycles on the back, were puffed out with damp and age so that they stacked drunkenly, spilling away from each other. Mary Lee was adding them in little groups to the pile of waste, letting them slide slowly out of her hand, like some card-trick into a hat. But she didn't notice where they fell; she was listening to the voices of the children, playing way down below her on the side-porch, waiting for supper to begin.

She couldn't hear what they were saying, so she gave a little jerk to her shoulders to tear her eyes from their blank staring and set to work again among the papers. The pulp books of ghost stories, the Church of God pamphlets, an advertisement of a Half Moon, a pile of unused Sunday School good-conduct cards, suddenly a peacock feather, long and loose among the trash, all but its bright eye worn to brown fringe, a poster of a revival meeting showing a young man with his hair slicked back like Wallace Reed, and his hands in doubtful attitude across his chest and

clasped together, SUNDAY Jesus Means Business.
MONDAY The Skeleton Key to the Golden Gates.
TUESDAY Die in the Canona Valley: RISE IN
CHRIST. Mary Lee threw them all on the pile, which
had grown so high that it tumbled backwards under one
of the brass beds.

She ripped the string from around a pile of letters,
settled herself more easily on the floor and let them drop
loose into her spread-out lap.

"Mary Lee? Mary Leeye?" Cinnybug called out in a
big half-whisper from the floor below, and almost as soon
as she had called, her head appeared above the floor of
the attic.

"Oh, there you are."

Mary Lee didn't answer. She had begun to sort the
letters, ripping each one through the middle and throwing
it on the waste paper.

Cinny looked around over her shoulder. "I'll declare,
it's still all I can make myself do to come up here. It sure
is scary, isn't it, Mary Lee?"

"It is for those that scare," said Mary Lee, throwing
another letter on the pile. Cinny settled herself on a pile
of quilts on the bed.

"What are you doing, Mary Lee? Hadn't you better
wait . . .?"

"Oh, it's just some junk of your mother's. No use to
keep it around littering up the place. Just a lot of junk
she had laying around here for years and wouldn't let
anybody lay hands on."

"Don't you think we all . . ."

Mary Lee sucked her teeth at the litter on the floor.

"There's nothing here hardly worth the burning." She
was scornful. "I'll declare, the things she kept! A lot of
trashy books and some letters from people I never even

heard of, sister this, and brother that." She tore at another letter and threw it on the rest.

"What's that?" Cinny's eye caught on to a bit of bright-ness as quickly as a magpie and she jumped down from the bed to pick it up. But it was only a Christmas card, bright blue, with the Wise Men of the East going towards a little sand-coloured village with the Star of Bethlehem hanging over it like a bright electric light. Inside there was a message, *God Bless Sister Anna Mary on Christmas 1929, Brother Beedie* in careful bad writing.

"Hunh," said Cinny, "I remember that year—that was when he got religion right after he came out of jail. Mother's had him laying around here ever since. What in the world would she of kept a thing like that for?"

"Don't ask me." Mary Lee had destroyed the packet of letters, and she picked up another one.

"Mother thought they were all just fine till she sneaked in one day on Brother Beedie's girl, only nine years old, stealing her Florida water and sprinkling it all over her little bare jezebel." Cinnybug giggled. "I thought it was some little bit of cloth," she explained, throwing the card back on the trash heap.

"What did you want to do? Sew yourself up some little old tacky collar? I'll declare you're as tacky as your mother." Mary Lee was already half-way through the next packet of letters.

Cinny watched the pile grow larger. "Mary Lee, it dudn't seem right on the very day, getting into all her things."

"It's about time, from what we heard this afternoon. You never can tell what your mother kept back from us all in her old age. I'm not going in there tonight without making sure, I'll tell you that right now."

"Well, I just thought it didn't seem right."

"You better be glad somebody around here is doing a little thinking. Are you going to help, or are you going back downstairs? Here, hand me that basket, and start helping to pile some of this junk in it."

Cinnybug bent over the pile, holding the basket close beside her. She made a little squeal of pleasure. "Look here, Mary Lee. Here's a picture of me when I was little. Mother musta kept it special, not in the album, I mean."

But when she drew it out Mary Lee had torn it in two, neatly, through the middle.

"Well, I'll declare!" Mary Lee held up a newspaper clipping, then put it down secretly into her lap and started to read, bending over it. Cinny craned over.

"What's that?"

"Nothing."

"Whyn't you throw it away, then?"

Mary Lee made a 'shhhut' noise to stop Cinny interrupting her. She went on reading.

Mary Lee Elecky, the daughter of Mr. and Mrs. Samuel J. Elecky, was married on Saturday at twelve o'clock at the First Methodist Church South to Mr. Nathaniel Longridge, of Palmyra, West Virginia. The church, banked with seasonal rambler roses, made a beautiful setting for the radiant bride, who was dressed in white voile, with a white lace veil which is a family heirloom. Miss Elecky was educated at Montmorency High School where she was valedictorian of her class. Her higher education took place at Miss Mimpson's Seminary. She has been for the past two years president of the Younger Women's Suffrage League, and is prominent in local theatricals. Miss Elecky's father has been for the past eighteen years associated with the Intercounty Fuel and Power Company. Mrs. Elecky, the former Miss Virginia Myers, is of a prominent local family. Mr. Longridge is associated with the Century Colliery Company.

He was educated at the State University where he took a degree of Bachelor of Arts. He is the son of Geoffrey Longridge, of Palmyra, a distant relative of Col. Longridge of Civil War fame.

Whatever more there had been to the clipping had been torn away.

"Gosh, what'd she want to keep all that kind of stuff for?" Cinnybug got back at Mary Lee for tearing her picture.

"Dammit, Cinny, gwan downstairs and let me alone. I came up here with a headache and I don't want to be bothered with you." Mary Lee looked at the clipping again, then tore it slowly across and threw it on the pile with the rest.

Cinnybug went off down the stairs, not daring to look behind her until she was past the first-floor landing. She found Amelia, still stretched out on her bed barefooted, watching the hillside out of the window.

"Mary Lee's up there into all Mother's things. I don't think . . ."

"Aw, let her alone. Nothing up there but a bunch of junk. Anything important Mother would of put in the bank vault." She turned her back on Cinny, heaved over in the bed, and closed her eyes.

Cinny slumped down beside her, just as Mary Armstrong slipped into the sewing-room next door. The whirr of the sewing-machine made both the women jump. Cinny ran to the door.

Mary Armstrong was pounding away at the fancy wrought-iron treadle with both her small feet, making the needle go so fast she couldn't see it dive and lift out of the table, sending the wheel skidding round so that the crossbars ran in and out of each other under her fist.

Amelia roused herself from the bed and called, "Mary Armstrong, I thought I told you to leave that machine alone." She said it so weakly that Mary Armstrong couldn't hear her through the throddle of the machine.

"It's not good for it to run without any material under the needle," Cinny yelled, explaining. Mary Armstrong took her feet off the treadle.

"Hell, she knows that." Amelia lay back down on the bed. The sewing-machine had run down and was silent.

"Now run on out, honey, I'm trying to have a little rest," she murmured to Cinny as if she were a child, too.

As Cinnybug started down the big front stairs, she heard the whirr of the sewing-machine, faintly behind her, starting up again. Amelia had evidently got past caring, because it went on and on until she was out of earshot.

She pranced out of the front door on to the main porch. Jellicoe and Cadwallader sat side by side in high rockers, watching the empty road.

"What are you two boys up to?" Cinnybug interrupted.

"Nothing, honey; setting and thinkin'." Jellicoe grinned at her but it changed into a yawn.

"Or sometimes you jest set!" hooted Cinny, catching on. She plopped down among the chintz pillows of the swing.

Nobody said anything. Cadwallader hadn't looked round or stopped the slight rhythm of his rocking.

But when Cinny started to swing lightly he said:

"For Lord's sake, Cinny, honey, can't you keep that swing quiet?"

"It needs a little oil." She looked up at the big hooks in the roof where the chains rubbed, and then sat very still, waiting for supper.

"Miss Mary Lee? Miss Mary Lee?" A'nt Elemere pulled her bulk up the stairs by the rails, calling all the time.

High above her she heard Mary Lee's voice.

"What do you want?"

Looking up, she saw her peering over the attic banisters down the stair well.

"Is it all right if we eat in the kitchen? Can't nobody but Solly put that dine-room table up again and he ain't coming back till morning."

"Well, I reckon we'll have to." Mary Lee was impatient. "Reckon we'll have to do everything in the kitchen if it comes to that. Oh, Lord." Her head disappeared, and A'nt Elemere saw just her fingers, tracing up the banisters back to the attic.

"Well, supper's ready, then," she announced.

Cinnybug heard her from the porch and jumped up.

"Come on, boys, let's eat this dirty little bite!"

"Come on, Cad, or we'll wait for you like one hog waits for another," called Jellicoe back to Cadwallader, who hadn't even moved in his chair.

CHAPTER XIII

BY the time supper was over, the twilight had almost ended, and in the near darkness the space between the house, the trees, the corn cribs, the chicken-coops, had lengthened like the shadows. A'nt Elemere, shaking the table-cloth out in great swinging flaps over the edge of the side-porch, could just barely see John Junior, running down among the trees near the creek. She turned back into the kitchen, folding the big cloth, took it back into the dining-room and stowed it into the early American sideboard.

As she was finishing the last of the dishes, Mary Lee came in from the dining-room, and switched on the electric light as she passed, making the twilight outside the window go completely dark, and signalling the start of the evening. The light sawed a path through it out of the windows and the screen-door, all the way down towards the coops, but petered out before it got there. John Junior's form disappeared.

"What you want to sit around here in the dark for, A'nt Elemere, I don't know. You'll end up breaking all the dishes."

Since A'nt Elemere's sitting around had consisted of washing-up after nine people, she didn't answer; she just thought.

Mary Lee drummed on the screen, looking out, then turned.

"Let me know when you're finished, so we can start."

A'nt Elemere went on drying up, stacking the dishes on to the big table.

"I'm almost washed-up, Miss Mary Lee. Almost."

Mary Lee bent down, searching through the kitchen cabinet.

"Where's the molasses can?"

"I ain't seen it."

"Everything gets all wheewhawed on a day like this. Everything gets out of place." She found the can, hidden behind the cereal boxes where it didn't belong, jerked it out and slammed the door.

"Lordy, I'm tired," she murmured as she went out of the screen-door. "I wish we'd start."

Cinny held open the dining-room door and looked in, but Mary Lee had disappeared, and there was only A'nt Elemere, drying the dishes in the harsh kitchen light.

"Where's Miss Mary Lee?"

A'nt Elemere motioned out of the window with her head.

"Out feeding the chickens."

Cinny came in.

"She's late."

"She reckoned Effie'd do it, but Effie went home."

A'nt Elemere had begun to put the dishes away, stomping back and forth across the floor so that Cinny had to get out of her way.

"She musta thought it was Sunday."

"Who?"

"Effie musta."

Cinny fidgeted around the room and then said quietly:

"Are you almost finished? We oughta get started."

"Almost." She went on putting away the dishes, neither slower nor faster than she had before.

Cinny ran out of the screen-door on to the side-porch, then seemed to forget why she was in such a hurry, for she sat down in the rocker, pulling it behind her to where she could get a good view of the kitchen. John Junior nearly walked over her, coming up to the door, carrying a large preserving jar.

"John Junior, come right back here and say excuse me," Cinny called after him.

John Junior backed up, still intent on the jar, and said, "Excuse me, A'nt Cinny," neither knowing nor caring if he'd passed in front of his aunt, or stepped on her foot. He flopped down at the kitchen table, put the jar in front of him and rested his chin on the table so that he could stare straight into it.

"What you got in there?" A'nt Elemere poked her head down near his.

"Lightning bugs."

"Oh." She straightened up and began to gather another stack of dishes to take to the cabinet.

"Ain't it time for you to go to bed, John Junior?"

He paid no attention, but after a while said:

"A'nt Elemere."

"Hunh?"

"Why can't you say dead when somebody is dead?" He straightened up and watched her.

"Why do you have to say gone before or passed over or gone to glory when it's a person?"

A'nt Elemere went on working, not looking at him.

"I don't know, honey. You just do 'cause the Bible says there ain't no such thing as dyin'." She knew before she'd finished that that hadn't been the right answer.

"You mean grandmaw might come back and ha'nt us?" John Junior was scared, but enjoying it.

"No, honey, no." She began to stack the glasses. "You dies in the flesh but you doan die in the spirit." She was still for a minute. "You pass over," she said, coming back to the table. John Junior was so still she thought she'd finished with him.

113

Then he said, "Over what?"

"Oh, the pearly gates. I don't know." She was annoyed. "You quit askin' so many questions. It just ain't polite to say dead when it's a person. That's why. And if you ain't got good manners Miss Mary Lee'll tan your hide." She stumbled and one of the glasses flew out of her hand.

"Now look what you went and made me do!"

"I did not." He forgot about humans and went back to watching his bugs, with his head down, his eyes against the jar.

"A'nt Elemere."

"Hunh?" She was sweeping up the glass, holding the dust-pan with her foot.

"Do you know what I'm gonna do?" He didn't wait for her to answer.

"I'm gonna take these lightning bugs and I'm gonna go out in the woods, and when I see something that needs looking at, if I have these lightning bugs with me in the bottle then I won't need a flashlight, I'll just use these lightning bugs. . . ."

"Unhunh," said A'nt Elemere, wiping away the last of the damp on the drain-board and wringing out the rag.

"If you squash a lightning bug the tail just keeps on being light for a minute. . . ."

A'nt Elemere filled the top of the coffee-pot with fresh grounds.

"It's dead in front, but it isn't dead at the back. . . ."

Mary Lee came in quickly from the back path.

"John Junior, why aren't you in bed?"

He had begun to unfold himself from the chair when he heard her voice. "Yes, ma'am." He began to mooch towards the dining-room.

She followed him out, speeding him up as she came nearer.

"You get a good wash. I'm going to come up there and look to see." She went out after him, swinging the door.

Cinny pushed open the screen-door and stood in it.

"Oh, I wish we'd go on and start." Then she noticed A'nt Elemere setting the coffee on the stove.

"What are you putting that on for?"

"Jest some coffee." A'nt Elemere lit the gas and it gulped into flame. She set the pot over it. "I'm gonna keep some coffee on all through."

Cinnybug's face curled with the intensity of trying to make A'nt Elemere understand. "A'nt Elemere, you can't stay! We've got legal matters to discuss!"

"Then I better stay," A'nt Elemere said shortly. She turned the gas down low.

Up in Miss Anna Mary's room, in the dark red plush chair across the fireplace from the matching rocker, where he'd sat a thousand times listening to Miss Anna Mary, Cadwallader sat in the mottled dark and waited for something to happen.

He'd laid the brief-case across his knees, and he patted it from time to time with the tips of his fingers, feeling to make sure he hadn't forgotten it. Nothing happened in the darkened room. The gas-fire, seeping through tiny symmetric holes in the imitation logs, made a slight hum, and shot patterns of light round the walls. Through the door, half-opened because Cadwallader had been afraid to shut it finally, afraid to throw himself full tilt after what he sought by shutting himself away from anything human, he could sense the emptiness of the hall. He almost got up and went downstairs to start, then he seemed to realise that the first movement out of the chair, out of the room, down to the others, wouldn't end till the fur was flying, so he shrank back a little into the chair, and waited.

He tried to feel something, tried to catch a sense of something, but his own senses never left him: the sound he heard was still the hiss of the fire, and the cold fingering his neck only the night draught through the half-opened door in from the empty hall. But there was nothing, nothing he couldn't feel before any job he had to do where he knew there'd be trouble; nothing special, no feeling of added strength that he was doing Miss Anna Mary's work. The very emptiness of the room was proof enough that Mr. Cadwallader Williams, and that the whole lot downstairs besides, were going to have to shut their own doors and start their own fights, for there was no nice feeling of surety in the air that he could tell himself came from Miss Anna Mary Passmore. She was gone; gone as if she'd been blown out; dead.

Cadwallader stirred in his chair, hearing the clock whirr, getting ready to strike. He'd had his last bit of help from Miss Anna Mary, and he knew it. Having failed with her, after sitting with his nose perked for half an hour hoping and fearing for something to happen which he wouldn't be able to explain, he eased himself awkwardly forward, put his head down on his hand, his arm resting on his knee, and began a short, embarrassed, lonely prayer. Then he reached on down and switched out the fire, so that Mary Lee wouldn't find him wasting gas in high summer, and got up to go on downstairs and get the whole thing over with.

Mary Lee heard the clock strike from the dining-room as she went through to the kitchen.

"Where's Cadwallader? Why don't we start?" Then she saw what A'nt Elemere was up to.

"What are you putting that on for? We just had some."

A'nt Elemere was heavily calm. "You all'll be needing

a lot more before you're finished tonight. I wouldn't feel right if I didn't stay and look after you."

Mary Lee was exasperated. "But we don't need you any more after you've finished with the washing-up!"

"Neb' mind." A'nt Elemere settled herself. "I know them legal talks. They doesn't end up until ever' fuss all the way back to birth done been dragged out and shook up, and ever'body's teeth is in ever'body else's neck." She never would have sat down in front of Mary Lee and Cinnybug, but she did the next best thing. She backed up and sat her bottom against the sink, managing to look immovable.

Mary Lee tried to humour her the best she knew how.

"A'nt Elemere, that's all foolishness! Now go on to bed."

A'nt Elemere didn't seem to hear her. She was rolling her head from side to side.

"Deeds! Ever time you starts unlocking that deed box, out come a knock-down-carry-out fight."

"What can we do with you? You're as stubborn as a mule." Mary Lee began to pace up and down in front of her.

A'nt Elemere remained calm; pleased with herself.

"Naw. A little sense jest rubbed off on me from Miss Anna Mary, that's all."

Mary Lee stopped.

"A'nt Elemere, you're going on upstairs out of the way or we're going to have our meeting in the front room."

A'nt Elemere heaved up straight. "No'm." She was too positive even for Mary Lee. "I'm stayin' right down here. You all'll all get to scrappin' and get so riled up there won't none of you be fit to drive a car without somepin' hot to drink." She played her final card. "There ain't a table big enough with the dine-room table down for all you all to get your elbows on anyway."

Jellicoe stuck his head in at the door.

"'Bout ready to start?"

"Can't you wait to carve up the estate a little bit longer?" Mary Lee slammed out to the side-porch and sat down in the rocker.

Jellicoe came into the kitchen.

"She sure is a mean woman," he almost whispered to Cinny.

But Mary Lee heard him and she called out:

"I just pride myself on speaking the truth. If you can't stand it, it's no skin off my nose."

Abraham, leaning against a tree with his legs outstretched, heard her high voice carry clearly across the dark yard. It was the first clear word he'd heard since he'd sat down to smoke, watching the house with all its windows lit, like a huge doll's house, the edges of it fuzzy dark against the night sky. He went on watching, relaxed against the tree, and took a long drag from his cigarette. Mary Lee, seeing the light move far away, took it for granted it was a lightning bug.

Inside the house, Cinny turned, almost tearfully, to Jellicoe.

"A'nt Elemere won't go on to bed. Oh, A'nt Elemere, I wish you would." She began to whine. "You're just getting Miss Mary Lee all upset."

"Unhunh." As if doing that were nothing to be worked up about!

Even Cinnybug saw then it was no use arguing.

Abraham lit another cigarette from the first, and went on watching the house, taking it in, what there was to notice in the dark: lights going out in far rooms as more of them came down to the kitchen, figures passing casually near the kitchen doors so as to be ready, to be on the dot, but not eager. He could hear the solid creaking of Mary

Lee's rocker, a high sound that was Cinnybug's voice in the kitchen. But he stayed where he was, in the dark, waiting by the tree.

Cinnybug leaned against the cabinet, looking out into the yard. She held her hand out, vaguely, towards Jellicoe.

"Gimme a cigarette, honey."

He felt around in his pocket and brought out a packet.

"Here." He lit them both and for a minute they stared, side by side, blowing smoke through the screen into the light behind Mary Lee's head.

"Jellicoe."

"Unhunh?"

"Do you think we could go to a new rug in the dining-room? I always did plan to have one when the early 'mercan sideboard came to me."

Jellicoe took a deep drag and sighed it out in a line through the screen.

"Well, honey, you know it'll be your money, so you gwan do whatever you want to."

But the sigh had ruined Cinny's dream. She snapped:

"Oh, now, Jellicoe, don't be that way! You never do seem to take any notice of the house."

She opened the screen-door to the back path and started out.

"After all, you been working a long time to keep the interest paid up. So, in a way, the home'll be part yours." The door slammed behind her and she sat down on the steps.

"Twenty-five years," said Jellicoe, following her out. He sat down beside her, waiting for it all to begin. Even Cinnybug was quiet at last.

Mary Margaret laid underclothes out on the bed in neat piles, while Julik sat and watched her.

"Mary, we only got two hours and twenty minutes until train time," he reminded her. "When do we start?"

She laid Julik's pyjamas out and began to fold them carefully. "There's no use being impatient, Julie. It won't be long."

She began to lay his toilet articles across a canvas bag; he leaned forward and took away a nose syringe and began to blow at his nose as he slouched back in the chair.

When he put it back, he noticed something funny about the clothes.

"Hey, Mary, what's the idea? You've separated everything."

"It's easier on the train." She laid her dressing-gown across the bottom of the smaller suitcase. "It gives us each a case to take into the dressing-room when we go to bed."

"Oh."

"Last time I waited nearly an hour for my tooth-brush."

"Well, I'm sorry, Mary." Julik was offended. "Do you think I like all this stuff? If I didn't take it you'd be the first to squawk."

She went on packing, hardly hearing his voice. "After all," he went on, trying to force kindness from her, "you're always belly-aching when I don't follow my doctor's orders, aren't you?"

She heard something that sounded like a question, so she murmured, "What did you say, Julie?"

"After all, you wouldn't get much sleep yourself if I didn't."

The truth of that was so much a part of their relationship that, not having heard what else he said, Mary Margaret wondered why he'd bothered to say it.

"Well, isn't it about time we went down?" He went to

the door and held it open for her. "These people make me feel like a pin in a bowling alley."

"Look, Julie, it won't be long. I wanted to come by myself, but you insisted."

"I only wanted to come to protect your interests, Mary. You need it with this bunch of vultures." He went ahead of her down the hall.

"The sooner we get out of here the better, while we've still got our hair," he smiled back at her. She started down the steps after him without answering.

CHAPTER XIV

A MELIA almost staggered into the kitchen.
"Let's get started. Where is everybody?"
Mary Lee was just getting herself out of the rocker when
she heard Amelia. She came into the room. A'nt Elemere
was answering Amelia's question with a grin. "They're all
at points around the kitchen, all watchin' and waitin' for
somebody else to sit down first."

Amelia took possession of a chair by falling into it.
"Well, I'm sittin' down!"

"You're practically lying down." Mary Lee passed close
to the chair and gave Amelia a look of disgust. She neither
noticed nor heard.

Abraham threw away the last of his cigarette and came
into the kitchen when he saw the others, through the
window, beginning to gather around the table.

"Hello, Mr. Abraham Passmore!" Amelia made an arc
with her arm, half-waving.

"Hello, A'nt Amelia, when do we start?"

"Pretty soon." She grinned. "Old home week. You
just wait." Then she laughed. "Wait till we get to
shootin'!" She stopped, began to dream. "Mother
wouldn't forget me. I'm going to have a little store."

Abraham sat down beside her and patted her arm.
"With another seven hundred dollars?"

She turned on him, jerking away so hard she nearly lost
her balance. "You leave him alone! Charles Truxton
was a fine man. Everybody can't be practical."

A'nt Elemere, watching the signs, interrupted them.
"Want some more coffee, Mr. Abraham?"

Julik and Mary Margaret came in from the dining-room and stood near the door, both wondering where they should sit. Amelia was staring at the ceiling. "I like to lie in bed and dance. Pretend I'm dancing."

A'nt Elemere handed the cup to Abraham. "You like sugar, I noticed." She set the bowl down in front of him.

"I like to dance until I'm almost asleep, so's I can carry it over into a dream—" Amelia looked sadly at Abraham, wondering—"but I never do!"

Julik was liking the smell of the new coffee, but he was still smarting from being told he'd taken too long in the toilet. "Mary, do you think there might be enough coffee for me to have a cup, or do they serve it to outsiders?" he asked.

Mary Margaret saw the mood and wondered what new thing had caused it. She tried, by habit, to make amends. "Julie, I'd have gotten you some, only I knew you never drank it at night. Do you think you ought to?"

"Oh, for God's sake stop fussing, Mary." He looked around, explaining. "She's all the time trying to nurse me."

She found a cup and motioned him to a chair opposite Abraham. She was too busy handing him the coffee to see that everyone was watching her.

Julik caught Abraham's eye and it made him speak, casually. "What kind of work do you do, Mr. Passmore?"

"I'm an oil man."

"Oh." Julik was careful. "I'm afraid I don't know much about that world." He tried to make it sound apologetic enough to make up for his lack of interest. Mary Margaret reached across and handed him the sugar.

"You prefer being a straw man."

"I don't get you." He was aware of the eyes of everyone in the room fastened on him, watching him being waited on by their Mary Margaret as if she was coloured.

"Have a good look. You want I should take off my clothes?" He tried to pass it off as a joke, but nobody smiled.

The door opened and Cadwallader came in quickly, with a business-like stride, as if the whole thing depended in the end on the sure pace of his feet at the beginning. The whole room was as still as a holding of breath, watching him come up to the table. As if by plan, they'd left the centre chair empty, and Cadwallader, taking the place for granted, leaned over it and placed his brief-case on the table, upright, so that the little brass lock and the gilt initials, C.J.W., were all that they could see.

"Clear these cups off the table," Mary Lee whispered stridently to A'nt Elemere. Then she sat down on the other side of Amelia, to keep an eye on her.

"Well, well, well! Here we all are!" Cadwallader looked round the table, checking them off. "Abraham, Amelia, Mary Lee." He looked round the other side of the table. "Mary Margaret. Now let's see. Where's Cinnybug?"

She opened the door, almost ran in, and sat down opposite Cadwallader, patting the chair beside her for Jellicoe. "Here we all are!" Cinnybug beamed round the table, but no one had heard her.

"I wouldn't smoke if I was you, Cinny, not during the reading." Cadwallader looked at her over the brief-case, trying to make rules as he went along so that the familiar kitchen would take on, by omission, an atmosphere of law and discipline he felt it sadly needed to curb them all. Cinny put out her cigarette with a great air of dignity, but Cad knew he hadn't quite made his point.

When the screen-door swung to behind Cinny and Jellicoe, a tall man detached himself from the tree-trunk by the gate. All that could be seen of him in the dark was the shadow of a bony, white face, his long, gnarled hands out in the air in front of his stomach, clutching his hat, and the faint outline of his shirt, light against his dark suit.

He was so scared they'd notice him that he tiptoed even so far from the house, opened the back gate slowly and sneaked up the path, waiting in the grass beside it, then moving a little forward through the dark, until he stood edged up against the rain-barrel, watching through the back door where he could see A'nt Elemere, back leaning against the sink, with her arms folded.

Inside, Cadwallader began to fumble with the lock of the brief-case.

"Now I'm sure you all want this to go off as smooth as I do," he heard him say. The tiny lock clicked back and Cadwallader locked it again in his hand, removed the little key, and put it in his watch pocket.

The man by the rain-barrel leaned forward, keeping out of the light, and cupped his hand to his ear, clutching his hat to his stomach with the other hand.

Slowly Cadwallader drew out the thick, white, folded document. Then he laid it in front of him, carefully, straight on the table.

"If you have any questions, save them until the end. Take your turns. I'm sure Miss Anna Mary wanted more than anything else for you to be satisfied as far as her duty could see to do it."

He started to pick the will up again, but only patted it as he remembered something. "She said to me, just before she died, she said, 'Cad, I hate to think of my family all splitting up and living in rented houses and not having any background when I'm gone.'"

Amelia forgot and lit a cigarette. Nobody noticed. Cadwallader's voice went on:

"You've got to see to it that there don't anything like

this happen. She had youall in mind. She certainly had you in mind."

Mary Lee moved in her seat. "Go on, Cad, stop running for office."

He turned away from the will altogether and began to rummage through his brief-case, making a quiet shuffling of papers like a mouse.

Amelia threw her cigarette down.

"For heaven's sake, Cad, go on!"

Cadwallader looked at her sternly. "Amelia, don't get impatient. These things all take time. I'm looking for a second paper I ought to have ready just in case any of you want to refer to it. You can't be too careful at a time like this."

Amelia blew smoke in his face.

"Amelia, I thought I said we ought not to smoke during the reading. I don't think it's right."

"What in the world difference it makes . . ."

"Oh, for God's sake, put it out, Amelia! Anything . . ." Mary Lee told her.

"Go ON, Cad!" Cinnybug echoed in a high whine.

It made him look up and arrested his arm in mid-air.

"Now, Cinnybug, don't you start getting het up."

Jellicoe half whispered:

"Cinny, honey, you know you ought . . ."

"Oh, hush up, Jellicoe." Cinny's eyes were fastened on Cadwallader's arm. He moved it down into the brief-case again. "Here it is. It's the old will your father left." He brought out another thick, rich fold of paper, this one richer because of the faint parchment colour of age. He began to unfold it and look carefully through it.

"Now I think we might go through this if anybody's forgotten it." He looked up over the will.

"Have any of you forgotten it?"

"No!" Mary Lee almost screamed before she could stop herself.

Cadwallader went right on slowly inquiring round the circle of faces.

"Perfectly clear in your minds?"

"Perfectly clear," said Amelia. He happened to look at her just at the end of the question.

He reached forward and buried the old will carefully among his papers, zipped the brief-case closed, put it down on the floor beside his chair, and picked up Miss Anna Mary's will again.

He held it up in one hand and began to pass his other hand gently across it.

"There's something I think I ought to tell you before I read you this."

Mary Lee shifted in her chair; it creaked like a groan.

"Miss Anna Mary wrote her own will in her own words. She brought it down to me to get it witnessed, and see if it was legal."

Slowly, as he talked, he let the will fall back on to the table again, but no one could stop him, no one could make him move faster. It was as if they were being charmed into a slow movement of their own, against their will.

"Of course it was legal! Miss Anna Mary knew as much about the law as I ever did . . . anyway about deeds and claims and wills and all the civil side. Rightoways! Just take rightoways. She was smart as a Philadelphia lawyer about rightoways."

He went right on, conjuring up Miss Anna Mary in his apologetic voice. Mary Margaret, sitting watching her hands folded in her lap as objectively as if they were little animals that might spring up and run away, couldn't shake herself free of Cadwallader's slow memory. There was not a sound round the table.

127

"Now this will has some things in it besides property. Some mighty fine things in it. Some sensible talk from the grave."

Mary Lee sat up and started to comment, then seemed to change her mind.

"Property isn't the only thing a woman can leave behind her. Not by long shot. She came in, and she said, 'Cad, I've made my will.' Just like that."

He looked round the table to confound them, but not a single one of them was looking up towards him any more.

"I'd been trying to get her to for years on and off, but she said she was in Jesus' hands and she'd be darned if she could do any better. You know how she was."

No one answered or agreed or looked up, not even when he grew quieter and less nostalgic and said:

"But something happened that changed her mind. So she came down . . . walked over from her usual trip to the bank one morning with the document in her pocket-book. But it was legal."

He caressed the long paper again.

"Air-tight!" He gave it a little slap and threw it open. "Here it is."

He adjusted his glasses and began to read, looking hard at the paper as if he didn't almost know it by heart, rehearsing this hour in his troubled dreams.

"*My name is Anna Mary Passmore.*"

Mary Lee gave a tiny snort. "What an ignorant way to start!"

Amelia waved her hand at her to shut her up.

But she was too late. Cadwallader had heard her and stopped reading.

"It's good enough. It's legal in spirit. Law isn't always a bunch of fancy words. Law is something better'n that. It's a spirchal contract too. The spirit meaning more than the words." Cadwallader was already lost in his own philosophy, so he came of his own accord back to the will.

"Now pay attention. . . . *Anna Mary Passmore. I am saner than any one of the people I come up against so I reckon this means I am of sound mind. All right. This is my will. Not my wish. My will.*"

There was not a sound in the room. All of their eyes were poised on Cadwallader and the words.

"*All you youngins have felt me crack the whip before so you know what I mean by the word will. I always swore I would write down what I wanted done with all this property. I didn't care.*"

Cinny couldn't stand it any longer. She began to wail, turning to Jellicoe.

"Jelly, this isn't a will at all! It isn't in any of the right words!"

"Now wait a minute," Cadwallader interrupted. "You just be patient and polite, Cinny, it's like your mother talking . . ."

"Long-winded!" Amelia said it, but she whispered it so low that no one but Abraham heard her.

Cadwallader looked at Cinny for what he thought was long enough to quiet her, then he began to read again.

"*This morning, this being the tenth of September, 1945, I have heard some news about Abraham at last which has changed my mind . . .*"

He felt, rather than saw, an interruption from Abraham, who had jerked his head up and was staring at him.

"Yes, Abraham, that's what it was. That's how long it took us to find out about young Abe. She possibly couldn't wait to hear any longer, so she had me try and track him down. Well, son, it was too late. Your dad had been dead on eight years. I always figured she must of sat right down in there in her room and written this within a few minutes after hearing. You'd think from that it didn't affect her much, but she was that kind of a woman, always took action, some kind of action, when things got too much for her. That's just the kind of thing she would of done."

He found his place on the paper again. Abraham was still.

"*My boy Abraham is dead. If I could of imagined in all my born days that I never was going to lay eyes on Abraham or hear from him again, I don't think I could of stood it. But there comes times when you have to face up to things. This morning I've got to face up to the fact that I won't see Abraham until I get to the other side. Ignorance makes you foolish; makes you stand for too much some times. I waited too long for that boy of mine to write to me. He went away mad. He had a reason for that. All of you youngins who are listening to this will of mine for the last time know in your hearts that he had a good reason. But he stayed mad too long. I can't do anything about that now, but what I can do I'm going to. This is the last time there's any chance of my family splitting up and running off to where you can't get back when you're in trouble and need a roof over your head. If I can't do anything else, I can provide that for you. So I want things divided up in the following way.*"

There was a stir round the table that made Cadwallader's voice falter as he read, but when he looked up to meet the wave of voices, no one said a word. He went on reading.

"*This is to insure that none of you turn your back on any of the others, for I've had enough back-stabbing and picking at to last us all many a lifetime, and I'm sick of it. If you won't love each other any other way, I'll tie up this land and property so you'll be legally bound to have some respect for each other anyway. I'll tie your hands and make you learn to love each other.*"

Abraham interrupted, as if by some pressure he could stand Cadwallader's voice no longer:

"Go back. I've got to find out something. Go back to the beginning."

"For heaven's sake, the damn thing's wordy enough without him having to say it twice." Mary Lee started to pluck at Abraham's sleeve to make him sit down.

"Abraham, son, take your turn." Cadwallader begged. "I've got to read it right through. It's the law. It's the way I've always done it. I'd lose my place."

Abraham sat down again; this time it was Amelia who plucked at his sleeve and kept her hand on his arm long after Cadwallader had started to read again.

"*First I want to say something to you, Mary Lee.*"

Her back went straighter, as if she had to sit stiff as iron to combat the woman when, for the first time, she couldn't talk back. Cadwallader went on, reading the last words in the argument, which Miss Anna Mary had simply insured by dying.

"*You've been a good girl in your own lights. You've taken over and run things, and made everything work for quite a while. In return I've given you a home. I'm not going to criticise the behaviour of a sick man like Longridge, but if he's as sick as all that, seems to me your best future is to go on home and look after him. Everybody'll get on all right here. There's lots of times I would have told you this, Mary Lee, but I had a selfish reason. I love that girl of yours. Mary Margaret reminds me of myself a way long time ago before I got myself a passel of youngins and then lost John and had to go killing snakes every day. I just couldn't sit by and see that youngin living with only you and a sick man and nobody to turn to when you bullied her.*"

Cadwallader felt, rather than heard the pressure of Mary Lee's anger, and his voice leapt ahead so that she'd find no gap to lash in and destroy his effort to finish the worst part of his job.

"*You always liked the sewing-machine. You can have that.*"

131

*You can have all the chickens except fifty White Leghorn spring
pullets and a Leghorn rooster. They look prettier around the back
yard and in my opinion they're the best fryers as well as layers.
You can have that rocking-chair on the back porch to take home,
too. It seems to belong to you in a way."*

Cadwallader stopped reading, waiting for the crash of
Mary Lee's anger. But nothing happened. She sat like a
pillar of stone, staring in front of her, the only evidence
that she had heard him at all was her hands, clutched in
her lap until the knuckles were dead white.

They waited until her silence had cast a kind of fear
in all of them worse than her violence would have done.
Cadwallader spoke as if he were waking her up.

"Mary Lee. Mary Lee!" She dragged her eyes from
staring to look at him.

"That's all about you, Mary Lee."

When she looked at him, it seemed to make her alive
again and Cadwallader was almost relieved when she
sprang half out of her chair and began to yell at him.

"How can you dare to stand there and tell me that the
senile ravings of an ignorant old woman are legal? Don't
you know your job? Haven't you got any sense?"

"Now, Mary Lee, you just please keep a little bit
quieter and let me read the rest. I'm sure we can iron
everything out at the end if we'll just keep calm."

Mary Lee sank back in her chair and closed her eyes.
Cadwallader was so relieved he could hardly drag his
mind back to the will, and took so long finding the place
again that Cinnybug reached up and pushed at his arm.
"Go on!" He found his place and began again.

*"Now there's a little bit of money. Not so much as all of you
thought there was gonna be so you might as well be prepared. The
combined savings and assets come to eleven thousand three hundred
and seventy-six dollars."*

Cadwallader stopped and looked up to explain.

"There's an addition here, made last week. Only last week! Do you know, she never lost track of her property right up to the last. Never missed a trick."

"How much is it?" Amelia pulled him back to the point.

"The new figure is," he found the place and began to read again, "*sixteen thousand three hundred and fifty dollars. In addition I've kept an insurance policy to be divided between all my grandchildren, however many there are by the time I die.*"

Cadwallader stopped again to look up sadly. "You know, she's the only person I ever knew who put that word down, just like that, in a will. . . ." But when no one answered he went on, "*It's for three thousand dollars. Now there's three of you so far. Abraham, Mary Armstrong and John Junior.*"

Julik jerked his head round to Mary Margaret.

"*So that makes a thousand apiece. If any of you are under-age when I die, I want your share held for you until you are of age and then a cheque is to be handed to you which none of your parents has any say in the spending of it. People need a little pocket money with just their name on it.*"

Cadwallader paused here, and Abraham smiled and began to get up from his chair again, but Julik's loud whispering to Mary Margaret stopped him.

"You're left out. There's no money. Mary, what did I tell you? You might have listened . . ."

Cadwallader interrupted him. "Wait a minute, Mr. Rosen. Mary Margaret's next."

He found his place in the will again.

"*Now for Mary Margaret. You're going to have to stand for a little bit of fuss over what I'm going to say. After all, you aren't as close kin as the others. But I love you. I always did.*"

Mary Margaret felt for Julik's hand to hold it, but he'd

put both elbows on the table and was leaning forward, swallowing the words of the will as Cadwallader stumbled through them.

"Now there's been a lot of things said about you lately, honey, but to show you I trust you and know that you wouldn't do anything to stain your girlhood,"

Cinny bit her mouth together to keep a giggle, like a nervous tic, from forming at her mother's phrase. But she stopped when she heard the next sentence.

"I'm leaving five thousand dollars to Mary Margaret Rosen, and I hope your marriage will always be happy."

Mary Margaret heard faintly a little cry from Cinnybug, and a sound from across the table, but she couldn't see. Her head was down, bowing in her lap, and she was crying a stream of tears, but silently, so that the rest, intent on Cadwallader after the first glances of surprise and anger at her, could not see. Only Julik, who had finished listening, sat back relaxed in his chair.

"Now another five thousand dollars is to go to John."

Cadwallader looked up. "She told me to write and tell him and I've already done it." He looked down at the will again.

"There's no use giving him a piece of the house when he's set on gallivanting around all over the place. He won't see a bit of use in a piece of farmhouse way out in the back woods. Write him my suggestion that he ought to send for his youngin. The boy needs him. Nothing good ever came of anybody that was raised entirely by women."

Cadwallader stopped. "I wrote him all that in the letter. Of course I told him how she said it was best for John Junior . . ."

But Cinny had counted up and she looked at Cadwallader, horrified, having no idea what he was talking about because . . .

"That's not enough! It's not enough! Cad, that only leaves six thousand dollars! Jellicoe, what . . ."

Cadwallader stopped her in mid-wailing, and she held her breath to listen . . .

"Now you wait a minute, Cinnybug." He found his place quickly this time and began to read again.

"*Now for the house.*"

The rest of the women swerved in their seats, and Cinny let her breath out loudly.

"*That's your house. The main thing, after all. I leave this house jointly to Amelia, Cinnybug (her real name is Thelma, I reckon I ought to put that in to make it legal), and to Abraham's son, the present Abraham Passmore.*"

The room was in its first uproar of the evening. Cadwallader had expected it. What he had not expected was Abraham's loud laughter over the lashing voices of the women. He went on loudly, and they quieted down again.

"*Here are the terms. It is to be owned jointly. None of you's to sell your share without consent of the others. In other words, it isn't sliced up, and one of you can't go off and sell up to some stranger. If you ever sell, you've got to agree.*"

Now the room was as still as it had been full of noise.

"*The rest of the money, six thousand three hundred and fifty dollars, is to be divided equally between the same three of you.*"

Cadwallader stumbled over the sum, and turned it slowly under the light, for Miss Anna Mary had done some of her figuring on the page, and crossed it out, so that Cadwallader, although he thought he'd memorised the figure, couldn't quite make it out, with the eyes on him, and the voices all ready to attack as soon as his own voice had stopped for a second to give them a chance.

So he kept on saying, "Wait a minute, just a minute now. Almost got it. Yes, that's the right figure." He saw a movement from Amelia out of the tail of his eye. "Wait a minute, Amelia, there's some more."

He found his place again. *"When I think of Abraham dying off out there somewhere, it pretty near breaks my heart. Well, his youngin's going to have a home to come to. He's got three thousand dollars, and now he's got a roof over his head. Little Abraham, it's what I would have done for your father, but he wouldn't let me—never wrote nor nothing. It's all I can think of to do for you, except to say I'm sorry we never did meet, and I hope you're like both your parents. I never did quite understand what all the fuss was about. If I had anything to do with it, I'm so sorry. But maybe I'll meet Abraham on the other side in God's Glory and tell him there wasn't no harm meant."*

Abraham did lean forward then, till his shadow, under the top light, had split the table.

"Cad, stop. You've got to stop a minute!"

"There's not much more. It has to be read. All of it."

Abraham waited, standing, ready for the last words.

"So youngins, it's the best I could do for you. I've tried to watch out for you and do what was right and also what wouldn't hurt you. May we meet in glory. Amelia, I wish you'd stop that terrible habit. Signed Anna Mary Passmore, witnessed Joab Wilson, Oliver Whitcome."

CHAPTER XV

ABRAHAM didn't move, and the silence, waiting for him to say what he had to, after all the impatience, got to the length that Jellicoe couldn't stand. He laughed and found something to say.

"Didn't know either one of them could write!"

In the silence after the witnesses' names had been read, A'nt Elemere roused herself from her own thoughts, which she was not prepared to voice, and from her comfortable fat wedge against the side of the sink, and began to pour the inevitable coffee and hand it round, passing it over arms that fell away from the table as she came near. Then she came to Cinny, who, coming alive, and throwing herself over in her chair, nearly upset the coffee cup.

"Jelly! Jelly! It isn't enough! It isn't enough! What are we going to do?"

"Now you know I'm not much good at this sort of thing, Cinnybug, I'd ask Cad if I was you."

Cinny turned to Cadwallader, accusing him.

"Cad, you told me I'd be all right. You told me last week!"

Cadwallader tried to pacify the quivering woman, who was turned, neck stretched, face half-grinning with fear, up into his face.

"Well, now, Cinny, that isn't a bad sum. The Passmore place is known to be one of the finest pieces of property in this county. Now you just think over how lucky you are."

Cinny's face was blotted with fear.

"I owe five thousand dollars to Mr. Crasscopper. I signed it! Signed it myself twenty-five years ago. It was all hinged on the fact I'd be remembered."

Cadwallader was fatherly with her, but a little shocked; for when it came to money, he knew where he stood and what was right and what wasn't and what was just plain sloppy.

"Now, Cinnybug, you told your mother that had been paid off down to two thousand dollars. That's what she left you this for."

Cinnybug found herself beginning to laugh, and hiccoughed for breath to shout, "Paid off! We haven't had our heads above water long enough ever!" But when she looked round at Jellicoe, sitting there all sorry and slack, she wailed, "Oh, Jelly, why can't you be some use?"

A'nt Elemere took her arm and put her down in her chair again, making her sit solid, making her drink something, whispering all the time, "Now come on, Miss Cinny, you just sit down there and drink your coffee."

Cinnybug did as she was told, but went on moaning still, "What are we going to do?"

Outside by the rain-barrel, the Reverend Beedie Jenkins slowly lifted his hat and pulled it down firmly over his eyes, so that even in the dark he tipped his head back slightly to pick his way along the path. It gave him a faint air of pride when his head was covered that he never had when his hat was clutched to his stomach and his head bent prayerwards.

He walked very slowly, and because he was completely alone he didn't even notice that the evidence of his feelings was falling down his sun-lined cheeks. He screwed up his eyes and his eyebrows hard to control his thoughts, but they came out anyway. He muttered to himself as he reached the gate, feeling for it in the darkness:

"Sister Anna Mary knowed me better'n that. She knowed me better'n that."

Brother Beedie forgot to be quiet, and slammed the gate behind him.

Abraham had not sat down again, but had stood, hovering over the table, waiting, still until there was a minute of peace for him to harrow. Now he spoke, but quietly: "Someone in this room tore up a letter from my mother to my grandmother. I want to know who it was."

They had all known trouble would come from him. But when the first of it did come, none of them caught the real sling of his question, they were so intent on their own troubles. The sound of his voice only reminded Cinnybug that he was there, and she looked up hopefully.

"Abraham, you've got money. If we could all agree maybe it would be all right." Then, with great effort, she smiled. "Maybe we could sell the house!"

Abraham no more heard her than she heard him; he was watching Mary Lee, who he knew had taken in what he'd said.

"Who tore up that letter?" He asked her, privately.

Mary Lee dismissed him. "I don't know what you're talking about."

He would have answered her but for the sudden noise as Julik jumped up and let his chair topple behind him. Abraham caught him poised, half-upright, trying to drag Mary Margaret to her feet. Then the whole picture moved. Julik was almost shouting for joy, "Come on, Mary, get the bags. We've got a train to catch!"

"What? What did you say?" She seemed drowsy with the shock of her news. "Is it time?"

"We've got to call the man who brought us from the station. There's no use sitting around here." Mary Margaret didn't answer. The silence Julik had created made him look from one to the other of them as they watched him. "Well, isn't it over? Isn't the whole thing over? What are we waiting for?" He tried to smile.

Mary Lee jumped up, shaking with anger, and ran round the table to bar his path.

"You wait, my friend, the whole thing has hardly begun!"

"Whoooom!" said Amelia, making a gesture like an explosion with her arms, ending with one hand patting Abraham's arm, absent-mindedly.

Mary Lee turned from Julik to Cadwallader.

"Cadwallader, can a will be broken if something isn't true. If it isn't true? You talked about the spirit . . . the spirit and the letter. . . ."

The question brought Mary Margaret to her feet, and she watched Mary Lee with such fascination at her that she was even without disgust.

"Mother!" Her voice was as soft as sighing.

"Well, can it?" Mary Lee motioned her to shut up.

Cadwallader was too upset to understand a word of what Mary Lee was saying. He'd figured it all out ahead of time, where the trouble would come from, who'd fight whom, and how he'd step between and what he'd have to do to keep the peace; but this was a thing he hadn't reckoned on, and to look at Mary Lee he could tell she was as near to having murder in her eye as ever he'd seen her.

"I don't quite get you, Mary Lee. Everything's very legal. Why Miss Anna Mary was as . . ."

"Look at what she said about Mary Margaret!"

Mary Margaret knew then that it was the end for whatever dreams she'd packed up and brought down and let loose in the house, and she sat down again, too defeated to more than half listen any more.

"Go on. Look at it. Go on."

"Well, here it is, Mary Lee. Look. Mary Margaret

Rosen. All legal. She'll get her money all right." He was relieved. There wasn't anything he'd done wrong. He put the will down on the table.

"That's not what I mean and you know it. What did the old fool say . . . 'stain her girlhood'? I'll throw that highfalutin talk back in both their damned faces." She swung round and asked the next question at Mary Margaret. "What if she wasn't married?" But Mary Margaret sat like a half-asleep girl, and didn't rise enough at the trouble to even look at her mother. Mary Lee leaned forward and began to pound at the will. "Wouldn't that put a different slant on the whole thing? Wouldn't it? Wouldn't that be what A'nt Anna Mary meant?"

"Well, now, let me see." Cad spoke slowly and picked the paper up again slowly, all to calm her down while he thought. He stared at the name, then took out a pencil, and put it back again into his pocket as he talked.

"I reckon the law would be that if it was left to Mary Margaret Rosen, and she wasn't Mary Margaret Rosen, but Mary Margaret Something Else—you know, a mistake. Well, I reckon . . ." He fiddled with the pencil in his pocket again.

"You reckon what?" Mary Lee's voice brought him back to the point, as cold and hard as a bit.

He took a deep breath and said what he had to.

"I reckon it would be that if that person named in the will was known by that name, well everybody would know who it meant. Wouldn't they?" Cadwallader asked hopefully. Now that he'd done what he had to, he turned and looked at Mary Lee, thinking he ought to make her understand. "But even if there was trouble you wouldn't get anything, Mary Lee. You see, you're not a direct heir." He could see as he told her that she knew already and that it wasn't the reason; the reason was something he'd never understand about. He waved both his arms, including them all, trying to get back to being a simple lawyer.

"But it's all right. I'm sure it's all right. I'm sure there's not going to be any trouble. We were so careful so there wouldn't be any trouble."

"What about the spirit? What about your fine spirit?" Mary Lee asked with a slight laugh.

Mary Margaret seemed to wake up, and she reached forward and tugged at Mary Lee's sleeve to make her turn round. But Julik had swallowed the trouble and gave her no time to speak. He turned on Cadwallader and began to yell.

"What's all this about? What's she talking about?"

Mary Margaret had attracted Mary Lee's attention.

"Mary Margaret, can you prove, can you swear and show proof that you are legally Mary Margaret Rosen? Are you married to this man?"

"No. I can't." Mary Lee, even standing above her, could hardly hear the answer, but she heard enough.

"I'm sorry. I can't."

Cadwallader leaned down to her, across the table.

"Mary Margaret, honey, I think you ought to have some legal advice. You don't want to lose your share, Miss Anna Mary'd of been awful upset. That phrase. It's kind of ambiguous. It crept in . . ." he ended, disappointed.

"Would she?" He couldn't hear her at all, only see her lips move.

Julik grabbed his arm and pulled him up straight to have it out.

"But a phrase! Some corny old woman's words! It can't stand between Mary and what's due to her!"

But Cadwallader didn't have time to answer. Mary

Lee had finally lost control and she pushed her face into his, spitting at him.

"I don't know about your kind of people, but in this family a word can stand for quite a lot. That word is marriage." She jerked round to Mary Margaret, bending closer and closer until she was close enough for the girl to see the spittle clogged between her false teeth and her gums.

"Do you mean to tell me you thought you could get by with flaunting yourself, nothing but showing yourself, nothing but acting as if you was naked in front of people! Dirty! Naked!"

"Stop her," Mary Margaret finally began to cry. "Somebody stop her!"

"Shut up, Mary!" Julik yelled at her over Mary Lee's anger and made them both turn towards him. But he spoke only to Cadwallader, who had the disaster in the palm of his hand.

"Let's get this straight. Wilson, is it true?"

If there was one thing in the world that made Cadwallader's blood rise above snake level, it was to be called by the wrong name. Julik had lost his last champion.

"My name, sir, is Williams," Cadwallader told him.

Julik only waited for his mouth to stop moving.

"Can Mary Margaret be kept from what's rightfully hers by a trick like this?"

"Well, now, Mr. Rosen, I know you've got Mary Margaret's interests at heart, but I don't think you ought to take on like that about it. There's no trick. There's certainly no trick. Just one of those unfortunate mistakes." He kept reading and rubbing at the will as if the words had changed into another language before his eyes.

"You mean she won't get anything at all?" Julik was so horrified that his voice squeaked like a little boy's.

Cadwallader cleared his throat carefully to gain time and calm everything down. "Well, I wouldn't put it like that, Mr. Rosen. No." He thought for a second, holding his breath. "No. Not just like that. It might mean that at the worst of course. It certainly means litigation." He sat down for the first time since the will-reading, as if the word had won and pushed him there.

"Litigation," he repeated sadly. "Long, drawn-out, expensive litigation. Maybe months. Oh Lord! I'm not clear on that point. I'm just not clear on that point." He hitched up his glasses with his knuckles and rubbed his dry eyes. Then he remembered he was talking to the strange young man. "I'm mighty sorry about this, wouldn't have had it happen for the world. But you see, if you could produce your marriage licence, everything would be straightened out in no time." This prospect cheered Cadwallader a little and made him sit up in his chair.

Mary Lee, frozen like a statue, stood looking somewhere over Julik's shoulder. Now she brought her eyes back to him and smiled, but said nothing.

Suddenly he was nearly crying, his throat tight with it. "I knew it would happen. I knew something like this would happen. I felt it coming! You're all glad, aren't you? You think I'm not good enough to touch your money!" He knew he was doing just what they would have expected him to do, but he went right on, hating them, loathing them, looking from face to lazy face, and hardly seeing them. "Aren't you satisfied now that a trick's been played?"

Cadwallader got to his feet again, insulted.

"Mr. Rosen, there was no trick. I wouldn't do a thing like that. It isn't ethical. I carried out the wishes of . . ."

"Ethical?" Julik looked at Cadwallader as if he wondered if he were quite sane. "Look, mister. Tell me something." He began to yell again and nearly choked. "What do you people know about ethical? What do you know about it? Where does ethical come to a man wanting something all his life and not able to get it? Where's the ethical, I'm asking you?"

He couldn't look any more at Cadwallader's long, grey face; he tried to focus on the others, at Jellicoe's flabby face, at Amelia, with a half-grin she'd left and forgotten, at Cinnybug, twisting and turning and obviously waiting for him to shut up and get out.

"Which one of you ever had any ambition to get someplace? Oh Jesus!" His oath was a cry. "Something like this would happen to me!"

Mary Margaret interrupted before he could say any more. "Julie. Oh, please, Julie . . ." She seemed to be moaning instead of speaking.

The sound of it stopped him at last. His terrible disappointment blotted out his anger and he was left high and dry, feeling hardly alive. He started for the door.

"O.K. O.K. I'll get our bags." He pushed it open and walked out without looking at her. It was only when he disappeared into the dining-room that Mary Margaret could make herself move at all. She jumped up and ran after him, catching the door with her shoulder as it swung back.

"Julie," she called by habit. "You can't lift those things."

Then she stopped on her way after him through the dining-room, and leaned against the wall as if she were too tired to move another step.

"What does it matter now?" He turned back to wait for her. "What does it matter about my hands? Don't just stand there." When she didn't move for him he called sharply, "Mary!"

"You go on, honey." She turned her face to the wall.

He wanted to shake her, but took her arm instead and tried to drag her along. "Mary, don't cause any more trouble. You don't expect me to spend the night in this hole, do you?"

She shook away from him. "No. You go on."

"Look, Mary, what's the matter?"

"Nothing. I'm not coming, that's all." All the trouble had set her back, like a little girl, and from the look on her face he knew there'd be trouble trying to reason with her.

"Mary, come on now. Just move on. Come on upstairs." He piloted her by the arm, and it wasn't until she set foot on the lowest step that she stopped again. "I just don't want to." She bit her lip, worried.

"Now, Mary, don't talk like that. You come on upstairs. We'll be on the train in a little while. Won't that be nice?" He found himself playing a crazy child game with her, just to get her to move on.

"I don't want to," she kept on saying as he took her up the stairs. "Everybody needs me and nobody wants me. I want to sit down."

It was like piloting a drunk. "Now don't you talk like that, Mary. What would I do without you?" He sat her down in the rocking-chair of their bedroom, then she remembered to say:

"Julie, I'm very sorry."

Looking at her, he realised at last that she was serious.

"Look, Mary, you can't do this to me right now. You just can't do it. After all I've suffered today I can't stand it. Haven't you got any feelings?"

"I'm sorry, Julie," she said again, and covered her eyes, even though it was night and both of them had forgotten to turn on the light, but had let the shaft from the hall guide them. "Oh, it doesn't matter," she mumbled into her hand.

"Christ, Mary, I can't stand this." Julik lurched down towards her. "I can't stand any more. Christ, don't you realise I'm thirty-four years old!" He fell against her legs and hung there in the air, trying to get his balance back. She wanted to pull her skirt away to free herself, but dared not, knowing how near he was to tears.

CHAPTER XVI

A S the dining-room door swung shut, Mary Lee began to move. She sat down in Mary Margaret's chair.

"I knew it. I knew they weren't married!"

Abraham leaned towards her, almost sick with disgust at her.

"You know a lot, don't you? Poor bugger! He asked for trouble and you were the girl who knew how to give it to him!"

Mary Lee started to speak, but Cinnybug had waited long enough for her answer from Abraham, with people interrupting and taking his mind off the important thing all the time.

"Abraham! If we could sell?"

But it was Amelia who interrupted and answered her before Abraham had a chance, leaning across the table until she was almost lying down.

"What about me? What if I won't sell?"

Cinny looked at her, surprised, wondering if the expression round Amelia's mouth was a smile, part of a joke or something.

"But, Amelia! You always did want a little money to start up something for yourself!"

Amelia laid her head down the little bit more until it was lying sideways on her arm.

"Thelma, look at me." She stopped smiling, or whatever it was.

"Look at me!" She raised her head, swaying a little, and sat watching Cinny. "Don't I just look like somebody who could pick up lock, stock and barrel and start on my own. Now, don't I?" Her mouth turned down at the edges. "Look at me!" She lunged forward with her final question. "Why do you think Mother left me a home?"

"But ever since Charles Truxton Edwards died, you been . . ."

Amelia took a deep breath.

"Charles Truxton Edwards was a son of a bitch!" she said, and then she laid her head down between her arms on the table.

Cinny swung back to Abraham.

"Abraham, persuade her! Please persuade her!"

His face was as cold as Amelia's had been bitter.

"Why should I?"

She clutched at the edge of the table and pulled herself up towards him.

"But you don't need this place! You've got money!"

He was so quiet for a big man that, when he answered her the way he did, Cinny thought for a minute that he'd come round to her way of thinking, and she sat back.

"You seem to have forgotten something. All of you have. I came down here for a certain reason. If there's a score to pay, I'll pay it. I want the truth. Then I'll decide what can become of my part of this."

But if his stillness had fooled Cinnybug, it had been like a red flag of danger for Cadwallader, still trying desperately to make everything go smooth, by refusing to recognise its going any other way.

"Abraham, I don't think this is quite the time . . ."

Abraham's angry interruption showed even Cinnybug she'd made a mistake.

"This is exactly the time. Williams, read that first part of my grandmother's will again. I want you all to listen."

Cadwallader unfolded the will and began to look over it, humbling in his throat for a call to order as he looked.

"Now, let me see. Let me see. Where is it you want?"

Abraham's finger jabbed to so exact a place that Cad's eyes had to be pinned to it. "There. Read it. Read it out."

Cadwallader wiggled the corner of his glasses by habit, humbled again in his throat, stalling just a few seconds more. Then he began to read again.

"If I could of imagined in all my born days that I never was going to lay eyes on Abraham or hear from him again, I don't think I could of stood it. But there comes times when you have to face up to things. This morning I've got to face up to the fact that I won't see Abraham until I get to the other side. Ignorance makes you foolish. . ." Cad looked up to see if he'd read enough, but Abraham said:

"Go on."

He found his place. *". . . makes you foolish; makes you stand for too much sometimes. I waited too long for that boy of mine to write to me. He went away mad. He had a reason . . ."*

"That's enough."

Mary Lee sucked her teeth. "We've heard all that before." She got up to go out on to the porch. Abraham was ahead of her, holding her close. From where Jellicoe sat, bored half to death, they looked like they were dancing. He wanted to turn it into some joke, but dared not with Cinnybug all hot and bothered as she was. He heard Abraham say to Mary Lee, "No you don't, sister." He pushed her back towards the table. Jellicoe lost interest.

"Six months before my father died, he wrote a letter to my grandmother. After he got sick, my mother wrote again. I helped her to write it. As you all know, she couldn't write English very well." He walked towards Mary Lee, his voice edged, as bitter as Julik's had been.

"Somebody here destroyed those letters before my

grandmother saw them." Then he was looking at Mary Lee and at no one else. "I want to know who it was."

"What do you think we are?" Mary Lee saw her chance, catching the quality like Julik in him, an Achilles heel.

But it wasn't going to work.

"Who did it?"

"Don't you use that tone of voice with me!"

"Who did it, goddamn you?"

She said nothing. Neither did anyone else.

Abraham let his own voice drop low. "Until I find out, I'm going to let the Passmore place sink and all of you with it."

Cinnybug found her voice and used it to accuse.

"This is all your fault! This is your fault, Mary Lee!"

Mary Lee stood her ground.

"I don't know what she's raving about." She turned to glare at Cinnybug, and her look made Cinny close her mouth with a snap. Then Mary Lee turned back to Abraham and took a stand to lay down the law on him.

"Listen here, young man, if you thought we were going to stand by and see Abe crawl to his mother behind our backs, you're vastly mistaken." She stopped, waiting to hear what he'd say, but when he didn't speak she baited him again.

"If he got his comuppins from being so high and mighty with us, then it wasn't any of our business."

Then Abraham found a way to say what had been on his mind from the first, what he was there to let them all know.

"If she'd ever seen those letters, he wouldn't have died."

Mary Lee's rage flamed up at him for it.

"That's just your mother in you coming out." She looked round the table for someone to agree with what she said, someone to back her up in her injured innocence. "Blaming us for something when we didn't even know anything about it. Did you ever hear tell? Isn't it just like her?"

But when no one answered she turned back. "We didn't know a damn thing about it." Then, to stop the silence that followed, "You act like we up and killed him!"

"You did!" Abraham bawled it at her, and then stood shaking, looking from one to the other of them.

"My father died because he couldn't pay for decent care."

No one answered a word. He walked to the screen-door, back again, pulled back his chair beside Amelia and sat down, all slowly, getting himself back into contact with them, and when he finally told them the rest, it was as if he were telling a story that hadn't happened, it seemed so far from him.

"A sick man can't hold a job for long. My mother went to work to look after him. He didn't ever want her to, but she couldn't do anything else, with him so sick. Well, it only made him get worse and worse. There seemed to be something in him, something heavy he never threw off, that kept him ever from getting on top of his sickness. I've always thought whatever it was came from here. Or maybe it was the war. Anyway, it was on account of her he finally asked for some help from his mother. When he got no answer he wouldn't try any more. Then she tried."

Mary Lee took in a gasp of breath to speak, but when Abraham looked up at her, she changed her mind.

"When he died, the doctor told my mother that. He told her that, standing in the room there with him. I was standing in the door and I heard him say it. 'Tuberculosis is a strange disease,' is what he told her. 'If he had had enough to eat and the right kind of care, he mightn't have died.' 'He gave in,' she was saying. 'He gave . . .' "

Mary Lee could stand it no longer. She destroyed the silence while Abraham recalled the story, with a critical, sentiment-damning snort. "Oh, mighty pitiful! Mighty long-winded and pitiful! So she thought if she sent you down here with a tale like that she could get something out of us anyway. Do you think we were born yesterday?"

Abraham was patient with her. "Now you don't need to worry about her. She died soon after he did. You can't share a bed with a man with T.B. . . ." But he stood up to face her, stretching himself, as if the moment had finally come to hear and not to tell.

"I was fifteen years old when Dad died. Some way I escaped it. And I've been waiting ever since to find out something. I want to know the trouble, all the way back. I want to know what happened to the letters. . . ."

"Go on, Mary Lee, tell him!" Amelia called at her. She grinned. "Or do you want me to?"

"All right. I'll tell you. I burned the letters. Now. Are you satisfied? Got what you come here for? I burned them."

But he left her to explain as she'd left him to, isolated, surrounded by watchers.

"I knew who they were from the minute I laid eyes on them. I knew they'd just be some begging stuff, and I didn't see a bit of sense dragging everything up again and worrying your grandmother. God knows she was worried enough with all the trifling family she had; I reckoned that if she got rid of one of them she ought to stay rid of him. Him and that woman!" Mary Lee's mouth curled into the smile of a woman who had heard the joke before. "Imagine! Trying to just come back and sit on their haunches . . ."

Abraham grabbed her arm to pull her to him across the table, but when he felt its frailty he dropped it again.

"I don't get it," he said so quietly that she thought all the anger had gone out of him, and kept on smiling. "All over America there are women like you. We raise our women in a hard soil and sometimes one of them goes crazy—" he watched her closely as if he could read the answer in the lines of her face. "She goes crazy with sadistic self-confidence and moral superiority. Nobody locks her up! They just hand her the reins and let her run things. . . ."

"If you know so much . . ." she began, but he wouldn't let her tell him.

"What in the name of God made you think you had a right to do a thing like that?"

"It was the right thing for me to do," she told him. "If you had any idea of the responsibility I had to shoulder . . ." but she didn't finish when she saw the way he looked at her.

He was too amazed, when he realised that nothing he'd ever say would make her see what she'd done, even to raise his voice. "So help me, you're too far gone for me even to want to punish you!"

"I don't care what you do." She walked past him close to him, but stopped when she got to the screen-door and was holding it open. "Why should I give a damn what youall do? This family can't do any more to me than they've done already." She was nearly crying, but they were tears of anger, not of grief. "I've worked my fingers to the bone and all the thanks I get is to be forgotten." She went out, trying to slam the door behind her, but it wouldn't slam. The screen only made a light complaining sound. They could hear the creak of the rocker as she sat down, but it was pitch-dark by then and she was lost to sight.

Cadwallader took advantage of her going to try to pull the meeting together, hoping to God that Abraham had stirred up enough trouble to satisfy whatever it was he wanted fed.

"Now I'm sure we can all come to some understanding, Cousin Abraham." He picked up the will again to remind them, and because it was all more businesslike if somebody had a paper in his hand. He slapped it against the table to get attention.

"Now, please, everybody, let's get down to brass tacks. After all, there's always a peaceful way to settle a thing if we just set ourselves to try and find it."

But when Abraham cut back to him, he knew that he had failed already.

"I want the rest of the story." He went close to Cadwallader, explaining.

"Now, look here, boy," Cad tried for the last time to stop him. "Now I'm sure a little falling out a long time ago couldn't mean so much to you. You were only a little boy, hardly dry behind the ears. Now you come on . . ."

Abraham shook him off and pushed him aside as if he were a curtain, gently. "Look, I want the whole story." He walked round the table. "You tell me, A'nt Amelia. I'd like to hear it from you." He leaned down to her, perched on a chair with one foot, leaning, getting nearer and nearer her face. "I'm sure that, in your present state, telling me a lot of fancy lies would seem a little silly."

But she didn't look at him. "Don't remember."

"Yes, you do." He let himself down, astride the chair, watching her closely, trying to draw the story out. "Now I've always remembered one thing. This kitchen, but not like this . . ." he looked around, still surprised a little at

155

the difference. "Everything in it used to be tall. There was a flutter of white dresses."

He caught something winging past in her memory.

"White dresses. That must have been the summer I came home to stay . . ."

"Where was Charles Truxton?"

She was bitter. "He lost his job. One of his jobs. He was looking around. I stayed here." She turned round, forgetting what it was all about, just trying to remember and gossip with him.

"You were still here, knee-high to a duck. You and your mother. We all wore white dresses, with little tucks in the front. Thousands of little hand-made tucks." She fingered the front of her black dress, as if she'd conjure up the rippling touch of them.

"Thousands of them. All hand-stitched. Seem to spend half our time washing and ironing white dresses. Clothes were a lot prettier then."

She caught his eye, and knew with a gust of sober sense what he was up to. She shut up and let her voice slur back to the evening's normal.

"That's all I remember."

"I don't believe you." He said it so gently she was almost fooled.

"I said that's all I remember, Mister Smart!"

CHAPTER XVII

EVEN Abraham stopped at the sound of the back screen-door.

Mary Margaret had opened it slowly, and she let it slide as slowly closed through her hand when she stepped through. She was alone.

She came and sat down again at the table, and Abraham asked her what they all were waiting to hear:

"Where's Julik Rosen?"

"He's gone."

Cinnybug laughed. "Gone? Where would he go? Number Nine doesn't come through till ten-fifteen."

Mary Margaret brushed her voice aside. "He's going to wait at the station."

Amelia began to roar with laughter, partly from relief because Mary Margaret had stopped Abraham getting nearer than he knew to her.

"I'd like to see that trifling bunch down at the depot when Mr. Rosen runs up with a chip on his shoulder and his hands in a flower muff." She bent forward, double, on the table, groaning with laughter.

Mary Margaret raised her voice for the first time then since the night had begun. She jumped up.

"Stop it, A'nt Amelia. Everybody can't be like you!"

Amelia stopped laughing, suddenly. A'nt Elemere, who had started to pour coffee when she saw Mary Margaret come back, brought it to her and pushed her back towards her chair.

"Here, drink your coffee and let your a'nt alone."

"I hate that attitude." Mary Margaret stood still looking at Amelia.

"Come on now, honey." She sat down, slackly.

Abraham came round the table and stood over her, forgetting, or not caring, that the others were there at all.

"So you've left him." He said it like the tag line of an old joke.

"I'm staying here for a few days," she murmured, not looking up at him.

But he took her by the shoulders and turned her to him, laughing at her in a way Amelia hadn't done.

"Move over all the Marys! Here comes another Mary!" He shoved her back into her chair.

"Take your place at the kitchen table. Drink away your life in coffee. Failures Row, Ladies only!"

He left her alone and went back to where he'd come from across the table. She thought he'd forgotten her till he leaned over and told her quietly.

"A few days! You've come home to roost!"

She looked up at him of her own accord then, defending herself.

"Where else can I go right now?"

"Go?" He was too excited to come away around the table again to tell her, so he went on leaning across, then sat on the table edge, telling her.

"Go to a hotel. Get yourself a room. Get a bottle of licker too and get like A'nt Amelia here if that does any good. You're starting out on a new life! You can't do it back here curled up in your Kiddie Koop." Then to the point. "Have you got any money, sweetie?" He was close enough to pull her head to his and kiss her, but he straightened up again.

"Oh, what's the use?"

She had forgotten his laughter for a minute and her face was alive again.

"Does it take long?"

"What? Oh—a second. That much time. You don't know. You're lost, strayed, not worth stealing. Then bingo! Like that! You know."

It was all beyond Cinny and she didn't care, and her whole tense body unwound like a catapult. She sprang up and yelled at Cadwallader.

"This is a business meeting!"

Abraham looked round at her, and then sat down again on the edge of the table, his body between her and Cadwallader so that she couldn't see anything else but him.

"All right, A'ntie, I told you I meant business. My business is a past to learn about. I don't know any more than I did when I came except that my grandmother was not responsible for my father's death." He turned to Cadwallader and pointed his finger. "Put it down. Item One on the agenda. Put it down in the minutes." He sat owning the table, watching all of them.

"Now. I want to know the answer to the next question on the agenda." He lashed at Cinny, who was sitting quaking with frustration and trying to get a word in.

"Who kicked my mother out of this house, and why did they do it?"

So when the words came they were an answer, not the question she'd planned, and a half tearful answer at that.

"We didn't kick her out. She left of her own free will." Cinny looked round wildly for someone to back her up. But there was only Amelia. "Didn't she, Amelia? Didn't she?"

Abraham leaned down to Amelia then, too, and shook her, hard, trying to make her talk.

"Was there a row? What kind of a row? Why? Go on, why?"

Mary Lee could be heard getting up from her rocker in

the dark. She strode in straight as a knife, looking like a woman with her mind made up. Abraham saw her over Amelia's bent shoulder, and let go of it, letting her fall back into her slouch again.

"Miss Burden on the Shoulders!" He went to meet her, but she walked past him to the table.

"You couldn't stay out there on your high horse for long, could you? You might miss something."

She stopped and stood rigid against the table.

"Sit down." Abraham followed close to her. "This is a business meeting. A'nt Cinny likes it better that way."

She didn't look at him, but said instead, watching the others, turning her head slowly, forcing agreement:

"I've made up my mind. I've decided to tell him."

No one answered her, but Cinny began to get up without knowing it, and sat down again. Amelia's head rose slowly from her arms.

"I'm going to tell him."

Mary Lee turned to where Abraham stood, waiting for what he'd come for.

"You are a bastard."

"Mary Lee, that isn't true!" Cinny wailed at the lie with some relief because Mary Lee hadn't said what she'd thought she was going to.

"So far as we know, it is." Mary Lee didn't bother to look at her, but kept on, quietly, at Abraham, making him stand there in front of her in the middle of the kitchen floor and take all she'd been meaning to say for a long time.

"Well, if you're so hell-bent on knowing, here it is. We got a white girl in. God knows it was a mistake, but the niggers got so trifling during the first war, just like they did this one, and we had to do something. The one we got spoke about ten words of English."

Amelia smiled. "She was pretty, in a kind of way."

"I don't know about that." Mary Lee went on, never taking her eyes off Abraham, saying the truth so hard that she didn't even bother with anger, plastering him with the truth, if that's what he wanted.

"She wasn't our kind of people. Well, she didn't need more than ten words of English to do what she set herself to do to your father. According to them they sneaked away and got married before he went overseas." She sucked her teeth for a second, remembering.

"A'nt Anna Mary always acted like she believed it, but I don't for a minute think she did. I'm sorry to have to tell you this kind of thing but you asked for it." Now in spite of herself her voice began to rise.

". . . I'm sick and tired of hearing you complain around the house." She jerked her head towards the back screen-door. "You've not stopped since you set foot inside that door!"

"Go on." Abraham dragged her back to the story.

"Well, she moped and sulked around after he left." Mary Lee wasn't telling it so well now, for the venom in her memory was making her re-live what she was telling, slurring her voice, creasing her face.

"She wasn't one bit of good. She'd been taken out of her place and I reckon she found it a little unfair to get put back into it."

Abraham was held still by amazement at the woman.

"But you could do that?"

Mary Lee sucked her teeth, slowly, and half turned, dismissing him. "I certainly could." She started to pull a chair back to sit down.

"My God!" He watched her like you watch a snake.

She plopped herself down in the chair and sighed, bored with him.

161

"Now you don't need to start that ghostly surprise act. It's just your father come out in you. He always did try to get what he wanted that way." She sniggered a little. "Didn't he, Amelia?"

Abraham stopped them all by shouting:

"I'm not a person with a purpose here! I'm a document! This little piece is a bit of my father; this of my mother; this of my Uncle Joshuay; this of my A'nt Susanna." He paced around, forgetting them, but still shouting.

"As far as you people are concerned I'm only a proof that my father, my mother, my aunts, my uncles, my little grey cousins, all lived and worked and had their being!"

Mary Lee knew of a final thing to say to shut the loud-mouthed man up and get back to business and she stood up and stopped his ranting.

"Do you want to hear the rest of the story?"

She had shut him up, and as he waited for what she was going to say, she let him stand there again, just waiting, until she knew she had him where she wanted him.

"Or are you changing the subject because you are finding it isn't the pitiful little yarn you were led to believe?"

She was enjoying herself, throwing remarks at him, making him wait.

"It's just what I expected." Something in his voice made her go on, pell-mell, at the rest of it.

"Well, in a few months it wasn't hard for any durn fool to see what was making the girl mope. You were born eight months after your father left. If you didn't look like the spit of him . . ." She turned away again, finished with him, just making comments almost to herself as she sat down. ". . . I wouldn't be sure you were even his son . . ."

Abraham caught her such a swinging slap with his flat hand against her ear that he knocked her sideways into Mary Margaret's lap. The slap brought them all to their feet, watching. But no one came to help her. No one said a word, waiting in the silence after the slap as loud as the slamming of a door. Abraham leaned over her, almost whispering, his voice shaking with rage:

"Then what did you do?" But when she didn't answer, just lay in Mary Margaret's lap, stroking the side of her head where the hairpins had jammed and he had slapped a grey braid loose, he dragged her up to her feet again, like a full sack, holding her close to his face.

"What did you do to her? I want it all."

"Nothing! Nothing!" Mary Lee was slobbering and she tried to turn her head away, to take in the others. "Somebody make him stop!" But he jerked her head back to him. "Nothing!" Mary Lee screamed again. "We didn't even speak to the girl. We never said a word."

Abraham dropped her and she nearly fell, clutched a chair and dragged herself on to it, crying and trying to do up her hair, poking pins into her crying mouth without realising what she was doing.

"Not a word." Abraham walked close to the table, so gentle they all thought he hadn't heard her, until they listened to what he had to say.

"That's the part I know. She used to say to me, 'Don't stand there, like one of them. Say something. Anything. Even if you hate a man enough to kill him, talk. Silence full of words is the worst form of hatred.' She would say it was the only thing she knew that could drive a person crazy. But she would never tell me how she knew such a thing."

No one dared to answer him; they knew from watching him he wasn't finished, even though he was silent for such a long time that Mary Lee looked up, out of her misery, her mouth full of pins, wondering what was coming.

His head went slowly back as if it were being pulled, and he opened his mouth wide and yelled like a shouting Baptist:

"So help me God, I'll let this house and all that's in it rot to pieces if it takes my last cent tying it up in court!"

Cinny screamed first, fighting her way to Cadwallader. "Can he do that? Cad! Can he?"

And Cadwallader's voice, even over hers, trying to keep the peace . . .

"Well, now, wait a minute, Abraham. That was a long time ago!"

Abraham's head came down, and he bent over Mary Lee, the tears streaming down his face but without a sob in his voice.

"Why did you do it? Why did you do it to that poor lonesome woman?"

The pins dropped out of her mouth and she spoke fast, words tumbling out too, explaining.

"She was poor white trash. We didn't have much money. Something had to be done. We couldn't have a scandal among the girls, and A'nt Anna Mary wouldn't hear of not having her right in with us after she knew about the baby. She just couldn't understand how important it was."

"What was? Come on, what was?" He held her by the arms again, shaking the real reason out of her. It came out yelling him down.

"Cinnybug was courting! She was courting! We couldn't have hired help sitting at the dinner table!"

"So you made it so she wouldn't want to."

"That was her own choice!" Her yell finally unleashed the others. Abraham stood back away from her and

watched them scream at each other like gulls, Cinny's
voice rising high over the rest, a soprano chant.

"You did it. You did it. You started it."

Then her voice swept under the general noise. Cadwallader stood over them, waving his hands for some kind
of dignity in the whole thing, but they couldn't hear him
nor see his lips move loosely, begging. Jellicoe, unaccountably, flicked a match under the table and made a
patch of bright light, lighting a cigarette, ignoring the
women face to face, tearing at each other in the middle of
the table.

"Mary Lee, you started it!" Cinny's voice won again.
"You said not to talk to her. You said she'd soon
learn her place. We didn't mean to do any harm." She
turned to appeal to Abraham, and he caught at her and
tugged her away from the rest, looking past her down at
Jellicoe.

"Do you mean to tell me you nearly ruined my mother's
life so you could catch this man?"

There was still so much noise that Jellicoe didn't know
he was being talked about. He blew out smoke and
wiggled with boredom in his chair. Cinny watched him,
then burst into tears.

"Stop it. Stop it, Abraham!" She sat down, feeling for
a handkerchief. "When we were courting, Jellicoe was
the cutest boy in this valley. He was the cutest and he had
a car, and he promised to take me on a honeymoon none
of the other boys would of. It wasn't our fault things
didn't go according to plan! It's all right for you . . ."
She waved her handkerchief at Abraham, then began to
twist it, stopping her crying and looking at Jellicoe as
if he were a stranger. "Everybody thought I was real
lucky." She looked, completely puzzled, at her knotted
handkerchief.

Abraham stood away from them until Mary Lee's and Amelia's voices ran down, and they leaned back exhausted into their chairs, as if they had been lovers instead of hell-catting at each other over the table-top, repeating and repeating accusations at each other, tiring themselves out.

Abraham caught Mary Margaret's eye. She sat there as still as she could be, with Mary Lee leaning half against her again. He looked away from her, to Jellicoe, to Cinny, still twisting and sniffling, to Amelia, on to Cadwallader.

"The family! Miss Anna Mary's family! Hold them together! Make them multiply! Keep them all eating out of the same trough no matter what it costs! If she had known what you were she'd never have tried to put a legal lock on our hating each other's guts. It'll take more than a letter from a tough old bitch to make us love each other. It'll take a goddamn miracle." He ended, looking at Amelia.

"Were you in it, too?"

Cinny flapped at her with the knot of handkerchief.

"Yes, she was. She was in it the same as the rest."

He turned to Mary Lee.

"And you. You were the ringleader. All in a woman's way, in the time women like best. Sewing! Rocking! Peeling potatoes! I can see it all so well."

He called Cadwallader back to power as gently as if he were asleep, instead of waiting to take over as impatient as a nervous man mounting a merry-go-round.

"Cad."

Only Amelia saw something in the way he said it of what he was thinking. She jumped up, yelling, frightened.

"What are you going to do?"

But he was still as gentle as ever, even when he said:

166

"I'm going to pay my mother back for all this family has done to her."

Then Cinny screamed, "What are you going to do?"

But he still didn't raise his voice.

"I own a third of this house and everything in it. From tomorrow morning I forbid the use of my third. My third of the chicken will die. My third of the cows will starve and take your two-thirds with it." He came close to Mary Lee.

"Try sitting and gloating on two-thirds of a rocking-chair," he called across the table.

"Lie awake nights thinking about it on two-thirds of a bed, hugging and beating two-thirds of a pillow!"

Mary Lee sprang at him and would have scratched his face, but he caught her hands.

"You fiend. You dirty fiend," she kept saying, trying to twist away.

"Don't blame me, sister." He pushed her down into her chair by her wrists. "It's the Mary Amelia Thelma Annie Coxey's Army Passmore coming out in me."

Cinnybug forgot even to cry. She tugged at Cadwallader's coat, jerking at every word, "Can he do it, Cousin Cad? Can he do it?"

He pulled himself loose.

"Of course he can't do it. He won't succeed." But nobody was listening to him, and he said to himself, sadly, "Oh, Lordy, why couldn't this all of been a little bit quieter?"

"I can't do it!" Abraham threw the law back in Cadwallader's face. "Of course I can't do it after it gets to the courts, but I can tie it up in court until the damage is done. I can do that and you know it."

He turned away from the table, through with them at last; when A'nt Elemere touched his arm as he passed, he shook even her away, and leaned his head against the screen, waiting, but too tired to think at all, just letting the sounds of the frogs croaking away down by the creek get to him and make a steady watery sound around him, resting in it, letting it engulf the women's voices behind him until they almost faded away.

Behind him at the table they'd run down, stuck, looking from one to the other, far too deep in trouble now to start accusing wildly at each other. Gradually, looking around, all three women's eyes lit on Cadwallader and stayed there. Cinnybug gulped quickly and got her words in first.

"Cadwallader, what did you let mother do it for? She musta been insane!"

Amelia's eyes were bright with tears, but she couldn't let them go, and her voice when she spoke was hard.

"She always was hard on us. You know that, Cad."

But before Cadwallader could defend himself or Miss Anna Mary, Cinny had broken in again, her voice beginning its steady rise.

"What are we gonna do?"

Amelia charged up, swinging the tears down out of her eyes, her voice breaking.

"Damn her! Damn Mother! Just like her, just like Charles Truxton, dying off without leaving me fixed."

Mary Lee was carefully buttoning her blouse at the wrists, but she looked up to interrupt. "You always knew your mother was turning into an old fool. Why'd you let her get away with it?"

She slapped her buttoned wrist.

"If youall had of listened to me, this never would of happened. I would of made quite certain she never get by with anything!"

168

It was her voice, rising over the others that made Abraham turn round, but the first thing he noticed was Mary Margaret, jumping up so quickly that she knocked her chair to the floor. This time her voice had lost its tight-rope balance and she was yelling louder than her mother.

"Leave her alone. Leave my grandmother alone."

She'd stopped their mouths, but not for long. Cinnybug set her right.

"She's not your grandmother. We've had just about enough of this grandmother . . ."

"Shut up, A'nt Cinny." Cinny's mouth gaped open. "Yes, I said shut up to you. I wondered when youall would start on her. You just leave her alone," she repeated, having stopped them, as if the words were magic to keep them quiet. Mary Lee had had enough of her little tantrum.

"You're in it the same as them. I don't know what you're blowing off your big bazoo for . . ."

"No, I'm not. I'm not staying here." She quit the table, leaving them, and ran towards Abraham, talking all the time.

"I'm going off tonight with Abraham. If he doesn't want me, he can drop me off beside the depot. Will you take me? Abraham, can I go with you?"

She couldn't notice that Mary Lee's face was going tight and dark, that she was being driven up from the table by her anger, for Cinnybug had squeaked at her, amazed, and she turned to look at her.

"Where would you go to?" Cinny was fascinated, watching her, big-eyed.

Mary Margaret burst into laughter at the look on her face, and couldn't answer her for laughing. Rather like a leaf that the wind of all the kitchen fury had disturbed, she swung crazily from one to the other of them, trying to stop her helpless laughter.

Amelia just shook her head back and forth.

"She's drunk."

"It's so funny!" Mary Margaret explained to Abraham through the laughter. He pulled her against him to quiet her, nearly upsetting them both.

"Take it easy," he almost whispered to her, and she was still.

Mary Lee's hard fingers bit into her arm and whirled her around from him. She was stiff, spitting, and her voice was tight and low.

"You'd do that? You'd do that? Flaunt yourself like that? I never expected any better of you."

Mary Margaret took away the hand from her arm, tore it away as if she were pulling a leech.

"Maybe that's why you never got any better."

Mary Lee stood stranded, not answering, the fear broken. Over Mary Margaret's shoulder, Abraham noticed for the first time that she had to look up to look into Mary Margaret's eyes. She looked sick and lonely and stripped of pride, and when she did speak, her voice rose and fell as if she were being sorry and righteous to a child.

"Mary Margaret, you've got no right to talk to me like this. You've got no right."

"What are your rights over me?"

Against the hanging top light, Mary Lee's face was in the shadow, but Abraham could see that she was no longer stiff, but bowing her head so that her hair made a thin grey halo.

"I've got the right to have my daughter married to a responsible man, haven't I, so I can be proud of you?" Her lip trembled gently, not in anger. "You've got no right to worry me to a frazzle like this."

Mary Margaret watched the change in her as coolly as if she were analysing the movements of an animal, and as coolly told her, "Look, Mother, all that talk's no good now. I've heard it too often. Now I'm going away. This time I'm really going."

Mary Lee's head shot up again. "You're nothing but an adulteress!"

"Let him without malice cast the first stone."

"I've always done the best I could for you!" Mary Lee's voice went up into a fine scream.

She had finally destroyed Mary Margaret's coolness, and her anger overwhelmed her and she began to shout, close to Mary Lee, backing her towards the table.

"Look, Mother, get this right." She choked, and tried again to speak. "You haven't! You've never loved me and that's all a mother can do! Not eat a child, or mould a child, or guide a child or blackmail a child. Just love it! Suckle it! Love it!"

Mary Lee sank into a chair, explaining, misunderstanding. "I couldn't feed you. I couldn't. I dried up. I couldn't help drying up! Could I? Could I?" She tried to force Mary Margaret to answer and when she wouldn't, she said, "You look like you hate me. Your own mother."

Mary Margaret had found her version of truth a pleasure. She went on, her face pink with excitement under the bright light.

"I hate all of you because you're professional land-poor, deed-grabbing southerners! I hate Julik because he's a professional down-trodden Jew."

As she watched them in the brash light, picking them out, one by one, her voice caught and calmed and seemed to withdraw from them.

"I'm not going to be walked all over. Listen! I thought

I was safe by now. I thought you couldn't do this to me. In one day you can shake me to pieces. I'm going because I'm too damn scared to stay here any longer. Poor old grandmaw. You got her, didn't you? Fed on her and used her to patch your nest. Look at youall!" She walked round the table, studying them each in turn. She stopped in front of Cinny.

"Little A'nt Cinnybug! Cute little thing! Just like a steel wire with a purpose."

She turned her back on her and caught Amelia's eye. "Poor old Amelia! Look at you! Using your memories as rent for a room and board.

"And you!" She was talking quickly now, almost running round the table. "Mary Lee the Right! Armed with disapproval enough to poison the intentions of a saint. And Julik! Julik the Great! Blackmailing his way through life with poverty and talent and a million dead relations."

She stopped, out of breath, watching them, but none of them had an answer. They sat, slapped down like fallen sandbag dummies. It was the look of them that made her decide, quietly again. "You may hate him and he may hate you, but Jew, Gentile and my Aunt Fanny, you're as alike as peas in a pod."

Amelia began to giggle. "Well, are you finished blowing your whistle, little Miss Mouse?" she asked and went on giggling, near to tears.

Mary Lee whispered bitterly to herself, "My own daughter. My own flesh and blood. Pushed away her dessert without touching it. Took it all for granted. Never picked up after herself. Took it for granted. Didn't 'preciate a thing done for her." She raised her head and howled at Mary Margaret for the last time. "You ungrateful little bitch. After all I've done for you!"

Mary Margaret was swinging towards the dining-room door when the shout caught her. She turned at the door. "Only the first birth is through the mother. The second is through the front door," she said, pleased with herself. She leaned against the door behind her, pushing it open. "Abraham, I'm going to get my bag, I've had enough of this, and if you've got any sense you'll come with me."

He came after her. "I'm not finished here."

"No, you're not, are you? O.K. You keep on. Wade in deeper. Up to your neck." She grinned at him, "What good do you think it will do?" She hadn't exactly called him a fool, but she had so looked it at him that he felt hot, remembering his anger.

He said nothing for a minute, and when he turned back to them, all sitting there waiting, he spoke only the end of his thought. "It's not mine. None of my business." Nobody understood what he meant, and when he went on, "My mother needed you. Sometimes I think it kept her going. But now that I've seen you . . ." he shrugged his shoulders in a little gesture that put them in mind of his mother.

He said to Mary Margaret, touching her, "Let's go."

"Good-bye, Passmores," he called out to them, but still no one moved. "Good-bye, Passmore Place!"

"Cousin Cad," he roused him by name, made him sit up from where he'd slumped down, too dejected to listen any more.

"You want me, son?"

"Cousin Cad, you can take my third of hell, and divide it up, exactly equally, between the resident devils!"

Cadwallader stood up and began to grope for the will again, by habit. "Do you really mean that, Abraham? It's quite a valuable piece of property. Your . . ."

Abraham stopped him. "No. I've found out what I

want to. That's all I want. It's my piece of property."

Cadwallader managed to grin. "Well, that's all fine, son, but you can't borry money on that!" He laughed feebly.

Abraham took Mary Margaret's arm, and then remembered A'nt Elemere. "Good-bye, A'nt Elemere," he called over his shoulder. "Thank you for all that good coffee."

"Wait a minute."

They both stopped at the sound of A'nt Elemere's voice.

"Come here to me, Miss Mary Margaret. You too, Mr. Abraham." She stood stock still and waited until they were standing in front of her, side by side, before she bothered to speak again.

"I ainta gonna let you youngins ramp off without finishin' what I got to do. It ain't fair on the Passmores, and it ain't fair on youall."

She hesitated to collect herself. "Now, don't go," she murmured, "I got a lot to say and I got to get it all clear. I'm getting old . . .

"Now I been listenin' to a lot of fine talk from you two young brats, and I ainta gonna have you talkin' that way. Walk out of here in scorn jest as bad as walkin' out of here in hatred. I ainta gonna have it. All this big talk . . . all this fancy laying down the law . . ."

She had found her stride and she went on, more strongly, her voice rising, "Ainta gonna have it. You know a mighty fine lot but you don't know about what nobody else might of been through. You don't know what Miss Cinny was like when she was a youngin, or Miss Amelia."

She brushed past both of them and went to the table where Cinnybug sat with her head down.

"Why, Miss Cinny was as pert and sassy as you could find

anywhere, all full of life, always talking about how she was gonna up and take the steamboat one day all the way to Cincinnati. That's how she come by that nickname, because she had such a bug to get to Cincinnati."

A'nt Elemere looked over Cinny's head at Jellicoe, slouched beside her.

"Well, she musta had. She married for it."

She shouted to Abraham across the room.

"Do you think a girl like she was would have hurt your maw ifn she'd knowed what she was at? Why, she didn't have sense enough to know." Her voice softened again. "You don't expect no little kitten to have horse sense, do you? Well, don't go waiting for it in Miss Cinnybug."

She caught the glint of Amelia's hair as she turned her head in her arms.

"And Miss Amelia. Prettiest youngin I believe I ever did see. Lord's love, you should have seen her ride. You would of thought anybody could ride like that wouldn't of been skeered of nothin'." She reached down and began to stroke her hair. "But she started out being skeered the very day she was married. Most gals does. But Miss Meely never got over it. She never had no chance. Never to know how you're gonna keep body and soul together. . . . Ain't none of youall knows about that marriage, and I ainta gonna tell you." Amelia turned her head a little and sighed in her half-sleep. "She knows. Miss Meely knows. Don't you, honey?"

A'nt Elemere straightened up and looked straight across the table into Mary Lee's eyes.

"As for Miss Mary Lee, I ainta gonna say nothing about her. I never knowed her 'fore she turned ornery . . ."

Mary Margaret tried to stop her by saying, "A'nt Elemere, we didn't mean to. . ."

But she got no further. "That's the trouble!" A'nt

Elemere looked up at her and trounced back across the room. "Don't nobody mean nothing when it's over. Let me tell you somethin', Miss High and Mighty, jest you try spendin' your life bein' bored and disappointed because you jest ain't got gumption enough to do somethin' about it! I seen people sicken and die of jest plain havin' no gumption."

She was very close to Mary Margaret. "I didn't reckon you had enough gumption to slap your mammy down and priss off, but I was wrong. Don't you start laying down the law, jest start thanking the Lord for your luck. Shamey on you! I thought you knowed better!"

"You know I'm ashamed."

"You downright ought to be. Seem like when the Bible say charity begin at home, well seem like to me so does pity."

She turned to the sink, trying to find something to do, because she suddenly realised how much she'd had to say; but still she went on, now softly, almost to herself.

"You learn on your own home-folks what gits on your nerves fore you start out practisin' on the rest of the world." She turned to them again, as if she were surprised that they were still standing there, watching her. "That's all I got to say to you youngins. Git on outa my kitchen. You're the two I ainta gonna worry about!"

"Lord knows why!" Mary Lee muttered, but nobody heard her.

Her voice only made Mary Margaret conscious of her, sitting there, and she was surprised somehow that Mary Lee had frozen back into her old straight-backed way already, as if she had only a memory of being alive since her last high words. She sat there with her hands twined together, straight out in front of her on the table under the bright white bulb.

"Mother."

Mary Lee neither answered nor moved.

"Mother." Mary Margaret bent down over her shoulder and kissed her cold thin cheek.

"Good-bye, Mother." She realised that, for the first time since she could remember, Mary Lee didn't draw back when she was kissed.

"Mother," Mary Margaret whispered again, and hugged her, mussing her hair. Mary Lee never said a word.

As Abraham held open the door for her, Cadwallader called out, "Abraham, don't you want to sign over the rights to your third?"

Abraham looked over his shoulder, "You don't need it, Cad," he called. "You've got three witnesses—twenty-five years of witnesses stuck to this fly-paper."

He shut the door behind him, and even as he started down the dining-room to the hall, he already had trouble remembering what they looked like, except that they were like bundles under the light.

Their footsteps echoed back from the wide, night-lit hall of the Passmore Place, and there was only the dining-room door where they had been, swinging behind them.

Cinnybug's bright voice splintered the silence of the kitchen they had left.

"Does he mean it? Does he really mean it? He must be outa his mind! It's a valuable piece of property!" She looked, pleading for reassurance at Cadwallader.

"We'll be all right now, won't we, Cousin Cad?"

But Cousin Cad had had enough of them. Mechanically, very carefully, he was putting the will back into his brief-case. He locked it and put the key away in his watch pocket before he answered Cinnybug.

"Don't worry about it now, Cinny. I'm pretty tired. I don't want any more fuss," he begged her.

Then, as he picked up the case, he relented a little. After all, it was his job to get things settled, once and for all, if things ever were settled that way.

"If you want me to, I'll drive to see Mr. Crasscopper in the morning and tell him you can pay off three thousand dollars right away. I'm sure Amelia'll see her way clear to helping you raise the rest."

Amelia raised her head out of her arms when she heard her name, and Cinny ran round the table to her. But Amelia didn't notice her at all, only when she said, "Will you, Amelia? Will you do that?"

Amelia was staring straight across the table at Mary Lee, just as A'nt Elemere had done, in judgment.

"Mary Lee, tomorrow you go."

Mary Lee patted her hair where Mary Margaret had mussed it, and pushed herself up from the table by her arms. She gave a long sigh, a yawn, and went to the dining-room door. "Oh, we'll see about that when the time comes, Amelia," she dismissed her. "I've got too much on my mind right now. I'm going to bed."

She was gone before Amelia could answer. She looked round at all of them left and complained, "I'll never get rid of her. Never will. That damn woman'll bury me from here." She put her head back down in her arms, still saying aloud, "Reckon I'd miss her anyway. She belongs here, same as the rest of the junk."

Cinny touched her shoulder to make her look up again. When she didn't, she shook it slightly.

"Amelia, you will let me have your half of the early 'mercan sideboard, won't you? I'll trade you my half of almost anything else!"

Amelia shook her hand away.

"Aw, for God's sake, let me alone."

Cinny kept on at her, begging for an answer.

"Please, Amelia, aw, please, honey . . ."

But Jellicoe, like Cadwallader, had had about enough of them for one evening, and he began to guide Cinnybug towards the back screen-door, coaxing her, "Come on home, honey, I got to go to work tomorrow."

Cinnybug looked longingly round the room for somebody to ease her mind. She asked A'nt Elemere, "Do you think she will?"

A'nt Elemere came round to her and began to coax, too. "Sure she will, sure Miss Meely will. Don't you worry. You git some sleep."

They had bundled Cinnybug to the door when she broke away from them and turned back, but only to say, as bright as a button for the first time since the evening had begun, "Good-night, Amelia, I'll be back up in the morning!"

From Amelia's arms where her head was cupped came a muffled, "I'll bet you will."

But Cinnybug and Jellicoe had disappeared and they walked down the back path, leaving a trail of fast conversation behind them.

Away from them, in the empty hall, Mary Lee stopped, rigid, forgetting for a second why she'd come out. Then she remembered that she was on her way to bed, the same as she had every night, as if nothing had happened. She dragged herself up the stairs slowly, tireder than she could ever remember being, but when she turned down the hall to her own room she forgot again and went past it, pulling herself on up the attic stairs, into the dark.

There, on the top step, the headache finally focused on her like a giant current, twisting even the darkness into a tighter thing around her, and she began to pace blindly back and forth across the attic floor.

In the kitchen Cadwallader stopped by Amelia and patted her shoulder.

"Good-bye, Amelia. It's been a sad day. Yes. Glad it's over."

He went out of the back screen-door and A'nt Elemere followed and watched after him, by habit, leaning worn-out against the door-jamb, breathing the night air in long tired sighs. She saw the shadows of Jellicoe and Cinnybug waiting at the gate, but Cadwallader passed them by, his voice floating faintly back, "Good-bye, Cinny, honey, don't you worry. Good-bye, Jellicoe."

Jellicoe's voice carried clear to her in answer in the still late air, "Good-bye, Cad. Come on, Cinny. Golly these things always take so long. Youall can talk the hind-leg off a mule when you get to discussing property."

She heard the car doors slam, and a long beam of light shot on; a motor started and the light came round in a circle, finding the porch, finding A'nt Elemere for a second, then was gone, leaving the darkness darker behind it.

The other car had not started when she came back into the kitchen. Behind her she could hear the kick and choke of a laboured engine. She went up to Amelia, still lying with her head in her arms in the now empty room, barren of any sound or movement.

"Miss Amelia, ain't you ready to go to bed?" There was no answer. She said again, "Miss Meely."

Amelia lifted her head.

"Look in the bread-box, A'nt Elemere; you and me need a drink."

A'nt Elemere got the bottle, and two glasses, and put them on the table as carefully as if she were setting it for a meal.

"Thank you, Miss Amelia," she told her, formally. "I

reckon I would like one to help me sleep." She waited beside the table.

Amelia laughed, a single snort. "That's a fine reason. We'll both have one . . . to help us sleep. Sit down."

A'nt Elemere had been waiting to be asked and now she sat down, as sedate as a tea party, and clasped the glass Amelia handed her in both hands, saying in a nice, strange, conversational voice, "I thought you was keeping it in the flour-bin today." She lifted the drink. "Thank you, Miss Amelia."

They both drank, and set down empty glasses.

"Miss Mary Lee got to find out."

Across the creek, the lights of the last car flashed on, lighting the trees for a minute until the car disappeared down the creek road. Neither of the women in the kitchen saw it; only Mary Lee, who had sunk to the low sill and was trying to cool her head against the glass pane of the attic window, saw, and knew which car it was.

But the car lights and the fireflies and the thing that had happened were all the same to her, nuisance. She asked one question against the window.

"Where in the name of God did I put my luminal?" and left her breath on the glass.

Then, as if the sound of her own voice in the dark, empty attic released her caged thoughts, she began to mutter, got up from the sill, and began to pace back and forth again in the soft darkness.

"What in God's name would they do without me? It's all very well . . ." she stumbled at the bed edge and knocked her shin on one of the brass knobs, making her call out in anger and quick pain, "Has a goddamn one of them ever even bothered to find out how many sheets there are in the house, or where the rugs are so worn out I've got to push the chairs over them every blessed time I go by? Do they think I like it . . ." She went on pacing the floor silently until she had returned to the window. She raised her small veined fist deliberately and drove it into the wooden window-frame, crying out:

"This is all the thanks I get, this is the thanks. . . . What do any of you know, goddamned trifling fools? What did any of you ever bother to learn about me? The whole damn lot of you—pigs in a pen!"

She turned away into the dark again, as if the Passmores were clustered outside the attic window, watching and listening, and she had decided to ignore the whole damn lot, saying to herself:

"They've no idea how lonesome a smart woman can get," then laughed a single, bitter laugh.

"When could they of spared me? When wouldn't they of let the whole damn place go to rack and ruin?"

Then she remembered the car that she had watched disappear down the road. "You think you're so damned smart!" she craned out of the window, stooped, and called to the road where the car had been in her frenzy. "Do you think I wanted you? Hanging around my neck when I was no more than nineteen years old?

"Jesus God, you little hussy, you don't know a damn thing about what somebody else might of been through!"

Nobody heard her but John Junior in the room below, who only woke and turned, not taking in the words, and went to sleep again.

"They haven't a notion," she said, drawing her head in again, calmer, finding the cool pane with her forehead. "Now, what in the world would they do if I just picked up and waltzed off?"

Then, as a last cry, almost not heard, into the room, "Where in the name of God would I go now?"

Like a stab of lightning the headache found and thrust

at the base of her skull, bringing a tidal wave of nausea. Mary Lee sank on to the attic bed among the piles of Miss Anna Mary's papers, her body dead quiet, but her head turning back and forth in the darkness like a hunter.

Only the wet mask of her forehead stayed for a little while on the attic window-pane.

Down below in the kitchen, A'nt Elemere was quiet for a while, sinking into her tiredness, but was roused by the crash of glass on the floor as Amelia pitched forward on to the table and lay still.

A'nt Elemere jumped up and shook her shoulders.

"Miss Amelia! Miss Meely! Wake up, Miss Meely!"

But she knew it was no use. She sighed, "Oh, well, it ain't the first time I put that youngin to bed."

Then, suddenly, it was all too much for her. She started to moan, and through the moaning stumbled snatches of her deep hurt, aloud in the still kitchen, ". . . all these youngins . . ." Her face screwed up, "Here you done went and forgot about me altogether . . ."

.   .   .   .   .

Abraham drove on down the now familiar creek road, which seven hours before had been so strange, intent on the tunnel of light ahead of him down the black road. What he thought were sobs came from Mary Margaret, lying where John Junior had lain, in the front seat beside him.

It wasn't until the main road that he realised she was giggling. He was furious, fooled. "For God's sake!"

It only made her giggle more, huddled, trying to stop.

"What's so funny?"

She stopped long enough to tell him, "I've got to go to the depot. It's no use . . ."

He drove on, silently, into his own headlight; the

road, the house, the whole thing dwindling and disappearing in the dark behind him; only the stranger cousin from it, like flotsam, left on the car seat.

"I've still got Julik's railroad ticket," she explained, and went on laughing.